RED-LINE:

MIRRORS

....

J. T. BISHOP

Eudoran Press LLC
Dallas, TX

Eudoran Press
6009 Parker Rd. Suite #149-913
Plano, TX 75093
www.jtbishopauthor.com

Publisher's Note: This is a work of fiction. Names, characters, places, and incidents are a product of the author's imagination. Locales and public names are sometimes used for atmospheric purposes. Any resemblance to actual people, living or dead, or to businesses, companies, events, institutions, or locales is completely coincidental.

Book Layout ©2015 BookDesignTemplates.com
Book Editing by Firstlookforauthors.com
Cover Design by Bespokebookcovers.com
Updated Cover by J.T. Bishop
Photos by rbvrbv, aarrttuurr, vikiri

Author photo by Mayza Clark Photography

Ordering Information:
Quantity sales. Special discounts are available on quantity purchases by corporations, associations, and others. For details, contact J. T. Bishop at the address above.

Red-Line: Mirrors/ J. T. Bishop. -- 1st ed.
ISBN 978-0692330418

To Cathy and Nick...

I don't know how we got to be so lucky to be siblings, but we did. You guys make me laugh, are always there for me, and I'm grateful every day that I got to grow up with you.
I love you...and to quote one of my own characters—
thank you for being there.

Other Books by J. T. Bishop -

The Red-Line Trilogy
Red-Line: The Shift (free at jtbishopauthor.com)
Red-Line: Mirrors
Red-Line: Trust Destiny
The Red-Line Trilogy Boxed Set

Red-Line: The Fletcher Family Saga
Curse Breaker
High Child
Spark
Forged Lines
The Fletcher Family Saga Boxed Set

The Family or Foe Saga with Detectives Daniels and Remalla
First Cut
Second Slice
Third Blow
Fourth Strike
The Family or Foe Saga Boxed Set

Detectives Daniels and Remalla Series
Haunted River
Of Breath and Blood
Of Body and Bone
Of Mind and Madness
Of Power and Pain
Of Love and Loss

The Redstone Chronicles
Lost Souls
Lost Dreams
Lost Chances
Lost Hope

ONE

....

THE PICTURE FRAME hit the wall with force, shattering and littering the floor with jagged shards of glass. Frustrated, Sarah Randolph paced the room.

Feeling her irritation, John Sherlock Ramsey watched her from his seat on the couch. He took a breath to keep calm, hoping it would help to relieve some of her tension. Looking at her though, it was apparent that no amount of calm from him was reaching her.

"Sarah..." he said.

She stopped and stared at him with a look that did not invite conversation.

"Never mind," he said.

She picked up her pacing where she left off. Not saying a word, he let her continue to walk. Finally, breathing deeply, she stopped and stared at him again. He expected a declaration or a question or a scream, but she just stood there.

"What?" he asked, determined not to push any buttons.

She put her hands on her hips. "This is stupid."

He made a monumental effort to show no impatience. "What is stupid?"

Sarah threw her hands up in the air. "This. All of this. It's just stupid. I'm stupid."

"You are not stupid."

"Yes, I am."

"You are not stupid."

"Don't argue with me."

Ramsey raised his hands in mock resignation. He'd grown fairly accustomed to her abrupt mood swings, but controlling his reactions to them challenged him considerably. "Forgive me," he said. "I am merely trying to argue the point that you are in fact not stupid. Would you rather I agree with you?"

Her hands went back to her hips, and she picked up the pacing again. "God, you are the most annoying person sometimes."

Biting back a caustic retort, he gave her as much space as possible. Feeling the presence of Declan at the door, he stood from his seat on the couch.

Sarah stopped. "Where are you going?"

"Declan's here," he said gently.

Her face reflected no change as she returned to her pacing and Ramsey resumed his forward movement.

"Great," she said. "More exercises."

Ramsey went to the door and opened it.

"Not bad," said Declan, walking up the entry. "You're actually paying attention."

Ramsey regarded his stepbrother. Declan's easy demeanor contrasted with his role as head of security for Sarah. Despite his laid-back style, he could be a formidable opponent—he was well-versed in the earthly martial arts and the Eudoran abilities of reading and manipulating energy.

"Well," said Ramsey, "when you've spent all day with Joan Crawford on steroids, even you can be an inviting distraction."

Declan's gaze caught Sarah's movement in the background. He frowned. "That bad, huh?"

"You have no idea."

**

It had been three weeks since they'd arrived at the new safe house. Declan had argued that a different location had no more advantages than their original one, but considering the events they'd experienced in the first house and its condition, they agreed that a change in venue was in order. The new house was located fifteen minutes closer to the city and was also built on a decent-sized lot, one which provided plenty of cover and privacy from the street. Morgana had insisted on twenty-four-hour security on the property, even though Declan believed it mattered little how many men were on the premises. Regardless, Morgana had demanded it, and Declan had picked his own team, all of whom were trained in his own brand of security, which included heightened-sensitivity awareness and energy intuition and manipulation. If he trusted anyone to pick up on a threat in advance of its arrival, it was the group he'd put in place. Even with their presence, though, he knew their adversary could overtake them with ease, which it was why it was important to get Sarah up to speed as soon as possible. As Declan entered the house and watched her now, he considered how difficult that was proving to be.

Within hours of arriving at the new house, after a difficult trip in which she'd painfully felt every energetic shift and mood from everyone she came in the vicinity of as she'd traveled, Sarah had succumbed to her mental weariness and slept for hours. After waking, though, it became evident that something had changed. Her previous sensitivities had lessened and her ability to manipulate the energy around her, which she had been practicing with Declan's help, appeared weaker as well. Assuming it would resume in time, he'd kept working with her, but her frustration mounted as her abilities continued to dissipate. Within days, they had disappeared altogether. Now, three weeks later, Sarah was cranky and housebound, and her mood reflected it. Even after continued attempts at reawakening her senses, nothing had worked, and even Declan had begun to wonder when, or if, they would return.

Declan entered the house. "Any change?"

Ramsey gave him a sour look. "Do you sense any change?"

Declan watched Sarah at the other end of the room. She had not acknowledged his presence. "Unfortunately, no."

"Well," said Ramsey, "pretty soon she's going to throw one of us into a wall, and she's not going to need any special powers to do it."

"I know, but what else do we do?" Declan asked, closing the door behind him. He spoke softly. "We don't know what this means. It may be entirely normal for her abilities to go dormant for a while. Or maybe it means something else. We're at a big disadvantage here. It's not like we can consult a Red-Line handbook."

"Well, threat or no threat, she wants to see her friend Rachel and her Aunt Gerry. If I tell her to wait one more time, I'm afraid she'll take my head off with her teeth."

Declan sighed. "I get it, but you understand that's probably what he wants."

Ramsey's mood darkened. "Y?"

"Yes, Y. Once enough time passes, he knows she'll come out in the open. He's waiting us out."

"Declan, much as I hate to admit it, if he wanted her, he could march in here and take her right now. She couldn't stop him, and neither could we."

"That's not the way he's playing it. He's a cool customer, and he wants to keep a low profile. He's not like his brothers."

"Yeah, well, it's working," said Ramsey. "She's either got to get her abilities back or she's going to insist on returning to her life."

"You know the Council will have something to say about that."

Ramsey glowered. "You mean Morgana will have something to say about it."

"Morgana or the Council. They want her under wraps and safe."

"No, they want her to read the mirror. That's all they care about. If she can't read it, then she's of no value to them."

"Well, she certainly can't read it now."

"No, she can't, but it won't be long before they start putting on the pressure. Time is not exactly on our side."

Declan crossed his arms. "What's Leroy hearing?"

"Exactly that. They're willing to take a wait-and-see stance, but they're already starting to get antsy. Morgana told him she wants to meet with Sarah."

"That's not an introduction I would recommend at the moment," said Declan, imagining the encounter.

"Actually, I might find it rather enjoyable, especially in her current mood," Ramsey answered, tipping his head in Sarah's direction.

Declan glanced at Sarah, feeling her anxiety. "I can't argue with that. I suspect Morgana and Sarah would be pretty evenly matched right about now."

"My money's on Sarah. I've been called names this morning even you've never called me."

Declan thought back to their teenage years. "And I've had some pretty colorful words for you."

"Unfortunately, said Ramsey. "I think you learned most of them from me."

Declan recalled their contentious past, which began in their teens after Declan's father married Ramsey's mother two years after Ramsey's dad's death in a car accident. Their experiences during Sarah's Shift had managed to bring them together after years of estrangement.

Declan gave a low chuckle, but he eyed Sarah as he advanced into the room. She paced with pent-up energy, still ignoring the two of them. Declan opened his senses and gently reached out to her. Despite her recent setbacks, he could still feel the power in her. He understood her need to pace. That much repressed energy needed an outlet. He wondered if they were doing the right thing by keeping her isolated. In the days after arriving at the new house, they had agreed to keep events as stable as possible. Ramsey continued to stay with her, and Declan remained close by as he maintained security. Leroy had returned home to his wife, but remained as the liaison between Ramsey and the Council, keeping his ear to the ground and Ramsey up to speed with any updates. He also kept the Council informed of Sarah's progress. Hannah had also returned home, but she checked in with Sarah every week to review her medical condition or, if needed, just to chat. During their time in the former house, they had grown close, and Sarah enjoyed having another Eudoran female to talk to, considering all the changes she'd recently experienced. Watching her now, Declan wondered if another phone call to Hannah was needed. Sarah appreciated his and John's presence less and less these days.

"Sarah?" said Declan as he walked into the room.

"What, Declan?" She kept up the pace, never looking at him.

Ramsey stayed quiet. Declan could sense his brother had had enough and was ready to turn the reins over. Ramsey moved to leave the room.

"Where are you going?" asked Sarah.

Ramsey stopped and turned back, keeping his face passive. "I thought I'd go to the kitchen, get something to drink, while you talked to Declan."

She stopped pacing. "What? You don't want to offer me anything? Maybe I'm thirsty, too. Besides, why would I want to talk to Declan? We've talked enough."

Ramsey looked at Declan, who gave him a wide-eyed look. "Sorry," he said, "Would you like something to drink?"

"No. I'm not thirsty."

His brother's face tightened, but to his credit, Ramsey stayed cool, but Declan could almost feel his brother's blood pressure rise. Ramsey spoke to Declan. "Would you like anything while I'm up?"

Declan almost smiled, but thought better of it. "No, thanks. I'm good."

Ramsey turned slowly, waiting in case there was another outburst. But getting nothing, he continued toward the kitchen.

Declan faced Sarah, wondering how to handle her.

Sarah scowled at him. "Well, I'm glad you're good, Declan. Now my day is so much better."

He heard his brother chuckle as he disappeared into the kitchen.

**

An hour later, Ramsey was still sitting at the kitchen table. He hadn't returned to the living room, letting Declan deal with Sarah. He'd needed the time to decompress. He'd believed getting Sarah through her Shift would be the difficult part, but this felt infinitely worse. Another week of this, and he might be tempted to hand her over to Y himself.

He berated himself for the thought. This wasn't her fault. They were just completely at a loss as to how to proceed. Taking a sip of his coffee, he mulled over the situation. On the other side of the door, he heard something hit the wall, and hoped it wasn't Declan. Not sensing a threat, he made no move to get up, knowing his brother would manage it. He didn't think he'd be of much help anyway.

His phone rang and he reached into his pocket to retrieve it. Leroy's name flashed on the display.

He answered. "Leroy?"

Sampson Leroy, Ramsey's best friend since his first days as a Protector, responded. "Sherlock? How's it going? Any better today?"

Once learning Ramsey's middle name, Leroy had called him by it ever since. Upon meeting, the two men had shared an instant bond and an easy rapport, a rare experience for Ramsey.

Ramsey groaned. "I didn't think it was possible, but it's worse."

"No change?"

"None. Declan's with her now. I can only assume he's still alive."

There was a sigh on the other end of the line. "What do we do if this keeps up?"

"Your guess is as good as mine."

"I can't put it off any longer. Morgana wants to meet with her."

They'd been delaying the inevitable conversation between the two women. Sarah had been through so much, and Ramsey wanted to give her some time to assimilate all she'd experienced. A meeting with the Councilwoman Morgana, who'd been instrumental in bringing them all together as Sarah went through her Shift and who remained a consistent thorn in Ram-

7

sey's side, seemed just one more straw to add the pile. Now, though, as he heard Sarah's raised voice come from the other room, yelling something undoubtedly unpleasant, he wondered if it might be time for a change. "I'd consider it, Leroy, if I trusted Morgana."

There was a brief pause. "What do you mean?"

"You think Morgana can honestly talk to Sarah without making this situation worse? You think she's got Sarah's best interests at heart?"

"She ought to. She needs Sarah at her best."

"She's not the type of woman to take things slow, Leroy. She'll walk in here and get in Sarah's face. That's not going to help anything."

"Maybe, maybe not, but Morgana knows a thing or two about navigating difficult situations. Just because she doesn't like to use those skills with us doesn't mean she won't use them with Sarah."

Ramsey didn't feel convinced. He played out the scene in his mind, feeling for a positive outcome, but felt nothing. "When does she want to do this?"

"She's coming tomorrow morning."

"What?"

"Sorry. I was trying to cushion the blow."

"It didn't work."

"Perk up, Sherlock. Maybe this will be a good thing."

Ramsey doubted it. "Well," he said, "if anyone's going to reignite Sarah's abilities, it'll be Morgana. That woman could make Superman fly with Kryptonite around his neck."

Leroy chuckled. "Maybe we should have set this meeting up sooner."

Ramsey rubbed his head. "Maybe. I'll try to prepare Sarah. Hopefully, she'll take it well. You'll know if you don't hear from me."

"Why?"

"Because she's likely ripped my vocal cords out and crushed them with her bare hands."

Leroy laughed. "Morgana might thank her for that."

"I have no doubt she would."

"See you tomorrow morning, then, around ten o'clock."

"Fine. See you then."

Ramsey hung up the phone as Declan entered the kitchen.

"Holy..." Declan started to say. He sat heavily at the table.

Ramsey leaned back in his chair. "And you've just spent one hour with her."

Declan eyed Ramsey's coffee. "You got anything stronger than that?"

"It's one o'clock in the afternoon."

"It feels a lot later."

"Yes, well, sixty minutes with Godzilla in there will do that to you. I feel like I've aged ten years."

"God," said Declan.

"I doubt even he'd want to deal with her."

Declan rested his elbows on the table and put his face in his hands.

"How'd you get out of there?" asked Ramsey. He waited for Declan to answer. "She didn't remove any vital body parts, did she?"

Declan's face fell.

"What?" asked Ramsey, not liking the look on Declan's face. "What did you do?"

"I couldn't take it."

"Couldn't take what? What do you mean?"

"I felt bad for her."

"Declan, what are you talking about? You didn't use some sort of Kung Fu on her, did you?"

Declan rolled his eyes at him. "Don't be ridiculous. Of course not."

"Then what is it? What are you not telling me?" Ramsey could feel Declan contracting his energy in some sort of attempt to cover up what he didn't want to reveal.

"John, before you overreact..."

"Overreact?" Ramsey's heart picked up some speed. "Why would I overreact?"

9

Just then, the kitchen door swung open. Sarah walked in with a jacket on and her purse in her hand. "Okay. I'm ready."

Ramsey swiveled and then glanced over at Declan. "What exactly is she ready for?"

Sarah's smile slipped downwards. "I'm standing right here, Ramsey."

Ramsey caught himself before addressing Declan again. He relaxed his posture. "Sorry, I was just curious about where you think you're going?" He kept his face tranquil, although the strain of doing so tested his reserves.

"John—" Declan tried to answer.

"Declan agreed to take me out of the house. We're going to the bookstore." Her stare dared him to argue with her, but her announcement pushed him over the edge.

"He what?" Ramsey stared at Declan. "What in the hell did you do that for?"

"John—" Declan tried again, but Sarah didn't back down. Her frustration brought her to the breaking point.

"Ramsey, don't you dare tell me I can't leave this house. Declan agreed to get me out of here and see Rachel, and I have every intention of doing so. You can't keep me cooped up in here forever."

"Sarah, listen to me," he said.

"I am tired of listening to you." She straightened and crossed her arms. "You are all I ever listen to. I see you in the morning, in the afternoon, and at night. It's all I ever do. I've done everything you've asked of me. Now, I'm just asking you for one thing. Just this one thing. I have to get out of here."

Ramsey set his jaw. "Sarah, it's too risky."

"Risky? What is risky? I'm beginning to wonder about this 'bad guy' of yours. He lacks motivation, if you ask me. If he wants me, then why doesn't he come and get me?" She put her hands on her hips for emphasis. "I'll tell you why." She leaned over and spoke directly into Ramsey's ear. "It's because I have *no powers*. That's why." She straightened. "Who wants me when I can't even heave a brick, much less anything heavier? There's no reason to take me anymore. Whatever you or your people wanted from me, it's not there. Show's over. Time's up. The buzzer has sounded. Let's admit defeat, people. I don't have it. I doubt I ever did. Maybe there was something there at first, but it's gone now. I'm not your answer. I am not your savior and there is no hope." She stopped and took a breath.

"You are not leaving this house," Ramsey said, his tone unyielding. "I don't care what Declan told you."

Her eyes flared, and her back stiffened.

"John, listen..." Declan tried again.

Ramsey pointed. "Don't argue with me, Declan."

Declan clammed up.

Sarah didn't say a word, but red-faced, she simply turned and walked out of the kitchen. A few seconds later, a door slammed hard and the whole kitchen seemed to shake.

Ramsey reached out with his senses to make sure she was still in the house. Feeling her close by and knowing she'd retreated to her room, he confronted Declan. "What the hell did you think you were doing?"

Irritated, Declan answered back. "Don't you think you're being a little hard on her?"

Ramsey ran a hand through his hair. "We're not protecting some helpless woman from her mean boyfriend, Declan. She's a Red-Line, for God's sake. Did you forget what happened three weeks ago?"

Declan raised a hand. "Of course, I haven't forgotten. Don't be stupid. I know the stakes here. But you can't keep her here forever. She's not your personal toy, John. You can't just lock her up and hope he never comes for her."

"You think I want to lock her up? I know she's going crazy here. Hell, I'm going crazy here. But we can't just let her walk out the door and pretend that life is normal."

"I'm not saying she can go out and never come back. I'm saying she needs a break. Everyone has their limits."

"You're the one who told me that's exactly what he's waiting for. For us to let our guard down. Now you're telling me we need to do just that? Make up your mind."

"I'm not saying there are any easy answers. But you yelling at her and telling her what to do is only making matters worse."

Ramsey held his chest. "So now it's my fault?"

Declan shook his head. "I'm not blaming anyone. I'm just trying to smooth the waters here. And you being an ass is not helping."

Ramsey stood, his anger building. "An ass? I'm here trying to keep this all together. I'm keeping her alive."

"What you're doing is treating her like some sort of porcelain doll." Declan's voice rose, as well. "She may be at risk out there, but you're putting her at risk in here."

"Oh, come on, Declan. Don't give me that psycho-babble crap."

"It's not crap." Declan said. He stood. "Think about it for one second. You're too caught up in the past. You're worried the same thing that happened to Mia could happen to her."

Ramsey dropped his jaw. "Mia? Why the hell did you drag her into this? She's got nothing to do with it."

"Doesn't she? You believe you failed her, and now you're worried you'll fail Sarah."

"Mia and Sarah are two totally different cases, Declan. Mia killed herself. Sarah's the target of an angry, vengeful Red-Line who'll stop at nothing to get her. You heard X. You heard what he said before he died."

"I heard what he said, and yes, I know Y's out there, but Sarah still has a life to live. How long do you want to keep her here? What if she never shows another flicker of ability? Never manages another show of strength? You gonna keep her here until we're all dead?" What's she going to do then, without her Protector to keep her safe?"

Ramsey shot out a hand. "I don't know, Declan. What do you expect from me? I can't keep her here, but I'm supposed to let her go home? Is that what you want? You think the Council will go for that? And what happens if she does go home, or she goes to the bookstore or goes for a cup of coffee down the street, and something happens. Something unthinkable. You think you're the one who's going to be racked with guilt? Are you going to be the one to explain it to our people, some of whom are already dying? Will you explain it to the Council?" He paused. "Will you explain it to your dad?"

At the mention of his father, Declan went quiet. Both were breathing hard, and the tension in the room was high. Ramsey's agitation got the better of him and he turned and banged his fist into it to vent his anger. Silence ensued as both attempted to calm down.

Behind him, Declan finally spoke. "And what are you going to do, John, when you continue to keep her here, treating her like some sort of prisoner?"

Ramsey's eyes shut.

"What will you do when she ends up hating you?" Declan paused. "And you end up losing her anyway."

Declan's words pierced him. He put his arm up against the wall, leaned on it and dropped his head. "At least she'll be alive."

"Not really," answered Declan. "Nobody's alive who isn't living their life the way they want to live it."

**

Declan watched his brother battle with himself. He didn't know what was best either, but he knew it couldn't keep going on like this. He knew it the minute Ramsey had left the living room and he'd spent some time with Sarah. He could feel her anger, fear, and doubt, and knew she blamed John, whether she realized it or not. If something didn't change soon, she'd turn on his brother and she'd lose the one person she needed the most. He knew that he couldn't let that happen. Some intuitive sense told him that, no matter how all of this played out, Sarah and his brother were critical parts of the equation. And if it meant getting Sarah out of the house for a little while, then it was worth the risk.

"We'll be gone an hour, two at the most," he said, staring at his brother's back. "It'll do a world of good for Sarah. It'll be good for you, too. Give you both some space."

Ramsey stood straighter and, his shoulders slumped, turned to face Declan. "Let me think about it. I just need to sit with it a while."

"Don't sit with it too long."

Ramsey frowned. "I hear you, all right?"

"All right," said Declan, happy that he'd at least made some headway. "How's Leroy?" he asked, deciding it was time to move on to another subject.

"I should have suspected you were mentally eavesdropping." Ramsey shook his head. "He's fine. He's bringing Morgana tomorrow morning."

"Really?" Declan did not hide his surprise. "You think she's ready for that?"

"Who? Morgana or Sarah?"

Declan wondered about that. "Good question."

"Care to join us?"

"You think I need to?"

"I don't know. We may need extra security."

"For whom?

"I don't know that either. Maybe for me."

Declan chuckled. "Considering how angry Sarah is with you right now, you may need extra security before tomorrow."

Ramsey groaned. "I guess I should go talk to her."

"I'd give her some space at the moment." Declan could still feel Sarah's emotional turmoil. "Give her some time to cool off."

Ramsey sat at the table, rubbing his neck and shoulders. "I have no idea what to say."

Declan empathized with his brother's plight. "You'll figure it out. You've always had a way with words."

"Something tells me I may have step up my game a little."

"Probably a lot."

Ramsey dropped his hand. "Thanks for the encouragement."

"You'll be fine. She has a soft spot for you, although you may not know it right now."

"Maybe, but I think that spot is currently about the size of a pinhead."

"If that big." Declan grinned, and the mood lightened.

Ramsey squinted. "Is this you trying to be supportive?"

"Sorry. I'm out of practice." Declan checked his watch.

"Going somewhere?"

"Yeah. I'm supposed to meet with the Council this afternoon."

"About Sarah?"

"Amongst other things. The realization that a second Red-Line likely lives among us has them a little squirrely."

"I can imagine it does. What, are you supposed to give them security tips?"

"Probably. Just give them as much information as I can to the degree that I know it, which isn't much."

"Well, you have fun with that. Sounds like a pleasant afternoon."

"About as pleasant as yours."

Ramsey sighed. "Don't remind me." He tapped on the table. "About your dad...How's he doing?"

Declan nodded. "He's better, actually. I got to spend some time with him yesterday."

"Good," Ramsey paused. "I didn't mean anything by bringing him up."

"It's okay. I know you didn't."

Ramsey picked up his coffee. "So, you'll be here tomorrow?"

"When's Morgana coming?" Declan asked.

"Sometime around ten."

"I'll come early. Make sure you're still in one piece." Declan headed toward the kitchen door.

Ramsey stood and followed.

"Wish me luck," said Declan.

"I would if I had any."

Declan opened the front door. "Sarah will be all right. She'll find her way."

"Isn't that what Mr. and Mrs. Borden said about Lizzy?"

Declan held his stomach. "I hope you didn't make her that mad."

"Guess you'll find out tomorrow."

"Should I bring a body bag just in case?" he asked, smiling.

"You're the intuitive one. You be the judge.

"See you tomorrow." Declan waved and Ramsey shut the door.

**

Several hours later, Ramsey found himself pacing the living room just as Sarah had earlier. She had still not emerged from her bedroom. His impatience grew as he realized she had no intention of speaking to him, at least not today.

He hated not having the chance to talk with her. He wanted to at least try and smooth out the bumps the two of them were experiencing, and didn't want to wait until tomorrow. He needed to let her know tonight about the meeting in the morning because if he didn't, she'd be angry with him for that, too.

Approaching her room cautiously, he wondered if he should try to break the ice. Arguing with himself, he decided he couldn't wait any longer. Standing outside her door, he knocked softly.

"Sarah?" He heard nothing and knocked again. "Sarah, can I come in?"

Ramsey thought he heard a muffled "no," but chose to ignore it. He slowly turned the knob and inched the door open enough to look inside. All he could see was darkness.

"Sarah?" He put his face closer to the door and opened it a little more to pop his head in. He hoped nothing would hit him in the face.

"Go away." He heard her muffled voice and discerned she was in bed although he couldn't see her.

"Sarah, I'm sorry. I didn't handle the situation very well this afternoon." He waited for her response.

"I don't want to talk about it."

"Please try to understand."

"Go away, Ramsey."

He heard the anger in her voice and knew the time for this conversation would have to be later.

"All right, I'll go." Thinking she hadn't been out of her room since midday, he asked, "You hungry? You want me to make you something?'

"What I want you to do is leave."

Imagining something being flung at him, he almost ducked back, but nothing violent occurred. "Okay. I'm leaving. Before I do, though, I need to tell you that Leroy is bringing Morgana here tomorrow morning. She wants to meet with you."

When Sarah didn't answer, he almost repeated himself when she quietly replied. "I don't suppose you could have bothered to ask me first."

"It wasn't exactly a request for either of us."

She sighed in the darkness. "Whatever, Ramsey. I honestly don't care anymore."

He hated that she wouldn't come out and talk to him. "Sarah," he said again. "Please be patient. This will all—"

"I said get out of here. I don't want to talk about it." Her outburst stopped him in mid-sentence. Hesitating, but fulfilling her request, he closed the door.

Remaining outside of it, though, he thought back to Declan's words that afternoon. *She'll end up hating you.* Realizing now what his brother had sensed, he wondered if she'd already reached that point. Had he already lost her? He had no answer as he turned and made his way to his own room.

T W O

....

T HE NEXT MORNING, the sun pierced the windows, cheering the house. Ramsey's mood did not reflect the brightness, though, as he sat in the kitchen, drinking his coffee. He'd been sitting there for a couple of hours, hoping to see Sarah, expecting her to be up early. She still remained in her room, though, and Ramsey, cranky from lack of sleep, felt his mood darken. He looked at the clock on the wall. Leroy and Morgana were expected soon. If he was going to talk to her before they arrived, then he needed to do it now.

Frustrated, he ran his hand over his face and debated waking her. He knew she had to be up, unless of course, she'd slept as poorly as he had.

Fifteen minutes, he thought to himself. Then he was going to check in on her, whether she liked it or not. This silent treatment had to end. Besides, after he'd tossed and turned last night, he'd come to the conclusion that Declan was right. Sarah needed some time out of the house, and as much as he hated to let her go, he would ease up a bit—for both their sakes.

A familiar presence permeated his fog of irritability, and he got up and unlocked the front door, then went and sat on the living room couch.

"It's open," he yelled, and the door moved inward as Declan stepped in-side.

19

Declan eyed Ramsey on the couch. "Please tell me you didn't leave this door unlocked all night," he said. He closed the door behind him and locked it.

"Give me more credit than that," answered Ramsey, staring at Sarah's closed bedroom door.

Declan entered the living room. "I see you're still in one piece. Things go any better last night?" He sat in the overstuffed chair next to the couch.

"Things are exactly the same as they were when you left. I haven't seen her since."

"She hasn't left her room?"

"No. I tried to talk to her, but she about took my head off."

"Does she know her presence is expected at any time?" He checked his watch. "Leroy and Morgana will be on their way by now."

"I told her last night. It didn't help."

Declan leaned forward. "Well, as much as I hate to bother her, we need to give her fair warning. We can't have her hiding in her room. It makes for difficult conversation."

That made up Ramsey's mind. He stood and made his way to her door. "My thoughts exactly," he said. He knocked twice. "Sarah," he said, "you awake?"

It was quiet and he tried again, knocking a little louder. 'Sarah, I don't want to upset you, but that meeting with Morgana I told you about? Well, we should talk about it before she gets here." When he got no response, he asked, "Can I come in?"

He put his hand on the door knob and slowly turned it, listening for any response or objections. Hearing nothing, he pushed the door open. The sunlight shown through her window and he felt a slight tinge in his belly when he didn't see her and worse, didn't feel her. He swung the door wide and entered. The bed was unmade but empty. The sunlight reflected on an object on the nightstand. Looking closely, he saw that it was her hummingbird necklace. She had asked Declan to retrieve it from her apartment not long after they'd arrived at the second house. It had belonged to her mother, and she wore it almost every day.

"Sarah?" He spoke urgently now, and went into the bathroom and flicked on the light. She wasn't there either, but what he saw surprised him just as much.

Declan stood in the doorway to Sarah's room. "She's not here, is she?"

"Declan," said Ramsey, "take a look at this."

Declan came into the bathroom and stopped, looking up at the mirror.

"What do you make of that?" asked Ramsey. Two towels had been pinned and hung from above, obscuring about ninety percent of it. "Not exactly what you'd expect in a woman's bathroom, is it?"

"Not in anyone's bathroom."

They stared at the covered glass. "I wonder what it means," said Ramsey.

"Well, how about we find her and ask."

That snapped Ramsey back to attention. "You getting anything about where she could be? It doesn't feel like she was taken."

Declan walked around the room and approached the window. He reached out to examine it. "The latches are undone. I think you have an escapee on your hands."

"Damn it. How did I not feel her absence?"

"You've been distracted. It's easy to miss. That, and her necklace is here."

"What does that matter?"

"Objects hold the energy of their owner."

"It's a necklace, Declan. It doesn't weigh more than a few ounces."

"Size has nothing to do with it. That necklace belonged to her mother and her grandmother. It's special to her. Sarah might as well have been with me while I carried it."

Ramsey touched the piece of jewelry beside the bed. "Yeah, well, no amount of bling right now is going to take the place of Sarah when Morgana gets here." He grunted in annoyance. "What the hell does she think she's doing?"

"Exactly what she wants to, I think. She's rebelling."

"Well, her timing couldn't be worse. I have to go look for her." Ramsey turned and left the room. Declan followed.

"Wait a second," said Declan.

"What?" said Ramsey, grabbing his keys off the counter.

"Let's just be logical about this. You going out and searching the streets for her is silly."

"Declan, don't argue. You know every second she's out there puts her at risk. I need to bring her back."

"I'm not saying we shouldn't find her; I'm saying let's make a plan here."

"A plan for what?" said a female voice at the doorway.

Caught up in their conversation, neither of them had noticed the new arrivals. Leroy stood in the doorway as Morgana entered the room.

Ramsey frowned at Declan. "I thought you locked the door."

"I have a key, Sherlock," said Leroy. "What's wrong?"

Ramsey debated how to word it, but knew there was nothing he could say to make it sound any better. "Sarah's..."

"Sarah's what, Ramsey?" said Morgana. She stood regally in the foyer, her air of authority radiating outward. She wore a red silk blouse, long black skirt, and a wide belt. A chunky silver necklace with red stones encircled her neck.

"Sarah stepped out for a moment," said Ramsey. "I was just going to look for her."

"She's gone?" Morgana's eyes widened. "You mean your charm lost its appeal? Imagine my surprise." Ramsey said nothing. "How did you manage to let her leave?" she asked. "What exactly do you do while you're here? Watch tv and water the plants?"

"I doubt the plants are thriving," said Leroy.

"Listen, Morgana," said Ramsey, "you and I can argue about my skills as a Protector later. Right now, I've got to focus on finding her."

Morgana flashed a glare at him. "If you can't manage to keep track of her here, how do expect to find her out there? She knows you'll come looking for her, and obviously, outsmarting you is not difficult."

Ramsey refused to let Morgana bait him. "There are only two places she would go. Her aunt's or to see Rachel. That narrows it down."

"Then let's approach this differently," said Declan to Ramsey. "Why don't you call the bookstore? See if Rachel is scheduled to work today. Call her aunt, too. See if she answers."

"Has anyone called Sarah's cell?" asked Leroy. "She still has it."

Ramsey and Declan regarded each other. "Good idea, Leroy," said Ramsey. He pulled out his phone and dialed Sarah's number.

"Brilliant," said Morgana.

"I'm going to check with our boys out front," said Declan. "See if they saw anything."

"I'll call the bookstore, then," said Leroy.

Ramsey listened as the number he dialed rang once, then went straight to voicemail. "She's got it turned off or the batteries are dead," he said, hanging up. A small swell of panic bubbled up, and he tried not to think about it. He didn't think she was in trouble, but he didn't want it to end that way. He watched as Leroy spoke on the phone with the bookstore.

"Call the aunt," said Morgana.

Ramsey searched through his phone contacts. When he'd first been assigned to Sarah, he'd added Rachel's and Aunt Gerry's contact information just in case he needed them. After finding Gerry's number, he dialed it and waited, wondering what he would say if she answered. He didn't have to worry about it, though, because it rang three times and the voicemail picked up for her, too. He hung up the phone, not leaving a message. "No answer."

Leroy got off the phone with the bookstore. "Rachel's shift begins in an hour."

Ramsey thought about it. "If she went to see Rachel, then she might be meeting with her now, before her shift begins. They frequently met at the diner across from the store." He wondered how fast he could get there.

"Yes, I'm sure she's going to meet with her friend at the exact place where you'd look for her first. Tremendous deduction." Morgana looked at Ramsey as if he'd lost his mind.

"If you've got any better ideas, lay 'em on me," said Ramsey, stifling the urge to say something unproductive. "I'm all ears."

Her response was cut off when Declan returned. "Guys out front didn't see anything. They saw a cab drive by about an hour ago, though. Didn't think anything of it."

"My, the ineptitude around here continues to reach new heights," said Morgana.

"They got the cab company," said Declan, shooting his own glare at Morgana. "I'll call them. See if I can find out where they dropped her off." He picked up his phone and walked into the kitchen.

"Great," answered Ramsey. "That's something, at least."

"What brought this on, Sherlock?" asked Leroy. "It's not like Sarah to up and leave."

"I can imagine what brought it on," said Morgana. "It no doubt had something to do with you." She narrowed her steely eyes at Ramsey. "I only hope she doesn't pay the price with her life."

Ramsey didn't know what to say to that, because his thoughts were headed in the same direction.

"Ease up, Morgana," replied Leroy. "Let's not jump to the worst possible scenario. We'll find her."

"I hope you're right, Leroy," said Morgana.

A few minutes later, Declan returned from the kitchen. "Records show the cab picked her up about a block from here, but they don't have an updated drop off point yet. Computers aren't showing it. Said they should have it soon."

"Unless she hasn't been dropped off yet," theorized Ramsey.

"Then that would point to Aunt Gerry," said Declan. "She's about an hour and a half away."

"Expensive cab ride," said Leroy.

"Doesn't rule out Rachel," said Ramsey. "Cab should have dropped her off about fifteen minutes ago."

"Perfect timing if she's meeting Rachel before her work shift," said Declan.

"All right then," said Morgana. "Declan, you and Leroy make your way to Aunt Gerry's. Ramsey and I will head toward Rachel and the bookstore. With any luck, one of us will find Sarah."

No one argued, deciding the plan sounded smart enough. Leroy and Declan headed out to Leroy's car as Ramsey and Morgana followed.

"We'll call you if I hear anything from the cab company," said Declan, opening the passenger door to Leroy's car.

"We'll do the same if we hear anything," answered Ramsey. Morgana made her way to his car and got in, not waiting for him.

"Wait a minute," said Ramsey before he got into the driver's seat. "What if she comes back and no one's here?"

Declan paused. "I'll call Hannah. See if she can come over and wait in case Sarah comes back first."

"Okay. And if she can't?" asked Ramsey.

"I'll have one of my security guys wait in the house until somebody shows up."

Ramsey nodded, got in his car and started the engine. He headed down the driveway and to the street, Ramsey turning one way and Leroy the other.

THREE

....

"**Y**OU'RE SURE YOU'RE all right? You had me worried sick." Rachel sat in the seat across from Sarah, her petite frame and short blonde hair contrasting with Sarah's taller frame and shoulder-length brunette hair. They had just finished eating a couple of scones and enjoying some coffee before Rachel had to leave for work.

The two women had become friends after Sarah began working at the bookstore over six months ago. Although opposites physically, they both shared common characteristics. They'd each lost both sets of parents and they had both ended up at the bookstore after unexpected events: Sarah after the loss of her corporate job, and Rachel after moving away from home to follow her boyfriend Todd to a new workplace.

"I know. I'm sorry," replied Sarah. "I was really sick, though. It took me by surprise. It was a week before I felt strong enough to even call you."

"Well, it's a good thing your Aunt Gerry was there to take care of you. I tried to call, but your phone wouldn't connect."

"Sorry. It died, and I was so out of it, I never thought to charge it." Sarah hated lying to her friend, but she knew she had no choice.

Rachel studied her with a worried gaze. "What about work? You planning on coming back? I could use your help with that awful computer."

Sarah smiled. Rachel never did have any success when it came to computers. "Arnie gave me a leave of absence for now."

"Why? Are you not able to come back? Are you still sick?"

"No, I'm better now," said Sarah, studying the table. "I'm just dealing with a few things that I haven't worked through yet. It may take some time."

Rachel stirred her coffee. "Well, I'm glad you called," she said. "I was beginning to think I'd never see you again."

"I know. I'm sorry it took so long."

"To be honest, I thought maybe you ran off with some guy." Rachel grinned. "I sort of hoped it was that man in the bookstore."

"That man?"

"What was his name? Ramsey? John Ramsey. The one you spilled coffee on?"

Sarah kept her face still, revealing nothing. "He stood me up. Remember?"

"Yes. But there was something about him. I felt sure he had a thing for you. I wondered if he might have showed up later and whisked you off your feet."

Sarah took a sip of her drink. "It's a good story."

"It's a great story. Part of me wanted it to be true."

"Yeah, well, sorry I don't have something more exotic to tell." *If Rachel only knew the truth*, she thought.

Rachel checked the time. "I hate it, but I need to go. It's going to take me a few minutes to walk to work."

They had met at a coffee shop a few blocks from the bookstore, one they'd been to only once before. Sarah suggested it, knowing that Ramsey would look for her in their usual meeting spots.

Sarah was surprised the time had passed so quickly. It felt as if they had just arrived. "Okay," she said. "Tell Arnie I said 'Hi.'"

Rachel stood and swung her purse over her shoulder. Sarah stood, too. The two hugged warmly.

"Don't make we wait so long before seeing you again, okay?" asked Rachel. "Keep in touch."

They broke apart. "I will," said Sarah.

Rachel held her gaze. "And whatever it is you're going through, I hope you figure it out. I'm just a phone call away, you know."

A well of emotion bubbled up, but Sarah didn't let it show. "Thanks, Rach. I appreciate that. You're a good friend."

"I mean it."

"I know you do."

"Okay, then. I'll see you soon."

"You will. You better get going. I don't want you to get in trouble with Arnie."

"Take care."

"You, too."

Rachel headed for the exit and Sarah watched her go. Her friend walked down the street and disappeared from sight.

Sarah felt the sadness of Rachel's absence. It was the first normal conversation she'd had in a month, and she missed her old life. Sitting back down, she battled her uncertainty. She knew she had to go back to the safe house, but the thought of going home, sleeping in her own bed, and being around her own things, made her homesick.

Ramsey would be looking for her and likely furious, but after his refusal to let her leave yesterday, she'd been so angry with him that she didn't care what he thought. And she was supposed to meet with that Councilwoman this morning. She imagined Ramsey's face when he'd found her gone. Earlier, the thought of it had given her satisfaction. Now, though, it made her feel guilty. She knew he would worry. Every action he took and every thought he had was intended to protect her. Considering the circumstances, she understood that, but everything they'd hoped to see in her had disappeared. All the sensitivity, heightened awareness, and surge of power she'd felt when she'd summoned it had ended. No matter what she did, it hadn't returned, and it didn't take extra powers to know that her new "special" friends were disappointed, even concerned.

The pressure of that weighed on her mind, and it had taken its toll until she'd finally snapped, using Ramsey's anger as the trigger. She considered calling him now, but looking at her phone, she saw only a black screen. At some point, the batteries had died. She thought that was odd, since she'd charged it last night. She realized she'd have to find a phone to call another cab or call Ramsey. She wasn't sure yet which one it would be.

"Excuse me. Do you mind if I sit?"

She looked up to see a man standing by her table. Holding a cup in his hand, he waited for her response. He wore a crisp white shirt, open at the collar, and nicely cut gray pants with polished black shoes. A large black and silver watch peeked out from the cuff of his sleeve. Caught by surprise, she viewed the room, noticing now that the little shop had grown busy and that all the chairs were occupied. Rachel's chair, now empty, had attracted his interest.

"Sorry," he said, "I don't mean to bother you. I'm just waiting for a friend. He should be here soon. I promise to leave you alone."

He smiled, and she noticed his pearly-white, perfectly straight teeth. His handsome features included shiny, well-cut sandy blond hair, gray eyes, and a closely shaved jawline. Even from her seat, she could tell he was tall. That, along with his slender build and the hint of musculature that his shirt only partially obscured, made him very attractive.

Seeing no reason why he couldn't sit there, she answered, "No, that's fine. I don't mind."

"Thanks. I appreciate it." He sat and sipped his coffee.

She went back to looking at her phone, wishing she had battery power so she could look busy. She didn't feel like making light conversation. Again, she thought of Ramsey, wondering where he was and hoping he wouldn't be too angry with her.

"You look like you've got a lot on your mind. Having one of those days?"

She hid her disappointment that he wanted to talk. Trying not to act distracted and choosing to be polite, she nodded. "You could say that. I've had better."

"I've been there. I hope it improves."

"Thanks. Me, too." She studied her phone.

"Anything I can do?"

She silently groaned when he kept talking. "Excuse me?" she asked, thinking his question sounded odd.

"I don't mean to presume anything. I just figured I'm sitting here, waiting. You want to talk?"

"Talk?"

"Yes. We don't know each other. Anything you say will be held in the highest confidence." He smiled again as if to convince her.

She didn't know how to interpret that. "No, thanks," she said, putting her phone away.

"Whatever you say." She could feel him watching her. "You waiting for someone?" he asked.

Apparently, the possibility of avoiding light conversation was too much to hope for.

"No. Not really."

·"Just taking time for yourself?"

Sitting there, holding her coffee cup, Sarah felt the first pangs of discomfort. She didn't have her alien extrasensory powers to rely on, but her basic human ones appeared to be working fine. Something about him made her feel uneasy. Her fingers sought out the comfort of her necklace but found nothing on her neck. She'd forgotten to put it on this morning in her rush to leave.

"I met with a friend earlier," she said, glancing up. "In fact, it's almost time for me to go."

Her anxiety evidently becoming obvious, his smile fell. "I'm sorry. I'm bothering you. Sometimes my personality turns people off. I can be a bit verbose."

That practiced behavior of always being nice kicked in, and guilt bloomed, but she couldn't ignore the anxiety in her gut. Suddenly, all the concern that Ramsey had expressed over her safety came into glaring focus. The discussions they'd had about someone coming after her played in her head. Goosebumps popped out on her skin.

"Don't worry about it," she said. "I'm just not feeling very social. Nothing personal."

"Well, I need to go anyway. I can't wait any longer." He sat for a second, his eyes on her, and her unease edged higher. When he stood to leave, she couldn't help but feel a sense of relief. Before departing, though, he leaned toward her, reaching out his hand. "By the way," he said, "my name is Yates. And no, I'm not named after the poet." His smile returned, but it didn't reach his eyes.

She considered not shaking his hand, but social convention won out and she took it. "Sarah," she said, feeling his fingers contact hers. His skin was soft, and his grip firm.

"Nice to meet you, Sarah."

He held her hand. She started to pull away when his fingers applied just enough pressure to keep her hand in his for another brief second. The subtlety of the action made her heart jump as warnings flared, growing stronger. Now regretting her decision to leave the house, she tried not to visibly react when he delicately grazed his thumb against her skin. Before she could pull away, he released her hand.

"I hope your day gets better." His intense stare relaxed and he straightened. "I know mine has." He stared for a few more seconds until he turned and walked away, never looking back as he left the shop.

Sarah released a held breath and swallowed, but her mouth was so dry, she could feel the inside of her throat stick. She brought her coffee up to take a sip with shaky fingers. The drink was cold, but she barely noticed, the man who'd left taking her full attention. She considered leaving, but decided to sit and wait, allowing her heart to regain its normal tempo. He's gone, she thought to herself. No harm done. Just some guy who thought he could pick me up.

Somewhere, though, in the back of her mind, she feared it was more than that. She continued to sit in the coffee shop, hoping he wouldn't come back but not quite ready to depart either, afraid he could be out there, waiting for her. She picked up her phone and ran her fingers over it, wishing she could call Ramsey.

**

Three blocks away, Ramsey's car pulled up into a metered spot just outside the bookstore. Declan had called about ten minutes earlier. Sarah had been dropped off at this very spot a little over an hour ago. He got out of the car and dropped some coins into the meter while Morgana finished her phone call. On the way over, she had contacted her assistant, Jenkins. While she waited on the phone, Jenkins pulled the files of research they had done on Sarah prior to her Shift. As Jenkins went through them, he gave Morgana the information she needed. After thanking him, she hung up the phone and exited the car.

"What did you find out?" asked Ramsey.

"We kept files on her whereabouts up until you took over. I'm hopeful they might lead us in the right direction."

Ramsey looked over at the doors to the bookstore and remembered walking through them that first day over a month ago. He hoped Sarah was nearby. He'd deliberately avoided any thoughts of disaster, knowing they served no purpose, but the longer they looked for her, the harder it became to push them back.

"Why don't you go in?" asked Morgana. "Look for Rachel. Maybe Sarah's in there right now talking to her."

He glanced back at her. "What will you do?"

"Based on the information I have, I'll do some looking around out here."

"I thought you said she'd never go to her usual places."

"That's not where I'm going." She moved away and headed down the sidewalk. "Let me know if you find her."

"You too," said Ramsey, watching her go.

He turned back to the doors, walked up, and went inside. The familiar kaleidoscope of books, shelves, and signs greeted him as he entered. He immediately looked for the register, almost expecting to see Sarah's face smile back at him, but felt disappointment when he saw only a young man behind the counter. Caught up in his work, the employee paid no attention to arriving customers.

Moving deeper into the store, Ramsey occasionally stopped at a bookshelf or magazine rack as if he were browsing, but kept an eye out for Rachel. He expected her to arrive at any moment.

As if on cue, a door marked "Employees Only" opened and out she walked, looking the same as he remembered her. He ducked behind a shelf and watched her move toward the Customer Service counter to assist a customer who was waiting there.

He debated his next move. Should he approach her? Doing so could stir up a lot of questions he didn't want to answer. Had she already met with Sarah? There was no way to know. He considered leaving the store, but visualized Sarah walking in just after he left. Looking at the large clock on the wall, he figured he'd give Sarah fifteen minutes. If she didn't show by then, he'd leave and look elsewhere.

**

Morgana walked down the sidewalk. Reviewing the information Jenkins had retrieved for her, she had noted that there were three places that Sarah and Rachel had frequented often. Ignoring those, she focused on the one place left. They had been there only once. Being no slouch herself when it came to certain abilities, she focused in on the location, letting the activity around her soften into a quiet buzzing and allowing her senses to provide her the confirmation she sought. Receiving it, she turned her attention back to the location indicated and headed that way. She picked up her pace, hoping to get there in time.

Turning the corner a few minutes later, she found the place. A big neon coffee cup blinked in the window. Looking inside, she perused the few tables within the shop. Seeing one of them occupied by the object of her attention, she opened the door and went inside.

**

Much calmer now that the man had not returned, Sarah began to think she may have overreacted. With all the warnings that Ramsey had given her, it was no wonder she jumped at the slightest concern. It surprised her that she didn't suspect everyone she came into contact with during this impromptu adventure. Taking a deep breath and releasing it, she relaxed.

"Hello, Sarah."

Startled, she looked up to see an older woman standing beside her. "Do I know you?" she asked. Did she have some sort of stranger magnet on her, she wondered?

"Not yet. But I know you."

The woman sat across from her. Sarah couldn't help but notice her polished look and how elegantly she carried herself. She moved with a lithe grace that belied her age. The woman pulled her chair in and put her hands on the table. "We've been looking for you."

Sarah slumped, and she instinctively looked out the windows, expecting to see Ramsey at any moment.

"He's at the bookstore, waiting to see if you'll show up."

Sarah eyed the woman across from her, admiring her stylish silver hair, which was swept up and held by a vintage clip.

The woman eyed the counter. "You want something to drink?"

Sarah felt no discomfort with this person in the way she had with the man who'd previously sat there. "Sure," she said. "Coffee. Black, please."

The woman stood and made her way to the counter.

Sarah's mind raced as she wondered how they'd found her. She could only assume they'd used some sort of as yet unknown alien tracking method, or they had a spacecraft watching her. Neither possibility made her feel better. Apparently, there was nowhere she could hide.

The woman returned carrying two Styrofoam cups with lids, one of which she placed in front of Sarah. She sat back at the table.

"Thank you," said Sarah.

"My name is Morgana," the woman said. "We were scheduled to meet this morning."

Sarah felt her face warm. This was the Councilwoman Ramsey had spoken of last night. As Sarah had prepared to leave this morning, she couldn't have cared less about the meeting, but sitting across from the woman now, she couldn't help but feel embarrassed.

"Sorry," she said.

Morgana's eyes never wavered from Sarah's. "Never apologize."

Sarah shifted in her seat. It was not what she expected to hear.

Morgana sipped her drink, and Sarah could not ignore her piercing gray eyes.

"Women of a certain stature never apologize, Sarah. It weakens them. Remember that."

Surprised, Sarah had no idea how to respond.

"Unless, of course," Morgana continued, "you think you did something wrong." She took another sip of her drink. "Do you?"

Sarah tried to keep up, but she was still back on the "never apologize" comment. The authoritative air that Morgana exuded held her in an almost trance-like state. Thinking about it, she responded with more confidence than she'd felt in a long time. "No," she said. "I don't think I did anything wrong."

"Okay, then," Morgana answered. "Let's move on."

Feeling the pressure on her lighten, Sarah took a sip of her drink and grimaced when the hot liquid touched her lips. "What is this?" She held her cup away from her.

"Green tea. Drink it. It's better for you than coffee."

Sarah put down the cup, picked up her napkin and dabbed at her lips. "Sorry. I wasn't expecting green tea."

"What was that?"

"I said sor—" Sarah stopped herself, realizing what she'd been about to say. "I mean... I didn't realize what it was."

"Understandable."

Sarah sipped her tea. Now that she knew what to expect, it wasn't too bad. "What happens now?" she asked. "You guys going to drag me back to that house?"

Morgana continued to watch her with that penetrating gaze. "Do I look like someone who drags anyone anywhere?"

She most certainly did not, thought Sarah. "Then what happens next?"

"That is entirely up to you."

"What?"

"I think you heard me."

"But..."

"But what?"

"I thought I was some, some...sort of super alien..." Sarah sputtered, not sure how to put it.

"How about we say that a little more quietly?" Morgana asked. "Let's use a different word, since we're in public. How about 'manager'?"

"Manager?"

"Yes." Morgana's posture never changed. She sat straight and tall across from Sarah as if they were talking about the weather.

"Okay," said Sarah, drawing out the word. "I thought I was supposed to be this great 'manager' or something?"

"You are."

"And I'm supposedly in danger."

"You very well may be."

"Ramsey says I need protection. That I can't be on my own. That I need to develop my, my 'management' skills as quickly as possible. He never lets me leave." Her frustration rose.

Morgana put down her cup. "Sarah, if there's one thing I detest more than anything else, it's when a woman blames all her troubles on a man."

Sarah sat shocked at Morgana's answer. "What? Are you saying I had some choice in the matter?"

"Didn't you?"

Sarah just stared, trying to understand. "You mean I could have left at any time?"

"What was stopping you?"

"Well, come on, Morgana," Sarah waved a hand. "Learning I'm a 'manager'—and apparently a higher level 'manager' at that—requires a little adjustment time. That, and discovering my new 'management' skills, was a little overwhelming. Not to mention I'm also apparently responsible for somehow saving all the other 'managers' out there."

"It's a lot to deal with."

"Yes, it is. It scares the hell out of me."

"Management work is difficult."

Sarah didn't know what else to say. She'd voiced her justifications, and Morgana had argued with none of them.

"What? That's it? I can go home?"

"Do you want to go home?"

"I...I don't know. I thought so."

"Then go."

Sarah's insecurities all fired at once. "But what about my 'management' skills?"

"What about them?"

"Don't you need me? Don't you need me to use them for some reason?"

"We do."

Sarah wasn't sure she understood. "But you're willing to let me walk away?"

Morgana leaned forward, resting her elbows on the table. "Sarah, you know everything you need to know, save for a few details here and there. Ramsey got you through your Shift and told you who you were. He also told you about a likely adversary, one we know very little about. Now I realize Ramsey is an intense man and he has a certain undefinable quality about him that some may find appealing, but he's still just a man. He takes his job very seriously, and because he does, he has made it seem as if you have no choice here. But don't let him stop you. You are now at a crossroads. As I understand it, your duties have ended for the moment. Unfortunately, we don't know much about your style of management, so it's difficult for us to assist you. All we can do is keep waiting and hope that at some point, your duties will be reinstated. But that being said, you still have the choice."

"The choice?"

"Yes. You can choose to walk out of here and reenter your life as it was. Return to the bookstore, your apartment, your life, leave all of us behind you. I can't promise that you won't be in danger. I have no idea what our other 'manager' out there plans for you, if anything. I can only assume if you make the choice to vacate your position that, in all likelihood, your duties will end and your value to the competition will be greatly reduced, if not eradicated completely. Or you can make the decision to embrace your new role at the firm. If you do that, though, then you leave your old life behind and you take on a new one, including all the responsibilities that come with the position. And I hate to say this, but you'll be stuck with Ramsey for a little while longer." Morgana sat back and crossed her legs. "But the decision is completely up to you."

Sarah sat quietly and so did Morgana. The silence ended when Morgana's phone began to ring. She took it from her purse and answered it. "I'm here," she said. She paused, listening to the caller. "No need. I'm with her now."

Sarah could hear a raised male voice coming from the other end of the phone. She knew immediately it was Ramsey.

"I'm telling you now," Morgana continued, listening again as Ramsey spoke, her facial expression unchanged. "It's not important where we are." Another loud shout emerged from the phone. "Your use of foul language changes nothing. I'll be there in twenty minutes." And with that, she snapped the phone shut and turned it off.

Sarah could only marvel at the woman across from her.

Morgana put the phone away. "Well?" She picked up her cup.

"Well, what?"

"What is your decision?"

"Now? You want me to decide right now?"

Morgana paused, but not for long. "You already know what to do."

"I do?'

"I find that most people know the answer to a question the moment it's asked. They only lack the courage to commit."

Sarah fiddled with the lid of her plastic cup.

"I'll give you five minutes. I'll wait outside." Morgana stood and picked up her purse. "If you choose management, then we'll return to the bookstore, find Ramsey, and head back. If you choose the other, then simply walk home from here. You know the way." Passing Sarah, she paused and turned back, "Five minutes. And I don't mean six."

She moved away from the table, headed for the door. A man in his mid-twenties stood from an adjacent table. "Excuse me, ma'am?" he asked Morgana.

She stopped. "Yes?"

"I couldn't help but overhear. I hope you don't mind me asking, but it sounds like your firm might be looking for some new management. May I give you my resumé?"

Morgana didn't bat an eye. "Did I give the impression we were hiring? How unfortunate." She turned and walked out the door, leaving the man staring vacantly after her.

He spoke to Sarah before returning to his seat. "Nice lady," he said.

Sarah checked her watch. She had four minutes left.

FOUR

....

RAMSEY PACED BY his car. Having been hung up on by Morgana fifteen minutes earlier, his worry grew as he replayed the conversation in his mind. She'd found Sarah. She'd been talking to her almost the entire time he'd been waiting in the bookstore. Since she had not told him where they were, he didn't even know what direction they'd be coming from when they returned. At least he assumed it would be the both of them. There was no telling though what Morgana would say to Sarah. Knowing her as well as he did, he had to admit that there was a chance that Morgana would return alone. If that happened, well, he didn't know what he would do.

He glanced again up and down the street, waiting for a flash of red to appear once Morgana turned a corner. A few minutes later, he was rewarded when he saw her, tall and stately, walking toward the bookstore. Based on what he could see, she was traveling alone. Other people on the street blocked his view, though. He continued to watch as she approached, hoping to see Sarah. Suddenly, the crowd parted and Sarah turned the corner that Morgana had just rounded. His body relaxed, and he breathed a deep sigh of relief. As Morgana neared him, she asked, "She's still behind me?"

"Yes, she is," said Ramsey. "Right behind you."

Morgana turned, watching Sarah's approach.

Reaching the two of them, Sarah stood there, not saying anything.

"You okay?" asked Ramsey.

"Yes," she said. "I'm sor—" She stopped in mid-sentence and looked at Morgana. "I mean...I hope you didn't worry too much."

Ramsey flicked his eyes between Sarah and Morgana, and wondered what the two of them had talked about.

"Me, worry?" he said. "I was the calm in the storm."

"More like the hurricane," replied Morgana.

Sarah remained where she was, as if unsure what to do next. Ramsey just wanted to get her in the car and back to the house.

"You ready to go?" he asked.

She didn't answer immediately, but finding her voice, she crossed her arms in front of her. "I've agreed to go back, but I have some conditions."

"Conditions?"

Morgana interrupted them. "I'll leave you two to figure it out. I'll call Jenkins to pick me up." She reached for the phone in her purse. Before calling, though, she looked over at Sarah. "I enjoyed our meeting. I look forward to hearing of your continued progress."

Sarah nodded. "Thank you, Morgana. I appreciate your... direction."

Ramsey could only stare in surprise. What had happened between these two?

Morgana waved her phone at Ramsey. "We'll be in touch."

"I'll wait with bated breath," he answered. He returned his attention to Sarah, who still stood with her arms crossed.

Speaking purposefully, she said, "First of all, you can no longer tell me where I can and cannot go."

Ramsey caught Morgana's slight smile as she put the phone to her ear, turned and walked away.

**

They argued during the ride back to the house, finally compromising just before returning. Ramsey agreed to give Sarah more freedom to leave the

42

house, provided that either he or Declan were with her. Sarah had argued for complete independence, but knowing that would only result in more arguments and that Ramsey only wanted her safe, she agreed to the compromise. She knew that in time, she would get what she wanted. She needed to let Ramsey adjust, though. It wouldn't happen overnight, but she was happy with the progress they'd made for now.

Just before arriving at the house, Ramsey asked her the question plaguing him. "So," he asked, sounding casual, "what's up with the mirror?"

"The mirror?" she asked.

"Yes. In your bathroom."

"You went into my bathroom?"

"You disappeared, remember? Logic dictates I would look for you. I couldn't help but notice."

She went quiet for a moment. "It gives me a headache."

"What?" he asked. "The mirror?"

"Yes. That's what you're asking about, isn't it?"

"How long has that been happening?"

"Since we moved in."

"You have not used your bathroom mirror since moving into the house?"

"No, I've used it. Just for brief moments. I prefer it covered, though."

He sat quietly. "Has that happened with any other mirrors?"

"How would I know? You've never let me out of the house."

He shrugged. "You have a point."

"Why does it matter?" she asked.

"Don't you think it's odd?"

She stared at him. "Seriously? After everything I've been through this past month? That does not rank in my top ten of weird things that have recently occurred."

He pulled up to the house and stopped the car. He didn't answer as she opened the door.

Before getting out, though, she turned back to him. "And don't forget about our agreement. I expect to be getting out of this house more often."

"How could I possibly forget?"

Seemingly satisfied, she exited the car and closed the door. Heading back into the house, Sarah was pleased to see Hannah. They greeted each other and went to sit on the couch.

**

Leroy emerged from the kitchen. "Welcome back," he said to Ramsey, who stood in the front entry watching the women. "How'd it go?"

Ramsey glared at Leroy.

"That well, huh?"

"I don't know what Morgana said to her, but now I seem to have a mini-Morgana on my hands."

"They talked?"

"Yeah, they talked." Ramsey shook his head. "Where's Declan?"

Leroy watched the two women now in full conversation, Hannah laughing at something Sarah said. "He had a client crisis. He'll be back later." Leroy regarded Ramsey. "Must have been a good conversation."

"Apparently."

"Sarah seems relaxed. Did she see Rachel?"

"Yes, she saw her. But that's not the only reason for her mood."

"No?"

"She expects to come and go as she pleases."

"And?"

Ramsey raised a brow at Leroy. "Oh, come on, Leroy, not you, too." Ramsey walked around his friend and into the kitchen.

Leroy followed him. "Sherlock, what did you think would happen?"

Ramsey opened the refrigerator and grabbed a bottle of apple juice. "I don't know, Leroy. Maybe just a little bit more concern about the situation here."

"I get it, Sherlock. I know we have reason to be concerned." Leroy leaned against the counter while Ramsey poured his juice. "Has she remembered anything more?"

"What? From her Shift?" asked Ramsey.

"No, from her tenth-grade birthday party. Of course from her Shift. About what happened, what she did?"

"No. She hasn't." Ramsey put the juice container back in the fridge. "She remembers nothing about X and Z. I think she has some vague understanding that she had a part in healing you, but that's it. I don't think she has any memory of me connecting with her either."

"Well, don't you think she should be told?"

"Why?" asked Ramsey.

"Why?"

"Yes, why?"

"Sherlock, you're my best friend, but sometimes you can be a total imbecile."

"Excuse me?" Ramsey put his glass of juice on the kitchen table.

"You are asking her to stay in this house, telling her she's in danger, and she doesn't even know why?"

"She knows why."

"No, she doesn't. You've given her the 'Red-Line' talk. She knows from the abilities she displayed at the other house that she's different. You've told her that there's potentially another Red-Line out there. But how is that supposed to prepare her?"

"Leroy, you know we don't tell Shifters about their experiences. That's not our job. We leave it to them to figure it out for themselves."

"We're not talking about a Gray-Line going through a run-of-the-mill Shift here. The circumstances are a little different."

"Leroy, you saw how she handled the Red-Line talk. She freaked out."

"That was over three weeks ago. I think you have reason to believe she can handle it now. I know you don't want to scare her, but if you honestly want her to understand where you're coming from, she should know why you're worried. She deserves to know everything before she makes the decision to leave this house again. That way, if anything does happen, she has the information she needs to react appropriately. You're not going to be able to protect her forever, so you better adequately prepare her."

Ramsey didn't say anything, but pulled out a kitchen chair and sat. He held his glass of juice but didn't drink it.

Leroy slid out his own chair and joined him. "What is it?" he asked. "To what do I owe this rare moment of quiet?"

"It's just…" said Ramsey.

"What?"

"I like her, Leroy."

"I know that."

"If something happens…"

Leroy paused. "I know this is difficult, Sherlock. You've got a lot more riding on this than just her safety. All of us do."

Slumping in his seat, Ramsey sighed. "All right, you win. I'll tell her everything."

Leroy sat back, smiling.

"Now what?" asked Ramsey.

"I'm savoring this rare moment of victory."

"Enjoy." Ramsey went quiet again, studying his juice.

"She'll be okay," said Leroy.

"You promise?"

"No."

"Thanks," said Ramsey. "You could humor me."

"You'll be okay, too."

Ramsey wasn't so sure. "You think so?"

"Yes, at least for the next twenty-four months. I hope it's longer than that, though, for all of us."

Ramsey swirled the juice in lazy circles. "Me, too, Leroy. Me, too."

F I V E

....

A WEEK PASSED with Ramsey telling Sarah nothing. He'd wanted to and knew he needed to, but found himself struggling to find the right time. Much to his surprise, he found himself enjoying his outings with her. The day after her impromptu visit with Rachel, he'd agreed to take her to lunch at a small diner close to the house. Even though the restaurant was close to empty, he'd spent most of the time watching and sensing the surroundings, ensuring that any threat would be immediately detected. Nothing happened, though, except that he'd successfully irritated Sarah, who'd spent the entire time eating while her table companion kept surveillance, saying almost nothing. After threatening to spend the rest of her outings with Declan, he'd agreed to try and relax.

Two days later, they went shopping. Sarah still wore the clothes Ramsey had grabbed from her apartment the day of her kidnap attempt, as well as what Hannah had bought for her and the few items Declan had packed from her apartment. Because of that and the fact she'd lost some weight from her Shift, she wanted to buy something new to wear. Reluctantly, he agreed to take her to the mall, though he dreaded the crowds. She agreed to go early, though, in hopes that the shops would be less busy.

While there, he sat and watched as she disappeared into the dressing room and then reappeared in her new items, asking his opinion. He wondered how she'd react to the mirrors in the store, but they appeared to have no effect on her. He worked hard not to go into security mode, although he kept his eyes open to the surroundings.

She scolded him a few times when she found him distracted and, his attention diverted once again, she disappeared into the dressing room and came back out. "Do you like it?" she asked.

"Hmm? Yeah, sure," he said, peering at something that'd caught his attention out near the register.

"Me too. I think I'll wear it tonight on my date with Declan."

"Good idea," he said, feeling relief when he realized his object of interest was a well-dressed mannequin. "Sounds great."

"Yes. He's taking me to a restaurant where they serve human remains. It's all the rage."

"Terrific," he said, finally turning in her direction. Seeing her outfit, he stilled. She wore a sleek, black off-the-shoulder mini dress that emphasized her curves.

She studied her reflection. "Now I appear to have your attention."

He watched her move in the mirror. "I like that one."

Turning, she viewed herself at various angles. The hummingbird necklace around her neck twinkled in the dressing-room lights. "You do?"

He scowled. "Did you say you were going on a date with Declan?"

Their gazes met through the mirror. "Yes, I did."

"The hell you are."

She smiled. "Well, then, how about we practice being better company. I feel like I'm here by myself."

Ramsey couldn't take his eyes off of her. He'd never seen her like this, and watching her now, he couldn't help but feel the strength of his attraction for her. He'd deliberately pushed it back these past weeks, knowing that those feelings would only distract him. Right now, though, they were vulnerable because he couldn't stop looking at her. Y could have been standing right behind him and he wouldn't have known.

"Ramsey?" she asked.

Snapping out of his reverie, he allowed himself a brief moment to drop the wall he'd erected when it came to her. "You look beautiful."

Her cheeks flushed. "You think so?"

"Yes," he said, sensing her mutual attraction. "And it's not because of the dress." They held eye contact through the mirror, and the room started warm. "Believe me," he continued, letting the moment play out, "if I let my guard down, I'd look at you all the time. You'd get sick of it."

She smoothed her dress nervously. "I doubt that," she replied. "I could get used to you looking at me all the time."

He shifted in his chair. "You could, huh?"

Her lips curved upward. "Yes. I've put up with you this long, haven't I?"

"The circumstances are slightly unusual."

Her gaze didn't waver. "They don't have to be."

His body heated and sweat popped out on his skin. He thought back to a previous conversation, one where she'd looked much more disheveled but just as attractive, and he couldn't help but ask, "I don't suppose you happen to own a Wonder Woman outfit, do you?"

Sarah made a quizzical face just as the saleswoman appeared. "Everything okay? Can I get any sizes for you?"

Ramsey lunged from his seat, knocking his chair backward and whirling on the unsuspecting employee, who jumped back at his unexpected movement. After losing her footing and flailing, she fell into a rack of clothes pushed against the wall.

Realizing his mistake, Ramsey moved forward to assist the woman as she tried to disentangle herself from the garments she'd yanked from their hangers.

Watching the disaster play out, Sarah held her hand over her mouth and ran forward to see if she could help.

Getting the saleslady back on her feet, Ramsey apologized, and Sarah assured her she would be up at the register soon to make her purchases. The woman looked relieved to leave the dressing area.

Sarah chuckled at Ramsey. "Little jumpy, are we?"

"Sorry. She took me by surprise."

"I guess you were a little distracted."

Remembering their discussion, Ramsey changed the subject. "I'll wait by the register. I think I've had all I can take for today."

"Poor guy," she said, patting him on the arm. "Okay, I'll be out in a sec."

Relieved that she didn't argue with him, he left the dressing area.

**

Sarah turned and headed to her changing room to take off the black dress. Passing the large mirrors, she couldn't help but take a last glimpse of herself in the mirror. She took a moment to enjoy the feeling of being out and spending time with Ramsey, time that didn't involve arguing. As she stepped away, a wave of nausea hit her and she grabbed at the wall. Bending over, she took a deep breath to settle herself. Looking back up into the mirror, she felt the familiar pain in her head, the pain that she'd felt when looking into her bathroom mirror at the house. She winced and looked away. The moment she turned, her head cleared and the nausea eased. She took a couple more deep breaths, straightened and headed into her dressing room, never looking at the mirror in there as she changed.

She grabbed her new clothes, left the room, and avoided the large mirrors as she passed them. Meeting Ramsey at the register, she completed her purchase, never mentioning to him her strange reaction. She knew it would only make him worry.

SIX

....

A FEW DAYS later, Sarah, agitated by the evening's events, strode into her room and closed the door behind her. Three days had passed since her shopping spree. She'd given Ramsey ample time to recover from his shock in the dressing room, but getting antsy again, she had asked him to take her to dinner.

Begrudgingly, he'd agreed. Now, dinner over, she reviewed the occurrences from the past hour. The evening had gone smoothly up until the end of the meal, but as they had prepared to leave, they realized the restaurant had grown busy. Outside, valet parkers had appeared and a row of vehicles idled out front, waiting to be parked. His car blocked, Ramsey attempted to work with the valet service to free it while Sarah waited inside at the bar.

She'd been standing there, watching the restaurant fill, and wondering if she'd ever again be able to enjoy the simple freedom of coming to dinner without having to look over her shoulder, when a man had approached her.

Remembering what happened next, she replayed the conversation in her mind as she changed out of her clothes and threw on a pair of sweatpants.

- - -

"Are you looking for someone?"

Startled out of her thoughts, she looked to see a man about her age, holding a drink and looking slightly inebriated.

"No," she answered. "I'm just waiting for a friend."

The man smiled. He was attractive enough, with brown hair and a mustache, his cuffed shirtsleeves and loose tie indicating his appreciation that the work day had ended. He waved at someone else at the bar. Sarah followed his gaze and saw another man of similar appeal. "Even better," said the man. "Maybe you and your friend would like to join us? Buy you two a drink?"

Sarah couldn't help but smile. "I don't think my friend would be interested."

The man's smile dropped. "Why not?" he asked. "She have a boyfriend?" He slightly slurred the word "boyfriend."

"Um, no. No boyfriend."

The smile returned. "Great. Then why don't you two join us? My name's Doug." He held out his hand.

"Sarah," she said, shaking his slightly sweaty palm.

Seeing his pal making some headway, the friend came over to join the conversation.

"This is Mark," said Doug.

"Pleasure to meet you."

Sarah shook his hand as well.

"Sarah's waiting for a friend." Doug raised a brow at Mark, who gave him a pleased look, as if somehow this meant they had scored for the evening.

"Terrific," said Mark. "You two want to join us for dinner?" He at least appeared slightly less intoxicated.

"I already asked that," said Doug, taking a sip of his drink.

"Oh, sorry," replied Mark.

"Actually," said Sarah, "We've already eaten."

"That's not possible," said Doug, holding out his arms as if showing himself off. "The main course has only just arrived." He grinned and attempted to wiggle his hips.

Mark put a hand on his friend's shoulder and, leaning into him, said something in his ear.

Doug's body posture stiffened. "I am not drunk," said Doug. "I'm fine. I'm just joking around."

Looking embarrassed, Mark said, "Sorry. It's been a long day. He's just letting off some steam."

"Don't worry about it," said Sarah, searching for Ramsey. The bar and restaurant were busy, though, and seeing her way through the crowd had become difficult.

Mark noticed her gaze. "Looking for your friend?"

"Yes."

"We'd love it if you had a drink with us," said Mark. "I know you've had dinner. How about a nightcap before you take off?"

"I don't think so."

"What's your friend's name, by the way?" asked Mark.

"That would be John." Ramsey came up from behind and stood between her and Mark. Sarah sensed his unhappiness.

"Who the hell are you?" asked Doug.

Mark instinctively moved his hand to Doug's elbow as Doug reacted to Ramsey's entrance. Doug pulled away and swayed, losing his balance. Reaching out to catch himself, he grabbed Sarah's arm and leaned into her, pulling her sideways. Now almost bumping heads with him, Sarah could smell the alcohol on his breath, and she tried not to breathe.

Ramsey reacted. He stepped forward and put one hand on Doug's midsection and another on his upper arm. Doug froze, a small strangled sound came from his throat and he doubled over. Ramsey caught him and lowered him into the closest unoccupied chair. Mark reached over and grabbed Doug before he tumbled out onto the floor.

"I think your friend's had too much to drink," Ramsey stated, letting Mark take over. He stood, and taking Sarah by the hand, cleared a path out of the restaurant. Sarah could only stare back at the two men as Ramsey led her out the door.

They walked into the parking lot. "What did you do to him?" she asked.

"Nothing. He'll be fine. He just needs to sleep it off."

"Don't you think you're overreacting?"

Ramsey opened the car door for her, and she slid in. He didn't answer her.

He moved to the driver's side and got into the car. "What the hell do you think you were doing?"

Sarah didn't understand. "Why are you angry at me? What did I do?"

"Why didn't you wait outside? I turn around to look for you, and you're gone." He put the car into drive and headed out of the parking lot.

"Because you were busy arguing with the valet people, and I wanted to wait inside."

"And why were you talking to those two?"

"Because they came up and talked to me. What was I supposed to do? Act like a deaf mute?"

"Yes. Why not? You didn't have to engage with them."

"I didn't expect them to approach me. I was just standing there."

"It's a bar, Sarah. You're an attractive single woman standing alone. What did you think would happen?"

"What? You think single women in bars have some sort of tractor beam or something?"

"Yes, actually. I think they do. Especially when it comes to men drinking alcohol."

"Ramsey, he was harmless. So was his friend."

"How do you know that?"

"Really? Please."

Ramsey focused on the road, but his tension was obvious. "Admittedly," he said, his voice calm, "he was not a mastermind of intelligence, but regardless, you cannot take risks like that."

"What risk? Passing out from his bad breath?"

"Sarah, I am not kidding."

"You really need to let up a little bit. I'm not going to live in a cage forever."

"Listen to me—" he started to say.

"No. I don't want to talk about 'danger' and 'be careful' and 'don't talk to strangers,'" she said. "It's getting to be ridiculous."

"We are going to talk about it. Whether you like it or not. Tonight. When we get back."

"Do I have a choice?"

"Unfortunately, no."

She debated arguing with him, but she heard the tone in his voice and she knew if she did, they'd only end up in a fight. To make matters worse, Hannah had conveyed to her last week that Ramsey's birthday was the next day, and Sarah had secretly planned to somehow surprise him with a cake and present. She didn't want to ruin it by having an argument tonight, so she chose to stay quiet, and they spent the rest of the ride home in silence.

Now, after heading to her room, she threw on a relaxed cotton shirt with her sweatpants and headed back out into the kitchen, determined to stay cool.

Ramsey sat at the kitchen table, unmoving.

She opened the fridge and pulled out a soda, pulled the tab back, and took a drink. "You want anything?" she asked.

"No. Thanks."

She took a drink and went to sit down across from him. He remained quiet.

"So?" she asked.

He pulled himself out of whatever well of thoughts he was wading in and answered. "How was your session with Declan this morning?"

Surprised that he had not dived straight into the "You need to be more careful" speech, she replied, "Fine. Nothing new to report. But I'm sure Declan told you that."

He remained impassive. "Not really. We didn't talk much."

"Oh. I thought you got a personal update every time."

He shook his head. "The Council might, but I don't. I live here with you. I suspect that if something new happens, I'll know it before Declan does."

"Yes. You probably would." She waited as he scratched at some invisible mark on the table's surface. "Declan did say my human sensitivities are progressing well. They're becoming quite acute, apparently."

"Really? That's something, I suppose."

"I suppose."

He still did not initiate the conversation she was expecting. After she took another sip of her drink, she asked, "So how long are we going to keep up with the small talk?"

"What do you mean?"

"Ramsey," she said with impatience. "What is it? What do you want to tell me?"

He straightened and clasped his hands together. "I need to tell you about what happened during your Shift."

She stared for a moment. "Okay. So tell me. What happened?"

**

Ramsey took a hesitant breath, debating with himself. He didn't want to frighten her, but he needed her to understand the risks. He realized now he should have told her sooner. Seeing her gone this evening when he'd turned to look for her in the parking lot had panicked him. That panic had escalated when he'd walked into the restaurant and seen her talking with the two men at the bar. It had taken much of his self-control not to grab her and pull her out of the room the moment he'd found her.

Pushing back his fear, he started talking. He told her about the events in the other house. How three men had broken in and threatened all of them. How one of them was her initial abductor, who had died in an encounter with Declan while gaining access to the house. How Ramsey and Declan had been subdued, and about Leroy's injury. He told her how she had emerged and protected Hannah, and how she had saved him and Declan from probable death. He told her how her counter-attack had resulted in the death of one man and the wounding of another, and how Declan had fought with the wounded man, but that he, referring to himself, had ultimately stabbed and killed that man. And lastly, he told her how she had saved Leroy's life, almost at the cost of her own, and he gave her a brief account of how he'd connected with her to save her.

Sarah sat still through all of it. Once Ramsey finished, she held her head.

"You okay?" he asked.

"I knew something big had happened, but I didn't imagine that. I have some vague recollection of helping Leroy, but it's foggy." She sat back, her face flat. "It's quite a story."

"Every bit of it is true."

"And those men...those men who came for me. You think they knew someone else who'll come back?"

"We believe they have a brother. He's the one we're afraid might come for you."

"And you think he's the other Red-Line?"

"Yes."

"How can you be sure?"

"That he's a Red-Line, or that he'll come for you?"

She leaned forward. "Well, both."

"X said he would before he died."

"Wait a minute. X?"

"Yes," said Ramsey. "The two men were twins. They called themselves X and Z."

"X and Z? How unimaginative. Who would name their children letters?"

"Well, we doubt they were born to a loving mother and father."

"Obviously not." She crossed her arms, thinking. "And he said they'd come for me?"

"Not they. Him. We assume he meant another brother."

"Were X and Z Red-Lines?"

"No, they were some sort of mutant form of Gray and Red. Something that we've never seen before. That, and the way they reacted to Y, makes us assume that Y is a pretty powerful fellow. More powerful than they were.

"Wait. Who?"

Ramsey realized he hadn't explained Y. "We figured if there's an X and Z, then there's probably a Y somewhere. The brothers pretty well confirmed it."

Sarah sat quietly, staring down at the table. "Y?" she asked.

"Yes." He waited, gauging her reaction. "Do you understand now why I'm a little cautious?"

Sarah stared off, her face pale, and held her elbows. Her eyes rounded and Ramsey detected a sense of alarm from her. She rubbed her arms as if chilled.

"Sarah, what is it?"

She shook her head. "Nothing. It's probably nothing."

"What is probably nothing?"

She hesitated. "I don't want you to freak out."

"Freak out over what? What happened?"

She didn't answer.

"Sarah…"

"I… In the coffee shop…there was a man."

"A man? What man? In the coffee shop?"

"Last week. When I met Rachel."

"There was a man?" Ramsey tried to stay calm.

"Yes. He sat down at my table. Said he was waiting for someone."

"And what happened?"

"Nothing happened. He only stayed for a few minutes. Then he left. Gave me the creeps, though."

"He gave you the creeps?"

"Yes."

"Why?"

"I don't know. Nothing specific. Just the way he felt."

A cold spike of fear crawled up Ramsey's back. "The way he felt?"

"Yes. I didn't think much of it at the time. Thought I was being overly sensitive. But then you said the brother's name was Y."

His heart thumped. "His name was Y?"

"No, not Y," said Sarah. "The man who sat with me called himself Yates. I remember because he said something about not being named after the poet."

"Yates?" Ramsey gripped the edge of the table. "Damn it. How come you didn't tell me this?" He stood and grabbed his phone off the counter.

"How was I supposed to know who he was? Besides, he may not be a bad guy. He may have been just as harmless as the two at the bar tonight."

Ramsey lowered his phone before completing the connection. "Is that what you think?"

Sarah hesitated, her eyes reflecting uncertainty.

Ramsey took a steadying breath. "Declan said your human sensitivities were acute. What did you pick up from this Yates? Be honest."

Sarah paused, her eyes shifting and she closed them, and for a second, Ramsey thought he detected a shiver run through her. She opened her eyes, her face clouded, and nodded.

"Make the call," she said.

SEVEN

....

THE NEXT MORNING began with Ramsey and Sarah up early. They'd stayed up late the previous night while Ramsey talked to both Leroy and Declan. After long discussions which resulted in few answers and even fewer decisions, they'd agreed that Y had made no other moves in the week since meeting Sarah and there was no reason to assume he'd make any moves that night either. Declan agreed to increase security at the house, and Leroy would meet with Ramsey in the morning after he updated Morgana and the Council. Going to bed after midnight, Sarah had debated wishing Ramsey a happy birthday but had stopped herself, still hoping to make it a surprise.

They'd been awake for a few hours, drinking coffee and saying little. Sitting back at the breakfast table, Sarah yawned.

"How'd you sleep?" asked Ramsey. He poured himself some more coffee.

"Probably as well as you did."

"That good, huh?"

"Yeah."

Ramsey had spent half the night imagining Yates sitting with Sarah and how easily it could have been for the man to take her. Then he spent the other half wondering why Yates hadn't and what sort of game he was play-ing. Ramsey's eyelids felt and probably looked like puffy pillows.

He sat just as the doorbell rang. "It's Hannah," he said. "Leroy must have called her."

Sarah went to the front door and opened it. "Hey, Hannah. Come on in."

Hannah entered, looking relaxed. Hannah had played an instrumental role in helping Sarah through her Shift. Her nursing background had enabled her to take care of Sarah through some difficult moments.

"Hi," she said. "Heard you guys had some recent developments." She took off her sunglasses and the baseball cap she wore and placed them, along with her keys, on the entry table. She shook out her long, straight au-burn hair, and the silver earrings she wore reflected the light.

"You could say that," said Sarah, shutting the door behind her.

"Hannah."

Hannah turned to see Ramsey leaning against the kitchen door. He sipped on some coffee. "What brings you out so early in the morning?"

"I think Leroy's worried about you two." Hannah eyed Ramsey's mug. "You got any more of that?"

"Sure. You take it black?"

"Just some cream. Thanks."

Ramsey disappeared back behind the door.

**

Hannah spoke softly. "You still planning your little surprise party?"

Sarah's shoulders fell. "Well, it might be just a little bit more difficult, now that his radar is up."

Hannah headed toward the couch, and Sarah joined her, telling her about her plans. "I was hoping to make just a quick run up to the market without him knowing."

Hannah dropped her jaw. "And just how exactly are you planning on do-ing that? With or without radar?"

Mirrors

"Well, since you're here, I'm hoping you might be able to help me out?" Sarah gave Hannah a look which Hannah knew could only result in trouble.

"Oh no," said Hannah. "Don't you dare pull me into this. Ramsey will kill me."

"Not once he finds out what it's for."

"Yes, he will. Birthday or no birthday."

"I'll back you up, and so will Leroy and Declan."

"Sarah, considering everything you've learned recently, don't you think you should stay close to home?"

Sarah didn't answer because Ramsey pushed the kitchen door open, carrying a coffee cup in his hand. He held the phone to his ear with his other hand and spoke into it. Approaching the couch, he handed the cup to Hannah. Still talking, he walked back out of the room and back into the kitchen.

Sarah waited until he disappeared. "I understand everyone's concern, Hannah, but keep in mind that nothing has happened."

"Something did happen. You met Y."

"Okay. Yes, I met Y, but he didn't do anything. He could have, but he didn't. Why didn't he? I couldn't have stopped him."

"I don't know, Sarah. But the fact that he's out there, that he actually made contact with you, is scary. He's up to something."

Sarah sighed. "Maybe. But I'm back to the same question. What? What does he want? What is he up to? And how long am I supposed to be at his whim in this house? How long do I have to hide here with Ramsey?"

"I don't think Ramsey's minding it too much."

"Believe me, I've given him reason to think twice."

Hannah could only smile. "Maybe you have, but I've been with him since this ordeal began, and I've seen the way he looks at you. He's not lying when he says he's not going anywhere."

"I know it. The guy is like glue."

"And it's not just because you need help."

Sarah stayed quiet for a while. "I like him too, you know."

"Well, I gathered that."

63

"But until something changes, nothing is going to happen. He won't let it."

"Things will change eventually. When the time is right."

"You're the eternal optimist."

"I try."

Sarah smacked her hand on the couch cushion. "Which is exactly why you should help me with this party."

"No way."

"Come on. You said it yourself. He likes me. I should do this for him. He's done so much for me."

"No," said Hannah. "It's too dangerous."

"No, it isn't. Everybody's just worked up right now. Please?"

**

Back in the kitchen, Ramsey spoke with Leroy on the phone.

"How'd the Council react to Yates's appearance?" asked Ramsey.

"Better than I anticipated," answered Leroy. "I think all this waiting's been getting to them, too. Everyone's been wondering what would happen next. Now that we have a face and a name, I think there's actually a sense of relief that we know something."

Ramsey sighed. "I know. At the same time, though, he met with her, Leroy. He introduced himself and shook her hand. It makes my skin crawl to think about it. And he did all of this within a three-hour window of her leaving. How did he know she'd left the house? How did he know where she'd be? How did he react so quickly? Is he somehow watching us? Watching her?"

"Try to relax, Sherlock," said Leroy. "You've got plenty of security at the house. Declan's got everyone on high alert. She's safe."

"Something doesn't feel right. I don't like it."

"You know what you need?"

"I'm afraid you're going to tell me."

"A nice big birthday hug."

Ramsey paused. "Oh, jeez."

"And a nice piece of birthday cake to go with it."

"How is it you never forget my birthday?"

"Because I'm your friend, you moron."

"You don't need to celebrate my birthday."

"What do you have against birthdays, aside from getting older?" asked Leroy.

"It's just the day I was born. So what?"

"It's the day the world was graced with your presence."

"Not a day most people would want to celebrate."

Leroy chuckled. "Who cares about them? I'm on my way over. We'll go out and celebrate."

"We will not."

"We'll discuss it when I get there."

"Leroy..." Ramsey talked to dead air when his friend hung up.

"Birthdays..." Ramsey griped to himself as he ended the call. He put the phone in his pocket and walked back into the living room.

"I don't think it's a good idea," he heard Hannah say from the couch.

"What's not a good idea?" he asked.

Sarah looked over. "I'm trying to convince Hannah to ask Declan out on a date."

"What?" asked Hannah.

"Really?" said Ramsey.

"I think they'd make a cute couple, don't you?"

"Wait a minute..." said Hannah.

"Don't ask me about it. Let me just forewarn you, Hannah. My step-brother can be a pain in the ass."

"You don't have to tell me," said Hannah. "He's a lot like his brother."

"It's just a suggestion," said Sarah.

The two women regarded each other as if exchanging more than just dating advice.

"What?" asked Ramsey, sensing something else. "What are you two up to?"

Just then, his phone rang. He pulled it out of his shirt pocket, saw Leroy's name on the display, and answered it. "Leroy. What's up? You get lost?"

The other end of the line was mostly static, but Ramsey could vaguely make out Leroy's voice. "Sherlock? Can you hear me?"

"Leroy?" asked Ramsey, holding his opposite ear closed. "The connection is terrible."

"Car...stuck on the road..."

Ramsey could barely make out that Leroy apparently had car trouble. "Where are you?"

The line briefly cleared. "Near mile marker 142, on the highway. About ten minutes away." The static came back. "I'll call....tow...be late."

"Leroy, I'll come get you. You're not far." He heard some muffled response before the connection broke. "Damn it," he said before hanging up.

"What is it?" asked Sarah.

"Leroy. Apparently has car trouble." He walked toward the entry and grabbed his keys from the table. "He's not too far. I'll go pick him up." He stopped and eyed Hannah and Sarah on the couch. "You two stay put. I'll be right back in twenty minutes. I'll tell security."

"Okay," said Sarah. "Be careful."

Ramsey opened the door and left.

**

Sarah immediately stood. "That's perfect. Let's go."

Hannah couldn't believe it. "Are you kidding?"

"No. We can run up to the store. We'll be back in plenty of time."

"We are staying here."

"Hannah, come on. We'll go together."

"Sarah, you think security is just going to let us stroll out of here? And even if they do, their first call will be straight to Ramsey."

Sarah's posture deflated, and she sighed. "Shoot. I can't seem to go anywhere without everybody knowing about it." She sat back on the couch.

Hannah felt bad for her, knowing she just wanted to do something special. "How about this?" she asked, trying to offer another option. "When Ramsey and Leroy come back, I'll run up to the store for you. I'll bring back a cake, candles, and a bottle of wine or something. I'll find some excuse to sneak it back into the house. Hopefully, security won't shoot me on sight."

"You will?" asked Sarah, leaning forward on the couch.

"Yes," said Hannah, putting her hand on her head. "But don't get mad if I screw up the surprise. I'm terrible at lying."

"You won't screw up. You'll be fine. Thank you, Hannah."

"How am I going to sneak in a cake and wine?" Hannah wondered.

Sarah's eyes lit up. "A box. You can put it in a box."

"A box?"

"Yes. Put it in a box. You can bring it in. Say it's for me. I'll bring it to my room. He won't know."

"Don't you think he'll wonder what's in the box?"

"You can tell him it's stuff from your place you thought I might like. He won't pay any attention to that."

"You think that will work?"

"Actually, yes. Long enough until I can spring the surprise."

"Where are we going to find a box?"

Sarah thought about it. "Look in my room. In the closet. I'll look in the garage. I think I've seen a box somewhere." Sarah and Hannah stood and Hannah headed into Sarah's room.

"In the closet?" asked Hannah.

"Yes," was the distant reply.

Hannah walked across the room and opened Sarah's closet. She pushed aside the clothes but saw nothing other than shoes.

"I don't see anything," she said. She scanned the room, wondering where a box could hide. She got down on all fours and looked under the bed. There was nothing there.

"Sarah," she said. "There's no box in here."

Hearing nothing, she walked back into the main room.

"Sarah?"

She entered the kitchen but it was empty. She opened the garage door, and it was dark.

"Sarah? Where are you?" Walking back out of the kitchen and into the entryway, she felt a tingle of worry. That was when she saw it. A small piece of paper on the entry table where she'd laid her keys, glasses, and baseball cap. Noticing the items were gone, she picked up the note. "Be right back," it read. "Don't worry!" A small smiley face was drawn below the text.

Fearing the worst but knowing what she would see, Hannah ran to the front window and saw her car was gone. How could Sarah have snuck out so quietly? She was more skilled than anyone was letting on. Hannah debated calling security and pulled out her phone, but dialed another number instead. It picked up on the second ring.

"What the hell do you think you're doing?" asked Hannah.

"I'm sorry, Hannah," said Sarah. "I promise I'll be right back. The store is right around the corner. I'll run in and run out. I'll be back in ten minutes."

"Sarah...this is a bad idea."

"Stop worrying."

"I can't help it. I don't like this."

"Nobody knows I'm doing this. Y is not waiting for me in the bakery section of the grocery store. I am fine."

"Ten minutes, Sarah. If you're not back, I'm turning you in."

"That's all I need. Thank you. I'll call you when I'm back in the car."

"Hurry, Sarah."

"I'm hurrying. Call you back soon."

"This better be a good cake."

"It will be. Bye."

Hannah heard the phone disconnect. She hung up and put her cell back in her pocket. Standing in the empty house, she heard only the tick of the clock on the wall outside the kitchen, and a pulse of unease ran through her. She started to pace, knowing she wouldn't stop until Sarah returned.

**

Ten minutes away, Ramsey neared mile marker 142. His phone rang. Picking it up, he expected to see Leroy's name on the display. Unexpectedly, it read "Unknown."

"Hello?" Static crackled on the phone.

"Sherlock?" Ramsey heard the broken, faint sound of his name before the static took it away.

"Leroy? Is that you?" The static cleared and the line sounded clear. "Hello?" he repeated.

"John Ramsey."

His name was spoken clearly, and the energy from the caller crawled up Ramsey's arm and he felt more than heard the voice. He didn't respond.

"Don't you just love technology?"

"Who is this?" he asked, his hand gripping the phone.

There was a pause. "Do you really need to ask?"

Ramsey's stomach flipped as he considered what to say. "Y?"

"Such a dull name," came the reply.

"What do you want?"

"You know what I want." There was another pause. "But that's not why I called."

Ramsey tried to keep an eye out for Leroy. "Then enlighten me."

"You can stop looking for Leroy."

Ramsey froze. "Why? Where's Leroy?"

"I don't know. Somewhere on the road, I suppose. On his way here."

Icicles of fear sent shockwaves through every one of Ramsey's nerve endings. "Here? Where's here?"

"Your little home away from home."

Ramsey slammed the brakes hard as he narrowly missed the approaching exit. He swerved the car into the right lane, exiting the highway and heard the car horn of the driver behind him. Accelerating again, he raced to do a U-turn and get back on the highway.

"Better hurry," said the voice on the phone.

"Don't touch her."

Y laughed. "She's not even here. You really aren't very good at keeping track of your assignments, are you?"

"Where is she?"

"I suspect she's making some sort of lame attempt to celebrate your birthday. Pitiful."

Ramsey completed his U-turn and slammed on the accelerator as he hit the on-ramp back to the highway.

"She'll be back soon, though. I guess Hannah will have to keep me company."

Ramsey held his breath. "Leave her alone, Y. She's not involved in this."

"But she is. All of you are. But you're right. She's not my main interest."

"What do you want with Sarah?" His car flew down the highway as he dodged traffic. On the phone, he could hear what sounded like knocking.

"I have to go now, Ramsey, but you better hurry. I'm waiting for whoever gets back first. You...or her." There was another brief pause on the line. "And I can't wait to see who wins."

The line and Ramsey's phone went dead. He punched the buttons, but his phone wouldn't work. Unable to call Sarah, he threw his cell against the dash in frustration and punched the accelerator to the floor.

**

Sarah raced through the store. She grabbed a chocolate cake and a bottle of wine, found some candles, and even grabbed a silly card as she ran through the greeting-card section. Standing at the register, she checked her watch. Hannah would be calling soon if she didn't hurry. Noticing a display of wristbands as she waited, she spotted one with black and tan colors. Small letters were etched into a narrow section of fabric on the band that spelled "Relax." She grabbed it instantly, knowing it would be a perfect gift. She had no idea if Ramsey would wear a wristband, but she knew he would get the point.

The customer in front of her completed their purchase, and Sarah waited while her purchases were scanned. After paying, she grabbed her bags and ran out to the car. She opened the door, threw the bags in, sat behind the wheel, and checked the time. Fifteen minutes had passed, and she expected Hannah to call at any moment. She placed the keys in the ignition and turned them. Nothing happened.

"No." Sarah refused to believe it. "No, please no. Not now."

She turned the keys again. Nothing. The car did not turn over. She kept trying, praying with each twist of the key.

"Damn it," she said, slamming her hand on the steering wheel. What were the odds that she and Leroy would both have car trouble? She stilled, thinking about it. Slim to none, she thought. A cold, wet shiver passed through her and she knew it meant something awful. Sarah grabbed her purse, found her phone, and hit the button to call Hannah. She listened as the phone connected and she heard it ring. It rang several times.

"Come on, Hannah. Pick up. Pick up."

It went to voicemail, and Sarah tried again, but with no luck. Hannah never answered the phone.

**

Hannah paced for several minutes, debating whether to call Sarah numerous times. Ten minutes, she thought. *I gave her ten minutes.* She made herself wait as she moved into the kitchen. She opened the refrigerator door and studied the inside but wasn't hungry. She considered calling Ramsey, but he was probably picking up Leroy by now and he wouldn't be able to do much other than yell at her. She sat at the kitchen table and considered another option. Accessing her phone, she called Declan.

He answered on the second ring. "Hello?"

"Declan?"

"Hannah? What's wrong?"

As usual, he picked up on her feelings as he did with everyone else.

Hannah tried to sound casual despite her worry. "You anywhere near the house?"

"Why?"

"Sorry. I'm not trying to freak you out or anything. I'm just nervous."

His voice tightened. "Why are you nervous? Are you with Sarah?"

"I was."

"You were? Hannah, what's going on?"

"Sarah snuck out in my car and went to the grocery store. She wanted to celebrate Ramsey's birthday. Ramsey doesn't know. I'm in this house waiting for her." Hannah knew she was rambling, but couldn't seem to stop herself.

"Where's John?"

"He went to pick up Leroy."

"Where's Leroy?"

Now she could feel his agitation.

"Somewhere on the highway. His car broke down. He's not far."

"His car broke down?"

"Yes."

"And John went to pick him up?"

"Yes."

"And Sarah's at the store to get a birthday cake?"

"Yes."

"And you're there by yourself?"

"Yes, I am."

There was silence on the line.

"Declan, are you there?"

She realized then that he was probably doing his "checking in" thing, where he went quiet and did some sort of connection ritual. She waited a few seconds.

"Hannah," he said, "listen to me."

Something in the tone of his voice made her hair stand on end. "What, Declan?"

"Just take it easy. Is the door locked?"

Now she knew he'd picked up on something. "Yes, of course."

"Okay. Leave it that way. Stay in the house. Don't open the door to anyone. You hear me? Not even me."

"What do you mean, Declan? You're scaring me."

"I'm going to the grocery store first. I'm not far. I'll find Sarah. We'll come back to the house. I have a key. I have no reason to knock."

"She'll be heading back soon."

"I'll find her. Just sit tight."

"Declan, are you not telling me something?"

He paused. "I don't know, Hannah, but something's not right. I can feel it. Try not to worry. Just do as I say. I'll let security know to stay alert."

"All right. Don't take too long, please."

"I won't. Call me back if you need to."

"Okay."

"See you soon. Just stay calm."

"I will."

They hung up.

Hannah checked her watch again. Ten minutes was up. Realistically, Hannah knew Sarah would not make it back in ten minutes. It would more likely be twenty. Declan must be close if he thought he could find Sarah before she left the store. She bounced her leg with nervous energy. Taking a deep breath, she tried not to let the conversation get to her. Declan had definitely picked up on something, and she wondered if he'd told her everything. As the twelfth minute clicked over, she couldn't wait any longer and she picked up her phone to call Sarah just as there was a knock on the door.

She froze in her seat. "No way," she said to herself. Her mind logically reasoned that it could be Sarah. Had she made it back from the store so soon? She had said ten minutes.

Hannah stood slowly and moved toward the kitchen door, then eased it open as if the person at the front entry might hear her. She listened but heard nothing. Trying to keep calm, she jumped violently when the knock came again, this time much stronger.

Rooted to the spot, her fear intensified until she heard a voice from outside. "Open the door, Hannah."

It was not Sarah.

Her first instinct was to hide, but when she went to move, her muscles would not comply. Panicking, she realized she was in trouble. As she struggled to step away, she began to feel a constriction through her chest. She took a breath and terror seized her when she found it difficult to expand her lungs. She reached out and grabbed at the wall, trying to keep her fear at bay.

"Hannah," she heard through the door, "I suggest you do as I say."

When she didn't move, the constriction through her chest tightened, and she couldn't take a full breath.

The voice from outside came again. "You know I'll only wait here until she arrives anyway, so you're preventing nothing."

Now feeling the lack of air begin to affect her, she had no choice but to move forward. When she did, the constriction eased.

"That's it," said the determined voice, muffled only by the closed entry between them.

Reaching the door, she prayed she'd have the courage not to open it. But the minute she hesitated, the tightening around her lungs returned and she found herself unable to breathe. She fumbled with the knob and unlocked the door, gasping as the air returned and the door opened.

"Hannah." The man at the door smiled and he slipped a phone into the pocket of his pants. He wore a crisp white shirt and perfectly fitted brown pants. His shirt was unbuttoned at the collar, and he wore a black and silver watch. He was taller than Hannah, and he raised a brow as she gaped at him. "May I come in?" he asked.

Hannah knew who he was. He bore a resemblance to his brothers, but he was not an identical match. Her mind went blank and she sucked in a desperate breath.

The wind ruffled his short sandy hair. He watched her, but she said nothing.

"I'll take that as a yes." He stepped past her and entered the house.

Instinctively, as he moved by, she felt the urge to run, hoping that she could make it to security. But as soon as she moved to leave, she panicked when the oxygen eluded her lungs again. Her legs stood rooted to the spot.

"Shut the door, please."

Fear making her fingers shake, she reached for the door and pushed it closed.

"Come sit on the couch. We'll wait together."

Still facing the closed front door and managing to take shallow breaths despite the pressure, she had little choice but to follow him into the living room. He sat in the overstuffed chair and she walked into the room. She tried to keep her fear under control, but her thoughts thwarted her and she imagined all that he could do to her. After reaching the couch, she sat, finally able to breathe normally again.

"Do you know who I am?" he asked.

She collected herself, but her heart was hammering so hard she wondered if she could talk. "Yes," she managed to say.

"Good. I hate introductions."

Sitting stiffly on the couch, she hated her vulnerability.

"Relax, Hannah. I'm not here for you."

"Why are you here?" She was surprised she'd made her vocal cords work.

"I have a few things I need to take care of. It won't take long. I'm not keeping you from anything, am I?"

"No."

"Good."

Hannah's phone began to ring. She had placed it in her back pocket after hanging up with Declan. Looking at the man in the chair beside her, she waited to see what he would do.

He picked a fleck of something off his pant leg, "Let it ring."

**

Ramsey ran the red light at the intersection near the house. He narrowly missed hitting a small SUV, which braked just in time and blared its horn. After turning down the quiet street that led to his destination, he approached the driveway. Doing his best to slow so he could manage the turn but still moving fast, he hit the entrance to the grounds. Looking for any signs of Declan's security team, he saw nothing and no one. Pulling into the front, he noticed Hannah's car was gone. He prayed that meant he'd arrived first.

Ramsey vaulted out of the car and ran up to the door. He stopped before opening it, somehow knowing it was unlocked. The sensations he felt as he stood there rattled him. Regardless of how unpleasant the energy was, he made himself feel it, knowing that he could potentially use this as an indication of Y's presence in the future. He hoped he'd never have to utilize it.

Taking a deep breath and closing his eyes for a moment, he gathered himself, raised his hand, and opened the door. Stepping inside, he saw nothing at first, but as he moved inside, he saw the back of Hannah's head and shoulders as she sat on the couch. Sitting in the chair beside her was a man he could only assume was Y.

Steeling himself, he stepped further into the room. Memories of X and Z returned, although this man looked different than his brothers. He had lighter colored hair and was clean-shaven. Whereas X and Z had appeared casual and unkempt, Y wore expensive clothes and was well-groomed, taking care with his appearance.

As he advanced, Ramsey used every technique he had to stay cool. He knew he would have to use his head to get them out of this alive, and that meant controlling his fear.

Y tipped his head at him, his gray eyes studying Ramsey. The man had an ankle resting on one knee. His elbows sat on the armrests, and his fingers were pressed together. The foot on his ankle bounced up and down.

"Welcome," said Y.

"Shouldn't I be saying that?" asked Ramsey. "It's my house." He eyed Hannah as he got closer, and although she looked scared to death, he was relieved to see she had not been harmed.

"Semantics," said Y, rising from his seat.

"You guys always bust into people's houses?" Ramsey stepped into the living room and stopped.

"I knocked. Didn't I, Hannah?" Hannah didn't answer. "She was kind enough to answer the door for me."

Ramsey took a breath. "More civilized than your brothers."

Y stilled, but didn't outwardly react. "Admittedly, my brothers were a bit more...aggressive." He spoke calmly.

"That's one word for it." Tensed and waiting, Ramsey watched Y move through the room.

"Nice house," said Y, picking up a magazine off the coffee table and then dropping it back down. "Plan on staying long?" He wiped his hands as if they were dirty.

"Why? You want to buy the place?"

One side of Y's mouth crooked up. "No." The man directed his sharp gaze at Ramsey. "I have no reason to hide."

"Really?" asked Ramsey. "You haven't exactly made yourself part of the social scene."

Y continued to walk slowly through the room. "I choose to stay secluded. That's different from hiding."

"Semantics," answered Ramsey.

Y chuckled. "Touché," he said, but his smile disappeared. He stood still, eyes narrowed. "So how about we get to the point of my visit? Unfortunately, we don't have time for small talk." Slipping his hands into his pants pockets, he stood as if speaking with an old friend.

Ramsey hoped Y was telling the truth and would explain his appearance. "That's a great idea. I'd really like to know what the hell you're up to."

Y cocked his head. "Yes, I suspect you've been getting a tad impatient. I know Sarah has."

The man's familiarity with Sarah bothered Ramsey, but he tried not to show it. "What do you want, Y?"

The use of his name got the first reaction. "Y is so mundane. I prefer the name Yates."

"Not named after the poet, though."

Yates's stare relaxed. "She told you, did she? I must have made an impression."

"Not the kind you'd tell Mom about."

"Nevertheless..."

"You were getting to a point?" Ramsey continued to hope that maybe this guy really did just want to talk. He needed him out of here, though, before Sarah returned.

Hannah's phone rang again, but they all ignored it.

Yates pulled himself out of his thoughts. "Yes, of course. The point of my visit." He walked closer to Ramsey, who stayed where he was. "I thought you should know that I have no plans to take her from you." His mood remained relaxed. "I know you've been expecting some sort of violent attack, but I assure you that is not my style."

Ramsey never broke his gaze. "No offense, but I don't believe you. Your brothers weren't exactly the harbingers of good will. They almost killed Leroy. And Declan, too."

"The situation was different at the time. I allowed them some latitude."

"Latitude?"

"We can argue over semantics again if you want, but we're wasting time." Stepping forward, Yates walked right up to Ramsey. Similar in stature, the two men faced each other, neither backing down.

Ramsey's brown eyes met Yates's gray ones. "What are you trying to tell me, Yates?"

Yates maintained his intense stare. "She'll come to me of her own free will."

"The hell she will."

"I will never force her to do anything. She'll make the choice to be with me when she's ready."

"Is this all you came to tell me?" Ramsey never blinked. "Because I'm getting bored."

"Has she gotten her powers back?"

Ramsey stiffened.

Y's eyes sparkled. "That's right. I know she can't use them, and I know why. I know a lot of things you don't."

Ramsey knew time was running short. Sarah would return at any minute. "Do you know how to get an unwelcome guest out of the house?"

Yates's eyes shifted, but he stayed motionless. "There is one more thing before I leave."

"Well, don't stop now." The energy in the room thickened.

Yates paused. "As I said, I'm not a violent man. I don't believe it resolves anything."

Ramsey didn't argue. "I believe we've covered that already. You're all for world peace."

An unseen ripple of energy permeated the air and Ramsey almost moved back.

Yates sneered. "But I have no problem with revenge." At lightning speed, Y stepped close and jerked his hand from his pocket.

Ramsey caught sight of a flash of steel, and before he could react, Yates sunk the blade deep into his side. The shock of the attack made him immobile, and he went numb as Y held the knife inside him.

79

Y clutched at Ramsey's shirt with his free hand. "That's for my brother," he said and yanked the blade out.

The numbness vanished and pain sliced through Ramsey. He gasped and grabbed at the wound.

Holding Ramsey up, Y leaned in and spoke into Ramsey's ear. "Hurts, doesn't it?"

Ramsey grunted and Y let go and stepped aside.

Ramsey dropped to the floor on his knees. Falling forward, he put one hand on the carpet and the other clutched at his wound. Blood flowed through his fingers. A white lance of searing pain hit him, and he fell forward and rolled inward, breathing hard.

Placing his foot on Ramsey's shoulder, Yates pushed him and rolled him onto his back, where Ramsey lay buckled and staring at the ceiling, sweat popping out on his brow.

His calm demeanor returning, Yates flipped the knife closed and returned it to his pocket. Seeing specks of blood on his sleeve, he wiped at them. "What a shame," he said. "You ruined a perfectly good shirt."

Watching from the couch, Hannah screamed.

EIGHT

....

L EROY DROVE FAST up the driveway. He'd been on his way to the house when he received the call from Declan. Declan had informed him of the conversation with Hannah, at which point Leroy had confirmed that he'd had no car trouble and was only a few minutes away. Arriving at the store at the time and finding Sarah, Declan told him to be careful. Declan had been unable to reach Ramsey or his security team, and Hannah did not answer her phone, so he suggested Leroy wait for him before he went into the house. Leroy told him what he thought about that suggestion and urged Declan to hurry if he wanted to help. Hanging up the phone, he picked up his speed. He tried to call Sherlock, but it went straight to voicemail each time.

Seeing his friend's car as he pulled up, a dark, heavy wave washed over him. He jumped out and hurried to the door, which stood open. Feeling the emotions from inside the house, his whole body tingled. Fear, anger, rage, and pain assaulted him. Walking in, he shoved the emotions back and shielded himself from them. Scanning the room, he saw Hannah kneeling over Ramsey, who was lying on the floor. Ramsey's face was pale and his hands bloody. One gripped his midsection and the other clutched the carpet.

Leroy almost stopped when the memories of his own situation a month earlier flooded him. Shaking off the flashback, he rushed to his friend's side and gasped at what he saw. Ramsey lay injured, his abdomen blood-soaked, as Hannah worked to staunch the bleeding.

"Sherlock?" he asked, breathless. Ramsey remained conscious but his eyes were shut tight. "Hannah? What happened?"

Hannah held what looked like a blanket against Ramsey's side. "Y," she said, her voice shaky. "He stabbed him. I've called an ambulance." Leaning hard over Ramsey, she applied pressure to the wound.

"How is he?"

"Not good, but he's hanging in there."

"Where's Y?"

"He's gone. You just missed him."

"Damn it." Leroy kneeled down, getting closer. "Sherlock? Can you hear me?"

Ramsey forced his eyes open and blinked. "Hey, Leroy," he said, sweaty and shaking. "How's your car?"

Leroy pulled off his jacket. He wiped Ramsey's face with a sleeve and then placed the jacket under his head. "My car's just fine. Looks like you got hustled."

"Appears so." Ramsey moaned and tightened his grip on the carpet. The color in his face drained more, leaving it ashy white.

"Take it easy," said Leroy. "Try to relax. Help is coming."

"Is it?"

"Yes. Hannah called an ambulance."

"Where's Sarah?"

"Declan's got her. Don't worry."

"You're sure?"

"Yes. I just talked to him."

Ramsey relaxed a little but breathed shallowly. "How bad is it?"

Leroy kept his face placid. "I don't know. How bad did he get you?"

Ramsey tensed when another wave of pain lanced through him. When Hannah pressed on the wound, he couldn't help but grab at her hands.

"Easy," said Leroy, taking one of Ramsey's hands in his and letting him grip it instead.

Ramsey groaned, trying to ride it out.

"Just breathe through it, Sherlock. I know it hurts."

"Hannah...ease up," Ramsey whispered, fighting to stay conscious.

"Sorry, Ramsey. I can't." Hannah pressed down. "I am not going to let you bleed out on me."

Ramsey released some air and held tightly to Leroy's hand.

In the distance, sirens wailed.

"They're almost here, Ramsey. Hang in there," said Hannah.

"Some birthday, huh?" Ramsey said, closing his eyes as he grimaced.

"I got you a birthday present," said Leroy.

"You did?" asked Ramsey. His eyes opened again.

"Yeah. It's in the car. But there's a catch. You got to live to get it. You understand?"

"You drive a hard bargain." Ramsey winced although he tried to smile.

"Do you understand?" Leroy asked again, more strongly this time.

Hearing the tone, Ramsey met Leroy's gaze. He nodded. "Yes, I understand."

"Good."

The sirens shrieked and went silent. The rush of footsteps could be heard as paramedics entered the house.

**

Declan's car joined the rest on the driveway. Sarah jumped out of the vehicle. "Sarah, wait..." he said.

But Sarah ignored him. He'd told her what he knew when he'd found her in the grocery store's parking lot. They'd left Hannah's car behind and rushed to the house. He knew it was bad the moment they hit the driveway. And he knew it was John who was hurt.

Following Sarah into the house, he was uncertain of what to expect. He barely had time to move as a gurney carrying his brother, pale and sweating, shot out of the house and into the waiting ambulance. Hannah moved out with them, speaking to the paramedics. They put Ramsey in the back and closed the doors. Starting the sirens back up, the ambulance headed back out of the driveway. Hannah turned and ran into the house to the kitchen, where she washed her hands.

Declan followed her inside. "Where are they taking him?"

Sarah stood with Leroy, who, looking pale despite his dark skin, held her and tried to calm her as he attempted to explain what happened.

"St. Mary's," said Hannah, drying her hands on a towel.

"That's thirty minutes away."

"It's a trauma center. It's the best place for him."

"How bad is it?" asked Declan.

Moving back in to the living room, she didn't answer him. Not finding her keys, she turned, looking focused despite what she had witnessed.

"Who's driving?" she asked.

**

Two hours later, Hannah and Leroy sat in the emergency room while Sarah paced the floor. Declan had stayed behind to find his security team and handle the police. The doctor had just been out to inform them that Ramsey had been taken to surgery. They'd managed to stabilize him after he'd lost a large amount of blood and suffered what the doctor called "significant" internal injuries. He explained that they would know more after the surgery. All they could do now was wait.

As their adrenaline dissipated, the effects of the morning began to take their toll.

"Why?" asked Sarah, pacing the room. "Why him? Why did he go after John?"

Weary from the morning's events, Hannah sat up in her chair. "Revenge," she said. "For his brother."

"His brother?" asked Sarah.

"X," said Leroy. "Sherlock stabbed and killed him." He rubbed his bald head. "X attacked Declan. And would have killed him if Sherlock hadn't stopped him. Didn't he tell you all of this?"

"Yes. Last night." She stopped. The image of Ramsey covered in blood and being strapped to a gurney by paramedics still echoed in her mind. "My brain's not thinking too clearly right now." She crossed her arms and looked at Hannah. Sarah had to ask the question plaguing her since they'd arrived, but which she'd been too scared to ask. "He's going to be okay, isn't he? I mean, they got him here in time."

Hannah made eye contact with Leroy, and Sarah noticed the silent exchange.

"What?" asked Sarah. When neither answered, she asked again, "What is it?"

"Perhaps we should take this conversation somewhere else?" Hannah asked as a couple entered the emergency room and took a seat. "Let's go to the surgical floor. There's a waiting room there. We'll talk more upstairs." Hannah stood and walked past Sarah toward the elevators.

Leroy joined her, and Hannah hit the up button.

Sarah said nothing as she followed, but the worry in Hannah's eyes stayed with her while they waited.

Four floors up, they entered another waiting room. Luckily, it was empty, and they closed the door behind them.

"Shouldn't Declan be here by now?" asked Sarah.

"He'll be here soon. He's on his way," answered Leroy. "I've been keeping him up to speed, so he knows what's happening."

Settling in for the long wait, Sarah asked, "Okay. What is it? What do I not know?"

It was Hannah's turn to walk the room. The worry etched in her face hit Sarah in her belly and Sarah could feel the same contraction of energy from Leroy.

When Hannah didn't answer, Sarah eyed Leroy who stood at the window looking out, his hands in his pockets. "Leroy?"

He turned. "It's more complicated, Sarah, than you realize."

A thought occurred to Sarah. "The doctors... They can treat him, can't they? They can help him, right?"

"Yes, they can treat him," said Leroy.

"Then what's more complicated?"

"Sherlock's injuries," said Leroy. "It's not just the stab wound."

"What? Is he injured somewhere else?"

"No," said Hannah. "That's not it."

"Well, what, then?" Sarah wrung her hands. "You two are scaring me."

"Sarah," said Leroy. "We told you that we were all in jeopardy, remember? Back at the other house? And that we needed you to help us."

"Yes. I know. But you said there was still time."

"Only if we stay healthy. If we're injured..." Leroy shook his head.

Sarah felt the blood run from her face. "What are you saying? He can't survive this?"

"We don't know," answered Hannah. She stood still, her face pale.

"What do you know?"

"Sarah, listen," said Leroy. "Long story short, our people, in order to survive on this planet, have been taking a serum. It protects us from the harshness of living for long periods of time on Earth. Many years ago, that serum was sent here, but it was lost when one of our ships went down. It was never found, and we never received a replacement for it. At this point, we've rationed as far as we can. There is no more left. What that means is that we are now more susceptible to illness or injury, especially those who are older. For us, since we are young and healthy, we will be the last to suffer the effects, unless..."

Sarah understood. "...unless you're suddenly not so healthy?"

"Exactly," said Hannah, studying the floor. "Ramsey's injury is severe." She sighed. "He may not survive it."

The shock hit Sarah in her gut and she went still. Even though she knew Ramsey was badly hurt, she'd not accepted the possibility of his death. He was in a hospital receiving excellent care, he was young and strong, people had survived worse injuries; she'd used all of that as reasoning to convince herself that he would live. But now, hearing this new information, she felt the bottom drop out and a new deep-seated fear hit her hard.

Ramsey could die.

"Oh God." She sat, trying to stay composed.

"Sarah." Leroy moved to sit next to her.

She clutched her stomach. "He can't die, Leroy. He told me he'd stay with me, that he wasn't going anywhere."

Leroy put his hand on her back. "Don't count him out yet. If anyone's too stubborn to die, it's Sherlock."

"That's true," said Hannah.

"What's true?"

Hannah turned as Declan entered the room.

**

"That your brother is stubborn," Hannah answered.

"No doubt about that. How is he?" asked Declan.

"In surgery," she said. "It's going to be a while."

"Did you find your people?" asked Leroy.

"Yes." He moved further into the room. "They'd received a garbled call from me telling them to meet at some abandoned lot ten miles away. When they got there, their phones stopped working and they couldn't reach me." He shook his head, still in shock. "Apparently, Y is handy at manipulating objects and voices."

"And people," said Hannah.

"How'd it go with the police?" asked Leroy.

"Okay. I told them what I knew, keeping out a few details." Declan looked at Hannah. "They want to talk with you."

"I expect that," said Hannah. "I'll tell them what I know, save the part where I was almost suffocated by unseen hands. That might be a bit much for them."

"I would suggest leaving that part out." Declan eyed Sarah, noting her faraway gaze and sensing her distress. "Sarah?"

"We told her, Declan, about the serum," said Leroy.

Declan understood and shifted his mood to bolster Sarah. Kneeling in front of her, he said, "Sarah, listen to me."

Her gaze moved to his, but she said nothing. He took her hand, instilling as much calm as he could with her, but she was tense and unable to receive the aid he offered.

He spoke softly. "I told the police that you and John were roommates and that you were staying with him for a short time while you recovered from an illness. I kept it as close to the truth as possible. They will want to talk to you."

She didn't acknowledge what he said.

"Are you okay with talking to them?" he asked.

She managed to focus and answered, "How do I explain Y?"

"You don't have to explain anything. You weren't there. You don't know anything about Y or who he is."

"So just act dumb?"

"Can you do that?" asked Declan. "We obviously can't tell them about who we are."

She nodded. "I can do that." Her eyes closed.

"Hey," he said. He waited until she opened her eyes. "He'll get through this."

Her weary face remained unchanged. "You don't know that."

"I know him. He'll fight to survive."

Gripping his hand, the emotion bubbled up and her eyes shimmered. "I hope you're right. Something tells me I can't do this without him." She moved to wipe a tear before it escaped her eye.

"You're a strong woman, Sarah. Don't doubt that."

"That's not what I mean, Declan." She let out a deep breath and sniffed. "That's not what I mean."

**

Three hours later, they still sat waiting when the door opened and a male doctor, wearing scrubs with sweat stains at the armpits and a surgical mask pulled down around his neck, entered the waiting area. By then, three other people had joined them in the room, also waiting for news on a family member.

"John Ramsey?" he asked.

"Yes. That's us," said Hannah.

They all stood to hear the doctor's update.

"I'm Dr. Young. He's just out of surgery and in recovery."

"How's he doing?" asked Declan.

"He's weak. He's lost a lot of blood, and we gave him a transfusion. He's lucky. No major organs were hit. His intestinal tract was punctured, though, and we've been working to repair the damage. Without going into a lot of doctor-speak, we managed to stop the internal bleeding, but with a wound like this, the greatest threat is infection. Bacteria spills into the abdominal cavity from the ruptured area. We've done our best to clean it out, but at this point, all we can do is load him up with antibiotics and hope the body will do the rest. We've put him in intensive care and placed him in an induced coma in an effort to put as little strain on his system as possible. The next twenty-four hours are key. If we can keep him from infection, it will go a lot better for him."

"And if you can't?" asked Leroy.

"Well, we'll do our best to fight the infection. In his weakened state, though, it could be a tough road."

"When can we see him?" asked Sarah.

"He'll be in recovery for the next hour at least. Once they get him settled, you should be able to visit for a few minutes."

A nurse poked her head in the room. "Dr. Young?"

He turned. "Yes?"

"They're ready for you."

"Thanks. I'll be right there." He turned back to the group. "Duty calls. I'll have the nurse let you know when he's out of recovery."

"Thank you, Dr. Young," said Hannah.

"Don't worry," he said. "He's young and in great shape. His prognosis is good."

They didn't say anything as he excused himself and left the room.

NINE

SARAH SAT BY Ramsey's bedside, her elbow on the bed and her head in her hand. It had been forty-eight hours since his surgery. He'd been moved out of intensive care six hours earlier. Seeing him for the first time after surgery in the ICU, it had been difficult to conceive how so many tubes and machines could be necessary for one man. She and Leroy had seen him first, since only two could visit at a time. They'd listened to the beep of the machine monitoring his heart and blood pressure and the whirring of the ventilator as it pumped oxygen in and out of his lungs. They'd only been able to stay fifteen minutes before Hannah and Declan saw him next.

Sarah did not want to leave the hospital, so Hannah had managed to secure two rooms at the hotel across the street, which catered to the families of patients. She and Sarah stayed in one room and Declan took the other. Leroy stayed the first night and each continued to take their turn to see Ramsey.

Thankfully, he'd remained fever-free and stable. They'd removed the breathing tube after the first twenty-four hours and reduced the sedation level, but he had not regained consciousness, so they'd kept him in ICU for another twenty-four hours. Because his vital signs remained strong and he showed no signs of infection, they'd moved him to a private room, believing he would regain consciousness as he gained strength. The private room allowed all of them the ability to stay during visiting hours, and it also provided a window, chairs, and a private bathroom. Now, sitting next to his bed, Sarah held Ramsey's hand, watching him and wishing he would open his eyes. With the number of machines required now reduced, the area looked less imposing, although his IV hung nearby and his heart rate, blood pressure, and oxygen levels continued to be constantly monitored. Sarah leaned her head and stretched her neck. Her eyes burned and her muscles ached. She'd slept little since they'd arrived at the hospital two days earlier.

The door opened, and Hannah entered, carrying two Styrofoam cups. "Here you go. I can't promise it's any good. There's no telling how long it's been sitting."

"Thanks, Hannah," said Sarah, taking the coffee. One of the benefits of being in a private room on a different floor was the family area. It contained a kitchenette with a microwave and refrigerator as well as a sitting room with a TV and magazines, and best of all, a coffee machine well stocked with cream and sugar.

Hannah sat in one of the extra chairs. She'd been questioned by the police the previous day, as had Sarah. Neither of them had said anything that would compromise who they were, but they provided as many details as the police could use to find Y, although they knew he would not be found.

"Heard from Declan and Leroy?" asked Sarah.

"No. Nothing."

Sarah looked at the clock on the wall. "They've been meeting with the Council for almost three hours now. I wonder what they'll decide."

"I don't know," said Hannah. "I honestly don't know what they can do."

Sarah sighed and closed her tired eyes. "Can I ask you something?"

"Sure."

Sarah faced Hannah. "How exactly am I expected to help you?"

Hannah rubbed the bridge of her nose. "What do you mean?"

"You said there was a serum."

"Oh, that."

"Yes, that. What am I supposed to do?"

Hannah held her coffee. "Ramsey didn't tell you?"

"No, he didn't."

Hannah hesitated. "The Council believes the serum still exists."

Sarah frowned. "Still exists? How?"

"The ship carrying it went down years ago, but the serum was not found at the crash site. We believe the captain likely dumped and hid it before the ship went down in order to ensure it would not be discovered by humans."

"Don't you think finding the ship would have been the bigger problem?"

Hannah made a face as she took a sip of the stale coffee. "Eudorans have a unique ability to remain concealed. She crashed, but she managed to put it down in a secluded area. She dumped everything that could further lead to our discovery had the ship been located."

"She?"

"The captain of the ship was female. Her name was Varalika."

"And if this serum is found, you think it's still good?"

"No reason it wouldn't be."

"There's no expiration date?"

Hannah smiled. "No. No expiration date."

Sarah leaned forward, trying to find a more comfortable position to ease the ache from sitting for so long. "And what can I possibly do?"

Hannah bounced her knee. "I wish Ramsey was awake."

"Well, he isn't," said Sarah. "C'mon, Hannah. I need to know."

Hannah nodded. "Varalika was a Red-Line, Sarah. Like you are."

Sarah waited. "So?"

"Red-Lines have unique abilities that Gray-Lines do not. I think you know about some of those abilities from what you experienced during your Shift. Another ability they possessed was to encode mirrors and use them as communication devices. They were an easy way to transfer information without fear of it being easily discovered."

"Mirrors? You mean like any mirror?"

"Yes. Any mirror. To a human or me, it's just a handy way to check out your face, but to a Red-Line, it's an effective and important tool."

"And why is that important?"

"Because Varalika's mirror was found near her body. We believe it contains the location of the serum. And we're hoping you can read it."

Sarah tried to take in what Hannah said. The room was quiet apart from the beeping of the machines. "You want me to read a mirror?" It was all she could think to say.

"Yes."

Sarah scrunched her eyes. "Hannah, maybe I'm confused, but nobody else could read it?"

"No. The Red-Lines in existence at the time all tried. None were successful. We assume she must have encoded it somehow."

"Encoded it? But why would she do that?"

"I don't know. She had to think fast. Her ship was going down. There's no telling what she was thinking. Stressed and scared, she may have accidentally transferred information to the mirror that created the problem. Or maybe she intentionally coded it for one person's eyes only. If that's the case, then they never found that person."

"Where is this mirror now?"

"The Council has it somewhere under lock and key, I'm sure."

"And why am I the only remaining Red-Line? Except for Y."

"Because the ship carried Gray-Line serum necessary for our survival. Once the ship went down, the Reds relinquished their remaining supply to us so that we could survive longer. Theirs was more potent, as I understand, so we've been able to stretch our reserves until these past few years. The Red-Lines died out soon after the crash. Only two survived."

"The Red-Lines sacrificed themselves?"

"Yes. They had to. Gray-Lines did not know they were taking a serum. They still don't, for that matter. Our host planet chose to keep it a secret. Only a select few knew. Red-Lines knew about the serum, though. In order to prevent a crisis and keep us alive long enough to find or acquire more, they let themselves die."

"That was noble of them."

Hannah chuckled. "Ramsey said the same thing."

Sarah put her coffee on the tray table. "I'm afraid to ask, but how is it that I'm here?"

Hannah put her coffee down, too. "That's a long story."

"I think we have some time to kill."

Hannah stood and stretched. "Yes, I guess we do." She bent over and touched her toes. "You should get up and move. It'll help."

"I will. But you haven't answered my question."

Hannah straightened. "Genetic testing."

"What?"

Hannah paused. "You sure you want to go down this road?"

"You can't stop now," said Sarah. "Tell me."

Hannah nodded. "Your human mother, Sarah, unbeknownst to her, married one of us, a Gray-Line. He was a genetic researcher. We'd been doing genetic testing for years with the hope that new Red-Lines could be born, but had little success. Your parents had been unable to conceive, so he suggested implanting your mother with Red-Line sperm. Your mother believed it was your father's. She agreed to the procedure and she got pregnant. You are the result."

Sarah widened her eyes. "I don't believe it."

"There were no other options. They couldn't make more serum, and they'd lost contact with Eudora. They couldn't expect more to arrive. So they did what they thought was the next best thing. Try to create a new Red-Line. One that might be able to read the mirror."

"They created me?"

"It's not like you're Frankenstein's monster," said Hannah, trying to downplay the news. "You're the result of a combination of Red-Line and human DNA. You're a one in a million shot that worked."

Sarah focused on Hannah's words, but she couldn't process them. "I'm a lottery ticket?"

"I wouldn't put it that way."

"How would you put it?"

There was a knock on the door, and Leroy poked his head in. He walked in with Declan behind him.

"Nice room," said Leroy.

"Better than the other one," said Declan. He walked to the edge of the bed. "How's he doing?"

"Still unconscious," said Hannah.

Declan looked between Hannah and Sarah. "What's the matter?" he paused. "Sarah?"

Sarah didn't respond. She'd been holding Ramsey's hand, but she released it and sat stiffly in the chair.

"Hannah?" he asked. "What's wrong?"

From the opposite side of the bed, Leroy spoke. "What's the problem?" he asked. "Other than waiting for our friend here to wake up from his beauty sleep."

"I told her," said Hannah, "about the serum. And the mirror. And where she came from."

Leroy's face fell. "What, you trying to put her in a coma, too?"

"She asked," said Hannah. "What did you want me to say?"

"Sarah, you okay?" Declan walked over to her and squatted in front of her. Sarah felt his perusal and didn't shut him out. He grimaced. "Sarah?"

Sarah didn't move, but her anger grew. Her mind raced with the newfound information regarding her origin. Everything she'd been raised to believe had been a lie. She'd been an experiment. A test dummy. She'd been made to save another species about which she knew nothing. Then, when they'd needed her, they'd pulled her out of her life, telling her only what they'd needed to, hoping she could save them. And now she'd befriended them and cared for—maybe even loved—one of them, and if she couldn't do what they needed, she would have to watch all of them die.

She felt used, as if she were a pawn or a toy. She'd had no control over this since the day she'd been conceived. And now there was nowhere else for her to go. Tingles of electricity pulsed through her arms and legs, but she ignored them. Her stomach clenched as her disbelief fueled her outrage. She wanted to stand and scream, even though she knew none of the people in the room were to blame. They had been sucked into this just as she had been, but she couldn't help herself. It was like a tidal wave of swirling energy was building within her and she couldn't stop it.

"Uh...Hannah, go watch the door," said Declan.

Sarah knew he could sense her fury, but she didn't care.

"What? Why?" asked Hannah.

A glass jar sitting on a shelf just inside the room began to tremble and shattered. It had been filled to the top with colorful candies, and a stick with a card attached had stuck out the top that read "Get Well Soon!" None of them had noticed it earlier. Now everyone jumped at the sound of the glass exploding and the small candies scattering everywhere.

Declan gripped the arms of Sarah's chair. "Now would not be a good time to be interrupted."

Hannah moved fast, avoiding the rolling candy. "Okay." She headed to the door, opened it, and went to stand outside.

"I'll help you," said Leroy, following Hannah.

Declan faced Sarah. "I need you to gain control, Sarah. Take some deep breaths."

Sarah stood abruptly and pushed past him. Every emotion swirled inside her and she wanted to unleash it. "Don't tell me what to do."

"Do you realize what just happened? Your abilities are returning. I can feel them."

Sarah whirled on him. "I bet that will make everyone happy, won't it?"

Declan held out a hand. "Listen, I know you've got a lot to process, but now is not the time. We're in a hospital, Sarah. In public. You've got to rein it in, or we'll have a lot of explaining to do."

"I don't care."

A sharp crack sounded. Declan looked horrified when a large fissure began to form on the side of the room's window.

"Sarah." He turned back. "Pull it together. You can't lose it right now."

"I'll do whatever the hell I please, Declan. I'm sick and tired of everyone controlling me, of expecting something from me." She paced at the foot of Ramsey's bed. "But what should I expect? I'm nothing but a lab experiment. Created to fulfill a purpose. Right?"

"That's not true."

She pointed. "Yes, it is."

The tray table rolled across the room and slammed into Ramsey's bed. Sarah's coffee cup fell over and brown liquid spilled onto the tray and floor.

"Sarah, please…" said Declan.

"My father wasn't even my real father." The chair behind Declan slammed into the wall, flipped, and fell on its side. Sarah gripped the foot rail at Ramsey's feet. "I'm such a fool."

Declan opened his mouth, but didn't respond.

The door opened and Leroy poked his head in. "Nurse is coming. Hannah's stalling her. Better hurry." His gaze shot between Sarah and Declan. "Everything all right?"

"What do you think?" answered Declan.

Leroy eyed the room, taking in the damage. "Okay," he said, assessing the scene, "we'll keep stalling." His head disappeared again.

Sarah knew she had to calm down, but the momentum carried her and she needed to lash out. She tried to redirect her energy, but wanted to break or throw something instead. She turned from Declan, not wanting to inadvertently throw him. She spied the small countertop in front of her with various containers of medical supplies sitting atop it, and felt the urge to shove it all off and smash it to the floor.

"Sarah, don't," said Declan.

An alarm sounded and Sarah turned toward the bed. The machine monitoring Ramsey's heart began to beat erratically. Declan looked, too. Breaking from the pull of the emotional onslaught, Sarah neared the bed, her heart racing.

Ramsey stared back, his eyes open but unfocused. "You two think you could keep it down?" His voice cracked.

Just then, the door opened and a nurse walked in, with Hannah and Leroy right behind her. "I'm glad that you're considering nursing school, Mr. Leroy," she said, "but I don't have time to discuss my career path with you. I have to make my rounds." She stopped when she walked into the room, heard the alarm, saw the broken glass, spilled coffee, and brightly colored candy littering the floor around an overturned chair and the room's patient, previously comatose, now awake. "Oh my," she said.

Nobody said a word until Declan broke the silence. "Nursing school?"

TEN

....

THE NURSE SWEPT candy and glass from the floor. After seeing Ramsey awake, she had taken his vitals and temperature, asked him some inane questions to make sure his brain still worked, gave him some water, and told him to continue to rest, as if he could do anything else. Another nurse had entered and asked everyone in the room to leave while the doctor came in and checked him again, asking similar inane questions and examined his injury, which—according to the doctor's opinion—was healing nicely. His brain was foggy, but he remembered his encounter with Y vividly. Remembering the pain, he tried to think of something else.

The door opened, and Leroy looked in. "We all clear?" he asked the nurse. "We promise to behave."

Leaning over to pick up the get-well card that had fallen to the floor, the nurse said, "Sure. Come on in." She placed the card on the bed beside Ramsey. She glanced at him. "I think he's ready for a little company." Leaning over, she picked up the dustbin full of candies and broken glass, walked to the trashcan, and threw the debris away. "Don't wear him out, though. He needs plenty of rest." She walked out as they all came in.

"Don't worry," said Declan. "We'll keep an eye on him."

Leroy walked up to the side of the bed. "Glad to see you back with us," he said. "How you feeling?"

Declan walked up from the other side. "You had us a little worried. About time you woke up."

Finally clearing some of the cobwebs from his brain, Ramsey blinked. "Glad I'm still among the living," he said, his voice still cracking.

They surrounded the bed, with Hannah and Sarah at the foot. Sarah watched him, but seemed reserved.

"You all right?" he asked, focusing in on her.

She nodded. "I'm fine. I'm just relieved you're okay."

"Give me a few days, and I'll be good as new."

"Give it a few weeks, at least," said Leroy.

"Try a few months," said Hannah. "You need to go easy, Ramsey."

Catching Hannah's eye, he unavoidably thought back to their encounter with Y. "You saved my life."

"I just did what I was trained to do."

"Regardless, if you hadn't been there..."

"But I was."

He didn't say anything, but the events leading up to his hospital stay replayed in his mind. His eyes narrowed as he considered the obvious question. "Where is Y?"

"Gone," said Leroy. "He disappeared after attacking you. No sign of him."

Ramsey wasn't surprised at the news. He spoke to Sarah. "You didn't see him? He didn't come after you?"

"We got there after he left. He was long gone," said Declan, speaking to Ramsey but watching Sarah.

Ramsey noticed the look. "What is it?" he asked. The more he came out of his fog, the more he began to sense something was off. "Something going on?"

"No, nothing," said Sarah, but Ramsey suspected she was lying.

"I wouldn't say that," said Declan. "We've had some developments."

"What developments?" he asked.

Declan waved a hand. "It appears our girl here has full power restored."

"What? You mean your abilities have returned?" He tried to hold his head up, but didn't have the strength to keep it level.

Leroy found the bed controls and adjusted it to a more upright position.

"Apparently so," Sarah answered, although not with the excitement that Ramsey would have expected.

"How? Why now?"

"I've been wondering that myself," said Declan. "I think I may have an idea as to why."

"Well, don't keep us in suspense," said Leroy.

"It's a theory, but I think it's probable," said Declan. "Think about it. When's the last time we've all been in a room together since Sarah completed her Shift and we moved to the new house?"

"The last time we were all together?" asked Leroy.

"It had to be when we left the original house," said Hannah. "You and Ramsey brought Sarah, and Leroy and I went home." She thought about it some more. "I honestly don't think we've all been in the same room together since then."

"Does that have something to do with it?" asked Ramsey.

"Well, based on the little we know about Reds, I believe that when they shifted, they were kept in isolation as much as possible."

"That wasn't possible with Sarah," said Ramsey.

"No, it wasn't," Declan continued. "Which makes me think she must have somehow connected to each one of us in the house. Used our energy in some way as she shifted. And now, at least for the time being, she still needs us around in order to access that energy."

"Which is why, when we all ended up in the same room, everything fired up," said Sarah, glad that there was now an explanation.

"Exactly," said Declan.

"Does this mean that she'll always needs us to be with her to do anything?" asked Hannah.

"For now, yes," said Declan. "Her reliance on us will likely decrease in time as she adapts and learns to utilize her skills without our help."

"I guess that means you all are stuck with me," said Sarah, crossing her arms and studying the floor.

"Or better said," added Leroy, "you're stuck with us."

Sarah offered him a half-smile and glanced at Ramsey, who still watched her from the bed.

"There's something else, though," he said. "What's bothering you?"

Nobody spoke, and Sarah regarded the floor again. "You don't need to worry about it. I'm fine."

Ramsey didn't buy it. "Is somebody going to tell me what is going on?"

Hannah sighed. "I told her about the serum and the mirror and where she came from." She paused. "About an hour ago, right before you woke up. And right when we realized her abilities were back. I have perfect timing, as usual."

"It's the reason the candy jar shattered," said Leroy.

"And why there's a foot-long crack in your window," said Declan. "Thankfully, I closed the shade before the staff noticed. Let's hope they leave it that way."

Hearing the news and finally understanding, Ramsey nodded. Sarah remained quiet. "You better now?"

"I've got it under control, if that's what you're worried about." Her rigid posture told him she was forcing herself to stand still and not pace. He knew she liked to move when she had something on her mind.

"That's not what I'm worried about," he said.

They exchanged a look before Declan interrupted. "We'll help her out as much as we can while you recuperate."

"I'm okay," Sarah said defensively. "Please stop treating me like I'm an egg about to break."

"Sorry," said Declan. "That's not what I meant."

Sarah dropped her arms, found the foot rail and gripped it. She closed her eyes. "Sorry. I didn't mean to be snappy."

"Don't apologize," said Declan. "You've got a lot on your mind."

"So, what happens next?" asked Leroy. "Do we all need to camp out in Sherlock's room for now?"

"That would be cozy," said Hannah.

"No. I don't think we need to go that far," said Declan. "I think it would be good for you, Sarah, to take an occasional break away from us."

Sarah could only nod.

"But we will need to plan on spending some time together for now. Let you adjust again to your abilities. Once we get that stabilized, we can focus on maintaining them when we're not all together."

"What about Y, though, Declan?" asked Leroy. "What do we do about him?"

Declan spoke to Ramsey. "You think you could tell if he was close again?"

Ramsey didn't hesitate with his answer. "Oh, if he's in the vicinity, I'll know it." His hand fell on something on the bed. He picked it up and saw it was a card.

"I think all of us would get some indication of his presence, so keep your feelers up," said Declan.

"What do we do if he shows?" asked Hannah.

"I doubt he'll show up here. He doesn't seem to like to come out in the open. He can't easily use his powers around humans without too much risk of exposure. He should stay under the radar."

"I'm not too sure about that," said Ramsey, his heart thumping.

"Sherlock," said Leroy, "you okay?"

Ramsey handed him the card.

Leroy opened it and read the inside. His posture straightened. "Son of a …" He handed the card to Declan.

"What?" asked Sarah.

Declan read it, his face paling. "It says 'Hope you feel better soon.' It's signed X, Y, and Z."

"Oh my God," said Hannah. "He was here?"

Declan pulled out his phone. "I'm getting you protection. I'll have someone outside your door at all times."

"You'll only get them killed, too," said Ramsey.

"Nobody's getting killed, Sherlock. Declan needs to take precautions, though. The more we can do to keep Y from coming around, the better."

"He's just messing with me," said Ramsey. "With all of us. He's trying to keep us intimidated."

"Well, it's working," said Hannah.

**

Declan left the room to make his phone call. Sarah could only stand and watch as the emotion in the room kicked up into high alert. She had almost forgotten what it was like to feel so many sensations at once. Once Declan left, though, she could feel her sensitivity decrease. She must have appeared lost in thought, because Leroy asked Hannah if she wanted to get some coffee, and before she knew it, she was in the room alone with Ramsey. Realizing it, she went to stand next to his bed.

"Pull up a chair. Sit a while," he said.

She grabbed a chair and pulled it up close. After sitting, she faced the bed and took his hand. Even though her sensitivities had lessened further since Hannah and Leroy left, she still felt that familiar pull whenever she was near him, as if she'd always known his presence.

He squeezed her hand, and she knew he felt the same.

"You sure you're all right?" he asked.

"You're in the hospital bed, not me."

"My wounds are healing. What about yours?"

"I'm not wounded."

"But you're upset."

She didn't respond.

"What is it?"

"I guess finding out you're a science experiment is a little troubling."

"You're not a science experiment."

"Yes, I am. I was created, wasn't I?"

"Yes, but so have numerous other babies. It's pretty commonplace now."

"I'm a little different than other babies." She fiddled with his bed sheets with her free hand.

"Sarah," he said. "Regardless of how you actually came to be, you were born to parents who wanted you. They could not conceive, and they wanted a child. You were very much loved by both of them. You made them very happy."

Eyeing their clasped hands, she moved her thumb across his skin. She couldn't deny what he said. She had been blessed with wonderful parents. "Did my mother ever know?"

"I don't know," he answered, squeezing her fingers. "From what I hear, though, she had some abilities of her own, so who knows?"

."She was an amazing woman."

He smiled. "Her daughter's not half-bad either."

Sitting with him, Sarah began to relax as his calm energy moved through her. Slowly, the heaviness began to lift.

"I know what you're dealing with is difficult," he said, "but selfishly, I'm glad they experimented. You wouldn't be here right now otherwise."

"You wouldn't be here either," she answered, patting the hospital bed.

"This is not your fault. Y did this, not you."

"But you're dealing with him because of me."

"And if I had the choice, I wouldn't change a thing. I'd rather have you here, with me fighting for you, than not here at all."

She almost called him a liar, but stopped herself, because she knew it wasn't true. His unwavering sincerity fluttered through her. "Will you say that if I can't read that mirror?"

"Nothing will change if you can't read the mirror."

"Nothing other than all of you dying off before my eyes."

"Hey," he said. "I just survived a battle with a knife, and I seem to be doing okay. Don't count me out just yet."

She appreciated his attempt to lighten the mood and take her mind off what troubled her. Deciding that there was little that could be done to change anything, she chose to let him. "You are pretty tough," she said.

He settled back against the pillow, looking weary. "Mom always did call me Superman."

"Is that so?"

"Yes." His eyelids drooped.

"Well, Superman. Looks like you could use some rest."

"Me? I'm doing fine."

"You are, but you still need some sleep. Close your eyes. I'll stay with you."

He managed to perk up at that. "You're not going anywhere?"

"No, I'm not going anywhere," she said, finding the controls and lowering his bed. She couldn't help but add, "Just consider me your Protector. And I'm good at what I do."

Laying fully back in the bed, he smiled softly and drifted off to sleep.

**

The next morning, Hannah and Sarah rode the elevator up to Ramsey's floor. Sarah had slept fitfully the night before. Nightmares of Ramsey lying in his hospital bed, looking pale and ghostly, had plagued her. She'd been at a window, looking in, but she'd had no way of entering his room. He'd looked at her and smiled, sending chills through her. Banging on the glass, she'd still found no way in. He'd started to cough uncontrollably, and blood dribbled from his mouth. Panicked, she'd heard alarms sounding, and she knew they came from the machines next to his bed.

From nowhere, a doctor appeared, carrying a large syringe. He'd approached Ramsey's bedside and inserted the needle into the end of Ramsey's IV tube. Now completely terrified, she tried to break the glass.

Hearing the sound, the doctor turned toward her, and Sarah's blood turned cold when she realized the doctor was Y. She'd screamed "No!" as Ramsey sat up in bed, staring at her and speaking in her head: "Trust destiny."

She'd awoken abruptly then, shaking and sweaty, and hadn't slept since. Now, riding the elevator, she couldn't get to his room fast enough.

The previous day had ended uneventfully, with Ramsey having slept through most of it. The police had stopped by to talk with him regarding the attack, and he'd spoken with them, telling them only what they needed to know. He'd been allowed his first bites of food that night, when he'd had some chicken broth and Jell-O. Visiting hours had ended soon after, and Hannah and Sarah had returned to their room at the hotel. Before they'd left, they met Marco, part of Declan's protection detail who was stationed outside Ramsey's door. Now, as they stepped beyond the elevator doors and headed toward Ramsey's room, they were greeted by a woman who watched them approach.

"You must be Sarah and Hannah?" she asked.

"Yes," said Hannah.

"I'm Mary. I have protection detail today."

"Nice to meet you, Mary," said Hannah. "Thanks for helping us out."

"Happy to be here. I'll do my best to stay out of your way."

"Don't worry about us. Just do whatever you need to do." Hannah went to reach for the door handle, but the door opened before she could enter and Leroy stepped out of the room.

"Leroy," said Sarah with surprise. "You're here early."

He stepped just outside the door. His usual confident demeanor was absent, and a wave of anxiety emanated from him.

"What's wrong?" she asked.

"We need to wait outside. The doctor's with him."

"Why?"

"Sarah," he said, "his temperature spiked in the night."

"What? But he was fine yesterday." The dream replayed in her head and Sarah's stomach turned.

"I know. Hopefully, it's minor. We'll see what the doctor says." Leroy's face conveyed nothing to ease Sarah's mind. Crossing his arms, he moved away from the door and paced in the hallway.

"How high is his temperature?" asked Hannah.

"One hundred and one," he said.

Hannah didn't say anything, and Sarah knew that her silence revealed her concern.

Ten minutes later, the door opened and the doctor stepped out.

They crowded around him.

"How is he?" asked Leroy.

"His temperature has climbed to one hundred and two. Right now, we'll continue to try antibiotics to see if we can eradicate the infection."

"Infection?" asked Sarah.

"Yes."

"But he was fine yesterday," said Sarah. "He's been doing so well."

"It's not uncommon for this to occur. Our hope is that the medicine will kick in and he'll improve within the next twenty-four hours."

"And if not?" asked Hannah.

"We'll need to run some tests. Make sure that nothing is wrong internally. If the wound has reopened, then we'll need to bring him back into surgery."

"Reopened?" asked Sarah.

"With an injury such as his, the area is repaired with internal sutures. If one has ruptured, he could be leaking bacteria back into the abdominal cavity, creating infection and fever. If that's the case, then we'll need to go in and repair it and clean it out." Seeing their worried faces, he tried to downplay the news. "That's only the worst-case scenario. More likely, the antibiotics will take care of the problem."

Sarah nodded and tried not show her fear. "Can we see him?"

"Yes. Just make sure he gets plenty of rest. I'll be back in a few hours to check on him."

"Thanks, doctor," said Hannah.

He turned and walked down the hall.

Sarah pushed open the door to Ramsey's room and went inside, with Leroy and Hannah behind her.

Ramsey lay in the bed, his face flushed and his eyes glassy, as if he'd rested little in the night.

"Hey," said Sarah, trying to mask her worry. "What are you trying to do? Stay in this hospital forever?"

He swallowed dryly. "Guess I just like all the attention," he said, but without the energy he'd exuded from the previous day.

"How do you feel?" asked Leroy.

Ramsey appeared to debate how to answer. "I wish I could say what you wanted to hear." Leroy's face conveyed what they all feared, but Ramsey didn't voice it. They all knew what his symptoms meant. "You up to watering my plants?"

Leroy released a pent-up breath. "You don't have any plants, Sherlock."

"Oh." Ramsey shifted on the bed. "Well, that's one less thing to think about then."

"Besides, I wouldn't water them anyway," said Leroy. "You can do it yourself when you get out of here." Standing close to the bedrail, he held eye contact with Ramsey until Ramsey finally looked away, the silent message communicated.

"That's the plan, Leroy," said Ramsey.

"Damn right it's the plan," answered Leroy.

Sarah stood on the other side of the bed. She listened to the two men talk, and heard and felt the message behind their words. She wouldn't accept it, though. It was entirely possible that the doctor was right. Ramsey could be better within the next twenty-four hours. His body might not be showing the signs of breakdown due to lack of the serum. It could be a ruptured suture. It could be an easily treated infection. Believing that he could survive this was crucial, not just for Ramsey's sake, but for hers as well.

Standing next to Hannah, though, and feeling the doubt arise from her, Sarah's hope faltered. Needing to do something, she grabbed the water glass by the bed and offered it to Ramsey. "Thirsty?"

Ramsey eyed her as if he felt her distress, but knowing there was little he could do. "Yes, thanks," he whispered, conserving his strength. His bed was raised high enough to enable him to sip from the straw.

The door opened again, and Declan entered. "I got your message," he said to Leroy. He stood at the foot of the bed. "You always did like to make things difficult."

"The easy way is boring," said Ramsey.

Declan shook his head. "You might reconsider that right about now."

"I would, but my body might need some convincing."

Declan glanced at Hannah. "What are the odds that this infection will clear up?"

"I don't know," said Hannah.

"You think this is because of the lack of serum?" asked Declan.

Hannah hesitated. "In all likelihood, yes."

None of them spoke. Sarah closed her eyes and took a breath, the emotion in the room ramping up with all of them together.

"Sarah," said Declan, "you okay?"

She opened her eyes. "I'm just dealing with all the energy. When you came in, it all sort of hit me." A thought occurred to her. "Declan," she said. "Do you think...?"

"What?" he asked.

A sudden flashback occurred. She saw in her mind's eye her hands on Leroy's belly, blood staining her fingers.

"Sarah?" asked Ramsey. "What is it?"

She snapped back to the hospital room. "Could I heal him like I did Leroy?"

The unexpected question surprised Declan and his brow furrowed. Before he could say anything, Ramsey spoke. "No. I don't think that's a good idea."

"Why not?" she asked.

"It almost killed you when you helped Leroy," said Ramsey.

"That was different," said Sarah. "Leroy was mortally wounded. You're not."

"Sarah," Declan replied, "the issue is you were shifting during that time. You had access to energy levels you have yet to experience since, energy levels over which you exercised control for almost an hour. I don't know that you have that ability at this point. I don't know that you could summon what's needed for the amount of time required." He paused when her face reflected her disappointment. "John's right. It could drain you. If you lost control, it could affect him, too."

"At some point, it may be worth the risk," said Hannah. "His condition is not as serious as Leroy's, so it shouldn't require the same amount of effort. The risk will be less to both of them. It can't hurt to try. Like you said, Declan, we don't know what she's capable of."

"Then we can wait," said Declan. "If he's worse tomorrow, then we can consider it."

"If he's worse tomorrow, then all the more energy required to heal him," said Leroy.

"I don't like it," said Ramsey.

"What's not to like?" asked Sarah, seeing his flushed face. "If I don't try and things go bad for you, I'll regret it for the rest of my life. I can't not try."

"We're all here in the room," said Hannah. "Why not now? We can stop it if we need to."

"How do we keep from getting interrupted?" asked Leroy. "If a nurse walks in at the wrong moment, it will be a problem."

"They come about every hour. They just checked on him. Should be a while before they come again," said Hannah.

"We have Mary at the door. She can keep an eye out," said Sarah.

Declan met eyes with his brother. "You up for this?"

Ramsey blinked heavy lids. "I'm pretty much at your mercy. I'm not up to putting up much of a fight." He sighed. "If you try this, you promise me you'll back off if gets to be too much?"

"I'll stop her myself if I sense she's endangering herself," said Declan.

"You're assuming you'll be able to stop her," said Ramsey.

"Stop worrying," said Sarah. "I'll back off if it's too much."

"I don't believe you," said Ramsey.

"We can debate this all morning, but if we're going to do it, we need to do it now," said Leroy. He pointed at Declan. "Tell Mary to keep an eye out. Let us know if we've got company."

Declan hesitated before finally deciding to act on Leroy's suggestion. He walked to the door and opened it. He spoke briefly to Mary and then returned, closing the door behind him.

"You're sure about this?" he asked Sarah.

"I'm not sure at all," said Sarah. "But I want to try."

"Okay," he said. Sarah found the bed controls and lowered Ramsey into a flat position. "Do you know what to do?" Declan asked.

"I have some recollection, but not much." Sarah went still, knowing that they waited for her guidance. Feeling anxious to start, she said, "Put your hands on him. Wherever you feel pulled to."

They all moved closer. Sarah placed her hands on Ramsey's stomach. Leroy leaned in and placed his hands on Ramsey's chest, and Hannah moved to his lower legs. Declan placed his hands between Sarah's and Leroy's.

Ramsey closed his eyes. "Man," he said, "if I felt better, I'm sure I'd have something creative to say."

"Just relax, Sherlock," said Leroy. "Try to rest. Let us do the work."

Ramsey took the suggestion to heart and succumbed to his fatigue. His eyes closed and Sarah felt him relax.

"All right," said Sarah. "Here goes." She took a deep breath, let it out, and told the others to do the same. "Everybody send him energy. Imagine him healthy and strong."

She closed her eyes and focused on the force emanating from the group, directing it throughout Ramsey's body. She didn't know exactly what she had done to help Leroy, but all she could do was trust her instincts. The heat within her began to build as her own energy joined with the others'. She gathered and guided it through Ramsey, focusing on his midsection and injury and then directing it up through his chest and head and down through his legs and feet.

"Is it just me, or is it getting hot in here?" asked Hannah.

"It's getting hot in here," said Leroy.

"It's the power she's generating," said Declan. "She's definitely building up the intensity." Sarah continued to work. "Her control is remarkable," he said.

Unaware of the conversation, Sarah continued to drive the energy through Ramsey, intent on removing any level of infection within his body. She visualized the flow as it traveled through and from him, taking anything that affected him negatively with it. Once she moved it out of him, she let it dissipate into the air. Maintaining her focus for several minutes and breathing deeply, she finally began to feel an inkling of completion, but she kept going, ensuring that anything that didn't serve Ramsey's health was removed. She sent several more rounds through him before she began to slow the pace. Taking another deep breath and allowing the energy within her to contract, she began to disengage.

"Sarah, how are you?" she heard Declan ask.

She opened her eyes and took a moment to center herself. Taking one last breath, she removed her hands from Ramsey's midsection and stood back. "That's it," she said. "I don't know what else I can do."

They all took their cue from her and stood back, too. Ramsey slept, surrendering completely to the experience.

"Did it work?" asked Hannah.

"I don't know," said Sarah. She shook her hands, ridding herself of the excess remnants of energy. "Strangely, I didn't feel much sickness in him."

"That must be a good sign," said Leroy.

"It may just be that he's not that sick. If you were expecting something as challenging as Leroy, then maybe it threw you off," said Declan.

Sarah wasn't sure what it meant, and shook her head to clear out any remnants of concern from her mind. She had to stay positive. "Well, all we can do now is wait."

The door opened, and Mary poked her head in. "Nurse is doing rounds. She'll be here soon."

"That's fine," said Declan. "We're good."

Sarah eyed the clock and was surprised to see that thirty minutes had passed since she'd begun to work on Ramsey. She could only wish the next twenty-four hours would move as quickly.

ELEVEN

....

MORGANA LEFT HER bedroom, moved through the dark hall, and walked into the living area. Ronald had notified her that her guest had arrived. It was late, and she'd left the lights off, save for the illumination in the entryway. She entered her office and saw that the desk light was on and that her guest was sitting in her office chair, facing away from her and toward the window.

"Drake," she said. She closed the door behind her.

He turned in his seat. "Good evening, Morgana."

"To what do I owe this late-night visit?" She moved to stand in front of the desk. She wore her long silk purple robe, which was tied around her middle with a sash, and no make-up.

He stared at her with his intense eyes. "You still look good, even now."

She raised a brow. "What does time have to do with it?"

He chuckled. Still wearing his unbuttoned overcoat, he held his hat in his hand, his thumb tracing over the brim. "You know why I'm here."

"You've heard?"

He stood. "Of course, I've heard." Moving to the window, he looked out. "He's in bad shape."

She knew the situation just as he did. "It doesn't mean he won't survive."

He turned back. "No, it doesn't. But it doesn't look good."

Standing there in the dim light, she determined the best way to handle his concern. "I see no point in doing anything until we know more."

"We could intervene."

"No, we cannot."

"If he dies..."

"Then he dies."

"And so could our chances."

"Our chances are a long shot at best, even if he lives."

"But if there's the possibility—"

She leaned against her desk. "Sarah is alive. We still have that."

"But we need him, too."

"We assume we do, but we don't know for sure."

"It's a risk."

"Everything's a risk, Drake. You just have to decide how much you want to gamble."

He stared at her, wide-eyed. "And you're willing to gamble our survival?"

She stood still, resolute in her decision. "I made a promise. I won't break it."

His anger flaring, he stepped forward. "You're being foolish."

His disapproval did not affect her. "You misunderstand," she said. "I want nothing more than to ensure our people's existence. If I thought by intervening it would change anything, then I would do it."

Confusion clouded his features. "Then why go to all this effort?"

"Effort? I've gone to no effort at all. I've simply put the necessary people in place. Beyond that, it is out of my hands."

"But you told me that the two of them—"

"Things must progress without intervention from outside sources. Doing so would only ensure our destruction. We must rely on the fact that whatever happens must be necessary. We can do nothing more."

His face fell. "And you're willing to trust in that? You have that much faith?"

She had only one answer. "Faith is all I have, Drake. It's all I've ever had. And so far, it's never let me down."

He fiddled with his hat before placing it back on his head and walked around to the other side of the desk. "Funny thing about faith," he said, heading to the office door. He reached it and looked back. "It can lead you into completely unexpected situations."

She held his gaze. "You need to make peace with the unknown, Drake."

He twisted the knob. "And if the unknown means we're all dead in the next twenty-four months? Can you make peace with that?"

Saying nothing, she watched him open the door and leave.

TWELVE

....

SARAH STIRRED AND opened her eyes. She sat at Ramsey's bedside, her head resting next to him while he slept. Eager to check on his condition, she'd arrived early that morning. The nurses knew her now and had allowed her in prior to visiting hours. He had slept most of the previous day, with little change in his condition. His fever lingered around one hundred and two degrees. She had slept with no nightmares, but the feel of him from the previous day still bothered her. It was as if sandbags were tied to him as he tried to swim. She had tried to clear away the sand, but apparently she'd had little effect.

Hearing him moan softly in his sleep, she raised her head. Seeing that he looked no better than he had when she'd left him yesterday, her anxiety cranked up a notch. She moved her hand to his forehead and pushed back his hair, and her fingers stilled when she felt the heat. Sitting up taller, her fear rose when she realized how hot he was. He mumbled something, but she couldn't understand him.

"Ramsey?" she asked. "Can you hear me?"

He moaned again, and she thought he said, "Dad." Moving his head slightly, his eyes opened to slits. He didn't focus on her at first, but blinked a few times. His skin and eyes remained feverish, and he lacked his usual vibrancy. Without thinking, she reached for the call button and pushed it.

She leaned in to him. "Hey," she said, trying to keep her voice calm. "You awake, sleepyhead?"

He seemed to remember where he was and managed to look over at her. "Morning," he said, his voice more of a croak. His face clouded. "Is it morning?" he asked, clearing his throat.

"Yes," she smiled, trying hard not to let him see her worry. "It's morning." She continued to stroke his forehead, wanting to touch him.

He closed his eyes for a moment but then reopened them. Finding her gaze, he held it, reading her easily. The lines of fatigue on his face softened. "It's going to be okay."

His insight into her, despite his illness, almost broke her. Tears sprung into her eyes. "It didn't work."

"You tried," he said. "Please don't feel guilty."

"You're getting worse." A tear threatened to escape, and she wiped at it. "There has to be something else we can do."

"Sarah, listen to me." He swallowed as if to gather his strength. "If I don't make it through this, you have to keep moving. You have a purpose and a destiny. You have to fulfill it."

Composing herself, she spoke again. "But you're part of that purpose. You're supposed to be with me."

"If I am, then I'll survive." He reached out with the hand closest to her, and she took it in her own. "My dad always told me to trust destiny. I've always believed in that. Now you have to do the same."

She stood and leaned over him, bringing her face close to his. She continued to stroke his forehead with her fingers. "You promise me you'll fight. Don't you dare give up."

With his free hand, he reached up and cupped her face. "I'll do everything possible, Sarah. I promise. But you promise me something."

"What?" Her hand moved from his forehead, and she rubbed her thumb along his cheek.

"You do whatever it takes to become the woman you were meant to be. Don't ever let me hold you back."

Now a tear did escape. It ran down her face, and he brushed it away. Their gaze held and she inched closer and lightly touched her lips to his. The instant they made contact, a spark of electricity sizzled between them, muted only by Ramsey's illness. Sarah sensed Ramsey's regret that he couldn't take her in his arms and kiss her the way he wanted to, without his weakness holding him back. Another tear trickled down her cheek and she held the kiss with him, neither wanting to let go.

The door opened. "Did you hit the call button?" asked the nurse, who stopped at the door. "Sorry to interrupt."

Sarah pulled away, but didn't let the nurse's appearance break the moment. Ramsey held her gaze, but tiring, he let his hand drop back to the bed. She turned toward the nurse. "I think his fever's worse."

The nurse moved in and checked the machines. She asked Ramsey a few questions and then left, saying she would notify the doctor. Sarah noticed the new reading on his temperature. It was one hundred and three.

**

Several hours later, Sarah paced the floor in Ramsey's hospital room. Leroy, Hannah, and Declan all waited with her. They had taken Ramsey thirty minutes ago to run tests. Despite whatever medication they'd given him, his fever had not lessened. Nobody said anything as they hoped that the tests might reveal anything other than what they expected.

"You talk to Morgana this morning?" asked Declan to Leroy. The silence unnerved him, and he needed to say something to break the quiet.

"Yes," answered Leroy, his mind elsewhere.

"What'd she say?"

"Nothing. What do you expect her to say?" Leroy glowered. "Sorry." He rubbed at his neck.

"Don't worry about it," said Declan.

They kept up the waiting and pacing for another thirty minutes, saying almost nothing, until two orderlies finally wheeled Ramsey back into the room and got him back into bed.

"So, what'd they see in there?" asked Leroy, referring to the tests. "Stale pizza and expired Beefaroni?"

Ramsey offered a weak smile. "Give me some credit, Leroy. I don't think Beefaroni expires."

"I think it does," said Hannah. "Probably in about twenty years."

"I rest my case," said Ramsey. A coughing fit seized him, and he grimaced.

Hannah adjusted the bed to an upright position to help ease the pain while he coughed. The others could only watch in dismay as they processed his continued decline. Sarah moved up next to him and took his hand, and Leroy and Declan moved closer, as well.

The coughing spell over, he sat back exhausted.

"You all right, Sherlock?" asked Leroy.

**

Leaning back and closing his eyes, Ramsey waited for the discomfort to subside. The heat in his body flared even though a chill moved through him.

Hannah pulled the blankets up to cover him, and she lowered the bed again until he was comfortable.

Taking a shallow breath, he found the strength to speak. "You want the truth?' he asked.

"Not really," said Leroy.

"Then I feel great." Another chill ran through him and he pulled the bed covers higher.

"Get some rest," said Hannah, tucking the blankets around him. "We'll be here when you wake up."

Drifting into a restless slumber, Ramsey could only nod.

"Here he comes," said Declan, standing.

They waited in the family room as the doctor who had examined Ramsey and presumably discussed his test results with him exited his hospital room and headed in their direction. They had been waiting for the results for what felt like hours while Ramsey slept, and now, watching the doctor walk toward them, they all held a collective breath.

"How is he?" asked Leroy.

Pulling his glasses off, the doctor rubbed the bridge of his nose. "I wish I had better news."

"What?" asked Hannah.

"The tests revealed no internal problems. We didn't see any issues with his injury. It's healed well. He has a secondary infection. Problem is, the antibiotics are not working. His fever is up to one hundred and four."

"Oh, God," said Sarah. She crossed her arms, and gripped her elbows.

"Damn it," said Declan, turning and moving away toward the wall.

Leroy could only stand and take in what the doctor said. "So, what next?" he asked.

"Nothing, I'm afraid," said the doctor. "We're using the strongest stuff we have on him. If he doesn't start to respond soon, then he'll likely develop sepsis, and then his other organs will start to shut down. He won't have long after that."

Leroy looked away at the news.

"How long? If he doesn't respond, how long does he have?" asked Hannah.

"Ideally, I'd like to put him back into ICU, but he's asked us not to. He signed a release asking that no extraordinary measures be taken. Based on that and the rate it's progressing, I'd say, optimistically, a week," he said. "Realistically, maybe two to three days. We've placed cooling blankets on him to try and keep the fever down."

"No," said Sarah under her breath. She wrapped her arms tighter around herself.

Nobody said anything as they each tried to deal with the doctor's devastating news.

"I'm sorry," the doctor said, seeing the distress of the people around him. "He asked to see Leroy. Said he wanted to talk to you privately."

Leroy slumped, dropping his head down. "Aw, hell," he said, putting his hands on his hips, knowing the conversation Sherlock wanted to have but dreading it. "Okay," he said, lifting his head. "Thanks, Doc."

With that, the doctor nodded and walked away.

Leroy stood where he was and stared at the floor, saying nothing.

Pensive, Hannah hugged herself, Sarah wiped tears from her cheeks, and Declan rigidly faced the wall. Each stood rooted to their space as they all tried to come to terms with the inevitable.

Taking the few moments he needed to compose himself, Leroy began to walk toward the room. "I'll be back."

As he neared the door, he took a deep breath and, gathering his courage, pushed it open.

His friend lay slightly raised in the bed, looking worn and frail. Even though blankets covered him and he blazed with heat, he shook with frequent chills. Hearing the door open, Ramsey opened his eyes. "Leroy," he said, sounding almost too weak to say the name.

Leroy stood for a moment just inside the door before moving closer. "Sherlock," he said in return. Instead of pulling up a chair, he sat on the edge of the bed. "Doc said your injury is healing."

"Unfortunately, that's the only thing that is." He coughed, and Leroy picked up the water by the side of the bed and let him sip from the straw.

Ramsey swallowed. "Thanks."

Unsure how to start the conversation, Leroy stayed quiet.

Ramsey spoke first. "Listen," he said. "I need to say a few things while I'm still lucid enough to say them."

"Sherlock," said Leroy, his voice rough, "there's nothing left unsaid between us."

"I'm dying, Leroy." Taking a shallow breath, Ramsey paused. "I need you to know that you're my family. You've always been a brother to me."

The sentence alone seemed to tire him. Leroy's chest tightened, but he let Ramsey finish.

"I need you to make sure that Sarah is treated right. Don't let the Council or Morgana use her. If she can't read that mirror, please make sure she's taken care of."

Leroy tried to keep his emotions at bay. "You know I'll do that."

"I know Olivia is your priority, but don't let them take advantage of Sarah. You have some sway with the Council, and I won't be there to get in Morgana's face."

Leroy could not imagine not having Sherlock around to argue with. "All right." He sighed. "I'll make sure she's taken care of. I promise."

"Thank you." Another chill traveled through Ramsey, and he shivered.

Leroy reached out and grasped the hand Ramsey had extended outside the bed covers. "You're my best friend, Sherlock," he said. "Who am I going to make fun of at their expense if...?" He closed his eyes, unable to finish the sentence.

Ramsey's own emotions surface. "I'm sorry," he said. "I wish I was stronger."

Leroy opened his eyes. "Don't. Don't do that."

"Don't do what?"

"Don't blame yourself."

Ramsey opened his mouth to speak, but hesitated. He looked away. "Sucks, doesn't it?" he asked, taking a long, shaky breath. "Being on that side of the bed."

Leroy squeezed his friend's hand. "It's absolute hell."

They sat in silence, listening only to the machines in Ramsey's room.

"Thank you," said Leroy, breaking the quiet.

Ramsey turned his head back to Leroy. "For what?"

Leroy's eyes filled with unshed tears. "For being there."

Ramsey his eyes filled, as well. "You, too," he said. "You, too."

Overcome with emotion, Leroy could only nod in return.

**

In the family room, Declan watched Leroy exit Ramsey's room and make his way back to them, wiping at his eyes.

"You okay, Leroy?" asked Hannah.

"No, I am most assuredly not okay." He sniffed, looking at Declan. "He wants to see you next."

Declan stilled. "He does?"

"Yes, he does."

Declan stared down the hall toward the door, finding himself frozen to the spot.

"You can do this, Declan," said Leroy, wiping away a tear, and following Declan's gaze. "You have to do this."

Declan nodded. "I know." He made himself move down the hall. At the door, he stopped as Leroy had, but put up his hand, pushed on it, and went inside.

Once in the room, he stepped to the foot of the bed, and waited until his brother opened his eyes.

"Hey," said Ramsey.

Declan swallowed hard. He did not expect or want to be having this conversation. "Hey, yourself."

"Sit," said Ramsey, and Declan moved to a chair by the bed. "No," he said, "sit next to me."

Declan hesitated until he realized what his brother meant. He moved closer and settled himself down on the mattress, careful not to sit on anything important.

Ramsey looked up with sad eyes. "You and I haven't always seen eye to eye."

Unexpected emotion welled up in Declan, but he held it back. "Yeah, well, we're stepbrothers. What'd you expect?"

Ramsey paused and Declan felt the years of tension between them finally uncoil. "I blamed you," said Ramsey.

Declan bit his lip.

"You had what I wanted." Ramsey took a moment to collect himself. "And I was jealous." A chill shook him, and Declan saw him grimace, but he didn't interrupt. "And you did it with such ease. Everybody loved you. My mother, my grandmother. It made me hate you even more."

"John..."

"Let me finish..." Ramsey swallowed hard. "I'm sorry. I was not a good brother to you."

Declan could barely contain his tears. "John... I wasn't exactly making it easy for you."

Ramsey smiled. "I know. That irritating ability of yours didn't help either."

"I may have used it to my advantage once or twice."

"Believe me. I know."

Declan hesitated, wanting to say something but stopping himself.

"What?" asked Ramsey.

"I'm not sure how to tell you this."

"Declan, at this point it's best to be direct."

Declan swallowed. "I called your mother."

"You what?"

Declan sighed nervously. "When you were in ICU and they didn't know how it was going to go, I called her."

"You did?"

"I couldn't not call her, John. She's your mother."

"What did she say?"

"She came to the hospital."

Ramsey's eyes reflected his surprise. "She did?"

"You were unconscious, but she sat with you for a few minutes. I waited outside the room. Nobody else knew she was here."

Ramsey frowned. "Did she say anything?"

Declan reached inside his jacket pocket. "She gave me this." He pulled out an envelope. "I wanted to give it to you, but it didn't feel like the right time."

Ramsey stared at the paper in Declan's hand. "Open it."

"What?"

"Open it."

Surprised, Declan ripped the side of the envelope with shaky hands. He pulled out a piece of loose-leaf paper. Another smaller envelope spilled out onto the bed. "John" was handwritten on the front of it.

Declan handed the paper to Ramsey.

"No," Ramsey said. "You read it to me."

Declan felt uncomfortable. "You sure about that?"

Closing his eyes, Ramsey answered, "Yes."

Declan hesitated, but seeing Ramsey wait, Declan lifted the paper and began to read.

My Dearest Johnny,

Seeing you now, my heart is breaking. I should have made the effort to say this sooner, but I thought I had more time. I know I have not always been the best mother to you. There was a time when I was, when your father and I were together. He was the whole world to me. But when he died, he took that world with him. When I looked at you, I saw him, and I allowed myself to push you away, as if it would ease my pain. It didn't work, though. All I accomplished was to ostracize you from my life, and now I've lost you both.

Declan paused, needing to stop. "You're sure you want me to read this?"

"Keep going," said Ramsey.

Lifting the paper back up, Declan continued.

I want to say that I'm sorry. If I could go back in time and change it, I would. I know that when I married Donovan, you saw it as a betrayal. Please know that I have never stopped loving your father and never will. Just as I will never stop loving you.

Declan stopped again, taking a breath. He looked at Ramsey, who remained quiet, before continuing.

I found this envelope in your father's things a few years after you left the house. I've always wanted to give it to you, but always found a reason not to. I'm giving it to you now, hoping it is not too late. It has never been opened. I hope that whatever words your father has for you will bring you the comfort you seek. Please forgive me for my mistakes. If you wish to see me again, and I hope you do, I would be happy to try and start over. Maybe I can do it right this time.

I love you,
Mom.

Declan held up the smaller envelope in his hands.

Ramsey looked over at it and, managing to pull his arm up from the blankets, took it delicately from Declan. "I'll read this one on my own."

"I should have given it to you sooner," said Declan.

"It's fine, Declan. Thank you." He held the envelope against his chest as if treasuring it, but after a few seconds, he started coughing. Declan took the envelope as Ramsey clutched at the sheets. Finally, the coughing spasm subsided and Ramsey lay back exhausted on the pillow. He searched for the envelope.

"It's right here," said Declan, placing it on the table next to the bed. "You can read it whenever you're ready." He folded the other note from Ramsey's mother and placed it back in the envelope, and laid it next to the other letter.

Ramsey's bloodshot eyes met Declan's. "There's one more thing."

"What?"

"I need you to take care of Sarah. You need to keep her safe."

Declan knew that what Ramsey asked was a tremendous responsibility. "You want me to do it? Not Leroy?"

Ramsey took hold of his wrist. "I'm asking you, Declan. Leroy can keep an eye on the Council, but I trust you to watch out for her."

"John..."

"Please, Declan."

"You know I will."

"No matter what happens, make sure she's okay. Promise me."

"I promise."

"Thank you." Ramsey let out an exhausted breath and rested back against the bed.

"John."

Ramsey turned his head toward him.

Declan could hardly get the words out, but he had to say them. "Despite all that may have happened between us, I've always considered you to be my big brother."

Ramsey eyes filled. "I know."

"I wish we'd had this conversation sooner." Declan couldn't help it as a tear escaped and ran down his cheek.

"We're just a couple of idiots."

Declan's breath caught. "Yeah, we are."

Ramsey closed his eyes and took a painful breath when another chill wracked him. "Declan," he asked. "Do me a favor."

"What?"

"Ask Hannah to come in?"

Seeing that their time was up and hating it, but realizing his brother's reserves were dwindling, Declan got up from the bed. "I will," he said wiping at his face and moving toward the door.

"Hey," said Ramsey weakly.

Declan turned. "Yeah?"

Ramsey found the strength to say more. "Thank you for bringing my mom to see me. Tell her that I love her, too. And that I'm sorry I couldn't see her." Another shaky breath made him pause. "You're a good brother, Declan."

Now the tears came easily, and Declan could only nod. Turning before his emotions overtook him, he left the room.

Declan returned to the family area, barely composed and wiping at his eyes. Walking past the others, he could only manage to say, "You're next, Hannah," and went to stand at the wall, leaning on it, arm outstretched, with his head hung low.

**

Leroy and Sarah let Declan process his time with his brother and waited for Hannah to take her turn.

Hannah stood uncertainly, as if doubting whether to go. But after a moment, she headed toward the room and entered it. Once inside, she moved to stand by the bed where Ramsey lay with his eyes closed. She was wondering if he was even awake, when he opened his eyes.

"Hannah," he said, patting the bed next to him.

She sat beside him. "Hey, Ramsey," Her voice shook. "Don't you think you've stirred up enough attention for today?"

He smiled. "You know me," he said. "Go big or go home."

"I'd rather you go home."

"Me, too." He swallowed and took a moment. "Bet you never thought you'd end up here that first day when you knocked on the door."

The memory of that day returned and Hannah shook her head. "No. I did not." Reaching her hand out, she pulled the covers up to his neck when he shivered. "If I'd known all the trouble you were going to cause me, I would have left the moment you answered the door."

"Now you can't get me out of your sight." He shook and tried to stifle a groan.

"There are worse things." Seeing his discomfort, she wished there was more she could do. "You tend to grow on a person. Like a weed."

He laughed easily at that. "Thanks."

"You're welcome."

He quieted for a second. "Now for the hard stuff."

Despite her intention to be strong, Hannah's defenses began to crumble. "Lay it on me," she said. She found his hand under the bed covers and took it, and he grasped her fingers.

"You're a smart and courageous woman, Hannah. No one can handle a crisis better than you."

She sniffed. "I'm not too sure about that."

"Don't doubt yourself. It's true. Anybody else would have turned tail and run. You never did."

She could only nod. "Once I commit, I like to see it through to the end. I couldn't leave."

"You and I are a lot alike. I see and feel the same way. I think that's why I like you so much." His fingers squeezed hers, and her tears begin to fall. "I'm making everyone cry."

She swiped at a tear. "I think it's unavoidable."

He paused. "I'm gonna need you to be the strong one, Hannah. Maybe it's not fair of me to ask, but that's what I'm doing."

"What do you mean?"

"I've got a group of people out there that are going to fall apart when…" He almost couldn't finish the sentence. "I need you to help them through it." His own breath caught when he spoke. "Can you do that for me?"

Wiping at her face with the back of her hand, she sniffed. "Of course. I'll be there for them."

"Thank you."

Hannah found a tissue and blotted her face.

"You're a good friend to Sarah," he continued. "She'll need someone to talk to after…" Stopping, he gathered himself. "You've been good for her."

"We're good friends and we'll stay good friends. I'll make sure she's all right. Don't worry."

She could see that her words brought him the relief he sought and he closed his eyes and relaxed. Taking a deep cleansing breath, he coughed, and opened his watery eyes. "I don't know what we would have done without you. You're the rock that keeps us all grounded." He held her hand as she cried. "I wish I could be there for you when you need someone."

Hannah let a sob escape. "You're here for me now. I won't forget that."

"Am I?"

"Yes. You're a good man, John Ramsey. Don't let the nurses tell you otherwise." She smiled through teary eyes.

He smiled back, and his eyes shimmered in the dim light.

"You want me to get Sarah?" asked Hannah, sensing he was ready.

"Yes, please." He closed his eyes again and Hannah knew the flood of emotions had to be draining him considerably.

Hannah stood and moved to the door. Before leaving, she saw him shiver again, his flushed face deepening in color. Feeling him weaken, she left, walking quickly away.

Leroy and Sarah watched her approach. Wiping her cheeks, she spoke to Sarah. "He wants you."

Sarah didn't hesitate. She jumped from her seat and hurried down the hall, pushing the door in as she made her way into the room.

Hannah sat next to Leroy and succumbed to her sorrow. Seeing her distress, Leroy put his arm around her, and she leaned into him. And as she dissolved into tears, Leroy sat with her as she cried.

**

Inside the room, Sarah moved to Ramsey's side. Sensing her, he opened his eyes. She sat with him, wishing she could be closer and rested her hand on his cheek.

Their eyes met and held, and she sensed his comfort now that she was near. She will herself to stay strong. "Say everything you wanted to say?"

His eyes mere slits with fatigue, he willed himself to keep them open. "Yes, except for one thing."

Holding it together, she forced herself not to fall apart. "What?"

He was quiet for a moment, but finally spoke, "I know the timing's lousy, but I thought I should tell you that I think I'm in love with you."

His words ruined her. She'd wanted to be brave to show him that she would be okay, that he didn't have to worry about her as she knew he would, but his vulnerability brought it all crumbling down. Fresh tears spilled over her lashes. "You know," she said, "you're making it really hard for me to be strong for you." Leaning over, she kissed his forehead and caressed his cheek.

He shut his eyes, but opened them again. "I don't want you to be strong for me. I want to be strong for you."

Her forehead touched his. "You are always strong for me. You're my hero."

"I'm not much of a hero now."

A shuttered breath escaped her as more tears fell. "You're more of a hero to me now than you've ever been." Lifting her head, she wiped a tear from his cheek that had fallen from her own. "And I love you, too."

Neither of them said anything. She stayed close, resting her forehead back against his own. Another flicker of pain seized him, making him suck in his breath, and she comforted him by gently rubbing his face, telling him to relax and that she would stay with him. Finally, completely spent, Ramsey allowed himself to let go, and he drifted into a deep sleep.

Seeing him give in and ensuring he rested, Sarah laid her head on his shoulder and cried silent tears.

THIRTEEN

....

S EVERAL MINUTES PASSED as Sarah lay there with him until her tears began to subside. She sat up and wiped at her face and nose with tissues from a box on the tray table, listening to the machines in the room. She was trying to pull herself together when she thought she heard what sounded like a low humming. Listening, she waited until she heard it again. It sounded like something vibrating on a hard surface. Looking over at the side table, she saw nothing that would account for the noise, but hearing it again, she pulled open the shallow drawer below the table top and she saw a small mobile phone. She didn't recognize it as Ramsey's or anyone else's. It buzzed again. She considered whether it could belong to a nurse or a doctor, but knew that made no sense. Something told her to pick it up, and she reached for it. She hit the button on the front and the screen lit up, informing her that there was an incoming text message. Unsure of what to do, she almost put it back down when some insight told her to open the message. The screen changed, and she sucked in a breath when she read the display.

Touching.

Her mind tried to make sense of it, but before she could think it through, the phone buzzed again in her hand and another message came through.

I have what he needs.

Her breath caught. She looked at Ramsey. Who was this?
As if reading her mind, the phone buzzed again.

You know who I am.

Her stomach tightened when she began to suspect the identity of the sender. Y. Her heart raced, and her hair stood on end. She debated whether or not to find Leroy and Declan when the phone buzzed again.

If you want to save him, then you must come and get what he needs.

She gripped the phone. The only thing that would save Ramsey was the serum. Had Y found the serum? A small flicker of hope blossomed. Could Y save Ramsey?
Another message followed.

There's a black car with a driver at the front entrance. Get in it. Tell no one and come alone.

Her mind buzzed, and she wondered what to do. Could she trust this man? The man who put Ramsey in the hospital in the first place? Intuitively, she knew the answer was no. The phone buzzed once more.

The car leaves in five minutes. Once it's gone, your choice is made. Ramsey's life is in your hands.

The last words moved her into action. She didn't have a choice. If there was a chance Y told the truth, she had to try. Even if it meant sacrificing herself to do it, then she would. She stood, careful not to disturb Ramsey, and leaned over to kiss his cheek. "Hang in there," she whispered, feeling her emotions well up again. "I'm going to get you some help. Please just stay alive."

Giving him one last look, she opened the door and left, heading to the elevators. She never looked in the direction of the family room.

**

Leroy saw Sarah leave. Hannah did, too. From behind Leroy, Declan said, "Where's she going?"

Sarah hit the elevator button, wiping at her red face and nose with her sleeve while she waited, never looking their way.

"Give her some time," said Leroy. "She needs to be alone for a while."

The elevator arrived and the doors opened. Sarah got in and, doors closing, disappeared from sight.

**

Down in the lobby, she headed for the front entrance. As expected, a sleek black car with a driver sat out front. She approached it.

The driver leaned out his open window. "You Sarah?"

She nodded her head.

"You comin'?"

Hesitating only for a moment, she opened the back door and got in. The driver pulled away and left the hospital grounds.

They drove for an hour, the driver saying nothing. She recognized little as they moved further and further away from the city. Her mind preoccupied, she paid little attention to where they were headed. Her thoughts remained on keeping Ramsey alive, and she prayed that Y told the truth, and that he had what Ramsey needed. She didn't think about what she might have to do to get it, but whatever it was, she wouldn't hesitate to do it.

She began to pay more attention when they left the highway and drove into a suburban neighborhood. Darkness had fallen, and the houses they passed were now lighted. She saw opulent gates at driveway entrances and knew they were in an upscale community. Large-trunked trees and high walls encircled wide-spread and well-maintained lots.

Finally, they pulled into a driveway with its own private gate and protected enclosure. As the driver approached, the gate opened, and they drove in. They followed the long entrance up to the front of the house, and Sarah could see the perfectly manicured front lawn, rounded shrubs which bordered the driveway, white flowers well placed among prominent statues, and tall, willowy trees. As they made their way to the entrance, an enormous water fountain with cherubs and angels locked in a wet embrace greeted them.

The driver pulled up and stopped. The car idled while the driver waited. Sarah opened the door. Getting out, she gazed up at the façade of the house. Even in the dark, it looked palatial. It stood two stories and had a Spanish influence, with stucco walls and a tiled roof. Gray pavestone led the way up a set of stairs that carried her eye to the two huge carved wooden front doors, each with a large flowering potted plant on either side. After closing the door, Sarah watched the car drive off and head toward the garages.

She gathered her courage before walking up the stairs. Reaching the doors, she rang the bell, hearing the chimes from inside as they rang.

A few seconds passed, and she heard the unlatching of the lock. The doorknob turned and the door opened.

A small man greeted her wearing black pants, a white shirt, and a black vest. He could not have been more than five foot three or four, and he had slicked black hair and a small mustache and goatee. "Please come in," he said. "You must be Sarah."

She tried to stay calm, and walking inside, she took a deep breath to make herself relax. "Yes."

"My name is Julian. It's a pleasure to meet you."

"Hello," she said, standing in the foyer of the house.

It was immense. A grand staircase welcomed her, and she followed its beautifully carved wooden handrail all the way to the second floor, where several rooms surrounded the railing above. Downstairs, hardwood floors covered with large oriental and Indian rugs and white leather furniture with glass furnishings adorned the interior. Massive pictures of mainly contemporary scenes framed the walls. She stared as she took it all in, unable to help but admire the beauty of the house. Heavy sea-green curtains were pulled closed over what she imagined were large windows looking out over what was likely a massive courtyard and backyard, if the size of the other estates they'd passed on the way were any indication.

A voice from above startled her out of her observations.

"Hello, Sarah." She looked to see Y, who'd appeared out of nowhere, leaning against the second-floor railing, "Thank you, Julian," he said to the man beside her.

Julian retreated from the room, leaving Sarah alone in the foyer as Y made his way down the stairs. He was dressed casually in relaxed dark jeans and a brown long-sleeved cotton shirt, his trim waist enhanced by the clothes. He wore no shoes. His tan face smiled easily as he neared, as if he was disembarking from a cruise ship. Reaching the bottom of the stairs, he walked up to her. She instinctively stepped back, but he kept walking and passed her.

"Hungry?" he asked before heading down a hallway and turning a corner.

Following with reluctance, she turned the same corner and found herself in an ornate kitchen with granite countertops, marble floors, a large gas stove, and an oversized refrigerator. An elegant glass breakfast table with an elaborate flowered centerpiece took center stage in the large room.

She saw him at the refrigerator with the door open. "I took the liberty of ordering out tonight," he said. "I got us a salad and chicken parmesan from the Italian place down the street. It's their specialty." He took the salad out of the fridge and put the main dish, which had been sitting on the counter, in the microwave. "It needs a warm-up. It won't take long."

After setting the timer, he picked up an uncorked bottle of wine from the kitchen counter. "I chose a wine for us. It should go well with the meal." He opened a cabinet and took out two large-mouthed crystal wineglasses and placed them on the counter.

She stared as he moved around the kitchen. "What are you doing?"

Looking over at her, he smiled. "I know you haven't eaten much lately, and I suspect you've had no dinner." He poured the wine. "Just thought you should eat something."

She narrowed her eyes at him. "This isn't a date."

Finished pouring, he held the second glass and put the bottle down. He picked up the other filled glass. "It's not a date, Sarah," he said. "But if you expect me to save your boyfriend's life, the least you could do is have dinner with me."

Holding his gaze, she realized that she was not in a position to decline his invitation. Despite her nervousness, she crossed her arms in front of her and answered him. "I agree to have dinner with you, and you give me what he needs?"

Leaning against the counter, Y rested one ankle over the other. "You impress me, Sarah, standing there as if you have a choice."

"I do have a choice." She hated that he was right, but she didn't want to show it.

"And what is it?" He waited for her answer.

Irritated that she'd have to waste time with him instead of rushing back to the hospital, she agreed. "I'll give you an hour."

Seemingly pleased by her answer, he reached out to hand her a glass, and stepping forward, she reluctantly took it.

"Have a seat," he said. "Get comfortable."

She felt guilty standing there holding a glass of wine while she knew Ramsey lay dying in a hospital bed. Deciding she could withstand this for sixty minutes, she went to sit at the table.

Carrying his glass, he went to join her, choosing to sit across from her. "Cheers," he said, holding up his wine.

Swallowing hard but going along with the charade, she lifted her glass and clinked it against his. He took a sip, and she did as well, barely tasting the wine.

"Relax," he said, sensing her impatience. "There's plenty of time. He's got at least twenty-four hours, probably closer to forty-eight." He took another sip of his wine. "Not bad, if I do say so myself." He stared at Sarah. "Do you like it?"

She tried not to react to his cavalier attitude about Ramsey's declining health. "I don't know much about wine."

"Neither do I. Julian buys all of it. He supposedly knows what he's doing."

Restless, she put her glass down. She found an ornamental clock on the wall and noted the time.

Noticing her preoccupation, he set his wine glass down, too. "You want what I have for him?" he asked. "Will that help you loosen up?"

She whipped her gaze to his. "You have it?"

"Of course. I wouldn't lie to you, Sarah."

"But you'd stab a defenseless man instead?" She couldn't help herself as she thought of Ramsey fighting to survive.

"I'd hardly call him defenseless. Besides, that was between us. It had nothing to do with you."

"Is that supposed to make me feel better?"

"And how is it okay that he killed my brother?"

"Your brother was going to kill him and Declan."

"If you'd done as they'd asked, that all could have been avoided."

"They were there to kidnap me."

He swirled the wine in his glass. "Sarah, do you honestly believe that the best place for you is with him?"

"You're changing the subject."

"No, I'm not. Everything that has happened stems from what occurred the day they came to take you." He studied her with a measured glance. "I'll ask again. Do you believe he's what's best for you?"

She didn't know how to handle this conversation, realizing that whatever she said would matter little. But having no other choice, she answered him. "Yes, I do."

"Why?"

"Why?"

"Yes. Why? What does he have to offer you?"

"I don't have to explain anything to you."

"You don't know, do you?"

"What do you mean?"

"You can't tell me what he offers you, can you?"

"He offers me everything."

"No, he doesn't."

Her anger began to build, and for the first time, she felt the energy churn inside her without the presence of the others.

Reading her, his expression changed. "You see that? You don't need any of them anymore, Sarah. You are already able to do what you were meant to do without their help. The only reason you're attached to any of them is because they got to you first. If I had been the one to help you through your Shift, you'd be in love with me right now."

His arrogance stunned her. "You're not serious, are you?"

"I am." He sat forward in his chair. "Think about it, Sarah. You're a Red-Line. I'm a Red-Line. We are ideally suited for each other. I was raised as one. I could teach you things you have no current understanding of, but which would amaze you. What exactly is it that you think Ramsey could teach you? How to help some hapless Gray through their Shift? You were meant for greater things, my dear. You were meant for me."

His own energy magnified, and she could feel it from across the table. Something about him made her want to pull away, and if she could have left, she would have. But she knew she had to finish this farce of a dinner in order to get what she needed.

"I'm not a doll, Yates. I don't just fall for any man that comes my way."

A smug look crossed his face. "You remember my name."

"I remember you from the coffee shop. I'm not mentally challenged."

Smiling, he said, "No, you are not. Except maybe when it comes to that protector of yours."

She set her jaw. "You know, if you went after Ramsey for your brother, you ought to come after me as well."

"Why is that?"

"Because it's my fault that your other brother is dead. I threw him against a brick wall."

He'd picked up his wineglass again, pausing before taking a sip. "That's different."

"Is it?"

"You were defending yourself, using powers you'd never used before. It's not surprising you lacked control."

"Who says I lacked control?"

He stared at her, his eyes glittering.

The intensity of the conversation was interrupted by the buzz of the timer. Shrugging off his mood, Y put down his wineglass and got up from the table. Needing to do something with her nervous energy, Sarah took another sip of her drink, wishing it was a glass of water.

Y pulled out the dish, placed it on the counter, and split out two servings, each on its own plate. He grabbed silverware and napkins and brought them to the table with the salad. He turned back to pick up both plates and then brought them over before handing one to Sarah. "Dig in," he said. "Dinner's served."

Taking the plate from him, she was careful to avoid contact, remembering their previous encounter when he'd taken her hand and lightly grazed it with his thumb. Picking up her napkin and placing it in her lap, and tried to look interested. She didn't know how she was going to eat, since she felt no hunger at all.

Y picked up the salad tongs and served her some salad before getting some for himself. Then he sat and took his fork and cut into his food. He watched as she left her food untouched.

"You should eat something if you want to keep your strength up. You don't want to collapse as soon as you come to his rescue." He lifted his fork and took a bite.

Refusing to take the bait, she didn't answer him, but picked up her silverware and forced herself to eat. Surprisingly, she didn't feel sick when she started chewing. In fact, it was as if her system kicked into gear and she suddenly felt ravenous. She had indeed eaten little since Ramsey's convalescence, and now her body told her she'd neglected it for too long.

Y smiled, and they sat quietly as they continued to eat and drink. The alcohol started to relax her, and she found herself sitting back further in her seat, without the coiled tension she'd previously held.

"Feel better?" asked Y.

She did, although she wouldn't admit it. Avoiding the question, she asked, "So where is it?"

Knowing what she referred to, he sipped his wine. "In due time, Sarah. Enjoy your meal."

The next several minutes were spent in relative silence while they finished dinner. Thinking of Ramsey as she ate, she told herself that what she was doing was only a means to an end. If this was all it would take to get him whatever it was Y had, then it was a small price to pay.

"So," Y said, wiping his mouth with a napkin, "want more?"

She'd eaten most of what was on her plate and finished most of her wine. "I've had plenty."

"Good." He put down his napkin and leaned forward, putting his elbows on the table. "Then let's discuss our options."

She didn't know what he meant. "Options?"

"Yes."

"What do you mean? I thought we agreed. I have dinner with you and you give me the serum, assuming that's what you have."

"I said the least you could do was have dinner. I didn't say that was all I wanted."

She didn't like where this was leading. "You want something else?"

"Yes, I do. I'm giving you Ramsey's life back. And considering my dislike for the man, I consider that to be a large gesture on my part."

"Considering you're the one who did this to him, it's the least you could do."

"He had it coming. But my interest is not in him, it's in you."

Shifting in her seat, a chill ran through her. "What do you want?"

"I want you to stay here with me."

Her eyes widened. "You're kidding."

"I am not."

"I can't do that."

"Yes, you can."

"I don't want to stay with you. I don't belong here."

"Hear me out, Sarah, before you decide."

"It won't matter what you say. I'm not changing my mind."

"Again, hear me out, please."

She sat nervously and sighed, determined to get through this. "Fine. I'm listening."

"Thank you." He got up and grabbed the bottle of wine. After sitting back down, he leaned forward and refilled Sarah's glass.

She started to object but thought better of it. Maybe if she could keep him drinking, she could get out of there sooner. As soon as she had the thought, though, she realized it could also make things worse. She stopped her mind from going down that road as he refilled his own glass.

"First of all, I think you should know that I have only your best interests at heart. I have no intention to force you to do anything. If after this conversation you wish to leave, you can. If and when you decide to be with me, you'll do it voluntarily, without provocation from me."

His words calmed her. She'd panicked when she considered what she would do if he held Ramsey's life as a bargaining chip for her compliance.

"But I want you to consider the possibility of living here."

"I don't—" she started to interrupt.

"Let me finish."

She stopped, telling herself that she only had a short time left with him, and if she let him talk, the sooner it would be over.

"Okay," he said, satisfied that she was listening. "As I said earlier, you and I are both Red-Lines. We have equal potential. Did you know that Red-Lines rarely mated with Grays? At least not until the very end. There's a reason why, Sarah. Because they weren't meant to. We are unique. Together, we could start over. We could take our place among the Council, become the leaders we were meant to be. Perhaps even make contact with our host planet, reestablish communication and travel back there once again. You do know that Reds were once the link between this world and our home?"

"This is my home," she said.

"That's beside the point. You and I have options, Sarah. The world is our oyster."

"This is a power trip for you?'

Ignoring her question, he kept talking. "What I'm trying to say is that Ramsey can offer you none of that. Yes, you may have some lingering attachment to him right now, but that won't last forever. After a while, you'll get bored. Besides, with the Grays on the way out, it won't be long until it will be just you and me, all on our own."

"Not if I can read that mirror and find that serum."

He laughed. "You don't honestly buy that load of crap, do you? That some mysterious mirror holds the key to their survival?"

"Why not?"

"Number one, the odds of you actually reading it are slim to none. Secondly, the likelihood of there being any serum to find is close to zero."

"There was serum on that ship."

"No, there was cargo on that ship. Nobody knows what that cargo was. For all they know, they're looking for a crate of Eudoran animal crackers."

"You don't know that there wasn't serum on that ship."

"And you don't know that there was."

"I'm still going to try."

"Let me give you another option."

"What other option?"

"You give my idea a chance. You stay here with me. I'll give you everything you need. Your own private room. You can come and go as you please. Visit your friends and your aunt. Go back to work for the bookstore. I don't care. Just give me a chance to work with you. Show you what's possible. And if you insist on reading that mirror, then read it. I have no investment in the matter. If you find the serum, hooray for you. If you don't, then so be it. At least you know you tried. But even if all your newfound friends die, you won't be alone. You'll be with me. It's a far cry from having nothing. It would be absurd to watch them die and for us to be the last two standing and never speak to each other."

Despite his logic, she couldn't even consider the thought of living with him. Somewhere under his layers of charm, she could feel a darkness, and if she pushed in the right spots, she suspected she would find it. She decided to see how far she could go.

"I acknowledge that you make a few good points."

"I make several good points, but thank you for at least conceding a few."

"But I have some questions."

He set down his wineglass. "Fire away."

Holding her wine, she held back from drinking more. She needed a clear head to deal with this man. "Where exactly do you come from? You obviously know my background, but I know nothing of yours."

Fingering the lip of his wineglass, he tipped his head. "I am much like you, Sarah. A product of many years of genetic testing. My 'father,' for lack of a better term, was Arnuff, one of the last two Red-Lines to survive. He and Emerson, as the last two remaining Reds, took it upon themselves to embark on their own line of testing, outside of that done by the Council."

"Why would they do that?"

"Because, my dear, they were not the innocent men they made themselves out to be."

"What were they?"

"Outcasts might be a more accurate term."

"What do you mean?"

"They were part of a small group of Red-Lines intent on eradicating the Grays."

She frowned. "What? Why would they do that?"

"How should I know, and why should I care? It was sixty years ago."

"But there must have been a reason."

"I'm sure there was. But it is not something they shared with me. All I know is whatever plan they had backfired, and somehow they ended up killing the Reds instead." He snickered. "Karma's a bitch, isn't it?"

Sarah couldn't help herself. "You should keep that in mind."

He raised his glass and peered at her over the rim. "My conscience is clear."

She decided to leave that subject alone for now. "And how does this secret involvement in destroying the Grays lead to you?"

"When it became apparent that the Council was getting closer to genetic success, they feared that if a new Red-Line were born, he or she would be a threat to them."

"How?"

"I suspect they were worried that the mirror contains information that may lead to the revelation of whatever plot they were involved in. My guess is that ship went down for more reasons than any of us know. By creating me and my brothers, they maintain the upper hand, or at least an even hand if they are discovered. Or at least that was their theory." He paused as if thinking about something. "We were born two years before you. Problem was they didn't take into consideration what to do with us once they succeeded. After we arrived, they kept us in hiding. Their only contribution to us other than their DNA was to train us as we grew up, to prepare us for some supposed takeover." He took another sip of wine, not hiding his sensitivity to the subject.

"Who raised you?"

"The only person I would even come close to calling a father."

"Who is that?"

"Eddie."

"Eddie?"

"Edward Bright. The man whose knowledge of genetics is the reason I sit before you today. His experiments resulted in the birth of triplets. Me, Xavier, and Zane. Or rather, X, Y, and Z." His fingers tightened on his glass. "Arnuff named us letters, as if we were test tubes. He called us that until his demise."

His anger blossomed, and she began to suspect that Arnuff's death was no accident.

"You're the middle child?" she asked, surprised.

He chuckled. "Actually, no. I was born first."

"They why are you 'Y'?"

"I asked the same question. Apparently birth order was not a consideration when it came to naming us." He stared off. "Fools."

"Who chose Xavier, Yates and Zane?"

"We chose them ourselves."

"You chose your own names?"

He nodded in reply.

Curious, she asked, "Why did you choose Yates?"

Looking serious, he said, "It means gatekeeper. I found it to be fitting." He managed to pull himself out of the intensity of his thoughts, and the room's energy lifted. "Anyway, after they learned about the Council's success in conceiving you, they began to wonder what your existence might mean for them. And for us."

"They were threatened by me?"

"They certainly were. They wanted to kill you."

She didn't hide her surprise. "Why? What could I do to hurt them?"

"You're a female Red-Line, just as capable as them if not more so. You risked exposing them if you read the mirror. But even if you didn't, you were still a threat."

"Why? I was a child. Nobody expected me to survive."

"When it was obvious you would survive, they had to prepare for the worst."

"What do you mean?"

"As the two remaining Reds, they were expected to participate in your..." He paused, looking for the word. "...assimilation."

"My what?"

"The Grays left you alone as you grew up, but as you got older and it was clear that you would go through your Shift, the Council looked to Arnuff and Emerson to assist in your transition. Problem was Arnuff and Emerson couldn't."

"Why not?'

"Because, as you realize by now, a Red-Line Shifter is highly volatile, highly sensitive, and highly intuitive, especially females. One look at them, and you could have read them like a book. They had to stay away." He stared at his wine. "They made up some excuse about remembering nothing and being too frail to assist. That meddlesome hag, Morgana, insisted on assigning Ramsey." He sat tensely at the table. "You can imagine my disappointment." He met her eyes, pausing as he shook off his memories. "By the time I realized what was happening, I had to take matters into my own hands."

A shudder ran through her when she thought about where she might be right now if Ramsey had not been assigned as her Protector. She had to ask the logical question. "Why didn't they kill me?

"I'm sure they secretly hoped that by staying away, you wouldn't survive your Shift." He gripped his glass. "I decided otherwise." Another wave of animosity rose from him.

"They could have killed me before my Shift."

The side of his lip rose. "We asked them not to."

"Why?"

"Because you offered us the one thing they couldn't."

"Which is?"

"A continuation of our line, Sarah."

A cold sliver of dread traveled up her spine. "You mean..."

He watched her react with displeasure. "Yes, that's what I mean. Children."

She didn't know what to say. "What, did you think I'd just willingly be your baby factory?"

He shook his head. "Don't be so dramatic. Of course not. If we had planned it properly and my brothers had not been idiots..." He glared. "Well, I believe things would have worked out differently for both of us."

She didn't want to know what he meant and she didn't ask, but one obvious question came to mind. "But how do you know I'm not your sister?"

"You're not. You are the daughter of Emerson. We are the children of Arnuff."

"How can you be sure?"

"Wasn't hard to figure out. Once we learned who you were, they got a hold of a DNA sample. Probably took hair from a hairbrush or bumped against you at school and got a blood sample. Simple to do."

"And I'm Emerson's daughter?"

"You are. Good thing, too."

"Why?"

"Otherwise you'd likely be dead."

She paled as she considered that, but she kept up the questions, wanting to know more about X and Z. "Your brothers," she said. "Were they Reds?"

"No. They were different. We were triplets, all born together. They were identical, but I was not. They had a combination of both Red and Gray DNA, so they were not complete Red-Lines, but they came with formidable abilities. Unfortunately, their uniqueness also made them unstable."

"Unstable?"

"Yes. They had violent mood swings and outbursts of aggression. They could be hard to handle."

Knowing what she knew of them, she believed that. "And you?"

"One hundred percent Red-Line, through and through. They learned the hard way to listen to me."

"It was you who kept them under control?"

"When they needed a firm hand, I could provide it."

"And Edward? How is it that he took care of you?"

"Our mother died in childbirth. Emerson and Arnuff, keeping up the pretense of being decent, rule-following Council members, rarely saw us except for training purposes. Edward stayed on, raising us."

"Where did you grow up?"

"All over the world. We rarely stayed in one place for long. They were terrified we would be discovered, and thus they would be discovered."

"And what was your purpose?"

"Ultimately?"

"Yes."

"To take up where they left off. They knew the Grays would die eventually, just as the Reds did. What better way to take over when you have three sons to take your place?"

"But take over what? With the Grays dead, what's left?"

"You have to think bigger than that, Sarah. The only thing that remains."

"What's that?"

"Humans, of course."

She blinked, not sure she understood. "Humans?"

"Yes." He took another sip of wine, as if they discussed who'd won the local high-school football game.

"They wanted to take over humans, as in the human race? But what about the big Eudoran thing about not revealing themselves?"

"Consider them rule-breakers."

"But why?"

"With the Grays dead, they would be all that's left. They didn't plan on retiring to Florida."

"But they were in their eighties. They weren't going to live forever."

"Unbeknownst to their fellow Council members, their life expectancy was quite good until recent circumstances changed that." He smiled as he finished his wine.

"It was?" she asked, choosing to not inquire about his involvement in their destruction. "Why? Because they were Reds?'

"Because they were Reds with serum."

Her heart rate picked up. "But I thought the serum was gone."

"Not all of it."

Now she knew her suspicions were correct. Y had more serum. Mustering all her strength, she fought not to over react with the anticipation that she might receive some. "What do you mean?"

He shifted forward. "Do you really think that those two survived the death of the Reds just on virility alone?"

"Isn't that what everyone believes?"

"Then they're bigger idiots than even I have imagined. Those two trusted no one. They had enough serum stockpiled to last them decades, which it has. It will last a few more decades, too, if I plan it right."

His revelation stunned her. "If they don't need it anymore, then why not share it? What do you need it for?"

"They're not the only ones who need the serum. My brothers and I didn't survive on bread alone."

His answer confirmed her suspicions. "You need it, too?"

"Of course. I don't have the benefit of human DNA to protect me." Pushing his empty glass aside, he sat back and asked the question he knew she wanted the answer to. "Which brings us full circle. Now that you know I have what you want, will I give it to you?"

Not knowing if he expected her to respond, she said nothing. She waited for him to speak, unknowingly holding her breath.

He looked at her glass. "You haven't finished your wine."

"I've had plenty."

"Have you considered my proposal?"

"To live with you?"

"Yes."

"I have, and I can't." Sarah waited, wondering if her honesty would prevent him from giving her what she came for. She believed, though, that lying would only make it worse.

"For now," he said.

"I won't change my mind."

"Don't be too sure."

"What does that mean?"

Not answering her, he changed the subject. "All right, then I want only one thing from you before you leave."

"What's that?"

He went to a desk in the den, which was adjacent to the kitchen. He opened a drawer, pulled out a black box, and brought it to the table. When he flipped it open, she saw a large syringe.

She jumped out of her seat. "What the hell is that?"

"Relax," he said, taking out the syringe along with a rubber cord. "I only want a vial of your blood."

She recoiled. "A what?"

"A vial of blood."

"What for?"

Sighing, he showed his first signs of irritation with her. "Sarah, you are a unique specimen. I myself am a bit of a novice scientist myself. I'd like to study your DNA. Find out just exactly how you survive without serum."

She continued to stand there, doubting his truthfulness.

He didn't back down. "Sarah, the three most important people in my life are dead because of my involvement with you. I find that I have been exceedingly kind in not immediately retaliating by wiping the earth clean of any semblance of Ramsey, or Declan, for that matter. Now, I offer you one dose of serum for one vial of your blood. Take it or leave it. It is my final offer."

She could feel the heat radiate from him, and she knew she'd used up whatever clout she'd had for now. Dinner over and his proposal denied, he'd become agitated. She'd pushed the boundaries as far as she could. Anxious to return to the hospital, she gave in to her fate, and stepping closer, she offered him her arm. "What about the wine?" she asked.

"I'm not taking a blood alcohol level, Sarah."

Turning her head, she felt him put the rubber band around her arm and tie it off. Closing her eyes, she somehow knew she was offering this man more than just her blood, but unable to do otherwise, she remained still and shut her eyes, wincing when she felt the prick of the needle against her arm. She stood unmoving as he filled the vial with the dark red liquid from her arm. He grabbed a tissue from the counter and held it against her skin as he removed the needle.

"There," he said, bending her arm against the tissue to put pressure against the puncture. "That wasn't so bad, was it?"

He capped the needle, put the syringe filled with her blood back in the box, and closed it. Setting it aside, he asked, "How do you feel?"

Feeling slightly nauseated, she said, "I'm fine. Now where's mine?"

He grinned at her. "You just can't wait to get back to him, can you?"

Saying nothing, she waited.

"Very well." He moved back to the desk from which he'd retrieved the black box. He opened a second drawer and pulled out a thinner, smaller gray box, and brought it over to her. Upon opening it, she saw that there was a small syringe inside.

Taking it out, he showed it to her. "This is one dose of serum." She could see a small amount of amber colored liquid within the vial. "Simply inject it into his IV. You should see results fairly soon."

She noticed that on the body of the syringe, the letter "Y" was written in black marker. She looked at him with confusion, and he understood.

"Just my flair for the dramatic. The thought of you thinking of me when you inject him, well, I find it pleasing." He put the syringe back in the box and handed it to her. "This will probably give him another year or two to spend with you as well. Lucky me."

Taking the box without saying a word, she opened her arm and removed the tissue.

He took it from her, stepped aside, and threw it away. "My driver will be out front. He'll take you back."

Relief flooded her because this ordeal was almost over, but she had a lingering doubt. Holding the box, she had to ask him a question. "This is the real deal, Yates? This won't kill him instead?"

"He's dying anyway. What would be the point?"

"It's your flair for the dramatic, as you say. It seems like it's something you would do just to spite me and hurt him."

He straightened, having no reaction. "It's up to you, Sarah, whether you trust me or not," he said. "Give him the serum or don't. It's your choice."

Realizing he had not answered her question but knowing he did it intentionally, she didn't respond. Pocketing the serum in her jacket, she took a step to leave, but an intense wave of nausea hit her and her vision spun. Sucking in a breath, she bent over, holding the kitchen counter to keep herself upright. "Oh," she said, holding her stomach and closing her eyes, hoping it would pass.

"Sarah," said Yates. "You okay?"

"I'm dizzy," she said, taking a deep breath. "Feel sick." It was all she could get out before another wave hit her and she buckled to her knees. "What's happening?"

Yates made no move to help her. "Probably the wine and the blood I took. It may have made you ill." He sat on his heels. "Take some breaths and keep your head down. It should help."

Doing what he said, she rested her hands on the ground, unable to stay balanced on her knees alone. She sat back as another intense wave washed over her. Fighting back the urge to vomit, she put her forehead all the way to the ground and felt the cold marble against her skin.

"Oh, God." Spots appeared before her eyes, spinning crazily. "What did you do?"

"Just relax, Sarah. It's almost over. Just give in to it."

Managing to turn her head, she squinted at him just as her body begin to give in to the darkness. "You lied to me." She fell to her side and curled into a fetal position.

He leaned over her. "I didn't lie. I simply augmented the terms of our agreement."

**

Sarah's body relaxed, her eyes closed and she went still. Yates moved closer to her and gently turned her on her back. Watching her still form for a moment, he brushed a piece of hair from her face, before putting his arms beneath her, and easily lifting her.

"We're not quite done yet, Sarah. I need you to do one last thing for me." Holding her body close to his, he walked out of the kitchen and carried her up the stairs.

FOURTEEN

....

LEROY SAT IN the room, listening to the machines that monitored Ramsey, who had not stirred since his conversations with each of them earlier that evening. The door opened, and Hannah entered, moving to sit next to Leroy on the small couch in the room.

"Where's Declan?" asked Leroy.

"Still on the phone," said Hannah.

"You haven't heard anything?"

Hannah pulled the phone out of her pocket. There were no messages. "Nothing."

"Where the hell would she go at a time like this?"

"Declan's got his people out looking, but it's a long shot."

"She wouldn't leave without a good reason."

"No, she wouldn't. Unless…"

"Unless someone took her," sighed Leroy. "I know."

They watched the bed and its occupant. A few minutes later, the door opened again and Declan entered.

"How is he?" he asked.

"Same," said Leroy. "He hasn't regained consciousness. Fever's still high."

Declan stood at the edge of the bed.

"You learn anything?" asked Leroy.

Declan glanced over. "No. Nothing. There's no sign of Sarah. I'm trying to get someone to pull security footage, but it's like pulling teeth. Probably won't be able to get to it till tomorrow."

"You think she was taken?" asked Hannah.

Declan shook his head. "I don't know. I can't imagine she would leave, though. Not with things as they are."

"She might have," said Hannah. "If someone got to her."

"What do you mean?" asked Declan.

"Think about it," she said. "Ramsey is dying. She's vulnerable. It's the perfect way to manipulate her."

"You mean dangle his life as bait?" asked Leroy.

"Yes."

"That's assuming he can be saved," said Declan.

"Regardless," said Hannah, "if Yates wanted to use her, that's one way to do it."

Declan ran a hand through his tousled hair, and moved around the side of the bed. He took a seat in the empty chair beside Leroy. "If that's the case, then we've lost them both," he said, shutting his eyes and rubbing at his face.

Leroy sat back. "Or she returns."

"Then I hope she makes it in time," said Hannah. Ramsey's labored breath echoed in the room. "Because if she doesn't..."

"Then we will have lost them both anyway," said Declan.

Leroy released a held breath. "What is it that Sherlock says?"

"I don't know," said Declan. "What?"

Leroy stood and stretched his legs. He moved to the side of Ramsey's bed. "Trust destiny."

Hannah held her head. "Now would be a good time to do that."

"Yes, it would, Hannah," said Leroy. "Yes, it would."

**

Sarah slowly opened her eyes, seeing sunlight. She could hear the soft cry of seagulls and the soft pounding of the ocean surf. Confused and having no idea where she was, she opened her eyes wider. Feeling the pressure of her bladder, she pushed herself up. Looking around, she saw she was in a large bed with a heavy wooden bedframe and an elaborate headboard. The windows were open and the curtains blew softly in the breeze.

Sitting up, she threw off the sheet that covered her. She still wore the clothes from the previous night. Thinking back, she remembered the events from the evening with Yates. Understanding dawned when she recalled that he'd somehow drugged her. Assuming she must still be in his house, her mind raced with frightening thoughts. Had she slept the night here? Considering that she might have done more than that without her consent, her belly flipped. Doing a check-in with her body, she didn't feel harmed in any way, but the thought of him touching her while she slept made her skin crawl.

She stood carefully, ensuring that any lingering dizziness had passed. Seeing that it had, she found the bathroom, although it could have passed for a separate room altogether due to its size.

Double sinks shared a wide granite countertop under two ornate mirrors with bright circular lights. A huge jetted tub and a large tiled shower shared another wall. The toilet itself had its own room, and she quickly entered it, then shut the door and locked it. Several seconds later, feeling better, she exited and went to wash her hands, expecting Yates to appear out of nowhere at any time. He didn't, though, and through the reflection in the mirror, she could see what looked like a closet behind her. Drying her hands on a lush hand towel, she gave in to her curiosity. She crossed the bathroom and pushed the door open.

The closet was a small sitting room with a couch and bench and two large mirrors. The walls held enough shelves and hanging rods to make a retail store happy, and in the middle of the room stood an island designed to hold nothing but shoes. Most of the closet was empty save for what must have been Y's clothes, which only required a small area of the closet. Feeling way too close to Y's personal space and realizing that she was in his bedroom, she left the closet and exited the bathroom. Back by the bed, she approached the windows, hearing the sounds of the ocean. She pushed aside the curtains and looked out.

She couldn't help but suck in a breath at the beauty of the view. A white sandy beach extended for miles on either side of the house. A large infinity lap pool with lush landscaping and a waterfall lay just outside a patio down below. She'd had no idea they had traveled to the coastline last night. She'd never heard the sound of the surf as she'd arrived, her thoughts only on Ramsey.

Thinking of him now, she closed the curtains and headed to the bedroom door, her sole purpose only to get out of there and get back to him. She opened the door and peered outside to see a large empty hallway. The house was quiet. Stepping out of the room, she moved toward what she assumed was the center of the home and hopefully toward the stairway. Something caught her attention, though, before she turned to head down the hall. It was a door, slightly ajar, just across the hallway from the bedroom.

Still working on reading and interpreting energy, she had learned to pay attention to anything that felt out of place. The room definitely had that feel. Even though all she wanted to do was leave the house, something compelled her to investigate the strange vibe. She moved across the rug, careful to not reveal herself, although she sensed that her presence had already been felt, so she moved fast. Reaching outward with her senses, she felt no one in the odd room, so she pushed the door open. It was empty except for two objects. A large, overstuffed chair and a freestanding mirror.

"Good morning, Sarah."

She turned and almost fell backward, but caught herself.

Y stood at the end of the hallway, wearing navy khakis and an open-necked white cotton shirt. "Feeling better?"

Taking a step back, she sensed his displeasure at her nosiness but then felt it disappear just as fast.

"Care for some breakfast?" he asked.

Anger flared within her. "What the hell did you do to me last night?"

His face projected innocence. "You needed rest. I simply helped you find it."

"By putting me in your bed?"

"Don't worry," he said with a smirk, holding up his hands in defense. "Your virtue is intact. You simply needed a decent night's sleep. I'm sure your lack of food and sleep these past several days has taken its toll."

"I don't need you to tell me when to sleep. You drugged me."

"Sarah, I don't need to drug anyone. I'm not a carnival act."

"You did something to me."

"I only had you spend the night. So you stayed longer then you anticipated. Don't worry. The serum is still in your pocket and Ramsey is still alive, awaiting your loving return."

Her fingers groped her jacket pocket, still feeling the small box in its proper place. "I want to leave. Now."

Sighing, he stepped out of the way. "Don't let me stop you." She hesitated, not trusting him, and he decided to help her out. "Head down the hallway. You'll see the staircase. I notified the driver when I knew you were awake. He's outside." When he said nothing else, Sarah moved to leave.

"Sure you don't want any food? I have a delicious egg breakfast waiting on the patio. The weather is perfect."

She walked by him without replying. She passed another bedroom and what looked like a media room and finally reached the staircase. Heading down, she saw the living area bathed in sunshine. The large living room curtains were now drawn back, the windows were open, and the magnificent view of the ocean greeted her as she stepped off the staircase. Taking no time to admire it, she headed straight for the front door.

"Give my best wishes to Ramsey," Y said from above. "I believe he's going to need them."

Sarah ignored him, opened the door and left, not even turning around as she shut the door behind her.

**

The car ride back seemed agonizingly slow. Sarah couldn't wait to get back to the hospital, and she prayed that what she carried would recover Ramsey's health. She pulled the small box from her jacket pocket and opened the lid, seeing the syringe and the liquid within it. Something within her stirred as if in warning. Staring at the Y written in marker on the base, she knew she had missed something important. Her mother had always taught her to pay attention to the small voice inside her head, and right now, it was chattering at her.

She pulled the plastic tube with its covered needle out of the box and grasped it between her fingers, feeling it. She tried to gauge whether or not Y told the truth. Would this save Ramsey? Holding it, she could feel nothing. Continuing to hear her mother's voice in her head telling her to trust her instincts, she tuned in and listened. Her initial sense of relief after leaving Y's house with what she wanted began to ebb as she considered that perhaps it had been too easy. Y had no interest in saving Ramsey's life, and she knew he had ulterior motives. Knowing that, though, did nothing to help Ramsey. She'd run out of options. If no other possibility showed itself, she would have to give him the serum.

She reached to touch her necklace, which she commonly did when something troubled her. Not feeling it, she searched for it with her fingers, but it wasn't there. She'd had it on when she'd left the hospital yesterday. Had it fallen off? Checking her pockets, she found nothing. She froze when she considered that it was likely at Y's house. Did he take it from her? She cursed herself for not realizing its absence before she left, knowing that if Y had kept it as some sort of trinket for his amusement, she would probably never get it back. Frustrated that she had let Y toy with her, she realized that she'd had no choice but to let him, and her thoughts returned to her current situation.

She dropped her hand from her neck and looked out the window as the car moved down the highway. She thought back from the beginning, wondering if, in all of the emotion of Ramsey's fast decline, she had somehow overlooked some important detail. A familiar jab flared within her belly, which she typically considered a yes response. It was a feeling she'd come to trust over the years, and she felt strongly that she should trust it now.

Putting the syringe back in the box, she replayed the events of the past twenty-four hours—her conversations with Ramsey and waiting for the doctor after the tests, watching Ramsey succumb to sleep after his emotional conversations with each of them, the buzzing phone. Her body chilled as she recalled the phone Y had somehow placed in Ramsey's room. Where was it? She reached for her pocket, where she had placed the phone after leaving the hospital the previous day. It wasn't there. Had Y taken it, along with her necklace, while she slept? She shivered at the thought that he had been that close to her without her knowing it. The text messages replayed in her mind. He'd told her that he'd had what Ramsey needed. That she would have to come and get it. He'd never used the word "serum." Did that mean that what she now held was not what Y was referring to in his texts?

Shutting her eyes at the lack of answers, she was annoyed that she couldn't determine what nagged at her. As the car neared the hospital, she knew her time was limited. If she didn't figure it out soon, she'd have to make a difficult decision. Trust Y or not? She laid her head back and stared at the car ceiling.

Fifteen minutes later, the driver pulled the car up into the semi-circular entry of the hospital. Sarah jumped out without a word to the driver, ran into the lobby and into an open elevator. The doors closed, and the elevator rose to her desired floor. Once the doors opened, she ran out into the hallway, headed for Ramsey's room.

"Sarah." She heard Leroy's booming voice before she could reach the door. Turning, she saw him just down the hall, not far from her. "Where the hell have you been?"

"Leroy." She stopped and faced him, breathing fast from her sprint. "How is he?"

He glowered. "Not good. Where were you?"

She debated how much to tell him. "I'll fill you in later. Right now, I have to see him."

"The doctor's with him right now. His fever's up to a hundred and five." His face fell. "He's barely coherent."

"Sarah?" She heard Declan's voice, and she looked behind Leroy to see Declan and Hannah walking down the hall toward her. "Where the hell were you? I've had my people out looking for you all night."

"I'm sorry, Declan. I had to go somewhere."

"Where the hell did you have to go at a time like this?" asked Declan.

He was irritated and she couldn't blame him. "I'm sorry. I didn't know I would be gone so long."

"Where were you?" His face showed that he felt her shielding herself from him.

She'd been practicing the skill, and she was working hard at keeping him out right now. She wanted to see Ramsey first. If she ended up giving him a fatal dose of some poison instead of serum, she wanted to be the only one who carried the guilt.

"You okay?" asked Hannah. "You scared us to death. We thought Y got you."

"I'm fine, Hannah." She stopped at that, saying nothing about Y. "I just want to see him."

Outside Ramsey's room, Marco stood watch. The door opened and the doctor emerged. Seeing them, he headed over.

"Doctor?" asked Leroy.

"I'm sorry," he said, hands on his hips. "He's declining rapidly. We've been unable to stop the fever. He's showing signs of kidney failure. It won't be much longer before he lapses into a coma." None of them spoke. "We'll do our best to keep him comfortable."

"I want to see him," said Sarah.

The doctor regarded her. "He's only semi-conscious. Be prepared that he won't know you."

Sarah's throat constricted. Giving Ramsey the serum was her only option, and she had to do it now. She couldn't waste time thinking about it.

"Sarah..." said Leroy, taking her wrist to offer comfort. "We'll go in with you."

"No," she said abruptly. Realizing she sounded harsh, she gentled her voice. "Please, I need to be alone with him."

The doctor excused himself and left the hallway.

"What's going on, Sarah?" asked Declan.

She felt his worry. "You have to trust me. I don't have time to explain."

Declan's eyes narrowed. "You know something."

Not answering him, she turned and moved toward Ramsey's room. "Please, just give me five minutes."

None of them argued with her, and she pushed the door open. Walking in, she was struck by Ramsey's declining state. Covered in blankets, he lay in the bed, his face red with heat. He looked small, as if he'd shrunk in size. Moving up close and sitting next to him, she put her hand on his head to feel his fever. Her heart raced, and she hated that she'd lost the last several hours with him. She wondered if he'd asked for her while she was gone.

As if sensing her, he stirred.

"Ramsey?" she asked. "John? Can you hear me?"

He made a small noise in the back of his throat, but didn't answer her.

"Please." She tried to talk, but the words stuck in her throat. "I'm not sure what to do." Her indecision tormented her. She laid her forehead on his shoulder. "What should I do?"

Hearing him make another noise, she looked to see his eyes flutter open.

"John? It's me. It's Sarah."

He made no reaction to her but only stared off, as if lost in another world. She tried to meet his eyes, but when she did, he looked blankly at her. He mumbled, but to Sarah's dismay, she thought he said, "Mom." He did not recognize her.

Panic set in, and she reached for the box in her pocket. She took it out with shaky hands, placed it on the bed, and opened it. The "Y" in black marker stared back at her and she pulled out the syringe and held it in her hand.

"I have serum, John. At least I think it's serum. I'm going to give it to you."

He didn't respond, and she doubted he'd even heard what she'd said.

Holding the syringe up, she pulled the plastic cap off the needle. She tapped at it and pushed lightly on the plunger to remove any bubbles. Her hands shaking, she located the IV on Ramsey's arm and placed the needle at the tip of it, ready to insert it and inject the serum.

Looking at Ramsey one last time, she wished he could give her some sort of affirmation that this was the right thing to do. That same twitch fired in her belly, and she hesitated.

Agonized, she dropped her head, still holding the needle at the IV. "Please tell me what to do," she said to herself. Huddled in doubt, she thought she heard a whisper. She lifted her head. "What?"

"Touching."

Ramsey had spoken. It was so quiet; she'd barely heard it. Ramsey continued to stare off at some distant point, his glassy eyes mere slits.

"Ramsey?" she asked. "Did you say something?"

There was no answer, but he blinked slowly before drifting off again.

She thought about what she'd heard. She'd been sure he'd said the word "touching." Something about it triggered a memory for her, but she couldn't place it. Why would he say that? Had he heard her? Was he simply responding to her plea for help?

Looking back down at the needle, she was readying herself to inject the liquid when it suddenly came to her. Her heart thudded and her mind whirled with the memory. The phone in the drawer had buzzed. She'd picked it up. The first text message had been, "Touching."

A piece of the puzzle clicked into place. The text message. Y had knowledge of her last conversation with Ramsey. How had he known? Sitting still, the needle still at Ramsey's IV, she concentrated as bits and pieces from the past twenty-four hours began to come into focus. The odd sensation she'd felt from Ramsey when she'd worked on him. The unusual vibe of the strange room at Y's house. Her headaches from looking at certain mirrors.

Another thought popped into her head, and she shut her eyes, thinking hard. Opening them again, she stared down unseeingly at her hands as segments of information and her own intuition came together. She whipped her head around toward the private bathroom. She'd never used it, instead always using the one in the hallway outside the family room. But now, she paid more attention. Just inside the door, she could see the sink and above that, the mirror.

The mirror.

Another image came to mind. The room at Y's house with the large chair and freestanding mirror.

She pulled up, moving the needle away from Ramsey's IV. "Oh my God," she said, the realization hitting her.

She hastily recapped the needle, put the syringe back in its box and into her jacket pocket. She brought both hands up and placed one on either side of Ramsey's face. Silencing her thoughts, she reached out to him, picking up on what she could but looking for something specific. Finding it, she dropped her hands and stood.

"Dear God," she said, her mind racing. Standing there, she made herself stay calm and keep a clear head while she wondered what to do. Closing her eyes, she took a deep breath and paced beside his bed as she tried to think. She walked several times back and forth, staying open to whatever messages came to her, keeping all other unhelpful thoughts out of her head. Declan had taught her a lot, but so had her mom, and she knew that the answer was there; she just had to be in the right place to receive it. Normally, she'd meditate, but that was hardly an option. A sudden image of her mother appeared in her mind's eye, and the answer came to her.

Her pacing halted. Could she do it? She studied Ramsey. If she had special abilities, then now was the time to use them. Before she could talk herself out of it, she moved into action, her plans for him changing rapidly.

She opened the hospital door. Hannah, Leroy, and Declan still stood outside, with Marco standing nearby.

"I need all of you. Right now." She spoke to Marco. "I need you to keep everyone out of this room."

"Sarah, what is it?" asked Declan.

Hannah and Leroy didn't ask questions and walked into the room.

"Declan," said Sarah. "I'll explain it, but right now we have to ensure we are not interrupted. Can you do that, Marco?"

Marco nodded. "If that's what you want, then no one will get past me."

Declan brow furrowed. "How much time will you need?"

"I don't know. This could take a while."

"Well, we can't have an army of nurses out here screaming for security if Marco won't let them in."

Sarah thought about it. She glanced down the hallway at the nurse's station where two nurses sat, one on a computer monitor, the other on the phone. A third one was likely on rounds. Taking a deep breath, she stilled herself, reaching out with her senses.

"What are you doing?" asked Declan.

Sarah didn't answer, but closed her eyes and focused, sending out a powerful wave of energy. Sarah opened her eyes and watched the nurse's station. Declan followed her gaze. The monitor at the station one nurse was using winked out and went dark.

"Hey, what..." said the nurse.

The other nurse, the one holding the phone, said, "Hello? Hello?" She held the phone out. "The phone just died."

"My computer went out," said the first nurse, hitting buttons on the keyboard.

The lights above them winked out as well, leaving them with no power at their station. "What the…" asked the nurse holding the phone.

"Great. Just what we need," said the nurse at the computer.

The third nurse appeared, asking what the problem was, and Declan dropped his jaw.

"Did you do that?" he asked.

Sarah relaxed her posture. "That ought to keep them busy for a while." She shook her head to refocus and saw Declan staring at her. "Guess I'm getting better at this."

"You guess?"

"We're not done yet." She turned back to Marco. "If someone wants in, you let us know.

"Will do," said Marco.

Declan marveled at her, followed her into the room and closed the door behind them.

"What is it, Sarah?" asked Leroy. "What's going on?" He waved at Ramsey in the bed. "Is this about Sherlock?"

"Yes, it is," said Sarah. "It's not an infection that's killing him."

"What do you mean?" asked Hannah.

Sarah stopped herself before saying more. "Leroy," she said. "I need you to go into that bathroom and cover the mirror. Use whatever you have, yank the shower curtain down if you have to, but it has to be covered. Then close the door behind you when you come out of the bathroom."

Declan gave her a strange look. "Sarah," he asked. "What is going on?"

Leroy didn't wait for an explanation. Hearing the urgency in her voice, he headed to the bathroom.

Sarah answered Declan. "It's not an infection. Feel him, Declan."

"What? What do you mean?"

173

They walked to Ramsey's bedside. He remained semi-conscious and unaware of the conversation going on around him. Sarah put her hands on his chest. Declan did the same.

"Now," said Sarah, "you remember how it felt when we got to the house? When he was stabbed?"

"Yes," said Declan.

"It's very much like that. You have to dig deep. It's subtle, but it's there."

Declan closed his eyes and focused, and Sarah could sense him opening up and probing Ramsey. After a few quiet moments, he sucked in his breath and opened his eyes. "What is that?"

Sarah felt it, too, much stronger now that she knew what to look for. "It's Y or something Y is projecting. I think he's using the mirror to do it."

Declan scowled. "The mirror? He's using the mirror? How?"

"It's a Red-Line thing," said Sarah. "They...we can use mirrors for more than just information storage. I don't understand it yet, but he can see us, Declan. He's been watching the whole time. That's how he knows so much. He can obviously use it to do this, too. He's been making Ramsey sick."

Declan stared at his hands, still sensing. "It's all over him." His face reflected his worry. "Can we get it out?"

Doubt crept in, but she kept it at bay. "If I have anything to say about it, we can. But I'll need everyone's help. I'm not sure I'm strong enough to do it alone."

Leroy came out of the bathroom and shut the door. "Mirror is covered."

"Okay," she said, straightening and taking her hands off Ramsey. She found the controls and lifted the bed higher, giving them all easier access to him, then found the bedrail and lifted it into place. Taking her cue, Declan lifted the rail on the other side. "This is the deal," she said to all of them. "Y has been using the mirror to project himself into the room. He's somehow been using this connection to poison John."

"What?" asked Leroy.

"How is that possible?" asked Hannah.

"I don't know," said Sarah. "But I think we can pull whatever is making him sick out of him, but we need to do it together."

Their faces froze, but no one argued. "What do we do?" asked Leroy.

Thinking for a second, Sarah felt for her next move. "Leroy," she said. "I need you up by his head." She spoke to Hannah. "Hannah, I need you by his feet." They moved into position. "Declan," she added, "you stay across from me. At his midsection."

Everyone at their positions, they waited for Sarah's next instructions. She took a breath and centered herself. "Okay," she said. "This is what I want you to do." Leaning over to demonstrate, she placed her palms on Ramsey's stomach. "I want you to put your hands on him, but it's very important that you are always pushing outward with your energy. Imagine a waterfall, or a beam of sunlight, or whatever works, moving through you. Imagine it coming through your head and out through your hands, but never coming back in. You don't want to suck any of this stuff into you. You must project forward at all times." She looked at Declan. "Pull it in toward his midsection. You and I will work on gathering it together into a single mass and containing it."

"How will we get it out once we do that?" asked Declan.

"We'll deal with that when the time comes. You just remember to draw the energy that Leroy and Hannah are pushing away towards John's midsection, but not into you. You have to be careful."

"I will," said Declan.

"Any of us gets this gunk into our system, and we may not be able to continue. You'll make yourself sick, too." Sarah regarded Ramsey, who showed no awareness of their actions, and prayed they could do this. "Take a deep breath and clear yourselves."

They did. Leaning forward, they put their hands on him, Hannah's on his feet, which lay beneath the blankets, Declan's on his belly, and Leroy's on his head.

Ramsey lay quiet, only his labored breathing breaking the quiet.

"How is this going to affect him?" asked Hannah.

Sarah hadn't thought of that. "I don't know. But we don't have a choice. If we're going to save him, then we have to get it out of him."

Hannah hesitated and Sarah felt her ambivalence, but Hannah nodded. "Okay," she said. "I'm ready."

"Me too," said Leroy.

"Let's do it," said Declan.

"All right," said Sarah. "Start pushing outward. You may not feel it at first, but as you continue to push it away, it's going to feel stronger or thicker to you." Sarah focused, pulling in the heaviness toward Ramsey's midsection, beginning to feel its thick consistency.

"My God," said Leroy, his senses beginning to pick up on what affected Ramsey. "What is that?"

"Some sort of dark energy," said Declan. "I don't know what else to call it."

They worked for several minutes.

"Hannah, you doing all right?" asked Sarah, feeling the mass begin to grow.

"Yes," said Hannah. "I can feel it now. I've gotten it past his ankles."

"It probably won't be as thick on his lower body. It's centered on his mid and upper torso." She continued to work. 'Leroy? How's it going?"

Leroy had his eyes closed. "This stuff is as thick as molasses. I've got it to his neck, heading to the shoulders."

"It's going to feel thicker the farther you go," said Sarah. "Just imagine a strong current moving through you, pushing it away. If you're a using a water image, make it a tsunami. You have to feel that it's easily removed."

"Got it," said Leroy. "I'm at his shoulders."

As they worked, Ramsey began to react. His eyes fluttered open, and he moaned low in his throat.

"Sherlock," asked Leroy, "you there?"

Ramsey blinked several times.

"Declan," Sarah asked, trying not to be distracted by Ramsey. "You doing okay?"

"Yes," he answered. "It's getting heavy, though."

"I know. Just keep it contained. Once we get it all in one area, then we can focus on pulling it out of him."

They continued for several more minutes on working to extract the dense substance attached to Ramsey's body.

"I'm at his knees," said Hannah.

"Working on getting it past the shoulders," said Leroy.

Ramsey jerked in the bed and gasped, his eyes wide now as he began to feel the effects of the sickness being drawn from him. He scrunched his eyes closed and then opened them. "Hurts…" he managed to say.

"Stay still, John," said Sarah. "Try not to move." The mass continued to grow.

Ramsey lifted his head off the bed despite the presence of Leroy's hands. "What's happening?" he said, dropping his head back down.

"Easy, Sherlock," said Leroy, keeping his voice steady. "We've working on making you better. Try to relax." He paused. "I'm at his chest now."

Ramsey went rigid and his back arched. He made a strangled sound and drew a constricted breath. "I can't breathe." His face paled. His hands shot out from the blankets, and he gripped the bedrails. Sweat began to pop out on his forehead.

"It's in his lungs," said Declan.

"I know," said Sarah. "Pull it down as much as you can. Keep pushing, Leroy. You can move your hands down to his shoulders. It'll help." She tried hard not to be distracted by Ramsey's pain, knowing it would only delay the process.

**

Ramsey wheezed, trying to find air to fill his lungs. A pain unlike anything he'd ever experienced burrowed into his chest. Panic set in, spots blurred his vision and an aching, gnawing, continuous spasm wracked his insides, making him feel raw, as if every nerve was exposed. He felt hands on him and through his blurry eyesight, he saw Leroy. "Leroy," he managed to whisper.

Leroy squeezed his shoulders. "I know it hurts, Sherlock. Just hang in there. We're going as fast as we can."

Ramsey shut his eyes and gritted his teeth. When the energy moved past his lungs and into his lower chest, he took a grateful breath but strained again when his midsection flared. Sweat trickled down his face and neck. Even though he could breathe again, he tried not to. Angry swipes of agony bit into him. "Oh God..." He couldn't help himself. His arms strained, and the rails creaked as he pulled on them.

"We're getting closer, John. Hang in there," said Declan. "Hannah," he asked, "how's it going?"

"Almost there," she said.

"Leroy?" asked Sarah.

"I'm just above you. Right at his upper belly."

"Declan?"

"Yeah, I'm containing it," said Declan. "It's getting big, though."

"I know," replied Sarah.

Ramsey lurched again and moaned. He struggled to curl inward against the agony, but Hannah kept a strong hold on his feet, keeping him in place.

"Don't move, John," said Sarah. "Leroy, can you hold him down? If we lose control of this thing, we won't get it back."

"I'm there," said Leroy, referring to the energy as he pressed down on Ramsey's shoulders. "I've met up with you guys."

"Me too," said Hannah.

Ramsey cried out. His body writhed, despite his restricted movement, and he breathed in shallow gasps. He clung to the rails in a death grip, and the bed sheets stuck to him from his sweat.

He lifted his head. "Please...stop... It hurts," he said in a whimpering voice. He dropped his head back down. He'd thought one knife to the belly had been bad, but now it felt like hundreds of knives stabbed at him, along with a white-hot poker that twisted his insides. He fought again to curl up against the misery, but the hands on him prevented it. A sob escaped him, and he sensed Leroy lean in close.

"Sherlock, listen to my voice."

He tried, but the searing pain made it almost impossible.

"Leroy…" It was all he could get out. His sweat drenched him, and his body shook in fear and pain. He tried to stay calm, but he let out an agonized breath, and tears clouded his eyes.

Leroy's whispered voice reached him. "You remember when I met Olivia?"

Ramsey tried to shift to the change in subject, but he could barely focus. He managed a shaky nod.

"You remember what you said when she broke up with me?"

**

While Leroy tried to keep Ramsey stable, Sarah and Declan contained the mass and Sarah wondered what to do next.

"Sarah?" Declan asked, staying quiet to keep Ramsey from hearing.

Sarah knew what he was asking. Tuning out Leroy's conversation with Ramsey, she felt for the next step.

"I need you to keep it stabilized. Hold it together," she said, deciding what to do. "Don't let it leak out. And don't let any of it get into you."

"I won't," Declan answered. "You got a plan on what to do now?"

Concentrating, Sarah heard Ramsey and Leroy's conversation.

"I'm not exactly on Memory Lane, right now, Leroy," Ramsey sputtered. He shook and drew another shallow, shaky breath, grimacing as he did so and looking even paler.

"You told me to suck it up," said Leroy. "That I should trust destiny. Remember that?"

"I did?" asked Ramsey. Another jab twisted him and he sucked in and groaned.

Sarah looked up at Declan. "We're going to lift it out of him."

"What?" Declan did not look convinced.

"We're going to lift it out of him," she repeated.

"And then what? Where are you going to put it?"

She spied the window.

Declan caught the direction of her gaze and looked at her in understanding. "You think it will work?"

"We're going to find out."

Leroy continued talking, trying to distract Ramsey. "Yes, you did," he said, his fingers curling into Ramsey's shoulders and holding him still. Despite what must have been difficult, Leroy kept his face flat.

Ramsey moaned again when another spasm hit. Tears leaked from his eyes and the muscles in his arms shook from the strain of pulling on the rails. "What are you trying to say, Leroy?" His voice shook and his face had lost its color.

"I'm telling you to follow your own advice," said Leroy. "Suck it up, my friend."

Just then, Sarah and Declan pulled the mass up and out of Ramsey's body.

Ramsey screamed. His body convulsed as if every nerve in his belly jolted in agony as whatever they took from him fought to stay where it was. Just as soon as they'd lifted it from him, though, he sank back into the bed and went still.

Containing what looked like a dense ball of gnats all flying in a circular motion, Declan and Sarah glanced at Leroy. "Move aside, Leroy," said Declan. "We don't want to throw this at you."

"Would appreciate it if you didn't," he answered, eyeing the swirling mass and stepping to Ramsey's side.

Declan looked at Sarah, holding the swarming energy at arm's length. "You sure about this?"

"No," she answered, "but we can't exactly walk it outside."

"What are you going to do with it?" asked Hannah.

Sarah and Declan counted down. "Three...two...one."

At one, they flung the mass at the window. The shade had been opened at some point, and the mass made contact with a smack. Expecting the glass to shatter, Hannah turned to protect herself. Declan and Sarah did the same. But to their surprise, the glass held, the swarming mass clinging to it as it began to dissolve. On closer inspection, though, they could see that the mass, although it was diminishing in size, was increasing in size outside the window. Once outside, it began to break up and disperse into the wind. The crack in the pane previously created by Sarah's burst of anger began to grow as the mass moved through it. It doubled in length, and tiny cracks spiraled outward alongside the larger fissure.

"It's gonna go," said Declan, watching as the window fractured into numerous lines.

"Maybe not," said Sarah. "The energy is almost gone."

The small black ball continued to decrease in size until finally, nothing remained, the wind taking away the last remnants. The window stayed intact.

Hannah let out a pent-up breath, and massaged her neck. "They don't teach that in nursing school."

"Let's hope they never have to," said Declan, who dropped his shoulders and shook out his hands.

The black mass gone, their attention turned back to Ramsey, who now lay in the bed, completely worn and pale with dark circles under his eyes. Drenched in sweat, his hair and hospital gown clung to him. He breathed heavily, as if he'd run a marathon.

"Sherlock," said Leroy, leaning over Ramsey with his hand on his friend's head. "Can you hear me?" Ramsey wearily blinked his eyes, staring upward. "How are you?""

Ramsey appeared to take in the room and the people around him. The poison now gone from his system, he seemed to be coming around, when he tensed and turned white. "I'm gonna be sick," he said weakly.

Hannah moved into nurse mode. She grabbed a plastic basin off the counter behind her. "Leroy," she said, "Help lift him up."

Leroy got his arms behind Ramsey, and with Declan's help, they lifted Ramsey's upper body just before Ramsey began to retch.

"Lean him over," said Hannah, holding the basin in front of him.

Ramsey had eaten little over the past few days, and there was nothing left in his stomach, but he gave in to his body's needs and threw up. Sarah watched in horror as he brought up a small amount of black liquid, which pooled thickly in the basin. He kept retching until the liquid turned clear, and then he collapsed backward, shaking from exhaustion. Leroy caught him and eased him back down onto the bed.

"Hannah," said Declan. "Wash that down the sink. Make sure you don't touch it. Then throw away the basin."

"I will," she said. She carried the container into the bathroom at arm's length.

Leroy covered Ramsey with the sheets. "Hannah," he said. "Bring a wet washcloth, too."

"How is he?" asked Sarah. Ramsey's flushed look was gone, but now he looked equally as pale.

"Fever broke," said Leroy. Hannah came out of the bathroom with a wet washcloth and handed it to Leroy, who wiped Ramsey's sweaty face and neck with it. "He's beat, but he'll live." He smiled at Sarah with gratitude. "You did it."

Before Sarah could respond, angry voices from outside the door could be heard.

"We're going to have company," said Hannah.

Declan stilled for a moment, and Sarah sensed what he was picking up from Marco outside the door. "Everybody stand around John," said Declan.

Leroy straightened and moved to the head of the bed, and Hannah returned to the foot. "Now hold hands," said Declan, going still as if communicating again. "Follow my lead."

They all grasped hands in a circle around Ramsey just as the door opened and two frustrated nurses rushed in past Marco. "What is going on in..." They stopped and took in the circle of people in front of them.

"Amen," said Declan and he lifted his bowed head.

"Amen," said Hannah, Sarah, and Leroy all at once. Sarah understood where Declan was leading them.

"I told you," said Marco to the nurses. "They just needed some time alone."

Declan dropped his hands, as did the others. "Everything okay?" he asked the nurses.

"Your...bodyguard," one nurse huffed as she looked at Marco, "wouldn't let us in. We almost called security."

"I'm sorry," said Declan. "We decided to have a prayer circle. We thought that with his illness and after the earthquake..."

"Earthquake?" said one nurse. "What earthquake?"

"Didn't you feel it?" asked Hannah. "We thought when the window cracked, we were all doomed."

"The window?" The nurses surveyed the damaged window. "That must have been what caused the power outage."

"Power outage?" asked Declan.

Neither one of them answered. They continued to look at the window.

"I never felt a thing," said one nurse.

"Me either."

A muffled cough brought their attention back to what they had originally come to do. Looking over at the bed, they saw their patient awake. Ramsey was sweaty and pale, but alert.

"Mr. Ramsey?" one nurse asked, walking closer to the bed.

The other nurse looked around at the group. "What happened in here?"

The four of them looked at each other, each wondering how to answer. Hannah finally spoke. "I'd say it was a miracle."

Sarah smiled, and knew none of them standing around the bed disagreed.

**

An hour away, Y sat down in the large chair, popcorn in a bowl in his lap, as he prepared to watch Ramsey's final moments. He'd waited for this for some time, and now he prepared to enjoy it. Quieting his mind, he relaxed, connecting to the mirror in front of him and then reaching out further, looking for the connection to the man he now knew well. Happy that this would be his final time to search for Ramsey, he felt almost giddy knowing his plans were taking shape exactly as he'd wanted. Pushing outward, he expected to easily reach his destination. Opening his eyes, he was surprised to see only a milky-white film across the mirror in front of him. Knitting his brow, he reached out again, wondering why the connection eluded him. Searching, he tracked the path and suddenly understood the problem. His conduit had been blocked. They had covered the mirror. She had figured it out.

Y stood, spilling his popcorn. Sarah had prevented his entry, and worse, if she'd followed the trail, she may have saved Ramsey's life.

His face passive but his anger fueled, he walked up to the mirror in front of him and punched it, shattering it into pieces.

FIFTEEN

....

SARAH STEPPED OFF the elevator into the quiet of the hospital corridor. She had not been able to sleep, and giving up on trying, she had dressed and left the hotel room, careful not to awaken Hannah. It was three-thirty in the morning as she crept toward Ramsey's door. She watched for a nurse, hoping they would not stop her from entering his room. After their impromptu prayer circle the previous day, the hospital staff had eyed them warily, as if not quite sure what to think. They'd been hastily moved into the hall after his recovery, allowing the nurses to clean him up and examine him. Not long after, two orderlies had transferred him to another room, since the current one had sustained apparent damage from a suspected earthquake. Once relocated, the doctor had appeared, ready to see his miracle patient. By the time they'd been able to get back in to see him, Ramsey had given in to his fatigue and had slept the rest of the day. He'd still been asleep when they'd left at the end of visiting hours.

Sarah saw no one as she entered. Seeing him in the dim light, she removed her jacket and placed it on the chair. She saw that the door of the bathroom was open, but the mirror remained covered. Leroy had taped paper over it earlier, making up some strange reason as to why the staff should leave it alone, which only gave more credence to the talk from the nurses after their circle.

She closed the bathroom door, preferring another layer of protection between the mirror and Ramsey. Returning to the bed, she watched him sleep and relief flooded through her at the sight of his healthy face. Dark circles still showed below his eyes, and he was thinner, but she knew that after he caught up on his rest and regained his strength, the effects on him would diminish and he would improve.

She took his hand, which lay outside the covers, and was surprised when he squeezed her fingers. She looked to see him watching her.

"Why aren't you sleeping?" he whispered.

"Why aren't you?" she asked in return. Her heart warmed to see him alert and awake again.

He didn't answer and she turned to pull up a chair.

"No."

She turned back.

"Lay beside me."

Something in the tone of his voice caught her attention. "You all right? You need anything?"

He shook his head. "Just you."

Knowing he was hiding something from her and sensing his need to have her near, she complied. She slipped off her shoes, sat on the bed, and leaned back, stretching out and moving on to her side. She moved close, and stretched her arm over his ribs, trying not to put too much pressure on his torso.

"It's okay," he said, noticing her carefulness. "You won't hurt me."

"You're not sore?"

"I am, but you make me feel better, not worse."

She settled her head into the crook of his neck and shoulder, her upper arm resting on his chest and he brought his hand up to interlace his fingers with hers. His other arm came up behind her back and he pulled her close. Closing her eyes, she breathed him in, smelling his familiar scent. "Better?" she asked.

"You have no idea."

She heard him exhale, his cheek nuzzling her forehead, and she snuggled in even closer. "You're comfortable?" she asked, wanting to be sure.

"You're kidding?"

Smiling, she relaxed. She expected to feel him do the same, but instead she felt tension, as if he was deliberately staying awake. "What is it?"

"Nothing," he said too fast. "Go to sleep."

She lifted her head. "It's not nothing," she said, but he wouldn't look at her. "Something's wrong."

He stiffened in response. "I'm fine."

The lie was obvious. "No, you're not." She watched him struggle to hide whatever bothered him. "What is it?"

He fought to find the words. "I...I don't know how to explain it."

That scared her. "You're not sick, are you?"

"No. No. I'm not sick."

A relieved breath escaped her. "Just try, then," she said.

He took a nervous breath. "I feel empty."

"Empty?"

"Not myself. I feel...invaded, like something was taken from me."

She heard the hollowness in his voice. Sarah pushed up so she could meet his eyes, but he wouldn't look at her. "Explain it. Tell me more."

He finally faced her. "What was that inside of me?"

Sarah began to consider the emotional effects of Y's toxic attack on him, rather than just the physical. "I don't know," she said honestly. "Some sort of projected energy. Designed to break you down."

His body shuddered. "Well, it worked."

Concern filtered through her. What else had that dark energy done to him?

He let go of her hand and rubbed his forehead. "I've been awake for hours. I haven't been able to sleep. I keep feeling it. Like it's coming back. As soon as I shut my eyes, it's there. When I try to think of something else, I can't. It's like I'm exposed, and I have no defenses." He sighed and shut his eyes. "It's like it's still in me, and I'm terrified that maybe it is."

The darkness Y had projected had been much more insidious than she'd realized. It hadn't just wrecked Ramsey's body, it had done a number on his mind as well.

"It's gone, John," she said, trying to ease his mind. "I felt it leave you. There's nothing left."

He didn't look convinced.

"Hey, look at me."

His gaze met hers.

"You're okay. It may not feel that way right now, but it's only been a few hours since you were on your deathbed. That stuff invaded you, and of course you feel defenseless, but you're not. Not anymore. You're stronger now."

"I wasn't strong enough to prevent it."

"You had a knife wound. You'd been operated on. Of course, you were weaker. It made it easy for him to prey on you." She searched for the words he needed to hear. "But that's not the case anymore. You're regaining your strength every minute, and we've put a stop to his method of transportation. He can't get to you anymore."

The energy shifted in him as some of her words penetrated. His energy still felt constricted to her, though.

"I hate this," he said, shutting his eyes but then reopening them to stare at the ceiling again. "I hate feeling so exposed."

Empathizing with him, she remembered how she felt during her Shift. "It's because you're so used to taking care of everyone else. You're always the strong one, the protector. How about you give yourself a break and let someone take care of you for a while?" Remembering what she'd brought with her, she reached into her pocket. "I have something for you."

"Yeah?" He waited. "What?'

"I never had a chance to give it to you." She showed him the "Relax" wristband she had bought for him on the day of his attack. "It's your birthday present."

"Really? You got me a present?"

His mood lightened and she smiled. "Yes." She slipped it over his hand. "It says 'Relax.' I think now would be a good time to wear it."

He raised his arm and admired it. "Thank you. It's perfect."

"You should do what it says."

He put his arm down, and she could feel his tension return.

She took his hand again. "Close your eyes."

He remained hesitant.

"You are safe," she continued, stroking his fingers. "I'll stay with you. Let me take care of you for once."

He tried to laugh. "You realize this is killing my image as a tough guy."

Glad that some of his humor had returned, she played along. "I won't tell a soul."

"Good," he said. "Leroy would never let me live it down."

Her energy began to help him unwind and he closed his eyes. Putting her head back down, she snuggled into him. He turned gently into her and rested his chin against her head. Continuing to project peaceful energy, she lulled him into a tranquil state.

"Go to sleep," she said, speaking softly. "All is well."

Within minutes, she could feel his breathing deepen as he succumbed and drifted off into much needed rest. Holding him close, she remained awake, hoping that whatever emotional effects this attack had wreaked upon him would be temporary but worried that they may be more difficult to deal with than she imagined. Finally letting go herself as his body heat warmed her, and listening to the peaceful sounds of his breathing, she joined him and slept.

SIXTEEN

....

"**H**OW IS HE?" asked Declan, coming up behind Leroy, holding two Styrofoam cups. He glanced out the window at Ramsey, wearing a robe and slippers, sitting in a wheelchair on the patio. He'd improved enough to be able to get up and move around. He'd been eating solid food for two days, and his strength had begun to return. The doctor had recommended physical therapy to help continue his recovery. They were releasing him tomorrow, which should have resulted in a happy patient. But Ramsey had been subdued, his personality not recovering as well as his body.

Leroy took a cup from Declan. "Same," he said. "Quiet."

"Not a word I would ever expect to describe him."

"I know."

Declan could feel Leroy's concern. "You think it's the attack?"

Leroy took a sip of his drink. "I don't know. He won't talk about it."

"He's been through a lot. He just needs time."

"It's more than that," said Leroy, putting his cup on the table beside him and crossing his arms. "He's doubting himself, I know, but..."

"But what?"

Leroy shook his head. "It's like he's lost faith, like he's giving up."

"Has he asked about what happens tomorrow?" asked Declan.

"I told him we were taking him back to his place. He didn't say anything."

"Did he ask about Sarah?"

"Not a word." Leroy sighed.

Declan couldn't believe it. "Now I know there's a problem."

"Yup."

"Does Sarah know he's upset?"

"She knows. Says he told her he felt defenseless that first night after we brought him back. Exposed. He hasn't talked to her about it since."

Declan considered that. "It makes sense. What happened to him would wig anyone out." He sipped his coffee. "You want to go out and talk to him?"

"I've tried. He clams up." Leroy looked at Declan. "You want to try?"

"Me?" asked Declan. "If he won't talk to you, then he likely won't talk to me."

"I'm not sure about that," said Leroy. "He may open up to you."

Declan studied his brother through the window. "I can try."

"Good," said Leroy. "We need to try and reach him. The longer he sits in this hole, the harder it will be to pull him out of it." Leroy paused. "I've seen him hunker down before, but not like this. This goes deeper."

Declan's senses heightened in alarm. He hadn't read too much into his brother's solemn mood, but then he figured John would snap out of it soon enough. Now, though, he wondered what else Y's poison had done to his brother.

"I'll go now." He took another sip of the mediocre coffee and dropped his cup into the trashcan. "Any advice?" he asked before heading out onto the patio.

Leroy took a moment to think about it. "Just be honest with him. He'll read you like a book if you sugarcoat it."

"Okay," said Declan. "I'll give it a shot." He moved toward the door.

"And don't be surprised if he gets in your face," Leroy added. "Sometimes you got a push a little to get past the wall."

"Great," said Declan, putting his hand on the door. "It wouldn't be the first time."

"Good luck," said Leroy.

"I'll take it," said Declan and he walked outside.

He headed toward the patio, and took a seat on a concrete bench near Ramsey's wheelchair. Ramsey said nothing at his arrival, even though he saw Declan sit.

"Nice day," said Declan, taking the initiative.

"I suppose," said Ramsey.

"I hear they're springing you tomorrow," said Declan. "You must be happy to hear that."

Ramsey had his head turned toward the courtyard, but now his eyes shifted toward Declan. "Leroy sent you?"

Declan chuckled. "Boy, and I thought I could read people."

"Sometimes you're an open book." Ramsey returned his gaze to the yard.

"Yeah," said Declan, watching him. "When I'm worried, it's hard to hide."

Ramsey didn't respond.

"Leroy's worried, too." Declan waited to hear a response, but none came. "What's going on, John?"

Ramsey took a few seconds before he answered. "Nothing," he said, trying to act relaxed. "You both don't need to worry." His words did not match his mood, though, and Declan felt it.

"Pardon my French, but that's bullshit."

Ramsey made no reaction, except to say, "Call it what you want."

Declan let a few moments pass as he considered his next approach. "You talk to Sarah about tomorrow?" His brother tightened his jaw, but made no other outward sign at his question. Inwardly, though, Declan sensed his sensitivity to the subject.

After letting the question settle in, Ramsey answered. "I'm going home to continue my recovery. I assume you and the Council will take over Sarah's care."

Declan had to bite his tongue at his brother's cavalier answer. He knew overreacting would only make him withdraw. "Actually, no. That's not what's happening."

Ramsey shifted his eyes toward Declan. "What do you mean?"

"She's going home."

"She's what?"

"She asked to go home."

Ramsey tensed in his wheelchair and Declan waited for the expected outburst.

"She can't go…" Ramsey started to say, but then stopped himself. Declan saw the display of emotions run across his face until he stilled and his shoulders slumped back down. "That's what she wants?"

"Yes," said Declan, deflated by Ramsey's response. His brother had completely pulled back and stifled his natural inclination to protect Sarah. "She says she's ready."

"You going to keep up your training sessions with her?" Ramsey asked, not completely able to disengage himself.

"In case you haven't noticed, she's progressing rapidly without my help. She could teach me a thing or two." His brother continued to withdraw, as if he didn't want to talk about Sarah. "We'll keep up security, though," he continued. "We'll have people at her place to keep an eye on her." Watching the tension move through his brother, Declan could feel the unspoken question and answered it. "Y said he would not come after her. That anything that happened would be voluntary on her part, so she's chosen to believe him."

Ramsey had learned of Sarah's trip to Y's house and how she had bargained for his life.

"Well," Ramsey answered, "I guess she knows what's best." The little amount of emotion he'd revealed moments ago now vanished, and his blank look returned.

Declan leaned forward and put his elbows on his knees. He had no idea how to deal with this. An angry brother he could deal with, but this silent one baffled him. "Talk to me, John. This isn't like you."

Ramsey put his hands on the wheels of his chair. "There's nothing to talk about, Declan. Sarah's going home, and so am I. Assignment over." He pushed on the wheels and turned himself. "I'm going back in," he said, wheeling himself off the patio.

Leroy met him at the door and held it open for him. Declan heard Leroy offer to help get him back to the room, but Ramsey declined.

After Ramsey disappeared inside, Leroy walked over and joined him on the bench. "Well?" asked Leroy.

Declan sat up and let go of a held breath. "You're right," he said. "This goes deeper. A lot deeper."

**

Ramsey headed down the hall, pushing on his wheels despite the tremble in his arms. His physical strength had improved, but he still had a long way to go. Sweat began to bead on his forehead and his breathing became heavy as he returned to his room. Wheeling himself through the open door, he stopped when he saw Sarah sitting on the bed.

Seeing him, she stood. "There you are," she said. "I was wondering where everyone went."

"Hi," he said, happy to see her.

Looking rested, she wore slim jeans and an oversized sweater and her brunette hair brushed her shoulders. He felt a pang of sadness move through him at the sight of her.

"Hi," she said in return. "How's today going?"

"Better," he said. "Every day is better."

She waved at this chair. "You go on a walk, or should I say roll?"

"Yeah. Leroy thought I could use some fresh air."

"Leroy's right. You need to get out of this room." She paused, and Ramsey knew what was on her mind. "Speaking of that," she said, "I hear you're getting out of here tomorrow." Her manner was subdued, as if the subject made her uncomfortable.

He understood. "I am," he said. "And I hear you're going home."

Her eyes rounded, and her posture sank. "They told you?"

Softening his look, he put up a wall to keep his emotions hidden. "It's okay, Sarah."

Her face projected her worry. "I wanted to tell you."

"It's okay," he repeated. "It's time."

Surprised at his agreement, she gave him a questioning look. "Time? What do you mean?"

He wheeled himself closer to the bed, and she stepped aside. His breathing had recovered from the return to his room, and he felt strong enough to stand by himself and sit back on the bed. "Sarah," he said, steeling himself for what he had to say. "It's time for you to return. I've done my job. You're ready."

Her eyebrows knitted at his response. "You've done your job?"

"Yes," he kept going, not allowing himself to think but just speaking the words. "I got you through your Shift. Your abilities are back. Y is going to leave you alone. There's nothing left for me to do." He froze, holding a flat stare on his face.

Her mouth fell open. "This isn't personal."

"I know it isn't."

"I just thought it would be good for me to be back on my own."

"I understand."

"I just need to figure out my life. I need to figure out what's next. Where do I go from here?"

"That's good."

She took a step toward him. "That doesn't mean you're not a part of that."

His gaze shifted away from hers. "Sarah," he said, clearing his throat. "I've got a lot of recovery time in front of me. I'll be pretty worn out with the physical therapy schedule they've got me on."

She stood stock-still. "I'd like to be there to help you through that."

Knowing the difficulty of what he was about to say, he forced the words out. "I think it would better if you didn't." Glancing back at her, he saw her stricken face.

She swallowed and crossed her arms in front of her. "You're shutting me out? Why?"

It took every ounce of fortitude he had to not take her in his arms, but he kept going. "I think I need to do the same thing as you." He stopped when he almost broke, but he pushed through it. "This 'illness,' or whatever you want to call it, has thrown me. I need a breather to sort things out." That was easier to say because it was the truth, but he hated saying the rest. "I need to take some time for myself." He hesitated. "Without any complications."

"Complications?"

He heard the disbelief and dismay in her voice, but didn't break, knowing if he did, he would lose this battle.

"Yes." It was all he could make himself say.

She bit her lip, and said nothing for several seconds. The room echoed the silence.

"All right," she said. "I'll give you some time." Her eyes shimmered and she wiped at an unshed tear, but remained composed. His heart raced as he fought to stay motionless.

"Thank you," he whispered, not trusting his voice.

Neither of them said a word, both processing what was happening, neither believing it.

Taking a deep breath, she cleared her throat. "I'd like to be here tomorrow, when they release you. Maybe take you home. Is that okay?" She eyed him, hopeful.

Ramsey wanted to say yes, but held back, knowing it was better to make the break now. He wasn't sure he'd be strong enough to deny her tomorrow. Holding his breath, he gave the performance of his life. "It would be easier for me if you weren't."

Her face froze, and he felt the emotional impact of what he'd said hit her. He had to look away and force himself to stay passive, although his heart ached at the pain he'd caused her.

Sarah nodded her head, but said nothing. Holding her elbows, she moved toward the open door but stopped. She turned to face him, and fighting back tears, she said, "I know there's more going on. And I know you're struggling." He refused to look at her, and felt her try to tune into him, but he blocked her. "You take the time you need," she said with a sniff. "But don't think this is it. I remember what we said to each other when you were sick."

He didn't move. "I said a lot of things I don't remember." Feeling her eyes on him, he forced himself not to look at her. From the corner of his eye, he saw her wipe a tear from her cheek, and he almost crumbled.

"I don't believe that," she said. "But it doesn't matter." She paused. "But you should know, I'm not giving up on you."

Listening, he fought to keep her out, not wanting to let her see or feel his torment.

"I'm not giving up on us." She stood there, standing tall, as if she dared him to argue with her. But when he didn't respond, she turned and left, leaving him alone to battle his demons.

SEVENTEEN

....

THE POT ON the stove bubbled, and bits of chili splattered the stovetop. Gerry stirred the pot and lowering the heat on the stove, she covered the pot and put the spoon aside. Looking out the window into her small backyard, she saw Joe. He was watering her vegetable garden wearing her pink bathrobe. Seeing that he was occupied, she opened a cabinet drawer and pulled out a canister. Images of red-nosed reindeers and tiny elves graced the top and sides, reminiscent of the fruitcake that had once resided within. When she popped the lid, she could still smell the orange aroma from the long-absent cake, even though the canister now held a pack of cigarettes. She took out the pack, removed one cigarette, threw the pack back in the canister, and returned it to the cabinet. Taking another peek outside and seeing she was still safe, she found a lighter in a drawer, lit up the cigarette, and took a long drag. She made a sigh of delight when the smoke reached her lungs. Then she exhaled, aiming the wisps of smoke out the open window. Closing her eyes, she took another puff and relaxed, feeling the nicotine rush through her body.

The doorbell rang and she swiveled in the direction of the noise. She wasn't expecting anyone and debated whether to answer it, but then she thought of Joe. She looked back out the window, hiding the cigarette from his view. She saw him turn and look toward the house. The doorbell rang again.

"I'll get it," she yelled out the window. "Keep watering, handsome."

He nodded and turned back, and she snuffed out her cigarette in the sink. "Damn. Foiled again," she said. Checking her faint image in the glass of the microwave door, she tucked a strand of her dark hair behind her ear and then, looking down, wiped a crumb off her sweatshirt. "Oh, well. It will have to do." She left the kitchen and went to the front door.

Gerry looked through the peephole, smiled and threw the door open. "Sarah," she said. "What are you doing here?"

Sarah looked apologetic. "Sorry, Aunt Gerry. I know this is unannounced. I should have called."

"Nonsense, honey. Come on in. It's great to see you." Sarah stepped inside and the two hugged warmly. Closing the door, Gerry followed her niece into the den, noticing that Sarah carried herself as if she wore a heavy cloak on her shoulders. "Come on in to the kitchen, hon. Have a seat."

Sarah did as she asked and sat at the breakfast table. Her eyes narrowed, and she sniffed the air. "Have you been smoking?"

Gerry reached for a glass in a cabinet. "Me? No. That Joe, though. Can't seem to get him to put those coffin nails down." She held out the glass. "You want something to drink?"

"You have any of your famous lemonade?"

Gerry smiled. "Always."

"Who's Joe?"

Gerry pulled out the lemonade pitcher and poured a glassful. "He's my current paramour. He's out back, watering the yard."

Sarah leaned to look out the window. "Nice robe."

"You should see him in my slippers."

Sarah chuckled.

Gerry handed Sarah the glass of lemonade and watched her take a sip. She noted the girl's slimmer frame and the hint of red in her eyes. Gerry took a seat at the table. "How've you been? I haven't seen you in a while."

Sarah didn't answer. She just looked at her lemonade.

"You okay?"

Sarah nodded and put down her drink.

"Oh, boy," said Gerry.

Sarah looked up. "What?"

Gerry sat forward in her seat. "It's a man, isn't it? You met someone."

"I..." Sarah shook her head. "Why do you think that?"

"I've seen that look before. Your mom looked the same way a few times after she met your dad. It's written all over your face."

"Is it that obvious?"

"Like an orange fish in an aquarium."

Sarah sighed, and tears sprang into her eyes.

"Oh, wow. You got it bad, hon." Gerry reached for a tissue. "Here."

Sarah took it, sniffed, and blew her nose.

"When did you meet him?"

"About two months ago."

"That fast, huh?"

"Yes."

"It happens that way, doesn't it?" Gerry asked.

Sarah dabbed at her eyes with the tissue. "What do you mean?"

"Is he 'the one'?"

Sarah stared, but then shook her head. "I don't know," she said. "Maybe." Fresh tears surfaced. "I don't know what to think."

Gerry put out her hand. "Let me see your palm."

"Gerry—"

"Don't give me any guff. Let me see your palm."

Sarah hesitated but then offered her right hand, palm up.

Gerry took it in hers. Her fingers traced over Sarah's skin. After she scrutinized it for several seconds, she let go and sat back in her seat. She studied Sarah. "What exactly have you been up to since I've last seen you?"

Sarah picked at the table cloth. "A lot has happened." She took another sip of her lemonade.

Gerry didn't say anything at first. "You still at the bookstore?"

Sarah shook her head. "I took a leave of absence. I'm thinking of going back, though."

"Why?"

"To get my mind off things."

"Don't."

Sarah frowned. "What?"

"I think you know the time for working at bookstores is over, Sarah."

Sarah gripped her glass. "What do you mean?"

"You know what I mean." Gerry leaned in and put her forearms on the table. "I found you work there to keep you occupied after your mom died and you lost the house and your job. You needed the distraction. But you've had enough time now. It's not a hiding place."

"A hiding place?"

"Sweetie, you can't escape whatever it is that's dogging you. If you're lost, then you need to find your way. You can't do that by wasting time in a bookstore."

"What do you mean? What's wrong with the bookstore?"

"Nothing's wrong with it, honey. But we both know that it's not your path."

Sarah held her head. "Why is it not my path?"

"You know. You've known it all along. So did your mom."

"My mom? What did she know?"

"She knew you were a special child."

Sarah swallowed and held her lemonade. "She did?"

"Of course. Anyone with any sort of ability could see it."

Sarah paused. "Did you see it?"

"Your mother and I talked about you all the time." She shrugged. "Of course. I wasn't as talented as she was, but I was no dummy when it came to reading certain people. Your palm has more interesting lines than a book."

Sarah stared at her fingers. "You can tell that much from my hand?"

"Hell, no. But your aura is like a beam of sunshine. It's easy to read."

"You're reading my aura?"

"That, along with other things. It's easy to see that you're unique."

Sarah clenched her hands together.

Gerry studied her niece. "You can do it too."

"Do what?"

"Read people. But somehow I think you know that already."

Sarah shifted in her seat. "I think I may have an idea."

Gerry's eyes narrowed. "I think you may have more than that."

Sarah thought of her mother. "Did Mom always know?"

"That you were special?"

"Yes."

"Since the day you were born. She knew."

It took Sarah a second to speak. "What if...?"

"What if what?"

"What if..." Sarah shook her head. "Never mind."

Gerry waited, letting her niece decide what to say next.

"What if I'm more special than you think?"

"What do you mean?"

"What if I'm different?"

"Different?" asked Gerry. "Different how?"

"What if I'm not who you think I am?"

Gerry didn't expect that question. "Well, unless you're some sort of space alien sent to conquer the earth, then I'm not too worried."

Sarah stilled and held her stomach. She wiped at a teary eye and sniffed. "You may not be that far off the mark."

Gerry reached across the table and took Sarah's hand. "Honey, I don't care if you're a cross-dressing Godzilla. I wouldn't love you any less. But if you are, then we all know Godzilla would not fulfill his purpose by working in a bookstore. He'd put on his pink lipstick, wrap his flowery boa over his massive scales, and rock his sexiness while he trampled Japan. You get what I'm saying?"

203

Sarah pressed her lips together and fought fresh tears. "I get it," she whispered.

"Good. Now tell me about this idiot that is making you cry. Do I need to find my shotgun?"

Sarah raised a brow. "Do you still own that thing?"

"Haven't cleaned it in years. But if I need to, I'll whip that puppy out."

Sarah shook her head. "No. There's no need."

"Do you love him?"

Sarah chewed her lip, and Gerry spotted the flush blooming Sarah's cheeks.

"Okay. That's a yes. Does he love you?"

Sarah squeezed Gerry's fingers. "I think he does. But he's pulling away. He's been through a lot recently. Most of which is due to me. He asked for some time."

"Then give it to him."

Sarah let go of Gerry's hand and sat back. "I am. But it's been over a week since I've seen him, and I miss him."

"I'm sure you do, but he'll come around."

Sarah made a sad smile. "I'm not too sure about that."

Gerry glanced out at the backyard and saw Joe pick a flower. "The good ones always come back." She looked back. "Something tells me he's a good one."

"He is."

"Then let him be. Give him the chance to sort things out. Sometimes men need to figure things out for themselves. Your being around him only confuses him more. He spends enough time away from you, and he'll know soon enough that he can't live without you."

"I wish I had your confidence."

"You do. You're just in the middle of the swamp right now, and it's hard to see through the muck. When the waters clear, though, you'll know exactly what to do and when to do it. Just ask your mom for advice if you need it."

Sarah fiddled with her tissue. "I wish I could talk to her. I miss our chats."

"You can. Hell, I talk to her all the time. We had a conversation this morning. She keeps telling me I put too much salt in the chili. I told her to mind her own damn business and go hang out with Buddy Holly or Moses or something."

Sarah smiled. "She always had a thing for Paul Newman."

"Who didn't, honey?"

Sarah turned melancholy. "I feel her around me sometimes."

"Why wouldn't you? She's with you just as much now as she was when she was alive. You need help, just ask."

"She's always there when I need her."

"Of course, she is. Where else would she be?"

Sarah ran her fingers down the side of her lemonade glass. "I know."

They sat in silence, until Gerry broke the quiet. "You hear that?"

Sarah looked up. "What?"

"Your mom just told me to offer you some of my salty chili. You believe that?" She stared at the air. "You are a total pain in the ass, Sis."

A soft breeze filtered into the room, and the rosy scent of Sarah's mother's perfume filled the air. Sarah sat wide-eyed, and her eyes shimmered again. "I can feel her." She sniffed and wiped her tears.

"I know you can," said Gerry. "You hungry?"

Sarah chuckled. "I'd love some salty chili."

"Comin' right up."

The patio door opened and a large man in a pink bathrobe sauntered in, holding a white flower in his hand. He glanced at Sarah. "How do?" he asked. "I'm Joe."

She extended her hand. "Sarah."

They shook hands and Joe turned and handed the flower to Gerry. "A flower for my flower."

Gerry took the offering and put it behind her ear. "Aww. Thanks, sweetie."

Joe smiled, but then frowned and sniffed. "Has somebody been smoking?"

**

The time passed with excruciating slowness for Ramsey. Leroy had taken him home after Ramsey had been discharged from the hospital, but Ramsey, who owned a small two-bedroom house on a wooded acre of land, had refused to let anyone stay with him while he recovered. Leroy's wife, Olivia, had stocked his kitchen with groceries and his freezer with frozen meals to be sure he fed himself, and Leroy saw him almost every other day to pick him up for therapy, since Ramsey had not yet been cleared to drive.

Their trips to the therapist's office were quiet ones, since Leroy had decided to wait it out until Ramsey was ready to talk, and so any conversation between the two consisted mainly of Leroy's work, or Ramsey's recovery, or the weather. Ramsey never asked about Sarah, and Leroy didn't offer, figuring he'd make Ramsey ask before he'd offer any information. Ramsey was stubborn, though, and after almost three weeks, he still remained in his funk, closed off from the world.

As per the established routine, Ramsey sat at home, waiting for Leroy, amazed that twenty days had passed since he'd left the hospital. They'd felt like twenty years. Feeling stronger, he no longer wheezed when the therapist put him through his paces. He was leaner, having put on only a small amount of weight since his hospital stay. He kept the house clean and he ate, but without any real appetite. His first week had been a difficult adjustment. There had been several nights when he'd drunk himself into a stupor in order to sleep, but he'd managed to go the past five days without needing more than one drink before he turned out the lights. Learning the hard way, he found that the nightmares were worse the more heavily he drank.

Not liking to leave the house, he departed only for his therapy sessions, but he'd forced himself to leave in order to have lunch with his mother a week before. Declan had set it up for him and had picked him up, driving him to the restaurant and dropping him off. He'd decided that after all he'd been through and because of his mother's letter, he needed to make the effort to reestablish a relationship with her. The meal had gone smoothly and was, in fact, the first time he'd talked with her in years without the conversation ending in an argument. When he'd left, he'd given her a warm hug, promising to stay in touch and see her more often.

Now, sitting silently on the couch, Ramsey was trying not to think about Sarah. A knock on his door sounded, and he stood and grabbed his jacket.

"You're late," he said, opening the door, but was surprised to see Hannah standing there instead of Leroy.

"Sorry," she said. She was wearing jeans with a fitted T-shirt with simple jewelry and make-up, and her hair was up in a ponytail. "I got a last-minute call from Leroy."

"Everything okay?" asked Ramsey, thinking of Sarah.

"Yes, everything's fine. He's just caught up at work." Hannah looked him over. "You seem well."

He picked up on her ambivalence. "That surprises you?"

"I'll be honest. I was half-expecting a Howard Hughes character from his recluse years, with long, dirty hair and fingernails."

Ramsey looked down at himself. "I'm not there yet."

"Not yet," she said quietly.

He didn't respond to her cynicism. "So, you're my ride?" he asked, closing and locking the door behind him. He felt the familiar pang of anxiety as he stepped off the porch, but pushed it back.

"You don't mind, do you?"

"Of course not. It's good to see you."

They walked down the driveway and got into Hannah's car. Ramsey slid in with little pain, a huge achievement since Hannah drove a little roadster that sat low to the ground.

Starting up the car, she glanced over. "You look a lot better since you left the hospital."

"Thanks," he said, buckling his seat belt. "I almost punched my therapist that first week, but now I'm starting to endure her grueling regimen with some measure of satisfaction."

"I expect you cussed her out a few times." Hannah pulled out and drove down the street.

"Oh, I did. Believe me, she heard a few things perhaps better left unsaid."

"They're used to that."

The two of them drove a few minutes in silence. Hannah had left the windows open, letting the cool air in, and Ramsey closed his eyes, enjoying the feel of it against his face.

"How've you been, Hannah?" he asked, opening his eyes.

"I've been fine." She hit the radio button, and The Rolling Stones began to play at a low volume. "Trying to get back into the swing of things."

"You still working with home health care patients?" he asked, launching into the routine of keeping his conversations light.

Keeping her eyes on the road, she said, "They want her to read the mirror."

Ramsey wasn't sure what she meant at first, but his mind quickly caught up. "Hannah..." he started to say.

"Or would you really rather talk about my work?"

Not knowing what to say, he answered with the first thing that came to mind. "How is she?"

Hannah tucked a piece of hair back that had come loose from her ponytail. "She's fine. I had dinner with her last night."

"You did?" He suddenly felt excited, as if his nearness to Hannah somehow brought him closer to Sarah.

Hannah paused. "She misses you."

Ramsey clenched his jaw, determined not to get pulled back into the emotional hurricane that thinking of Sarah created for him. "Did she go back to work?" he asked, determined to keep it light.

Hannah raised a brow at him and Ramsey knew he wasn't fooling her. "No. She left the bookstore."

"She did?"

"Yes. She's been spending time with her friend, and a few days with her aunt. She's trying to figure out what's next."

"That's good."

"Morgana called her yesterday."

Ramsey couldn't help it then as his protective side kicked in. "About the mirror?"

"Yes."

"Hell." Ramsey sighed and made a mental note to talk to Leroy about it, but just as quickly changed his mind. That wasn't his job anymore.

"She wants to do it."

Ramsey put his elbow up on the window and made the continued effort to remain detached. "Is she ready?"

"How do you know if you're ready for something like that?"

Ramsey didn't know how to answer her. "When's this supposed to happen?"

"Sometime next week. Not sure of the day."

Ramsey sighed.

"I'll ask the obvious," said Hannah. "You going to be with her when she reads it?"

Ramsey tensed, and stared straight ahead. "Why should I be?"

"You're serious?"

"Hannah," he said, realizing he sounded harsh but knowing he had to in order to stay away. "Sarah and I are..." He wasn't sure what to say.

"Are what?"

"We're taking some time to be apart right now. It's better if I don't see her." He tuned out the feeling of dishonesty in his gut.

Not believing the truth of it either, Hannah spoke plainly, as she usually did. "Well, then, you're a damn fool, Ramsey."

Ramsey could only shake his head as his fingers came up to rest in his hair. "You're probably right, Hannah." He watched the traffic, his mind convoluted with thoughts. "You're probably right."

They said nothing else for the rest of the drive.

**

Several hours later, Ramsey was sitting on the couch finishing his microwavable meal. The TV was playing, but the sound was muted. He had planned earlier to actually make something for dinner, but his difficult conversation with Hannah that morning still weighed on him. The drive home had been quiet, with no further conversation about Sarah. Ramsey had met with the doctor during his visit and had been cleared to drive, so he no longer needed anyone to take him where he needed to go. If he wanted to, he could shut out the world, and no one could stop him.

Wondered if that were possible, he was interrupted by the ringing of the phone. Picking it up, he froze when he read the caller ID. It was Sarah.

The phone ringing, he debated for several seconds whether to let it go to voicemail, but was unable to stop himself from answering. The thought of hearing her voice sent a chill through him.

He raised the phone. "Hello?"

There was a brief moment of quiet, and she spoke. "I thought you weren't going to answer."

He closed his eyes, not prepared for the impact that hearing her voice would have on him. God, he missed her. Just as fast, though, he shut it down, knowing she would pick up on it.

"Sorry," he said, offering no explanation. "How are you?"

There was another hesitation, but then she said, "I'm good. How are you? I hear you're making great progress."

He made a concentrated effort to breathe normally. "I'm doing all right. Starting to regain some of those rippling muscles."

She laughed, and his stomach flipped. "I'm sure you are."

"I hear you left the bookstore."

"I did. It didn't feel like the place to be anymore." She paused. "So much has changed."

He heard the pensive tone in her voice, as if perhaps she thought that things had not changed for the better. "I know," he said, feeling certain that they were worse. "Just take your time. You don't have to know everything right now."

He could hear her take a breath. "Well, so long as this Council is helping me pay my bills, then I guess that's true."

Ramsey smiled into the phone. "The Council has deep pockets. You can definitely take your time and have some fun while you're at it."

Sarah didn't respond, and he picked up on her emotions through the phone. He knew what she wanted to say; that the only fun she wanted to have was with him, but she had stopped herself from saying it, and he could empathize, because he knew how it felt.

"Yeah," she answered. "I suppose."

Ramsey wanted to reach out through the line and comfort her, and if she'd been there, he probably would have. He did not expect a conversation with her to be so difficult.

"You know I'm reading the mirror?" she asked.

"That's what I hear," he said, glad to change the subject but not sure if this topic was any better. "You ready for that?"

She sighed. "I don't know. I have to read it sometime."

"You read it when you're ready, not because you're being pressured. Don't let Morgana decide what's best for you."

She hesitated again. "You mind if I ask you for a favor?"

He felt himself wanting to give her everything. "No, of course not."

"Can I come over there for dinner tomorrow?"

Taken off guard, Ramsey stilled, not knowing what to say to her request.

Not hearing him answer, she kept talking. "I know you can't drive. I'll bring the food. You don't have to do a thing."

"Sarah…"

"Please, John? I just need to talk this through with someone. And the only one I want to talk about it with is you."

The plea in her voice broke everything down in him, and he couldn't say no. "Actually, I can drive now," he heard himself say. "You want me to come over there?"

She must have been surprised at his answer, because it took her a second to respond. "Oh, God, no. This place is a mess."

Ramsey couldn't help but laugh. "I don't care."

He could hear her laugh too, probably in relief that he had agreed to her request. "I suspect your kitchen's bigger than mine anyway," she said, "so is your place okay?"

The thought of her walking around in his home almost made him change his mind. "It's fine," he heard himself answer, knowing it would take every ounce of his self-control to have her here. "What time do you want to come over?" He thought ahead and realized that the next day was Friday and that made it feel like a date night, but he tuned out his thoughts, not wanting to think of it like that.

"How about six o'clock? That'll give me some time to start dinner."

"That's fine. You want me to provide the wine?" He regretted the words the moment he said them, knowing now that it did feel like a date.

She showed no reaction to his suggestion, though. "That would be great. Something red."

"Okay."

They both remained quiet on the phone before Sarah broke the silence. "Thank you," she said.

His heart aching, he closed his eyes. "You don't have to thank me, Sarah. It's not like we can't see each other."

Again, it felt like she wanted to say one thing but ended up saying another. "Good. I'll see you tomorrow."

"See you tomorrow."

He hung up the phone and fell backward onto the couch, already dreading the next day. He didn't know how he was going to get through a whole meal with her without pulling her into his arms and carrying her into the bedroom. Shutting his eyes tight, he refused to let his mind wander. Eyeing the time, he realized that it was late and that Sarah had been up too, probably debating whether to make the phone call she had just made. Rubbing his face with his hands, he stood, turned off the TV and the light. Making his way into the bedroom, he groaned, knowing it would be a long night.

**

Ramsey searched the aisles. They seemed to stretch for miles, like rows in a cornfield. All he needed was a bottle of wine. He looked around for someone to help him, but strangely, the store looked empty. Impatient, he continued to walk, passing several aisles of food. Finally spotting what appeared to be the alcohol section, he entered it, seeing the colored bottles and displays as he moved further in. He searched for the red wine, wanting something nice but not too expensive. Eyeing the labels, he hoped to see a brand he recognized. He decided on a merlot, mainly because the sea of merlots were in front of him, and looking down the never-ending aisle, he didn't feel the urge to explore the section for anything else. Checking the aisle, he found it strange that he was alone. He expected on a Friday that this section would be one of the busier ones.

Leaning over, he read some of the labels. Seeing a possibility, he pulled it from the shelf, debating his choice.

"Funny. I always took you to be a beer man."

The unexpected voice startled Ramsey, and he straightened, holding on to the bottle, glad that he hadn't dropped it. He turned and froze, seeing the man who stood behind him. Y.

His heart rate picked up its pace. "What are you doing here?" He didn't know what else to say.

Y smiled. "The same thing as you, I suppose. Looking for the right bottle for that one special lady."

213

Ramsey narrowed his eyes. "And you just happen to show up in the same place as me?"

"Total coincidence."

"I doubt that."

They each sized up the other. Ramsey checked to see that Y's hands were not in his pockets.

"How's the belly?" Y asked. "Everything back in its proper place?"

At the mention of his injury, Ramsey could feel the ache in his gut. His anger flared. "It's great. Too bad your aim was off."

Y's lips turned up. "Oh, if it was off, you wouldn't be standing here right now."

"That's right," answered Ramsey, willing his thudding heart to slow down. "You planned on offing me with poison." He looked down at himself. "Looks like you failed at that, too."

Y's grin fell, and his attention returned to the display of wine. "In due time," he said, reaching for a bottle and pulling it from the shelf. "This is a nice one."

Ramsey watched Y hold the wine while reading the label. He debated turning and leaving. Every instinct told him to, but he couldn't help himself. "What are you really doing here?"

Y glanced over. "Doing exactly what I said. Getting a bottle of wine for that special someone."

A cold shiver traveled up Ramsey's spine. "And who would that be?"

Y's eyes sparkled. "I believe you know her." He turned his head. "Sarah?"

Ice water ran through his veins when he saw a woman turn the corner and move down the aisle toward them. His brain wouldn't process what he saw. Well-dressed but casual, her hair in soft waves, Sarah approached them.

"Hey, honey," she said, linking her arm with Y's. "I lost you. This store is huge."

Y pulled her close. "I found a nice cabernet." He held the bottle out to her. "What do you think?"

She glanced at the bottle. "I would have no idea."

Y smiled. "Me either. But it's expensive and the rating is good."

Ramsey stood glued to his spot. He couldn't make his voice work, and every nerve ending in his body suddenly came alive. He managed to whisper one word. "Sarah."

She looked over, but without recognition. "Yes? Do I know you?"

Ramsey couldn't move, but his nerves began to itch and his heart skipped.

"Sarah, my dear," said Y. "This is John Ramsey."

"John Ramsey?" Her brow furrowed. "Have we met?"

Ramsey's body trembled and a scream began to build in his throat.

Y's grin returned. "Yes, honey. Once or twice. Don't you remember?"

She shook her head. "No, I can't say that I do."

"Well, no matter." Y cocked his head. "You want to go check out the cheese aisle?"

She laughed. "Wine and cheese, huh?" she asked. "You trying to woo me?"

"Is it working?" he asked.

"Are you buying strawberries, too?"

"Whatever your heart desires."

"Then I'd say you're on the right track."

They held each other's gaze, and Ramsey watched in mute horror as Y leaned in and kissed Sarah gently on the lips. His nerve endings throbbed, and he grimaced at what felt like needles stabbing at him throughout his body. "Sarah...please." It was all he could say.

She took her eyes off Y. "What's the matter?"

"He's not who you think he is."

She squeezed Y's arm. "He's everything."

The buzzing grew in Ramsey's body, and sweat popped out on his skin. "No, he's not. Listen to me..."

"I have to go now," she said.

Ramsey raised a shaky hand. "No. Don't go."

His hand on Sarah's back, Y led her from the aisle.

"Sarah, wait."

Pivoting, she looked back.

"Please, listen to me." Ramsey could feel his body heat rising as the needles jabbed harder at him.

Y spoke into her ear and she reached down into her purse, and pulled something from the inside. Looking up at Y, she showed him what it was, and he nodded. She began walking toward Ramsey.

His relief that she now approached was muted only by his hypersensitivity. He fought to stay motionless. Every nerve stretched thin, and any movement felt as if it plucked at a raw wound. Sweat dripped down his back.

As she neared, she stretched out her hand. "Sarah..." he said.

"This is for you." She held a small mirror, and it reflected his face in the glass. Horrified, he saw his discolored skin bubble up in angry black pockets. Realizing that he'd been infected and panicking, he reached up, trying to rub off whatever had invaded him. His feet were frozen to the ground. His insides twisted, and he felt the pain of the toxin inside him. He tried to scream, but it stuck in his throat.

Sarah, seeing his fear, began to laugh. She turned and walked back to Y, who was waiting for her.

The pain assailed him as the toxin worked its way through his body, but the torment of watching her go felt worse. Another sharp spasm pierced him, and he gasped and dropped the wine he was holding. It hit the ground and shattered, sending streams of red liquid and glass spraying in every direction.

Ramsey jumped in his bed; his throat frozen in a silent shriek. Breathing hard, he opened his eyes. The hot sheets stuck against his damp skin and he pushed up, blinking, the rapid thump of his heart beating against his chest. Shoving aside the sheets, he sat up and put his feet on the floor. He rested his head in his hands while the nightmare faded, but his fear did not.

After several minutes, his breathing slowed, and he stood and moved into the bathroom to splash cold water on his face. His hands shook from the effects of his adrenaline rush.

Willing himself to calm down, he walked into his living room and flipped on the TV. He kept the sound low and found a station where Katherine Hepburn, in black and white, was arguing with Cary Grant. After heading into his kitchen, he poured himself a fingerful of vodka, and he sipped on it as he settled himself on the couch. Fingers still trembling, he watched Katherine and thought of Sarah, wishing she was there.

**

The next afternoon, Leroy pulled into the driveway outside his home, surprised to see Sherlock's car out front. Hannah had told him that the doctor had cleared Ramsey to drive, but Leroy had not talked to his friend in a couple of days and they hadn't made plans to see each other. He'd thought to call him this evening, but apparently that would not be necessary. Leroy hoped this was a good sign and that maybe Sherlock was finally ready to open up. He headed to his front door and opened it with his key. Walking inside, he saw no one until his wife poked her head out from the kitchen. Her dark hair was pulled back and she wore his apron with the saying, "Kiss the Cook," emblazoned on it. A dusting of flour smudged her cheek and she smiled at him.

He entered the kitchen. "Hey, babe," he said. "Where's our guest?"

"Hey, honey. He's in your office."

The smell of something delicious wafted through the room, and he knew dinner would not be disappointing. "He okay?"

She stirred something on the stove. "Seems to be. He's quiet, though."

Standing behind her, he kissed her neck. "It's a recurring theme with him lately." He put his arms around her. "You smell good."

Laughing, she leaned back into him. "That's dinner." She looked back at him. "You should invite him to stay. He could use a good meal. Put some of that weight back on him."

"Hmm. I'll ask him." He nuzzled her neck. "And it's not just dinner that smells good." He gave her butt an appreciative squeeze and she giggled. "I'll go talk to him."

"Take your time. Dinner's not for a couple of hours."

He left the kitchen, walked past the living room, and into his large office. Ramsey stood at the far end of the room, looking out the wide picture window, encircled by Leroy's wide array of potted plants. Leroy closed the door behind him. "Sherlock?"

Ramsey turned. "Hey, Leroy. Sorry to bother you at home. I called your office, but they'd said you already left."

"Don't be ridiculous. You're welcome here anytime. You know that." Leroy noticed his friend look around as if distracted. "You all right?"

Ramsey didn't answer at first, but put his hands in his pockets.

"Sherlock," said Leroy, beginning to worry. "What is it?"

"I wanted to talk to you about something. And not by phone."

Leroy knitted his brows together. "Okay." He motioned to the couch across from his desk. "You want to sit?"

"I'd rather stand."

Leroy could see his friend's tension, and he waited to hear what Ramsey had to say.

Ramsey faced the window again. "I've been doing some thinking, and I've made a decision."

"What decision is that?"

There was a brief pause. "I'm leaving the program."

Leroy wasn't sure he understood. "You're what?"

"I'm quitting. I'm not going to be a Protector anymore."

Leroy stared at his friend's back, unsure where Sherlock was going with this. "You mind if I ask why?"

"Because I'm done. I can't do it anymore."

"Why not?"

Ramsey turned. "Because..." He took his hands from his pockets and crossed his arms.

Leroy waited. "Because why?"

Whatever Ramsey had started to say, he stopped, as if he'd changed his mind. "Because it's just time for me to move on."

"Move on to where?" asked Leroy, his voice on edge. "What are you going to do with all your newfound free time?"

Ramsey studied the floor, his body rigid. "I'm moving away, Leroy. I'm going to sell the house."

Leroy couldn't believe what he was hearing. "You're what?"

Ramsey set his jaw. "I'm leaving."

Leroy could only stare, unsure of what to say until that gnawing feeling that he'd been pushing back for some time when it came to Sherlock reared up and he decided that enough was enough. "What the hell is the matter with you?" he asked, not holding back his anger.

Ramsey's own anger surfaced at Leroy's confrontation. "Nothing's the matter with me. I've made a decision. That's all. It's nothing more than that."

"The hell it is," said Leroy, ready to yank the truth out of his friend with his bare hands if it came to that. "Why don't you tell me the real reason for all this moving away crap?"

"The real reason?" Ramsey asked, raising his voice. "What do you mean? Why do I need another reason? I'm done. I've had enough. That's reason enough."

Knowing he had to get through to his friend, Leroy did not back down. "If I believed you, Sherlock, I'd be the first to congratulate you on a job well done and recommend a real estate agent. But you're lying to me, and more importantly, you're lying to yourself."

Ramsey shot out his hands. "Don't tell me, Leroy, what I am and am not doing. If I wanted your opinion, I'd ask for it."

"I don't give a damn whether you asked for it or not. You're going to hear it anyway."

Ramsey moved for the door, but Leroy blocked his exit. "Get out of my way." Ramsey shouted.

Leroy stayed put. "Tell me the real reason," he said, ignoring his friend's outburst. "Why?"

Frustrated, Ramsey walked away and faced the window. "Damn it, Leroy." he yelled. "Leave me alone."

Leroy shouted. "I will not leave you alone." He knew it was now or never. If Sherlock walked out that door, he didn't know if he would ever have the chance to reach him again. He watched his friend's back and saw him breathe deeply, as if some heavy weight held him down. Walking up to his desk, Leroy decided to make an impact, and he slammed his hand down on its surface. "Tell me, damn it, what the hell is the problem?"

Something snapped in Ramsey at Leroy's words. He turned furiously, swiping at a stack of books on Leroy's desk and shoving them all onto the floor, taking his desk lamp and a stack of folders with it. "Because I'm useless. That's why."

Ramsey kicked at a book and sent it flying into the wall. The dam having broken, Ramsey kept going. "I'm totally helpless. I can't think straight. My head's a mess. All I can do is just try to stay in my own space and try not to think about some...some..." He flailed his arms. "...black poison to come and mess with my body and my mind." He paced as if trying to burn off the energy erupting from him.

Leroy didn't say a word, letting him vent.

"Do you know what I've done in my house?" Ramsey held his chest. "I've covered every mirror. Every single one." Still moving, he seemed unable to stop. "The thought of that happening to me again..." He shuddered. "The first week I had to drink myself to sleep every night. I have nightmares. I wake up in a cold sweat, thinking I'm infected, and I'm panicked. I don't want to leave the house, but I force myself to because I know I'm being irrational." Breathing heavily, he allowed his emotional turmoil to surface. "I think I'm going crazy." He made another kick at a book as he rubbed his hands over his face and through his hair. Then he clasped them behind his neck and sighed deeply. "And that's not even the worst of it."

Still pacing, he dropped his hands to his hips and shut his eyes.

"What's the worst of it?" asked Leroy.

Ramsey swallowed, and his whole body trembled. "It's Sarah," he said. He opened his eyes and stared off. "She risked her life for me." He took a breath. "And…" He paused for a second, as if hating to say the words.

"And what?" prompted Leroy.

Ramsey stood still. "…he used me to get to her." Ramsey dropped his head as if he couldn't bear the guilt. The energy seemed to run out of him. "And I can't live with myself knowing that I'm her weak point. That he can get to her through me."

Completely spent and out of words, he walked to the couch and sat, putting his head in his hands. "That's why I have to leave."

Leroy didn't say a word. He watched Sherlock sit in misery on the couch and finally understood what had his friend tied up in knots since his hospital stay. Stepping over the books on the floor, Leroy went to sit next to him, offering comfort, but without words.

They sat for a few minutes until Ramsey's breathing slowed and resumed its normal rhythm. Eventually, he straightened, and leaned back into the couch. "What?" he asked. "No pearls of wisdom?"

Leroy saw the vacant stare. "Oh, I've got 'em," he said. "I just want to be sure you're ready to hear them."

Ramsey let out a ragged breath. "I could really use little advice right now."

"Okay," said Leroy, relieved that his friend was ready for help. "First of all, you're not going crazy. I don't know why I didn't suspect this, but what I think you are dealing with here is a not-so-surprising case of post-traumatic stress."

Ramsey smiled, but it didn't reach his eyes. "PTSD?" he asked. "Come on, Leroy. I didn't go to war."

"This is not limited to veterans, Sherlock. It's common among victims of any traumatic event." He paused. "It makes total sense."

Ramsey studied his hands. "You think that's what I have?"

"You were stabbed and poisoned. I'd call that stressful." Leroy used his fingers to count Ramsey's symptoms. "Trouble sleeping? Heavy drinking? Nightmares? It's textbook. You've obviously experienced some agoraphobia."

"I'm not scared of spiders, Leroy."

Leroy smiled. "Actually, you are, but that's arachnophobia. I'm talking about you not wanting to leave the house."

"Well, close enough." Sitting back, Ramsey leaned his head on the couch pillows. "I suppose I'm not a fan of spiders either."

"Suppose?" asked Leroy. "I've killed more than one bug in your defense." He watched Ramsey roll his eyes. "But aside from your fear of spiders, you've been through a lot and you've had trouble processing it. But it's not a reason to throw in the towel. You can get through it. It's only been a few weeks."

Staring at the ceiling, Ramsey considered Leroy's diagnosis. "If that's what it is, then I'll find a way to deal with it."

Leroy pointed. "And don't do that either."

"What?" asked Ramsey.

"Stop telling yourself you can solve all the problems in the world. You need to reach out and ask for help once in a while."

Ramsey moaned. "That's not my strong suit."

"Tell me about it," said Leroy. "I was about damn near ready to tackle you to the ground if you didn't talk to me today."

Ramsey lifted his head off the back of the couch. "I hear you," he said. "I'll see what I can do about asking for help."

"You can talk to somebody if you want. I'm sure Hannah can recommend someone."

"No, thanks," he said. He waved a hand.

"Sherlock..."

Ramsey ran a hand through his hair. "If I need to talk, I'll let you know, okay?"

Leroy knew he'd gone as far as he could on the subject for now, so he didn't push it. "Okay," he said. "But you let it go too long like you did with this, I'll drag you to someone myself."

Ramsey nodded. "I hear you."

The tension in the room, although diminished, still felt unresolved. "What else?" asked Leroy.

Still looking conflicted, Ramsey leaned forward again and rested his head in his hands. "That still doesn't solve my problem with Sarah. I can't risk her safety because Y can get to me whenever he wants."

Leroy chose to tread easily on this subject, knowing that this is what had taken a true toll on his friend. "Listen to me."

Ramsey dropped his hands, but studied the floor.

"There's no way to know what Y has up his sleeve. Yes, he did get the upper hand and put you in the hospital. Yes, he almost killed you. But the fact is that he didn't succeed. He failed."

"He failed because Sarah went out to meet him," said Ramsey. "She put her life on the line for me."

"You would do the same for her. You did do the same for her."

"It's not the same, Leroy."

"Why isn't it?"

"Because it's my job to protect her."

"Not anymore, it isn't."

Ramsey sat up, surprised. "What do you mean? You know why I backed off."

"That's not what I'm referring to."

"What, then?"

"You want a relationship with her?"

Ramsey hesitated, and went quiet.

"Sherlock?"

Ramsey closed his eyes. "You know I do."

"Then you've got to drop the protector act."

Ramsey opened his eyes again. "Why?"

Leroy leaned forward, elbows on his knees, thinking back. "You remember, right after I started dating Olivia, we went through a rough patch, and she broke up with me?"

Ramsey's face fell. "You're not going to tell me to suck it up, are you?"

Leroy smiled. "No. I'm not."

"Good," Ramsey answered. "Okay. I'll bite. I remember."

"You want to know why she threatened to leave me?"

"Why?"

"It was because I kept trying to fix everything, to fix her, too."

Ramsey sighed and shook his head.

"She was my assignment when I met her. It was my job to look after her. Problem was, after I started dating her, I couldn't drop the role. It worked fine when I was on the job. Not so fine in a relationship."

Ramsey played with the band around his wrist. Leroy recognized it as the gift Sarah had given him in the hospital. "What am I supposed to do, act like I don't care about what happens to her?"

"I wouldn't go that far. You just need to drop the tough-guy persona. Let her see the real you."

Ramsey huffed. "That might be difficult."

"But it's necessary," said Leroy. "It's not as difficult as you might think."

Ramsey paused. "That doesn't solve the Y problem."

"You're still the one Sarah wants. He didn't succeed. All he did was push Sarah away from him and closer to you."

"Doesn't mean he won't try again." He frowned.

"What?" asked Leroy, feeling another wave of angst from his friend.

"I hate to say this..."

"You're on a roll. Don't stop now."

"I've been having these thoughts."

"What thoughts?"

Ramsey clenched his hands together and his face tightened.

"Just say it," said Leroy.

Ramsey swallowed. "I...," he groaned, and whispered. "I've wondered if maybe she would be better off with him instead of me."

"Why do you say that?"

Ramsey looked down as if embarrassed. "He's a Red. She's a Red. He can show her things I can't. If, God forbid, we're all dead in two years, I don't want her to be alone." He stopped, but Leroy sensed he wasn't finished. "I can't give her what she needs," he continued. "Maybe he can." He set his jaw, and closed his eyes.

Leroy took his time in answering, wanting to be sure he conveyed the message Sherlock needed to hear. "Understand something," he said. "I've watched you two together, and I know without a shadow of a doubt that she would rather spend the next two years with you than a lifetime with him." He waited to be sure Sherlock had heard him. "Yes, he is a Red, but he's a dangerous Red. He has no interest in her other than to control her."

Ramsey didn't respond.

"And what I find ironic is the very thing you're trying to do to protect her is the very thing he would want you to do."

Ramsey looked up, his eyes wide.

"By pushing her away, you push her closer to him. It's exactly what he would want, for you to leave her alone. Why do you think he came after you in the first place?"

Ramsey sat still, and Leroy allowed him time to think it through. Ramsey rubbed his temples. "I'll be damned," he said. "It seems either way I risk hurting her."

"Well, then," said Leroy, "if that's the case, then the answer seems pretty simple. You might as well be with her. And let the chips fall where they may."

The weight seemed to lift from Ramsey's shoulders as some of the pieces began to fall into place. He visibly relaxed.

"Feeling better?" Leroy asked.

Ramsey sat back, and nodded. "I do."

"Still plan on leaving?"

Ramsey smiled, but Leroy could tell it wasn't the usual big smile he knew his friend possessed.

"What?" Leroy asked.

"Sarah. She's coming over for dinner tonight." He shook his head. "That's the reason I came over and made that stupid decision to leave—because I was terrified."

"I thought you were avoiding her."

"I tried. But she asked."

Leroy nodded. "What are you going to tell her?"

"I don't know, Leroy." He sighed. "I don't know."

"What time is she coming over?"

Ramsey eyed the clock on the wall. "Shoot. I have to go, or I'll be late." He stood.

Leroy stood, as well. "You all right?" he asked. He knew Ramsey was better just by the feeling in the room.

"Yes," he said, and eyed the room. "Sorry about your books."

"The books will live. I just want to be sure you do, too."

Ramsey patted him on the arm. "I'll be okay." He paused. "Thank you."

Leroy smiled, too, glad that he was finally getting his friend back. "You don't have to thank me."

"Yes, I do. You've been putting up with my mood these last few weeks. Nobody should have to endure that."

"It has been brutal," Leroy agreed. "I may have PTSD myself."

Ramsey gave a brief chuckle. "Well, if you ever need someone to talk to—"

"—I know where to go," interrupted Leroy.

The two hugged warmly, and Ramsey's energy felt the lightest it had since his hospital stay. As Leroy walked Ramsey to the front door, Leroy asked him to wait and disappeared back into the back bedroom. Finding what he wanted, Leroy quickly returned, holding a small potted plant. Olivia popped her head out from the kitchen and asked Ramsey to stay for dinner, but he politely declined due to his other plans and Olivia wished him well and returned to the kitchen.

"This is for you," Leroy said, handing the plant to Ramsey.

Ramsey stared at the plant as if it had just arrived from Eudora. "What is that?"

"It's a plant, you idiot. They grow in the ground. They're typically green. Surely you've seen one before."

"What's it for?"

"It's your birthday present," said Leroy. "Remember what I told you?"

Ramsey stared at Leroy as if he'd lost his mind. "Remember what?"

Leroy rolled his eyes. "I said if you wanted your birthday gift, you'd have to live to get it."

Ramsey's face dropped. "And that's what you got me?" he asked. "This is what I fought to survive for? You know I've never been accused of having a green thumb."

Leroy touched a leaf. "It's an African Violet. Just set it on a windowsill without direct light and keep it lightly watered. Give it some fertilizer now and then. It's simple enough."

Ramsey took the plant from Leroy. "What do you have against the plant?"

Leroy groaned. "Would you just try to humor me here? It wouldn't hurt you to have something green in your house."

"You could have bought me a green blanket or a green picture? Heck, what about green tea?"

Leroy shot out a hand. "Would you take your plant and get the hell out of here?"

Ramsey smiled, and Leroy finally saw the grin his friend had lost. Glad to have it back, he opened the door and Ramsey stepped out.

"Let me know how it goes tonight with Sarah," he said as Ramsey walked away.

Ramsey looked back, carrying his plant. "I will." He opened his car door. "Thanks for the gift, and the talk."

"You're welcome. Take good care of it, and yourself."

"I'll do my best," he said, and he got in his car and drove away.

EIGHTEEN

....

R UNNING LATE, RAMSEY drove fast to the house. Despite his nightmare the previous night, he'd stopped for a bottle of wine and then got stuck in traffic. He texted Sarah, telling her he would be there by six-fifteen at the latest and to wait for him. She'd texted back and told him not to worry about it. Finally pulling into the driveway, he saw her car, but did not see her, although a second vehicle with one occupant inside it sat parked across the street.

When he got out of his car, he recognized Mary, one of Declan's security people, as the person in the car. She was outside his house, apparently assigned to keep an eye on Sarah. He remembered Mary from the hospital when she'd kept watch outside his room a few times, and he waved at her as he walked up to his door. He wondered where Sarah was, since his front door had been locked. Despite the fact that Mary was watching from the street, his imagination wanted to kick in and think the worst. He tried to relax, but some habits died hard, and his heart pounded when he walked in and still didn't see her.

"Sarah?" he asked, closing the door behind him. He put the bottle of wine and the potted plant on the kitchen counter, took off his jacket and threw it over a dining chair.

Hearing movement, he turned to see her walk into the room from the bathroom. "I'm here," she said.

Seeing she was okay, his heart continued to thud, but for an entirely different reason. She wore a long chocolate-brown belted coat, and red high-heeled boots peeked out from beneath the low hem. As she neared, he could sense an energy radiate from her that he had not felt before.

"Hi," she said, stopping a few feet from him.

Her presence almost prevented him from speaking and he allowed himself a moment to adjust. They'd always shared an instant connection, and that had not changed. In fact, it seemed magnified as they stood facing each other.

Forcing himself to open his vocal cords, he spoke. "How did you get in?"

She made a guilty face. "I hope you don't mind. I find that I'm skilled with locks."

"You mean you opened it on your own?"

Still looking guilty, she nodded. "Yes."

"Well," he said, "I'll sleep even better knowing that."

"You don't mind?"

Unable to take his eyes off her, he couldn't help but think how beautiful she was. "As long as it's you." He wondered about her coat. "I thought we were eating in. You want to go out instead?"

Her eyes flashed, and something stirred in the air. She moved closer, reached for her belt, and pulled on it. The coat opened, and she slid it over her shoulders, letting it drop to the floor and revealing what she wore beneath— a fully-fledged Wonder Woman outfit.

Ramsey stood slack-jawed. The red corset with gold sparkles covered her waist and breasts snugly, and the blue-starred bottom sat high on her hips but covered her from the tops of her thighs to the bottom of the corset, leaving her long legs uncovered except for her knee-high boots. She even wore gold bracelets. The only thing she didn't have was the headband and lasso.

"If memory serves," she said, putting her hands on her hips, "you had some interest in wanting to see me in this?"

His vocal cords locked up, which didn't matter because he had absolutely no idea what to say. She stepped forward and he managed to string some words together. "What about dinner?"

Sarah's nearness pierced his personal space. Not prepared for her assertive approach, and still unsure as to what he wanted to do about her, he backed up. She kept coming, though, and he moved backward until he found himself bumping up against the wall of the hallway.

She raised her arm and placed her hand on the wall near his head, leaning her weight on it. Her boots brought her face level with him, and she looked directly at him, her eyes never wavering, her face only inches from his own.

He was completely taken aback and couldn't utter a word.

Her eyes boring into his, she said softly, "I thought we might eat a little later."

His mind went blank, and he didn't know what to make of this unexpected turn of events. Was she seducing him? He couldn't help but wonder about this startling change in her.

"Are you okay, Sarah?" he asked. His breathing began to pick up as her proximity and her outfit started to affect him. He could smell her perfume, her hair was soft and shiny, and a whiff of shampoo reached his nose. Taking in a deep breath, he calmed himself, maintaining his control.

She gave him a knowing smile. "I am most certainly okay." She brought a hand up and played with a button on his shirt. "I just know what I want, and I'm tired of waiting for it." She licked her bottom lip, and Ramsey almost moaned. "And we have the whole weekend, which I hope we put to good use."

Frazzled by her response, all he could do was stare. He had not expected this when she had made dinner plans with him. What had happened to the shy, quiet lady he had met two months ago? Who was this strong, assertive, sexually-charged woman now standing so close to him?

"Sarah—" he started to say, still pulling back, unsure if this was where he should go with her.

"Don't," she said. "Don't start with the 'I'm not sure if this is the right thing' story."

He tried again. "But—"

"Just listen," she said, still leaning on her arm but now focused on explaining instead of seducing. "I know what you've been through. It's been hell. Because of me, you were stabbed, poisoned and almost died—"

"That's not true—"

"Let me finish," she said.

He stopped.

"I know you've suffered because of me. You've sacrificed a lot to protect me, to keep me safe, and I appreciate that. I love that about you. I also know you blame yourself for most of it, if not all of it. I know you want to slay all the monsters and keep me from harm, so much so that you're willing to leave me to do it."

She paused to collect herself, and he was surprised by how well she understood him. Finding himself staring at her lips, he wondered what they tasted like.

"But you have to understand something," she said, and he made himself refocus. "That can't happen. You and I are in this for the long haul. I'm not going anywhere, and neither are you. You're not getting rid of me that easily."

He closed his eyes, struggling to figure out how to handle this, but then opened them again. "So," she said, leaning in a little closer, "I know you will always want to protect me and be my hero, and that's fine, but there's something you need to know."

Ramsey could barely breathe now she was so close. "What?" he whispered.

Her eyes never wavered from his. "I know your mom always called you Superman. But it's not Superman I want." She bent her arm and moved up against him, and he sucked in a breath. "I just want the man."

Hearing her words, the last floating pieces that remained in Ramsey's mind moved and clicked into place, and he realized how lucky he was to have this woman standing in front of him, after all they'd been through, wanting him as much as he wanted her. His body seemed to take on a life of its own, and he straightened.

**

Sarah witnessed the transformation—something in his eyes shifted, and his demeanor changed. Holding her breath, she waited, hoping she'd reached him, when he suddenly stood taller and, pushing back against the wall, moved his body weight toward hers. Now it was her turn to move backward. She let him walk forward, bumping her up against the opposite side of the hallway as his hands came up to rest on the wall on either side of her head. Sarah let him take the lead, because she knew he needed to feel right about this. She wanted the old Ramsey back, and she had to know that this was the man who was leaning in toward her now, his face mere inches from hers.

Her heart hammering, her breathing quickened when he moved his mouth near hers but stopped mere millimeters from touching her. His body pressed into her, and she couldn't help it when a moan of satisfaction escaped her throat.

Hearing it, Ramsey's eyes turned dark, and he brought a hand to her shoulder and traced a finger down her bare skin. He took his time, and Sarah understood he was taking it slow, and she forced herself not to move, although she wanted him to rip her costume off and take her to the bedroom. She bit her lip as he trailed his finger down her arm and back up, where he delicately ran it up her neck and chin. His lips were so close to hers that she could feel his breath on them. "You're sure about this?" he asked.

She heard the question but could barely process it. Feeling every inch of him against her and finally feeling his familiar energy course through him and into her, she knew that whatever doubts he'd held these past weeks were gone and he was back. Making herself speak, she whispered, "I'm wearing a Wonder Woman outfit. I'd say that's a yes."

**

His heart almost bursting out of his chest, Ramsey pressed his body harder into hers and heard her draw in a breath. Keeping a hand on the wall, he wanted to swoop her up and carry her into the bedroom, but he chose to stay right where he was, with his lips just barely touching hers, and his finger caressing her jaw.

Moving her face closer, she tried to kiss him, but he pulled away, not letting the kiss happen, letting the energy grow. It felt like a huge tidal wave was building, and when it crashed, he knew it would be unforgettable. Lingering near her lips, her hot breath mingled with his own and she whimpered, wanting the contact. Drawing out the moment, he slid his mouth down alongside her cheek and jaw, grazing them until his lips found the sensitive skin beneath her ear. He kissed her there, taking in her taste and scent, and his whole body tingled. Her body stiffened and he heard her gasp.

Something in the house shattered, and they both turned at the noise. "Oops," she said, breathing hard. "Guess I'm still working on some control issues."

Breathing hard himself, he understood. "Don't worry about it," he said, and he returned his mouth back to her neck. She reached for his waist, found his hips, and pulled him close as she arched into him. The movement made his desire for her rocket into the stratosphere. Forcing himself to take it slow, he moaned, still nibbling her neck, and felt her grip his back. He trailed his lips further down her throat, and tasted and teased her with his mouth and tongue.

Sarah clung to him, running her hands up his back while he trailed his tongue down her sensitive skin. Sucking in a breath, her fingers pulled on his shirt and her breath tickled his skin below his ear. Moving against him, she moaned again.

Reaching the hollow of her collarbone, he leisurely explored the contours there. He brought one hand to the other side of her head, cupped the back of her neck and pulled her closer while he continued to nibble her with deliberate slowness. She gasped and wiggled against him, and enjoying her torment, he slid his lips down further, his tongue tracing the line just above the top of her corset. Her head fell back to give him access, and her hand moved into his hair, directing him to go lower.

He changed direction though, and directed his lips upward, and dotted more kisses up her throat and chin until he found himself back at her lips. Breathing fast, he anticipated the kiss, knowing she was waiting desperately. Savoring the moment, he brushed his lips against hers.

The surge of ardor that hit him prevented him from being gentle, and with the passion between them escalating fast, he pressed her against the wall and kissed her hard. His mouth slanted over hers, and she shifted with him, returning the kiss with equal fervor. Something nearby broke again, but they ignored it as their tongues met and the kiss deepened. His other arm slid down, and he wrapped it around her waist. She moved her hand to grasp the back of his neck, her other arm locked behind his shoulders, and they both fought to pull each other even closer, the wall acting as their only support.

They prolonged the kiss, both of them eager for more and enjoying the feel of finally coming together. The energy between them burned like a torch, which only burned brighter as they held each other. He lifted his mouth briefly from hers, and her hot breath brushed his skin, but unable to hold back, he found her lips again. Their hands grasped at each other over their clothes, wanting to feel everything, seduced by the power of the energy between them.

Ramsey couldn't get enough of her. The feel of her lips and tongue against his scorched him, and the smell and taste of her drove him wild. He'd never felt anything like it before. All rational thought disappeared. He moved his body against her while his lips slanted across hers again and again. Her fingers pulled at him, and he dropped his hands, moving them down her back to the curve at her waist and then her buttocks, pulling her tightly against him. He groaned into her mouth and she stilled when his hands continued to travel around to her front, just below her breasts, and lingered there, teasing her. Even though he still ravaged her mouth, he knew she felt every sensation as he let his fingertips graze over her costume.

Pulling back, she eyed him hazily while he ran his hands up to the back of her corset and found the zipper there. Beginning to unzip it, he lowered his head to capture her lips in another kiss.

"Wait," she said, gasping.

Ramsey stopped, but could feel the hammering of her heart against his own. "What?" he asked, itching to kiss her again.

She tried to catch her breath. "Take the boots off first," she said. "My feet are killing me."

He smiled seductively, and chuckled. He lowered his lips back to her neck. "My pleasure," he said into her ear.

He trailed more kisses down to her shoulder, sliding his fingers along her arm. Bending at the knee, he grazed his lips over her sternum, and dropped lower. Lifting his head, he slid his hands down the curves of her breasts and waist. Once there, he took his time while he trailed them over the lower part of her costume. He touched her hips and buttocks, and sliding his fingers lower, he caressed her upper legs as he went to his knees. Grazing her thighs with his lips, he roamed his hands downward and kissed his way down to the tops of her boots. Her legs trembled at his touch.

**

Letting her head fall back against the wall, Sarah wound her hands into his hair, and she felt his fingers, with agonizing slowness, glide down her legs until they reached her boots. He slid the zippers down on each, and removed each shoe from her foot. She wore thin socks, and he removed each one, gently caressing her foot as he did so, his thumb working in circles along the arch. Hot fire shot up through her legs and into her belly when his fingers moved from her feet and back up her legs. Laying another trail of hot kisses from her knees and back up her thighs, he stood, once again avoiding her most intimate areas, and his hands followed to stroke wherever his lips had been. His arm encircled her waist, and he brought his face back to her throat. He dragged his mouth along her skin, his tongue tasting her. Taking his time, he found his way back to her lips and captured them again in another searing kiss.

She came undone then and completely gave herself over to him. Her mouth moving over his, she grasped at his shirt and pulled it up. Wanting to feel his skin against hers, she raked her hands underneath the fabric and touched his belly.

**

Feeling her hot fingers move over his stomach and up to his chest, Ramsey groaned. No longer able to contain himself, he found the zipper at her back, lowered it, and explored her body beneath her costume. His hands roamed over her, making her gasp, every touch between them turning the fire into an inferno.

Another object shattered in the house, but neither paid attention and he bent and reached down with one arm to slip it under her knees and pick her up. Her lips found his neck, and she began to claim it as he carried her to his bedroom. Glass crunched beneath his shoes.

She lifted her lips and whispered heavily into his ear. "Sorry. I hope I didn't break anything important."

Trying to catch his breath despite his rapidly beating heart, he didn't hesitate. "Honey," he said, feeling her nibble his lobe, "it is my sole plan that by the end of this weekend, this house will have to be condemned."

Sarah giggled into his ear.

Knowing he was the luckiest man on earth, Ramsey carried her into his bedroom and, using his foot, slammed the door shut behind them.

**

Y closed the door to his basement lab, where he'd spent most of the last three weeks working hard to find the exact specifications needed to create the serum he would require to get what he wanted. It had taken longer than he had expected, but now he knew he was close. He'd been blessed with a scientific mind, as were most Eudorans, but his was special. Edward, his pseudo-father, had cultivated his abilities as he grew up by teaching Y everything he knew. Eddie had a brilliant mind of his own, and when he realized Y showed a unique ability in the area, he had delighted in showing the child the wonders of science.

Now, with a full laboratory in the basement of his large oceanside home, he'd used his gifts to his advantage over the years and had spent many hours developing several varieties of interesting toxins, some of which he'd used and some he hadn't. He'd found that due to his abilities as a Red-Line, he could direct the use of these toxins in particular ways. This had proven useful on more than one occasion. His intelligent mind, along with his maniacal way of removing any obstacles in his path, had resulted in the lucrative and immediate success of his private research corporation, called XYZ labs. It was one of the largest in the U.S. and his company's research had led the way in discovering a number of medical breakthroughs in various areas, everything from improved face cream to curing cancer.

Rubbing his eyes, he left the lab and walked up the stairs to the main floor of the house. The breeze from the open windows fluttered through the room, and he smelled the ocean. Living in hiding most of his life, he hated feeling closed in, and so he lived in a vast space where he could enjoy the beauty around him.

Walking into the kitchen, he saw that Julian had left him a plate of food. He put it into the microwave to warm it, and poured himself a glass of wine and sat at the kitchen table. As he had come to do lately, he pictured Sarah sitting across from him, recalling her visit from only a few weeks before. He let his mind travel back, and envisioned her there, holding her glass of wine, looking at him. The microwave dinged, but he ignored it. Seeing only her, he imagined what it would be like when she sat there every night, eating dinner with him, laughing, and enjoying his company.

Admittedly, he'd not handled her interference well. He had not anticipated that she would discover his mode of poisoning Ramsey, and he'd battled his rage for days after he'd learned that Ramsey still lived. But looking back now, he realized that he had been mistaken. As usual, things had worked out for him, because he now relished the knowledge that he could make Ramsey suffer even more. He'd break him down bit by bit until he lost the one thing that he loved the most—Sarah.

Smiling to himself as he stood, he took his food from the microwave and sat to eat.

**

Sarah turned in the bed, snuggling into Ramsey. Resting her head on his chest, she heard his heartbeat. She draped her arm over his midsection and felt his fingers trail over her lower back. She sighed, thoroughly satisfied with the moment and their amorous activity throughout the night. They'd slept little, waking each other after only brief periods of sleep, ready to resume their lovemaking as if they'd never touched each other before. She felt consumed by him, unable to get enough of his touch. Even now, she could feel desire stir again in the pit of her stomach.

**

Ramsey felt the same. He'd never encountered anything like what he felt with her. It was as if they'd always been together. They knew how to move, where to touch, what to kiss, when to go slow and when to go fast, allowing one to bring the other the maximum amount of pleasure. They were like a meteor in reverse, only burning brighter as time passed. Sleep was only an annoying impediment, allowing them just brief moments of respite until they were ready again. Amazed at how he could want her over and over, he marveled at his stamina. Grazing his chin over her head, Ramsey smelled her hair and he craved her again. But he held back, enjoying the feel of her in his arms.

They'd never eaten dinner, but had made the effort to muster breakfast a few hours earlier, when their bodies growled for food instead of each other, but they'd only ended up making out in the kitchen over soggy cereal and cold coffee. Never finishing, they'd wound up back in the bedroom.

Still hungry, but not just for food, he looked down at their clothes on the floor and saw the red corset and blue-starred bottoms discarded there.

"Did you rent that or buy it?" he asked, feeling her leg move against his.

"Hmm?" she asked.

"The costume."

"Oh," she said. "I bought it."

"Good thing," he said, thinking back to when he'd taken it off her. "I don't think it's returnable."

She giggled, and his desire grew. "Well, I thought we might use it more than once." Moving her hand over his belly, she lightly touched the pink scar there, and he sucked in a breath. "Does it still hurt?" she asked.

Feeling her fingers on his skin, he made himself relax. It wasn't the first time she'd touched it. "No," he said. "Not really. It aches sometimes, but it's not bad."

She eyed the gray mark just above his hip and caressed it. He recalled her licking it hours before and he groaned. He was about to pull her into his arms when he heard a faint buzzing.

"That's your phone again," she said, still moving her fingers over his belly.

He sighed, not wanting to answer. "It's probably Leroy, checking in on me."

She kissed his chest. "You better talk to him, or he'll just keep calling."

After their conversation yesterday, Ramsey knew Leroy wanted to make sure he had not gone off the deep end again. His friend probably wanted to know how things had gone with Sarah, too. Smiling at that, he rolled over and reached for his pants leg on the floor. "You're probably right." He grabbed the pants, pulled them over, and took the phone out of the pocket. "If we plan to resume without interruption, I better speak to him." He hit the answer key and lay back in the bed. "Hello?" he said as Sarah started to pepper kisses down his chest. Holding his breath, he tried not to moan.

"Sherlock?" answered Leroy. "You okay? I've been trying to reach you."

"I'm fine, Leroy." He bit his lip as Sarah found his gray mark on his body with her tongue.

"How'd everything go with Sarah?"

Ramsey took a shaky breath. "It's still going."

There was a pause before Leroy's chuckle traveled over the line. "Well, it's about time."

Ramsey couldn't continue the conversation since Sarah's lips were doing unbelievable things to him. "I've got to go," he said, hitting the hang-up button before Leroy could respond. Throwing the phone down on the ground, he gave himself over to her as the fire in his belly grew to a fever pitch and his mind went blank.

** **

A little while later, after a few more hours of enjoying each other, Ramsey jumped back into the bed carrying a jar of peanut butter and crackers.

Sarah laughed. "That's what you got up to get?"

"You're hungry, aren't you?"

"What, no breakfast in bed?"

"It's after noon. Time for breakfast is over. Besides, I wouldn't last that long. The eggs would only go untouched." He unwrapped the crackers while she sat up next to him.

"You do know you're not supposed to eat crackers in bed, don't you?"

He crooked an eyebrow at her. "Considering everything we've done, I think crackers is the least of our offenses." Leaning in, he kissed her.

"You make a good point," she said. "Give me one."

Not having brought a knife with him, he tried to dip the cracker into the peanut butter, but it broke. Instead of getting up to get a knife, he dipped a finger into the peanut butter and smeared it on the cracker.

"What are you doing?" she asked.

"I don't have a knife."

"That's your cracker, then. I'll get my own."

He widened his eyes. "After last night, you're worried about my finger in the peanut butter?"

A mischievous grin on her face, she dipped her own finger into the jar. She scooped out a dollop, but instead of putting it on the cracker, she put it in her mouth and proceeded to eat it off her finger. He couldn't stop watching as she licked until the peanut butter was gone. "Mmm," she said. "That's good."

"Is it?" he asked, barely able to speak.

"Can I have some of that?" she asked, leaning towards him, aiming to eat what was on his finger.

He backed off, though, and wouldn't let her have it. "That's mine," he said, but instead of eating it, he reached over and smeared the peanut butter on her breast. He leaned in and licked it off her, capturing her sensitive skin in his mouth.

Gasping, she arched back and pulled his head toward her. Leaning forward, he pushed her back on the bed, pulled more peanut butter from the jar, and after placing it on the delicate areas of her body, proceeded to eat it off her.

They continued like that, each intermittently licking peanut butter off the other, crackers crunching beneath them as they explored each other, enjoying the food and each other's touch until they wound up in the shower, where they continued their exploration until the water ran cold.

After getting out and drying off, Ramsey changed the bed sheets, and they ended up back in them again. This time, though, they fell asleep and slept for hours, exhausted after their busy but sleepless night and morning. Waking in the evening, and famished for an actual meal, they'd ordered pizza. Now, sitting in Ramsey's living room with the fireplace lit, they each munched on dinner and enjoyed a glass of wine as they sat in robes on a large blanket Ramsey had pulled from a closet.

They said little while they ate, listening to the crackle of the fire and sipping wine, enjoying the food and each other.

Leaning back on the couch, Sarah reached for another piece.

Ramsey sat back next to her. "Better?" he asked.

"Much," she said, biting into her pizza. "I was starving."

"Me, too." He turned to face her, and watched her as she ate. "I guess feasting on you wasn't enough to keep my stomach happy."

"Well," she said, "it certainly kept other parts happy."

Inspecting the room, he took in the damage. A few picture frames, a vase, and from what he could tell, some dishes in the kitchen were broken. The most noticeable damage was to the glass coffee table, which sported a large crack down its middle. Thinking back, he suspected what had caused the crack and recalled Sarah's moans of pleasure. "It certainly shows."

Sarah blushed, and he guessed she was remembering the same thing. "It was worth it," she said.

Ramsey grinned. "It sure as hell was." Her eyes sparkled in the firelight. "I can't wait to see what else we can break."

Laughing, she put her pizza down and wiped her mouth with a napkin. "Me, too." After taking another sip of wine, she set the glass on the table and moved up next to him, cradling into his side and he wrapped his arm around her and held her close.

"Can I ask you something?" she asked.

"Of course."

She played with the sleeve of his robe. "Will you go with me to read the mirror?"

He didn't answer at first, but didn't react negatively, either. "Are you sure you're ready to read it?"

"I don't know."

"Have you tried to read anything else?"

"Anything else? Like what?"

"Like other objects?"

"No, I haven't."

The conversation made him think of something else he wanted to ask her but had been too distracted to do so earlier. "By the way, speaking of objects, where's your necklace?" He felt her tense up. "What?" he asked. "Did you lose it?"

Sighing, she said, "Not really, no."

"Then what? Did you leave it home?"

"No."

He couldn't understand her strange reaction until he realized that she didn't want to tell him. "Sarah, what is it?"

"I left it somewhere."

"Left it where?"

She hesitated. "I think it's at Y's house."

Ramsey went still, but stayed calm. "Why is it at Y's house?"

"Because when I went there, I had it on, but when I left, I didn't."

Ramsey's mind whirled. "You haven't told me much about what happened when you went there."

Sarah closed her eyes and he sensed her anxiety. "It wasn't that big a deal. He told me he had something to cure you, but he didn't, so I left."

He didn't believe for a second that it was as simple as that. "Somehow I think there's more to the story."

"I don't want to upset you."

That did bother him, knowing now that something had occurred that he wouldn't like. "Please tell me," he said, "because right now my imagination is making it pretty awful."

Sitting up, she met his worried gaze. "Don't freak out. It's not as bad as you think." He waited. "A car picked me up and took me to Y's house. He said he had serum for you. He made me eat dinner with him. All I wanted to do was leave, but he said if I wanted the serum, I had to have dinner. So, I did. Then he asked for a blood sample from me. I allowed it because I wanted the serum, which he gave me after he took my blood. When I tried to leave, he…"

"He what?"

"He drugged me or something. I don't know."

He scowled. "He did what?"

"I woke up the next morning."

"The next morning? You spent the night there?" His heart thudded.

"I woke up in his bed—"

"You what?"

"Nothing happened. He wasn't there. I was fully clothed."

"Sarah, that doesn't mean—"

"Stop," she said. "Don't go there. Give me some credit. I do have some intuitive ability. I checked in with myself and felt fine. I would have known if he'd taken advantage." Ramsey rubbed his head in frustration. "When I got up and started to leave, that's when I saw the room."

"The room?"

"Yes. In his house, with the large mirror. It had a chair in front of it."

"This is the mirror he used to get access to me?"

"I suspect so, yes, but I didn't know it at the time. Afterward, he found me and let me leave. His driver brought me back to the hospital. It was then that I realized my necklace was gone."

There was so much Ramsey wanted to say, so much to react to, that he didn't know where to start. Y had taken her blood? He had drugged her and made her spend the night? He'd taken her necklace? What the hell was the man up to? "Sarah—"

She held his wrist. "Before you get mad, just know that everything is fine. I am fine. He told me he would not force me to do anything. He wanted me to stay, but I said no and he let me leave."

"He wanted you to stay?"

"Yes."

"And what about the serum? Did he have it?"

"Yes, he did."

"He did? But I thought you said he didn't have what I needed."

Sarah shook her head. "I didn't trust him. He gave me a dose of what he said was serum, but I didn't need to use it."

"And how does he have serum in the first place?"

"Because he needs it."

"He needs the serum?"

"Yes. He's a Red-Line. Emerson and Arnuff stashed serum away when they realized they might need it. It's how they survived all these years."

"Wait. What?"

"Yes. They've been involved from the beginning. They were part of some covert plot to knock off the Grays, and when they realized they were in trouble, they held back some of the serum the Reds were giving to the Grays, and that's how they survived. Then, when the genetic testing started, they got nervous and went out on their own, starting their own testing and resulting in the births of X, Y, and Z."

Ramsey dropped his jaw. "Have you told this to Leroy and Declan?"

"Yes. I told them everything."

"And what did they say?"

"Well, they were as surprised as you. They've told the Council, but at this point, there's not much that can be done."

"He's got serum."

"He does, but it certainly would not be enough to save the Community. He said if he continued to conserve, it would only last him for a few more decades."

"A few decades? Sounds like plenty of serum to me."

"Well, he's not exactly going to turn it over to us willingly."

Ramsey didn't doubt that, and he expected that if they tried to take it, it would only result in the destruction of the serum and likely someone's life as well. He tried to understand everything coming at him at once. "I don't like this, Sarah."

"What?"

"He's up to something. Why take your blood?"

"He said he's an amateur scientist and wants to study my blood to see how I survive without serum."

"He's lying."

"Maybe he is, but at the time, it seemed like a small price to pay for your life."

Ramsey slumped and looked away.

"Hey," she said, tipping his jaw back toward her. "This isn't your fault."

"Yes, it is. He used me to get to you."

"If it wasn't for me going over there, you'd be dead right now."

"If it wasn't for me, you'd never have had to go there in the first place."

"And if it wasn't for you, I wouldn't have survived my Shift to even get there. In fact, if it wasn't for me, you'd never have been injured."

"Don't say that."

"Listen," she said, breathing hard in frustration. "We can play this game all night. Who did what when, and who caused what. But at the end of the day, it's still just you and me trying to find our way through this. And if we have to take a few risks along the way to protect each other, then so be it."

He understood, but it was still difficult to grasp.

"We're bound to make mistakes along the way," she said, "and God knows, I'm sure I'll make plenty more and so will you. But what else can we do? We don't know what's going to happen next. All we know, all I know, is that I love you and I want to be with you. And I'm not going to let some madman get between us. He's got enough power already. Let's not give him more."

Ramsey wished he knew what to say to argue with her, but he couldn't, because he knew she was right. They were just doing their best with the circumstances they were given. He reached up and cupped her face, his thumb tracing her cheek. "I don't want to lose you."

Leaning into his touch, she rested her hand over his. "You are not going to lose me."

He prayed that was true. Feeling the familiar energy in his belly ignite, and suddenly desperate for her, he dropped his hand to her leg. Sliding it up under her robe, he ran his fingers up the side of her thigh. Her eyes flared, and after moving her hand behind his neck, she kissed him. His fingers traveled up to her hip and with his other arm coming around her, he lifted her at the waist and pulled her over until she straddled him. She moved her mouth eagerly over his, and he tasted pizza and wine while she nibbled his lips. He slid his hands up, undid the belt of her robe and opened it. He reached inside and caressed her skin from her waist to her neck and she moaned and rocked against him. The energy building fast, their kiss intensified, their breath intermingled, and they pulled at their robes, freeing themselves. And as the fire slowly burned out, they passionately made their own.

**

Sometime later, after making it back to the bedroom, they fell back into an exhausted sleep. Wrapped around Ramsey, Sarah slept soundly, but sometime before dawn, she awoke, feeling something amiss. Laying on her side, she faced the wall, but not feeling him against her, she turned in the bed to see that she was alone. Hearing the sink running in the bathroom, she sat up. The air was chilly, so she grabbed the top sheet and wrapped it over her shoulders. She walked to the bathroom and stopped at the doorway, where she saw Ramsey leaning over the sink splashing cold water over his face. From where she stood, she could see the tension in his body, and by the glow of the nightlight she noticed the sheen of sweat on his skin. Something was wrong.

She stayed silent and didn't move, not wanting to frighten him by coming up behind him. She couldn't see his reflection because his bathroom mirror was covered, as all his mirrors were. He turned off the faucet, and she could hear his ragged breathing as he reached with trembling fingers for the towel.

He must have sensed her presence, because he spoke as he wiped his face. "I'm okay. Go back to bed."

She came up behind him instead, opened her arms, and pressed up against his back, bringing the sheet around him and encircling him as her chin came to rest on his shoulder and her cheek pressed against his ear. He dropped the towel and reached up with his hands to encircle her wrists, grabbing tightly as if needing to hold on to her.

"What's the matter?" she whispered. "You all right?"

His breath shook and a shiver ran through him.

"I'm okay," he said, leaning back into her. "Just need a few minutes."

His anxiety worried her. Feeling his distress, she pulled him closer and brought her arms securely around him. "What is it?"

He hesitated and she hoped he would open up to her. Before, he would have kept his secrets closely guarded, but she sensed his need to get past that, and she waited. He took another shuddered breath. "Nightmares," he said. "I've been having them since the hospital."

"Nightmares about what?" His body went rigid and she squeezed him. "Tell me."

Sighing, he closed his eyes. "Usually, it's me being attacked or infected with that poison again. I see it on me or it gets near me, and I can't get away. I try to get rid of it and it just grows, and I panic, and I wake up in a cold sweat with a scream stuck in my throat." He opened his eyes and gripped her wrists.

She began to realize some of what he'd been dealing with. "Is that what you dreamed about tonight?"

He hesitated to answer, and she sensed it had been bad. Feeling his fear, she moved her hands and settled them over his chest and abdomen, and she fired up the energy in the pit of her belly, infusing it with all the calm and softness she could muster. She directed it up through her heart and down her arms and into him, trying to help him relax. Taking a deep breath, he started to talk again.

"It was awful." He paused. "You were there. We were in bed and I woke up, and it was on me. I tried to get it off, but it just grew. You woke up and saw what was happening, and you tried to help me, but..."

His tension radiated from him. "But what?" she whispered.

"But it got on you. I saw it move from me to you, and I lost it. I couldn't stop it, and I watched it take you. I tried to reach for you, to help you, but you kept moving farther and farther away. And you were screaming..." He clenched his eyes shut.

Feeling him tremble, she nuzzled into him, sending another wave of energy through him. They stood there silently for several minutes while she kept up her ministrations, until finally, she felt his heartbeat slow, his shoulders come down, and his arms and hands, which clutched at her wrists, relax. "Better?" she asked.

A held breath escaped him, and he swallowed. "Yes."

Giving him another squeeze, she looked up at the mirror and regarded the sheet hanging over it. "You know," she said, diverting the subject, "you make it really hard for a girl to check her lipstick."

He smiled. "I know."

Snuggling into him even more, she said, "You don't have to keep that sheet up. He can't get to you. Home mirrors have enough energy from their owners to keep him out."

His hands moved up and down her forearms. "Maybe so," he said, "but the thought of him seeing through it, well, it bothers me."

"I can show you how to feel one-hundred-percent safe."

"You can?"

"Yes. I figured it out when I went home. I didn't know for sure what he could see or not see, so I blocked the mirror."

"You blocked it? How?"

Holding together the sheet that encircled them, she took his hand from beneath and directed it toward the mirror. He let her guide him.

"Put your hand against the mirror," she said, feeling his doubt and hesitation. "It's okay," she added, and he pushed the sheet aside. He moved his hand up under it and placed it against the cool surface.

She followed by placing her hand over his. "Now," she said, "summon up some genuine John Ramsey energy, right here." Sarah pressed against his stomach with her other hand that clasped the sheet. "Let it build."

Ramsey did as she asked and she sensed the energy within him grow and blossom.

"Good," she said. "Now bring it up through your chest and down through your arm and into the mirror."

He did as she instructed, and his energy moved through his body and into the mirror, and diffused into the reflective glass.

"Keep going until you feel it's enough," she said.

His hand against the mirror, he continued.

"You feel that?" she asked.

He nodded. "It feels different now. Like something closed." He dropped his head and he exhaled. "I don't feel so exposed anymore." He dropped his hand from the mirror, and hers came with it.

"Better?" she asked, wrapping her arm back around him.

"That will keep him out?"

"Yes. If he tries to use the mirror, all he'll see is something like a giant poster board with your picture on it."

"That ought to make him happy."

"You can do that with all your mirrors," she said, giving him a reassuring squeeze. "Because a man should be able to admire his rippling muscles."

**

Laughing softly, the tension drained from Ramsey's body. He felt ten pounds lighter and he marveled at Sarah's ability to soothe him. Eyeing the mirror, a thought occurred to him. "Since we're opening up here, you want to try something?"

"Hmmm," she moaned in his ear. "What exactly have we not tried?"

He chuckled but didn't let her distract him. "That's not what I mean, but hold that thought. I mean why don't you try to read the mirror?"

"What? This mirror?"

"Sure. Why not?"

"Well," she paused, hesitant, "doesn't it have to be encoded or some-thing?"

"No," he said. "Red-Lines did use mirrors to encode information, but you can still read one without a message in it. It's an object with energy, like anything else."

"You think I should?"

Her wariness surprised him. "What's stopping you?"

Now she was the one who was tense and he could feel it.

Looking up at the mirror, she asked, "What if I can't?"

Understanding, he attempted to alleviate her doubt. "I don't think you have to worry about that."

"You don't?"

"Sarah," he said, "so far you've met every challenge you've faced. You have abilities you don't even realize you have yet. I think this mirror will be easy for you." Her hesitation remained. "But if you can't, then we'll know, and you won't walk into that Council room next week and be blindsided. It may be that you just need a little practice. And what better way is there to find out? Standing here with me now, or in a crowded room with a bunch of strange people standing around?"

She took a wary breath. "I'd rather be with you."

"Then let's go for it. I want to see what you can do."

"Don't get your hopes up."

"Stop doubting yourself." Ramsey found her hand under the sheet and took it in his own, guiding it out and back toward the mirror. She let him direct her until it was her hand on the mirror, with his over hers.

"What do I do?" she asked.

"I suspect you need to relax a little. I can feel your tension." Her body eased as she leaned against him. "Good," he said. "Now just take your time. Close your eyes. Let yourself be guided. Quiet your mind."

He stood still, now trying to send her peaceful waves of energy as he glanced sideways at her. He saw her close her eyes. "That's it," he said. "Tell me what you feel."

Not saying anything at first, she continued to stand, her hand against the mirror, her front leaning up against his back, while he held her hand gently against the glass. Suddenly, she smiled.

"What?" he asked.

"I see you."

"You do?"

"Yes. You don't wear a lot of clothes around the house, do you?"

He grinned. "Well, what for?"

She went quiet again for a second. "You're not home a lot."

"No. Not usually." Not surprised that she was picking it up fast, he encouraged her. "Keep going."

After another pause, she said, "The house is old."

"Yes. Fairly."

He waited again as she listened to what only she could hear. "And there's someone else."

Ramsey had wondered how much she'd pick up, and she didn't disappoint. "Who?"

"A woman."

He didn't speak, not wanting to give information away.

"She's older."

"Yes," he said.

"Very kind."

"Uh-huh."

"She smiles a lot. Laughs, too."

His heart warmed as memories returned.

Her eyes furrowed, but then relaxed. "She loved you very much."

His heart stammered. Sensing the swirling energy in Sarah, he began to connect through her to the energy in the mirror, feeling but not seeing what she did.

"You were troubled," Sarah continued and he didn't interrupt. "She took you in. She helped you." She stopped for a second, a realization hitting her. "It's your grandmother."

The energy Sarah felt from the woman who took him in years ago flooded in, and his smile blossomed. "Yes," he said.

"She lived in the house?" she questioned. "No, she owned the house."

"Yes, she did."

Sarah opened her eyes. "She gave it to you."

Amazed by what she had done, he confirmed her reading. "Yes. When she died three years ago, she left the house to me."

Sarah dropped her hand from the mirror, taking Ramsey's with it. "She has a beautiful energy."

"She certainly does." Her hand went back below the sheet. "Not bad," he said, feeling her wrap around him again, "for a first timer."

Her energy sizzled through her and Ramsey felt the tingles against his skin. "That wasn't so bad, was it?" he asked, feeling the electric charge in the air. He leaned back into her, all thoughts of his grandmother disappearing as she pressed back into him. "You want to read more?" he asked, hoping she'd say no.

She didn't disappoint him. "I'd rather read more of you."

He gave a pleasurable sigh, feeling her hands travel over his chest and belly. The tone in her voice and her body against his made all thoughts of mirrors disappear, and he turned in her arms, his arms encircling her while hers moved up and around his shoulders. She wrapped the sheet closer, letting it envelop them both. Finding her lips with his own, he kissed her as he leaned back against the bathroom counter, bringing her with him. Before it became too hot to stop, though, he pulled back. "God, you are so beautiful," he said, laying his forehead against hers.

She closed her eyes and pressed against him. "So are you," she whispered.

Savoring the feel of her, he thought about what she had done before she'd read the mirror. "You helped me tonight," he said. "Thank you."

She opened her eyes. "I'm glad I was here to do it."

He caressed her back with his thumbs and a thought occurred to him. "Stay with me."

She brought her nose to his. "I am with you."

"No," he said, kissing her forehead, "I mean stay with me. Move in with me. Don't leave." He trailed warm kisses down the side of her face to her cheek and jaw.

She sighed softly. "Okay," she said, and moved her lips to find his and captured them with her own, encircling her arms around his neck.

He pushed himself off the counter and wrapped himself around her. He let his tongue find hers and the kiss rapidly turned passionate. Breaking away, breathless, he looked at her, his lips grazing hers.

'What?" she asked.

"I love you." And before she could respond, he moved back in to capture her lips again.

Unable to speak, she answered him by meeting his kiss hungrily. With the heat building fast between them, he reached down and lifted her and her legs wrapped around his waist. Still kissing him, she dropped the sheet onto the bathroom floor as he carried her back to the bed.

NINETEEN

....

SARAH PULLED HER suitcase out of the car, and Ramsey grabbed several grocery bags and carried them into the house. They had finally managed to leave the bedroom after a lazy Sunday, during which they did nothing but order take-out, talk, eat, catch an old Hitchcock movie on a local TV channel, and enjoy each other throughout the day. Their conversations involved no mention of Y, serum, or mirrors, but their time together allowed them the chance to get to know each other better. Sarah learned about Ramsey's love for road trips, how he liked to camp when he needed to relax, about his troubled teenage years and his Nana Rose, who took him in after his father's death. Ramsey learned about Sarah's knack for computers, how, after her own father's death, her mother had brought in extra money as a psychic medium, and that she wanted to one day travel to exotic places. He discovered she liked horror movies, cheesecake, and gardenias, and she learned his favorite color was blue, that he liked chocolate cake, and that he'd never liked science, much to the dismay of his father. She also discovered the source of his middle name; his dad had been a huge Arthur Conan Doyle fan.

The weekend had ended with Leroy calling that night, confirming the Council's plans to meet with Sarah on Tuesday. They'd spent Monday morning going to Sarah's apartment and packing the things she'd needed, and they had stopped at the grocery store in order to restock the shelves in Ramsey's kitchen.

Upon walking into the house in the late afternoon, Sarah dropped her suitcase and pulled her cosmetic bag off her shoulder and let it fall to the floor. Their amorous activities that weekend had worn her out, and she took a second to rest.

Ramsey carried in the remaining grocery bags and closed the door. He set the bags on the counter and turned to look at her, crossing his arms in front of him.

"Something on your mind?" she asked.

He'd been quiet since they'd left the grocery store. "You all right?"

"Yes. Why? Do I look like I'm not?"

"No," he said, leaning against the counter. "You look great. It's just that I know there's a lot going on right now." He looked around the house. "You're moving in here. You're supposed to read the mirror tomorrow." His eyes held a worried expression. "It's just a lot to process. I want to be sure I'm— we're—not pushing you too fast."

Reading the doubt on his face, she walked up to him. He opened his arms and she walked into them, wrapping herself around him. "You're not rushing me into anything. I can't imagine being anywhere else." Warming herself in his arms, she breathed in his scent.

Ramsey gave a contented sigh. "Good," he said. "Because you don't have to do anything you don't want to do."

Smiling, she stared back at him. "This coming from the man who wouldn't let me leave the house six weeks ago?"

His eyes turned dark, and he gave her a stormy look. "Yeah, well, I had to protect you back then." Leaning forward, he hugged her close, his mouth moving to her ear. "I couldn't let anyone take advantage of you." He nibbled her earlobe with his teeth.

Feeling his warm breath on her neck, her insides shuddered. "I think the only one I need protection from is you." Her hands gripped the back of his shirt, and she let her head fall back. He trailed his lips to her neck and kissed her there, making her shiver.

His mouth moved over her skin, turning her insides to mush, and she felt his hands find their way under her shirt. "We need to unpack the groceries," she said, trying to catch her breath.

"They're not going anywhere," he said hotly. He flicked his tongue behind her ear and grasped her top and pulled it up. She raised her arms, and he took it off her. Reaching down, he picked her up, capturing her mouth with his lips as he lifted her.

Unable to deny him, she wrapped her arms around him on their way back to the bedroom. Between kisses, she said, "Maybe eventually we'll actually eat a meal with our clothes on."

Ramsey grinned, and kissed her back. "Now where's the fun in that?" he asked, and he deepened the kiss.

Sighing and teasing him with her tongue, Sarah accepted the fact that the ice cream they'd bought would likely melt before it ever got to the freezer.

**

The next morning, after they shared a satisfying shower, they had breakfast fully clothed, much to Ramsey's disappointment. They'd managed to get up the previous evening to put away the groceries and prepare some dinner before they'd both succumbed to their appetite for each other again.

Now as they ate, Ramsey watched Sarah pick at her food from across the table. "Nervous?" he asked, sensing her distraction.

Putting her fork down, she said, "A little. I'm not very hungry."

He checked the clock on the wall. They had to be in front of the Council in two hours. He wished he could speed up time so he could get her there and get the ordeal over and done with. Before he could respond, though, his phone rang and he picked it up. "Hello?"

"Sherlock?"

"Hey, Leroy."

There was a short pause. "Sherlock..."

Ramsey straightened, sensing Leroy's distress. "What? What's wrong?"

"I'm sorry. I hate to tell you this..."

Ramsey's heart picked up its pace. "What, Leroy?"

"It's Declan. His father died this morning."

Ramsey shut his eyes at the shock of the news. "What?" he said. "I thought he was better."

Sarah saw Ramsey's reaction. "What is it?"

Ramsey opened his eyes. "Declan's dad died this morning."

"No..."

Leroy continued. "They thought he was better. He took a turn for the worse this weekend. They took him to the hospital, and Declan's been with him."

Guilt sliced through Ramsey when he considered what he had been doing while his brother had been at his father's bedside. "Why didn't he tell me?"

"He knew you were with Sarah. Her security detail has been in front of your house for three days. He didn't want to bother you."

"Damn it." Ramsey put his elbow on the table and ran a hand through his hair. "What about Mom?"

"I don't know. I only spoke with Declan briefly a few minutes ago."

"How is he?"

"About as well as can be expected."

Ramsey cursed. He considered his options. "Leroy..."

"What do you want to do, Sherlock?"

Ramsey looked over at Sarah.

She knew what he was thinking. "You have to go over there."

"Sarah..." he said.

"No. He's your brother, and it's your stepfather. You need to go."

"I can't leave you. I told you I would go with you."

"Don't worry about me. You have to go."

"Leroy," said Ramsey, trying to think of another option. "Can we re-schedule?"

"I've got a room full of Council members expecting her." Leroy hesitated. "It would be best not to cancel."

"Nobody's rescheduling anything," said Sarah. "I'll be fine."

"I'll be with her, Sherlock. Hannah's coming, too. I'll swing by and pick Sarah up. She won't be alone."

Ramsey felt completely torn. He wanted to be there for Sarah, but knew he had an obligation to his family. Hating his decision, he reached out his hand. "Sarah..."

She reached across the table and put her hand in his. "I understand. Go. I'll be fine. It's only a mirror. If I read it, great. If I don't, I can try again later. This isn't a one-shot deal."

He squeezed her fingers. "You're sure?"

She nodded. "Yes. I am."

Ramsey spoke back into the phone. "You'll pick her up, Leroy?"

"I'm leaving now. I'll be there in thirty minutes."

"I'll wait till you get here."

"Okay. See you soon."

"Thanks." He hung up the phone.

"You all right?" asked Sarah.

"I'd be better if I could go with you."

"I know, but this is unavoidable. You have to be with your family."

"I could go with you first. Then go to them."

"That will be at least another three hours. I know you. You'll be distract-ed and a wreck. I'll feel guilty, too." She shook her head. "No, you have to go now. You don't need to wait for Leroy, either."

Holding her hand, his turmoil ate at him. "No, I'll wait." He sighed. "I'm sorry."

"You don't need to apologize. This isn't anyone's fault."

"You sure you'll be okay?"

"You're not leaving forever. I'll see you tonight. I'll give you a full recap."

"I want you to call me as soon as you're out." He rubbed his thumb over her palm. "You promise me?"

She reached up and took his other hand. "I'll call. I promise."

They shared a gaze across the table. "Everything will be okay," he said, "no matter what happens." He wasn't sure if he said it for her benefit or for his.

"As long as we have each other," she answered, "I know it will be."

**

Ramsey stood on the sidewalk and stared up at his mother's house. It was his first time home in three years. He hadn't been here since his Grandmother's funeral, when they'd all gathered here afterwards. Contemplating why death seemed to be the only reason for his visits and thinking perhaps he should change that, he walked up the drive to the entrance, and knocked. A few seconds passed, the door opened, and his Uncle Phillip stood in front of him.

Phillip looked him up and down. "Well, hell," he said, "look who's here."

Ramsey regarded his uncle, his mother's brother, standing there in a beige corduroy jacket, striped yellow shirt, and baggy jeans and holding a glass of something most likely alcoholic in his hand. His mustache and thick glasses helped mask his puffy face, and Ramsey noticed he had a lot less hair than the last time he'd seen him.

"Hi, Uncle Phil."

His uncle scrutinized him. "You here to cause trouble?"

Ramsey heard the tone in Phil's voice, realizing it wasn't altogether undeserved. "No," he sighed. When his uncle didn't say anything, he asked, "Can I come in?"

His uncle appeared to debate the matter, but then stepped aside and let Ramsey enter.

The house looked the same, with the familiar furniture and paint color. It was quiet and empty. "Where's Mom?"

"She's in the bedroom with your Aunt Margaret. The doctor gave her a sedative. She's been up the last two days sitting with him in the hospital, and she's exhausted and grief-stricken. She needs to rest."

Ramsey stared back toward the bedroom, wondering if he should poke his head in, but thought better of it. "How are you?" he asked his uncle.

"Me?" His uncle sloshed his drink. "Do you really care, or are you just trying to be nice?"

Ramsey remembered Phil as always being more of a burden than a support to his mother. Although the guy carried the typical Eudoran affinity for science—he taught biology at the local high school—he'd unfortunately also developed some of the less desirable earthly traits. Phil and Ramsey's dad had never seen eye to eye, since Phil's brotherly attributes consistently fell short of his sister's expectations. Ramsey recalled Phil as being a drinker, and apparently that had not changed.

"I'm just trying to be nice," Ramsey said, feeling old emotions surface.

"That's a first," said Phil, not catching his nephew's slight.

Ramsey didn't respond to that, knowing this was not the time or place to get in an argument with a tipsy relative. "Where's Declan?" he asked, hoping to find a reason to get out of the room.

Phil pointed to the back yard, spilling his drink as he did so. "He's out back."

"How is he?"

"How do you think? You should know what it's like to lose your dad."

Trying to hold his tongue, Ramsey put his hands in his pockets. "I'm going to go talk to him." He walked toward the sliding glass back door.

"Try not to be an ass," said Phil as Ramsey opened the door and stepped outside, remembering now why he never visited.

"Thanks, Phil," he said, closing the door behind him.

New patio furniture had replaced the worn old deck chairs and table he remembered from his youth. The yard was barren save for a few shrubs alongside the house and a patch of grass with an empty bird bath near the back fence. Ramsey had inherited his mother's lack of interest in anything green. It had been his father who'd tended the yard and garden when Ramsey was a child, and vague memories of houseplants and hanging baskets surfaced as he walked toward the side yard. Turning the corner, he saw Declan sitting in a lounge chair with his feet up, staring at the surrounding fence. Ramsey walked over and took a seat in the chair beside him. There was a small table in between them, with an untouched glass of water on it— or at least Ramsey assumed it was water. Saying nothing, he let his presence settle in, listening to the soft breeze as it rustled the leaves of a large tree in the neighbor's yard.

"Hey," Declan said, finally acknowledging Ramsey.

"Hey," Ramsey answered, leaning back in the chair, staring at the same wooden fence that held Declan's attention.

Declan spoke quietly. "You didn't have to come."

"Yes, I did."

The two remained quiet, not feeling the need to fill the silence.

"How's Charlotte doing?" Declan finally asked. He'd never been able to call Ramsey's mother "Mom," just as Ramsey had never called Declan's father "Dad."

"She took a sedative. Margaret's with her."

Declan paused, as if speaking hurt. "Is Phil drunk yet?"

"He's well on his way."

Declan nodded and Ramsey let Declan decide whether he wanted to talk.

"Where's Sarah?" said Declan after a few minutes.

Ramsey debated his answer but finally settled on the truth. "I'd say right about now, she's either reading or not reading the mirror."

Declan turned his head. "What? Why didn't you go with her?"

Ramsey met his look. "Because my stepfather died."

Declan studied the fence again. 'You should have gone with her."

Ramsey sighed. "I wanted to, but I need to be here." He paused. "Leroy and Hannah are with her. She'll be okay."

Neither spoke, both lost in their thoughts, and more time passed.

"I hear you two made up," said Declan, still reserved but trying to engage.

Ramsey considered that one way to describe it. "You could say that."

Declan allowed himself a brief smile. "Was it everything you thought it would be?"

"And then some."

"Good," said Declan. "I'm happy for you."

"Thanks."

More quiet minutes passed and Ramsey felt Declan withdraw despite his attempts at conversation. Deciding to try and reach out, he asked, "How are you?"

Declan showed the first signs of discomfort when he shifted in his chair. "I'm okay," he said, but it was without his usual calm demeanor.

Ramsey heard and felt the lie but didn't challenge him on it. "You want to talk about it?"

"Talk about what?" Declan asked. "What's to talk about?"

Ramsey turned, sitting up and sideways in his chair. "Your father's death?"

Declan set his jaw and hardened his features. "No, not really."

Ramsey didn't push. "Okay," he said. He turned and sat back, regarding the fence again.

"You don't have to stay," said Declan, his voice strained. "You can go be with Sarah."

The thought of leaving Declan to the care of his Aunt Margaret and Uncle Phillip seemed worse than death itself. Ramsey remained where he was, ready to be there when Declan finally gave into his grief. Reaching out to Declan empathically, Ramsey felt the sharp pain of despair and knew he was exactly where he needed to be.

"No," he said. "I'll stay."

**

Sarah sat at the round conference table, with Leroy on her right and Hannah to her left. She and Leroy had arrived twenty minutes earlier and met Hannah there. They'd been ushered into a large room by a man named Jenkins, who, according to Leroy, was Morgana's personal assistant. Nervous, Sarah shifted in her seat.

"Relax," said Leroy. "They'll be out soon."

"They?" asked Hannah. "Are they all coming?" She wrung her hands.

"Yes," said Leroy. "Why wouldn't they? You've seen them before, so what's the worry?"

"That was a different meeting," said Hannah, "and I basically sat in the back and kept to myself."

Leroy smiled. "They're just like us. Nothing to worry about." He glanced at Sarah. "They're probably just as nervous about meeting you."

Sarah took a deep breath. "Yeah, well, somehow I feel like they're setting themselves up for disappointment." She wished Ramsey was there but tried not to dwell on it.

"You'll be fine," said Leroy.

"How many of them are there?" asked Hannah.

"Usually eleven," said Leroy, "but they're down to nine without Emerson and Arnuff."

"Nine," said Sarah. "That's not so bad."

"Is there a secret handshake?" asked Hannah, trying to lighten the mood.

Leroy widened his eyes. "Yes. Don't you know it?" Hannah shot him a worried look, and Leroy chuckled. "I'm just kidding."

"Very funny," said Hannah.

"Is there a grand wizard or something? A head council person I bow to?" asked Sarah.

"Where do you two think we are? Oz?" asked Leroy. "No. There's no great wizard. There's not even one designated leader. The council members take turns leading meetings, but all decisions are made by a majority decision. They keep it pretty simple."

Sarah bounced her knee. "Well, I wish they'd hurry it up. My stomach's in knots."

Just then, the door opened and Morgana stepped in, with several more people behind her. They were all older, mostly appearing to be around Morgana's age, and dressed professionally, as if they were meeting an important client with whom they wished to do business—which Sarah supposed she was. She didn't know what she had expected, but it hadn't been this. Somewhere in her mind, she must have anticipated an ornate room with heavy curtains and huge chairs, with members wearing long robes and carrying scrolls or ancient texts or something. Watching them as they sat, she thought they looked more like a board of directors about to vote on who would become the next board president.

Morgana took a seat across from her and the others found their places at the table. Jenkins came into the room and placed a nameplate in front of each of them, assumingly so that Sarah could refer to them by name.

Morgana spoke first. "Good morning, Sarah." Regal as usual, she perused the three of them, and Sarah picked up on a flicker of what felt like concern emanate from her. It felt out of place, since the woman rarely exuded anything other than assured self-confidence.

Pleased to get the proceedings under way, Sarah tried to follow Leroy's advice and relax. "Good morning," she said.

"Hannah. Leroy," said Morgana, acknowledging them as well.

"Good morning," said Leroy.

"Good morning," said Hannah.

"Well," said Morgana, "now that we're all here, let's dispense with any more formalities." She glanced around the table. "To spare you the obligatory introductions, we've used nameplates so that you would know who we are." She eyed Sarah. "And we all know who you are."

"Apparently so," said Sarah, feeling like a circus oddity.

Morgana addressed Hannah and Leroy. "While I'm glad you're both here to offer support, I'd like to know where Ramsey is." She interlaced her fingers. "I expected him as well."

"Declan's father died this morning, Morgana," said Leroy. "He needed to be there."

Morgana showed no reaction other than a brief silence. "I'm sorry to hear that," she said. "Please convey our condolences."

"I will," said Leroy.

Morgana turned her gaze back to Sarah. "Very well. Are you ready?"

"Morgana," said a voice from down the table. The nameplate in front of him read "Drake." He was a lanky man with a graying goatee and equally graying hair who exuded a powerful and intelligent presence.

Morgana shifted her gaze. "Yes, Drake?"

"Perhaps we should wait until circumstances are more ideal?"

Sarah picked up on the unspoken message between Morgana and the Councilman, but she had no idea what it meant.

"Nonsense," said Morgana. "Circumstances are what they are. I believe we should proceed." Scanning the rest of the room, she asked, "Any objections?"

The other members at the table all shook their heads.

"I have a question."

All eyes looked down the table at a Councilwoman with a nameplate that read "Daphne."

"Yes, Daphne?" asked Morgana.

Daphne was a petite woman with obviously dyed black hair and heavy make-up. Her chunky charm bracelet dragged against the table as she leaned forward and spoke to Sarah. "What makes you think you can read it?"

"Daphne, this is not the time to play games," said Morgana.

"What makes you think I can't?" replied Sarah.

Daphne stared back, debating whether to answer, while the rest of the table watched the two women. "None of the other Reds did," she said. "I don't expect you to be any different."

"Daphne, please," said a man named Randolph, who sat next to Morgana. "Let's not be so dramatic."

"Look at her, Randy," she said. "Does she look like a Red-Line to you?"

"What exactly is she supposed to look like?" replied Randolph. "Wonder Woman?"

Sarah remained expressionless, wishing Ramsey were there to hear that comment. If they only knew, she thought to herself.

"Who cares what she looks like?" asked Drake. "We all know who she is, and according to all that we now know, she is indeed a Red-Line." His hands moved as he spoke. "So how about we get past this inane discussion and get to the task at hand. I'm sure Sarah is as anxious as we are." His gaze found her from where he sat. "Would you like to try and read the mirror?"

"Why don't you offer to buy her dinner, too, Drake?" Daphne's attitude exuded antagonism.

"That is enough, Daphne." Morgana's sharp-edged voice carried across the table. "If you are unable to maintain a professional demeanor, then we will have no choice but to ask you to leave these proceedings."

Clearly angry, Daphne glowered, but she didn't argue with Morgana. Sarah felt the contempt from the woman and couldn't help but wonder why. Now she was glad Ramsey was not there, knowing he would have offered a colorful response that would only have made the situation worse.

Morgana waited until she was satisfied that her fellow council member had backed off. Once convinced, she returned her attention to Sarah. "Now," she sighed, "as Drake was saying, are you ready?"

Sarah swallowed, not feeling ready at all but not prepared to admit it. "As ready as I can be."

Daphne huffed in response.

"Very well," said Morgana, and she pressed a button on a small console built into the table. "Jenkins," she said into the box, "you may bring it in."

Within seconds, the door opened and Jenkins walked in, carrying with him a small red velvet pouch. He walked up to Morgana and handed it to her, but she waved him off and nodded at Sarah. He turned and handed Sarah the bag when he neared her chair. She took it from him, and he left, never saying a word. Sarah could feel the weight of the object inside but made no move to retrieve it.

"Open it," Morgana prompted.

Sarah looked at Leroy, who looked back at her, nodding his head. Now she wished more than ever that Ramsey was present. Her fingers trembled as she opened the pouch. She reached inside and felt the cold surface of the object, then pulled it out, seeing for the first time the mirror that had been her main focus of thought since she'd first learned of its existence. It was small and silver and in the shape of an octagon. A beautifully engraved letter D in calligraphy graced its surface. Turning it over, she only saw the back of the silver encasement. Realizing the mirror was inside, she pulled open the top and saw the mirror within, revealing her reflection.

"It's small," said Hannah.

"It's a pocket mirror. It was common for Red-Lines at the time to carry one," said Morgana.

"What's the letter D for?" asked Leroy.

"We're not sure," answered Drake. "We assume it's a family heirloom."

"And you're sure this was hers?" asked Sarah. "The pilot's?"

"Varalika," said Morgana. "Yes. She was the only one on the craft. It was found in her hand."

Sarah held the mirror carefully, touching only the silver portion. "And no one else could read it?"

"No," answered Morgana.

Sarah tried to tune into the object without touching the mirror itself. Strangely, it felt oddly blank. Since her abilities had returned, she'd become accustomed to feeling something when she'd held objects of some significance. She hadn't read them, but they'd always contained an energy. This felt strangely empty.

She hesitated, but knew they were all waiting to see what she would do. Trying not to judge anything based on her initial sense of the item, she decided it was now or never. Taking a breath and centering herself, she raised her hand, closed her eyes and brought her fingers to the glass.

Feeling jittery, Ramsey's voice echoed in her mind to relax. An image of the two of them pressed up against each other in his bathroom while she read his mirror flitted through her. Feeling his calming presence, she let her mind go quiet. The cool glass warming from her touch, she let go of the swirling emotions around and within her, opened up her senses, and listened.

TWENTY

....

AFTER A LONG and difficult day, Ramsey opened the door to his house, happy to be home. It was late, but he knew Leroy was there because his car was out front, as was Sarah's security detail. He'd heard what had happened with the mirror not long after Sarah had tried to read it. She'd had no luck, getting nothing from it, just like every other Red-Line before her. They'd talked, and he'd encouraged her, reminding her that there would be other opportunities to try again. It was still early in her development, and she could practice with other objects to see if it would help. Her voice didn't hide her doubt and disappointment, but to her credit, she didn't complain. Ramsey knew that she didn't want to add to his burden, and he appreciated that, but he didn't want her to pretend with him either.

Leroy was on the couch, and he stood when Ramsey entered. "Sherlock?"

"Yeah, Leroy, it's me." Throwing his keys on the entry table, he eyed Sarah as she came into the room. Leaving his front door open behind him, he moved into the living area where Leroy waited.

"Everything okay?" asked Leroy. "How's your mom?"

Ramsey stopped in front of Leroy, and Sarah walked up and took his hand, waiting to hear his answer. Her fingers felt warm in his, and he gave them a reassuring squeeze.

"She's out of it. She took a sedative before I got there. I barely saw her except for a few minutes before I left and we made her get up and eat something before she took another pill and went back to bed." His tired eyes felt heavy, and he rubbed them with his free hand. "My Uncle Phil got drunk and cussed me out before he passed out on the couch, and while her husband snored, my Aunt Margaret gave me her secret family recipe for chicken noodle soup. Apparently, it cures everything, including grief, because she didn't seem too bothered that her sister-in-law's husband just died." Groaning, he stretched his achy midsection, making a mental note to take some aspirin when he had the chance. "All in all," he said, "not all that unexpected when it comes to the Ramsey family."

"And Declan?" Leroy asked.

Ramsey waved at the open front door. "Why don't you ask him?"

Declan walked in carrying a small bag, his eyes red-rimmed and his face fatigued. Dropping his bag, he shut the door. His tired eyes spoke volumes. "He wouldn't let me go home."

Ramsey smirked, hearing the annoyance in Declan's voice. "I pulled big-brother rank on him. Told him he had to stay in the guest room at least for tonight."

"I can stay at my place," said Declan, but his argument held little fervor.

"We talked about this," said Ramsey. "You're not going back to an empty apartment, and you're sure as hell not staying with Phil and Marge at my mom's."

"He's right, Declan. You should stay here," said Sarah.

Declan eyed his brother and Sarah as they held hands. "I'm intruding."

"The hell you are," said Ramsey. "I have a guest room with its own bathroom. It's private, and you can have your space." He watched the indecision run across Declan's face.

"Or you can stay with me and Olivia," said Leroy. "We have a guestroom, too."

Declan threw his hands on his hips and closed his eyes. "Now I've got the both of you ganging up on me." His eyelids lifted but drooped as if he could barely keep them open.

"Nobody wants that," said Leroy. "It's a losing battle."

Sarah had let go of Ramsey's hand and had walked into the kitchen after speaking to Declan. She returned holding a glass of water and two aspirin and held them out to him. "Here," she said.

Ramsey stared at her, amazed that she had picked up on his thoughts. Too tired to think about it and needing the aspirin, he didn't say anything as he took the pills and swallowed them, the water following close behind.

"Thanks," he said, but she had already moved away toward Declan, who was still standing in the entryway looking like he'd rather be anywhere else.

"I'm sorry about your father, Declan," she said, and she moved in to give him a hug. He froze at the unexpected gesture, but reached up and returned the hug. "Stay," she said. "You shouldn't be alone tonight."

Unprepared for her response, Declan's emotional wall started to crumble, and his face tightened, but he held it together.

"Besides," said Sarah, stepping back, "if you stay, we can make a big breakfast tomorrow and maybe you can give me some tips on reading mirrors."

Declan swallowed and Ramsey sensed his brother was grateful for the subject change. "I heard," he managed to say.

"It doesn't compare to your day," she said. "But it still sucks."

Completely spent, Declan relinquished the fight. "All right," he said. "You win."

"There really wasn't any doubt about that," said Ramsey. "You're already here." He put the empty water glass on the table next to him.

"Good," said Leroy. "I'm going to head out and see my lovely wife."

"Thanks for staying, Leroy," said Ramsey.

"Of course." He reached for his jacket on the couch and pointed. "What happened to your coffee table?"

Ramsey eyed the crack and answered nonchalantly, "I slammed my shin on it."

Leroy raised a brow. "You cracked the table with your shin?"

"I guess the right amount of force in just the right spot will do that." Ramsey made glancing eye contact with Sarah.

Her face flushed, and she stared at the floor.

Leroy knitted his brows. "That must have left a mark."

"Amongst other things," said Ramsey.

Leroy put on his jacket, missing the hidden exchange. "What's the plan for tomorrow?"

Declan massaged his temples. "I'm going to the funeral home to make arrangements."

"I'll go with you," said Ramsey.

"You need to check in on your mom," said Declan.

"She needs to be there, too," said Ramsey. "I'll pick her up and we'll all go."

Declan looked like he was about to drop where he stood. "Okay," he said. "That's fine."

Ramsey read him easily. "You know where it is. Go hit the hay."

Declan did not have to be told twice. He grabbed his bag and headed down the short hall. "Goodnight," he managed to say before entering the guest room and shutting the door.

"How is he?" asked Leroy.

"He's a mess, but he'll make it," said Ramsey, seeing Leroy out. Sarah walked up and put an arm around him.

Before he left, Leroy turned and seeing Ramsey and Sarah, offered a contented smile. "And how are you?" he asked Ramsey. "Better?"

Ramsey couldn't help but smile back despite his fatigue. "I'm a mess, too, but in a good way."

Leroy nodded. "Then I'd say you're back to normal."

"Your plant's still alive," said Ramsey. "That should tell you something."

Leroy walked to his car. "I'll call Guinness," he said, and he waved, got into his car and drove away as Ramsey shut the door.

Turning, Ramsey pulled Sarah into his arms. She reached up and returned the embrace, holding him close.

"So," he said into her ear, smelling her shampoo, "tell me about your day."

Loosening her hold, she brought her face to his and gave him a gentle but urgent kiss. "Later," she said, meeting his eyes, sending him an easily interpreted message. Dropping her arms, she took his hand and led him to the bedroom.

**

The morning dawned as Sarah opened her eyes and saw soft light filter in through the curtains. Moving in the bed, she stretched after a decent night's sleep. She'd expected to toss and turn, thinking about her failure with the mirror the previous day, but Ramsey had effectively managed to take her mind off her worries, and they'd fallen asleep after they'd both found comfort in each other's arms.

With Ramsey's arm draped over her midsection, she turned and watched him sleep. She considered waking him to resume their activities from the previous night, but she knew the day before had been difficult and he needed the rest. Lying there, she heard a noise coming from the center of the house and felt Declan's presence. Listening closely, she heard a drawer close and the sound of the refrigerator door opening. Knowing he was awake, she edged her way out of the bed and put on her robe.

Entering the kitchen, she saw Declan sitting at the kitchen table with a glass of orange juice and eating toast with butter. "Good morning."

He looked up. "Did I wake you?"

"No," she said. He appeared more rested than the previous day but still looked like he carried a heavy weight. "You're up early. Did you sleep?"

"Yes, pretty well. I'm just an early riser."

She found a glass and helped herself to the orange juice still on the counter.

"John still asleep?"

"Out like a light."

She put the orange juice back in the fridge and joined him at the table.

"How's he been?" asked Declan. "Is he finally getting past what happened?"

"He has his moments, but he's doing better."

"I'm sure you have a lot to do with that."

"Well, for a while there, I didn't think he was going to give in to my charms."

Declan smiled. "He can be stubborn."

"So I've learned."

Declan took a bite of toast, but without much enthusiasm.

"You want me to make some eggs?" she asked.

He put the toast down, then took a swallow of orange juice. "No, I'm fine. Thanks, though."

Sarah watched him fiddle with the toast, though he didn't make the effort to eat anymore. "How are you?"

He didn't answer but continued to stare down at his plate. She caught how he was gripping his orange juice.

"What?" she asked.

"Nothing." He stood and dumped the leftover toast in the trash, then put his plate in the sink. "I should get my stuff and head out. I've got a lot to do today."

"Declan," she said, and he stopped before he left the kitchen. "Wait."

He shoved his hands into the pockets of his jeans. "I should go."

"Why?"

His shoulders hunched and his head down, he didn't answer her.

"It's seven o'clock in the morning," she said. "What exactly is it that you have to do right now?"

Lifting his head, he finally acknowledged her. "I can't sit and dwell on it. I have to get up and move, do something."

Sarah knew he was grieving, but she suspected something else weighed on his mind. "What's bothering you?"

He leaned back against the fridge, laying his head against it, his eyes closed. "I don't understand."

"Don't understand what?"

"What happened." Sighing, he opened his eyes but stared at the ceiling. "He was doing great. He'd seen the doctor and got a clean bill of health. He'd been feeling good, a lot like his old self." Declan dropped his head. "And then out of nowhere, he takes a nosedive."

Sensing there was more, she let him process what he was feeling.

"I should have known," he said.

"Known what?"

His head came up. "I didn't sense it. I know my dad. He felt good. I could feel it in him. How come I couldn't tell he was sick? I could always tell before if he wasn't himself. How come not now? If I'd sensed it, maybe..."

She understood then. "This isn't your fault. There's nothing you could have done to prevent this."

He took his hands out of his pockets and crossed his arms. He let out a deep sigh. "I'm not so convinced."

She waited a few seconds to let him settle. "Sometimes information is kept from us for a reason." She paused. "We aren't meant to know everything."

He pushed off the refrigerator, walked across the kitchen, and gripped the countertop. "That's not the answer I want to hear."

"No," she said. "I know it isn't."

Seeing his lost look return, she wished she knew what else to say, but having lost both parents herself, she knew there was nothing that she could offer that would give him what he wanted. The only thing that would help was time.

"Sit," she said. "If you leave now, John will just go out and find you."

His face creased in a sad smile. "He probably would."

Collecting himself, he returned to sit at the table as Sarah took a sip of her orange juice. "Your turn," he said. "What happened with the mirror yesterday?"

Sarah put down her glass. She felt she'd handled it pretty well, but she couldn't deny her deep disappointment that she'd proven just as unsuccessful as everyone before her. The thought that her failure would result in the deaths of her newfound family hounded her, but she'd kept her emotions at bay. At some point, though, she knew it would rear its ugly head and she'd fall apart.

"I guess what I said is true," she said, swirling her drink. "Sometimes we aren't meant to know everything."

Declan went quiet and she felt him tuning into her. "What exactly happened?" he asked.

Staring at her glass, she recalled the previous day. "We met with the full Council." She looked up. "I assume you've met them."

"Yes, I have." He nodded. "They can be intimidating."

"They're not the most welcoming group."

He smiled. "No."

"One of them—her name's Daphne—is not my biggest fan."

"Daphne?"

"Yes. She was acrimonious at best."

Declan sat back. "I suspect I know why. She had a relationship with Emerson for a short time."

"She did?"

"Yes. The fact that he's lying in a coma and is suspected of betraying our Community is probably not sitting well with her."

"That's not my fault."

"No, it's not, but sometimes it's easier to deflect your pain onto someone else."

Realizing now what had caused the woman's antipathy, Sarah's aggravation with the woman subsided. "I suppose so."

Declan eye's narrowed. "What else happened?"

Her mind replayed the moment. "They brought out the mirror."

"What did it look like?"

"It was small, octagonal, and silver. It had this engraved letter D on the lid." She took another sip of her drink, not really tasting it. "It looked just like a woman's cosmetic mirror, only fancier than the ones you see today."

"How did it feel?" he asked.

"That's what was weird," she said. "I didn't feel anything."

Declan furrowed his brows. "Nothing?"

"Nothing. It felt like a piece of plastic."

He shook his head. "That doesn't make sense."

"I didn't think it did either. Shouldn't I have felt something? I mean if it was Varalika's mirror, it should have her energy all over it."

"It should." He tried to think of a possible explanation. "They're sure it's hers?"

"They found it in her hand."

"Maybe it has something to do with what she went through. If her ship was going down and she was panicked, maybe she somehow transferred that energy to the mirror, somehow affecting it."

Sarah had another thought. "Could she have blocked it?"

He frowned. "I suppose she could have, without realizing it."

"I mean intentionally."

"What do you mean?"

"I mean maybe she doesn't want us to read it."

Declan thought about it. "I know it's possible for a Red-Line to code it in a way to prevent another from reading it. And maybe she did, but my question would be why? Why would she do that? She's about to crash. She's carrying serum. She's in trouble. There's no worry about a human finding and reading the mirror. So why intentionally block it?"

"I don't know." Sarah began to wonder. "How much does the Council know about why her ship went down?"

"What are you thinking?"

She sat forward. "We know Arnuff and Emerson were involved in some sort of plot against the Grays. Y even suggested that there was more going on than we know."

"You think Varalika knew something?"

Sarah sighed and squeezed the bridge of her nose. "I don't know. I could just be grasping at straws."

"Maybe not."

"There's no way to know, anyway," she said, realizing she could assume anything but never know the truth. "It's just weird that the mirror feels blank." Sarah went quiet.

"What?"

Sarah thought back. "There was something else. Some sort of communication between Morgana and Drake."

"The Councilman?" Declan asked.

"Yes," she answered, remembering what had caught her attention. "It had to do with John."

"John? What do you mean? He wasn't there."

"That's exactly it. They expected him to be there. They were surprised that he wasn't."

"Why would it matter?"

"I don't know. But I distinctly felt some sort of communication between them. Drake even suggested we wait."

"Wait to read the mirror?"

"Yes, but Morgana disagreed, so we went ahead."

Declan tapped at the table. "Well, now you've got me flummoxed. What would John have to do with the mirror?"

Ramsey walked into the kitchen. "Good morning," he said. He was dressed in sweats, his hair was wet, and he smelled of soap. "Did I hear my name?" He saw their glasses of orange juice on the table. "Did you eat?"

"Good morning," said Sarah, watching him open the refrigerator. "No, we haven't eaten. We were waiting for you."

"Any coffee?" he asked, closing the fridge.

"Not yet," said Declan.

"What? No caffeine? I thought I could count on you two." He opened a cabinet and pulled out a container of coffee grounds.

"Sorry," said Declan. "We dropped the ball."

Ramsey grabbed a filter. "I'll let it slide this one time, considering you both have other things on your mind." He scooped out the grounds. "Everything okay?" he asked, apparently not missing that they were deep in conversation. "You're not hitting on my lady, are you?"

Declan chuckled. "If I thought I had a chance, I'd be tempted."

Ramsey stepped over to the sink to fill the coffee pot with water. "Yeah, well, for some reason, I think she kind of likes me."

Sarah thought back on their amorous weekend. "You do have some attractive qualities."

"You're one of the few that can put up with them," added Declan. He shifted in his seat. "Sarah was telling me about her day yesterday."

Ramsey finished up with the coffee and flipped on the machine. He went to sit down at the table with them. "Anything I should know?"

Sarah reached over and took his hand. "Any idea why Morgana was missing you yesterday?"

His eyes widened. "I would have no answer to that. I would have thought she'd have been pleased by my absence." His fingers encircled hers. "Why would she want me there?"

"I don't know," she said. "It's probably nothing."

"You picked up on it. I doubt it was nothing."

"Well, I suppose next time we see her, we can ask her," said Declan.

Ramsey glanced over at him. "You always were the smart one."

Declan didn't deny it. "What does that make you?" he asked.

"The good-looking one, of course." He got up from his seat. "Anybody hungry?"

**

They made a big breakfast and talked, keeping the subject matter light, knowing that the day would be a difficult one. After eating, Sarah showered and they drove to Ramsey's mother's house. Ramsey was glad to see his mom awake and alert. Phil had sobered up and said little after they arrived, and Margaret took him home soon after, since Ramsey and Declan were there to help. Sarah's introduction to Charlotte went smoothly, with both wishing it could have been made under better circumstances. They headed out to the funeral home around lunchtime and made arrangements for the next day's service. Declan stayed quiet, making suggestions where needed but letting Charlotte make most of the decisions. Afterwards, they stopped for lunch, eating little although they were hungry. The emotions of the day hampered Sarah, and she tried to keep them at bay, but her attachment to those affected made it more difficult. Ramsey knew she could feel it, but he also knew she wouldn't leave. Staying close, he did his best to bolster her when he thought she needed it.

They made it back to Charlotte's house in the late afternoon, all of them emotionally drained. As Declan sat with Sarah, Ramsey finally found some time to talk with his mother alone. Their conversation went better than Ramsey had anticipated, each of them opening up about Ramsey's father and how his death had affected them both. The discussion ended with a comforting hug between them, as they both allowed years of hurt feelings finally dissolve.

Before leaving, Ramsey offered to stay with his mother at the house that night, but she refused, asking to be alone and wanting the time to process her husband's absence. Making her promise to call if she needed anything, Ramsey agreed to let her be. He planned to pick her up the next day for the funeral.

The three of them left in the early evening, saying little as they drove back to Ramsey's house. Ramsey had called Leroy and Sarah called Hannah, letting them each know the plans for the following day. Back at the house, they tried to get Declan to stay for dinner, but he declined, asking for the same space as Charlotte had, wanting to be alone to prepare his thoughts for the words he would say at the service. When he got in his car and left, Sarah and Ramsey wished they could say the words that would ease his pain, though they knew there were none.

**

The funeral was simple, attended by family, a few close friends, and the members of Declan's security team who were not on duty. Leroy arrived with Olivia and Hannah, and Marge and Phil sat together. There were others present whom Ramsey recognized, but few whose names he remembered. He and Sarah sat in a front pew, with Declan on the aisle, staring ahead and saying little. His mother sat with Phil and Margaret in the front pew on the opposite side of the small chapel. Ramsey held Sarah's hand and kept an eye on Declan.

Seeing movement, he looked up with surprise when, at the end of the pew, Hannah appeared and stepped in, moving around and sitting beside Declan. She reached over, took his hand, and sat with him. His brother glanced at her, his lost look briefly fading, and squeezed Hannah's hand in return. Sarah noticed the gesture too, and she looked at Ramsey, their eyes communicating their curiosity. When the pastor began to speak, though, their attention was drawn elsewhere.

During the service, Ramsey caught another profile in the chapel. He was surprised to see Morgana, with Drake sitting next to her, seated behind the other attendees. He remembered Drake from the few Council meetings he'd attended. Seeing them glance his way, he tipped his head in her direction, and she acknowledged him in return.

After the pastor and Declan had spoken their words of remembrance, they carried out the coffin, with Ramsey, Declan, Leroy, Phil, and two family friends acting as pallbearers. They placed it in the hearse and made their way to the cemetery.

Once there, they sat in chairs and listened to the pastor as they prepared to say their final goodbyes.

**

Standing far enough away not to be seen, but close enough to watch, Y observed the proceedings. He wore a designer black overcoat, belted at the waist, a gray scarf that matched his eyes, and his black and silver watch gleamed from his wrist. Putting his hands in his pockets, he kept his eyes on the small group, studying each of them one at a time, reviewing his tactics, reveling in their perfection. His preparations complete, he anticipated the unveiling of his plans and smiled with satisfaction as the group wallowed over Declan's loss.

A thrill of excitement swept through him. In only a week's time, he would have what he wanted, and he would begin to exact his revenge. Turning to leave, he couldn't help but laugh.

TWENTY-ONE

....

RUNNING LATE FOR his therapy appointment, Ramsey walked through his house, looking for his keys. He'd missed the previous session because of the funeral two days before, and now, if he didn't hurry, he would come close to missing this one. Finally finding his keys in the pocket of a pair of jeans he'd thrown in the laundry, he rushed out to the entryway.

Sarah held the door for him. "Find them?"

"Yes," he said. "In the pocket of my jeans."

"You usually put them on the entry table."

"Well..." He leaned in and kissed her. "...if I hadn't been so distracted by you when we came home yesterday, I probably would have."

She smiled. "I can't help that I'm so desirable."

Hearing her, he made a sudden reverse move, throwing his arm around her and pulling her up close. He brought his lips to hers, making her legs buckle and she brought her arms come up around him.

He broke the kiss, breathing hard. "Maybe I should reschedule."

Sarah caressed his cheek. "As much as I'm tempted," she said, "you can't. Your therapist would not be pleased. And you need to keep up your regimen. I need you in tip-top shape." She kissed him again to emphasize her point before pulling back. "Plus, I'm meeting Hannah for lunch. I can't cancel on her." She played with a button on his shirt and something in her

287

tone caught Ramsey's attention. The energy she exuded felt feigned. "What is it?"

She fiddled with his collar. "Nothing. I'm fine."

He could feel her tense up. "No, you're not. What's wrong?"

She made a nervous laugh. "I'm not very good at cloaking myself, am I?"

"Hey." He tried to catch her eye. "I don't want you to cloak anything with me."

"It's nothing." She tried to pull away, but he held on. When he kept staring, she relented. "Morgana called."

"She did? When?"

"While you were in the bedroom, looking for your keys."

"What'd she want?"

"She wants to meet soon."

His face clouded. "About the mirror?"

She nodded. "She wants you to come, too."

"Damn it. She's putting too much pressure on you."

"No, she's not. She's got the fate of her people on her mind." She stared at his shirt. "So do I."

He realized then what had her on edge. "Hey. There's plenty of time. A lot can happen."

She tensed against him. "Don't humor me. Two years will disappear in a flash." She dropped her head on his shoulder and he pulled her in and hugged her. She whispered in his ear. "What if I can't read it?"

He wanted to tell her that everything would be all right. But he knew she wouldn't believe him. He spoke softly. "Listen. I know you're scared. There's a lot riding on you reading that mirror. I wish I could tell you I knew what was going to happen, but I can't. All I can say is that we've made it this far." He pulled back and cupped her face. "I don't know what will happen, but what I do know is that you and I will find a way. Trust destiny, remember?"

She nodded. "Keep reminding me, okay?"

"Whatever you need. You and I are in this together. I'm not going anywhere."

She tightened her grip on him. "Promise?"

"Promise."

"You'll go with me to Morgana's?"

"Wouldn't miss it. She and I can catch up over tea."

Sarah relaxed and he could feel her worry begin to dissipate. "I'm sure she'd like that."

He dropped his hand from her face and wrapped it back around her. "Feel a little better?"

"I do. Thank you."

"Anytime." He watched her. "And I want you to talk to me about this. Don't hide it from me to spare my feelings."

She moved her hands up and down his back. 'It seems as if I don't have a choice. I'm not good at hiding anything from you."

"As it should be." Leaning in, he stole another kiss before giving her an evil grin. "And you can't hide that Wonder Woman outfit either. Maybe tonight we can put it back to good use."

"Hmm," she said, her humor returning. "Maybe I need to find you a Superman cape."

He grinned. "I hardly think I'd do the uniform justice."

"Don't sell yourself short, strong man." She rubbed his shoulders. "I've seen those rippling muscles of yours."

Ramsey growled as he moved in for another kiss. She returned it, wrapping herself around him. Before he could pick her up and carry her away, though, she pushed back. "You need to go."

He groaned and let her go. "We'll pick up where we left off when I get back."

"Promise?"

He touched her jaw. "I'm going. But I'll only be thinking of you." He stepped away. "I'll miss you."

"I'll see you when you get back."

"Say 'hi' to Hannah." He headed out and down the drive.

"I will." She paused. "I love you."

Reaching his car door, he looked back. "I love you, too."

**

Sarah waved and watched him drive off. After closing the door, she headed for the bedroom. She had only a short amount of time before she had to head out to meet Hannah, or she would be late, too.

They had planned to meet at a Greek restaurant near Hannah's current job placement. It was a little farther out, and Sarah would have to drive about thirty minutes to get there. Moving through the house, she threw on her earrings and put on some last-minute lipstick and perfume, grabbed her purse and phone, and left the house, glad to see she was on time.

Twenty minutes later, and nearing the location, her phone buzzed, telling her she had a text message. Stopped at a light, picked up the phone and saw it was from Hannah.

Had an unexpected change. Want to meet at Sullivan's?

Sullivan's was a nearby old dive of a restaurant that had been open for over twenty years. She had been there once before with Rachel, and Hannah had always wanted to try it. Locally, it was known for its steak burgers and loaded fries, and it was a great place to go for comfort food and a beer. Considering the difficult week they'd been through, it sounded like the perfect place.

Before the light changed, Sarah texted back.

Sounds great. It'll take me ten minutes.

After the light turned green, Sarah changed direction, and headed back the way she'd come. Checking the rearview mirror, she saw the car following her. Declan and Ramsey still insisted she have someone with her whenever she was alone, and so Marco followed her now as she drove. Should something occur, they determined that the best tactic would be to have someone nearby who could call in the troops if Sarah needed help. Her security had always provided a layer of distance, giving her some privacy, while also keeping an eye on her.

Her phone beeped again, and she looked down at the message.

Great. See you soon.

The thought of a greasy hamburger and fries made her stomach rumble as she drove.

Ten minutes later, she pulled into the restaurant's parking lot. The usual busy lunchtime crowd had dissipated, and she found a spot up close. Marco parked nearby. She didn't see Hannah's car but figured her friend would be there soon. She walked inside and saw that there were tables available and that they would not have to wait. The hostess asked to seat her, but she declined, saying she would wait until her friend arrived. Taking a seat in a booth in the empty bar area, she put down her purse and kept an eye on the entry, waiting for Hannah. She noticed Marco come in behind her and he followed her into the bar.

"Everything okay?" he asked.

"Yes, fine. Thanks, Marco. Hannah had a last-minute change in plans."

"Okay. I'll wait with you until she gets here."

Despite the fact that she'd had security for several weeks now, it still felt odd to have a bodyguard. "Okay," she answered, and he went to stand next to the bar.

After five minutes turned to ten, and then fifteen, Sarah pulled her phone out, wondering if she had missed a text or call from Hannah saying she would be late.

Marco came over. "Is she coming?" he asked.

"I hope so," said Sarah. "I was just checking to see if she'd tried to reach me."

Seeing no message, Sarah began to type one when her phone buzzed again and a text from Hannah appeared.

Where are you? Everything okay?

Before she could respond, Marco put a hand on her shoulder. "Stay here," he said, eyeing the front of the restaurant.

"What is it?" asked Sarah.

He stood still for a moment, and Sarah followed his gaze but saw nothing. "I'll be right back," he said. And before she could object, he left, walking out toward the hostess stand.

Puzzled by the text message and Marco's strange behavior, she began to text Hannah back when she felt a new, but familiar, presence. Looking up, she almost dropped her phone when she saw Y standing next to her wearing an expensive navy suit with a gray and blue striped tie. His eyes reflected the light as his hands slipped into his pockets and he smiled at her.

"Hello, Sarah."

She froze in her seat.

"You mind if I sit?"

Without thinking, she grabbed her purse and tried to stand, but he stood over her, making it impossible for her to get up without touching him.

"Relax," he said. "I just thought I'd say hello. I was on my way out after a lunch meeting when I saw you sitting here. Imagine my surprise."

"I was just leaving," she said, her heart racing.

"It looks like you just arrived."

"I'm still leaving. Please move." Sarah tried hard to stay calm.

"There's no need to leave. I'm on my way out." His eyes scanned the restaurant. "Don't tell me. You're meeting my favorite person. How is he?" He pulled a hand out of his pocket and studied a fingernail. "Or are you two still on the outs?"

292

Sarah refused to be pulled into the conversation, and she certainly didn't want to talk about Ramsey. "I'm not interested in chatting. I am meeting someone, and I'm late."

His expression flattened. "Very well," he answered, and something cold emanated from him. It felt like a wet, black cloth had draped itself over her, and she felt claustrophobic. Stepping back, he gave her just enough space to stand without getting too close. Pulling her purse up over her shoulder, she grabbed her phone.

"It's been a pleasure to see you, Sarah."

Biting back a sarcastic retort, she moved around him, wanting only to get out of there. She began to feel a sense of relief, but it faded when he gripped her arm.

"Before you leave," he said, "would you mind giving Ramsey a message for me?"

Something sharp pricked against her skin above her elbow, and a strange numbness moved up her bicep and into her shoulder. She began to panic. "Let me go," she said, trying to pull away.

He didn't, though, and she could only stand there as a wave of heat enveloped her and she felt nauseated. Overwhelming dizziness hit her, and she felt her knees buckle. He pulled her up against him and held her as she reached for the table for support. Spots appeared in front of her eyes, and she did panic then, resisting and trying to free herself. "Please. Let me go," she said again, her voice shaky. Her strength had vanished.

His arm came around her. "It's okay, honey," he said. "You're just having a dizzy spell. Sit down."

Another wave of nausea hit, and she shut her eyes as her head spun. She would have fallen then if he had not been there to hold her up. He guided her back to the booth, and lowered her down into the seat. She put her forehead against the table top. Breathing deeply, she tried to ease her rolling stomach.

"Everything all right?" said an unfamiliar voice.

Managing to turn her head, Sarah saw a man standing next to Y. He held a bar towel in his hand, and when she squinted, she thought his nametag read "Dave."

She heard Y say, "She's fine. She's just dizzy. It should pass soon." Y kneeled down in front of her, brushing the hair from her face. "Just relax, sweetheart."

Sarah tried to force out the words that she was not his sweetheart and that she needed help, but her limbs were heavy and her muscles wouldn't respond. The only sound she could muster was a low moan. Another wave hit her, and the room spun again. She closed her eyes.

"Does she need a doctor?" asked Dave.

"No, thank you," said Y. "You're very kind. But my fiancée is just having a dizzy spell due to a medical condition. It should only last a few minutes. Would you mind getting us a wet cloth?"

"Sure," said Dave, and he left.

Terrified, Sarah gripped the table. Sweat popped out on her brow, and she tried to summon the strength to move or scream, but failed.

Y moved closer, and spoke into her ear. "Just relax, Sarah. It will pass soon." He slid his hand down the back of her head, and she shivered. Thinking of Ramsey, she reached out to him with the little energy she had, wishing he could hear her plea for help, but knowing it would not help.

"You said you'd leave me alone," she said, managing to whisper. "Please."

"I can't do that, Sarah." Leaning over, he kissed her head. "You mean too much to me."

Her body trembled, and she wanted to pull away, but couldn't.

Dave returned with a wet towel and handed it to Y.

"Thank you, Dave," said Y.

"How is she doing?"

"Better," Y said, moving to lift Sarah's head and gently wipe her face.

Sarah remained helpless to prevent him from touching her. Her body would not comply, and her vocal chords would not speak the words she needed. All she could do was breath in gulps of air as he dabbed at her face with the cloth, moving in swipes from her forehead to her cheeks.

"How does that feel?" he asked her.

Her frightened stare was her only weapon as she watched him pretend to soothe her, and she told herself to stay calm, that this would pass, that he would leave her alone after he had scared her sufficiently.

Dave appeared satisfied that Y had the situation under control. "If you need anything, just let me or someone else know."

"Thanks, Dave," said Y. "I appreciate your help."

Dave disappeared, and Sarah felt much of her hope for rescue go with him. She thought of Marco and could only pray he was in the process of contacting Declan.

Y turned his gaze back to her. "How are you feeling?" he asked, putting the damp cloth on the table. She managed to keep her head up, but couldn't respond. Sarah didn't know if it was because of the sickness or her fear. Her eyes clouded with unshed tears, and he reached out and took her hand. She tried again to pull away, but he held tight.

"It's okay," he said. "Try not to be scared." He stroked her hand. "It was the accident, remember?"

She narrowed her eyes, having no idea what he was talking about.

He kept going. "You had a car accident and a brain injury. Your memory's been affected. Remember, Sarah? We were going to be married, but we had to delay it."

Her fear swelled and her heart slammed against her chest. What the hell was he saying?

And then she felt it again. Another stab of pain, but this time on the meat of her hand where he held her palm. Her hand went numb, and another wave of intense nausea and dizziness hit her hard. She moaned again as her vision blurred and then went dark, and a loud buzzing sounded in her ear, and then she heard nothing at all.

**

Y held her as she went limp, and then gently rested her head back against the booth. He reached into a pocket and pulled out his cell. After hitting a button, he waited until he got a response and said into the phone, "Bring the car around."

He snapped the phone shut, and put it back in his pocket. Y grabbed Sarah's purse, put one arm behind her and another under her knees, and lifted her. She was unconscious, and her head rolled into his neck. Standing motionless, Y held her with her forehead resting against his jaw, and he got a whiff of her perfume. He breathed it in, relishing her flowery scent. Moving his lips down to her hairline, he closed his eyes and kissed her gently.

Opening his eyes, he whispered to her, "Never mind about the message to Ramsey, Sarah." He raised his head, and his chin grazed over her skin. "I'll deliver it myself."

He stood for a few silent seconds, savoring the feel of her body against his, and then walked out of the empty bar, passed the vacant hostess stand, and exited the restaurant. A sleek black automobile was idling out front. After carefully laying Sarah in the back seat, he slid in next to her, closed the door and seconds later, the driver drove away.

∞ ∞ ∞

What happens next? Y has an evil plan to keep Sarah by his side and destroy Ramsey. Will he succeed? Find out in *Red-Line: Trust Destiny*. Enjoy an excerpt below...

Want access to a free copy of the short story *Red-Line: Prelude to the Shift*, plus excerpts, missing scenes, free books and extra content? Visit jtbishopauthor.com to find out more. Follow J.T. on her Amazon Author page to be notified of new releases.

And after the Red-Line trilogy, prepare to enjoy the sister series to the Red-Line trilogy. *Red-Line: The Fletcher Family Saga* includes *Curse Breaker, High Child, Spark* and *Forged Lines*. There is a boxed set, too! The Fletchers are a gifted family, but it comes at a cost. When a distant but dangerous enemy wants them dead, they'll join forces with the Ramseys to survive. Will they all pay with their lives?

And after the Fletchers, get ready for some mystery thrillers with a touch of the supernatural. Check out the *Family or Foe Saga*, which introduces the charismatic Detectives Daniels and Remalla. They'll pursue a killer with unique abilities who's out for revenge against those he believes wronged him. *First Cut* is followed by *Second Slice, Third Blow*, and *Fourth Strike*. A boxed set is available for this one, too!

Not ready for *First Cut*, but would love to read a mystery thriller ghost story? Then look into *Haunted River*, which kicks off Detectives Daniels' and Remalla's own series. The ghost of a woman haunts a small town where she lived and died. When a second woman turns up dead, Daniels and Remalla become suspects and potential victims. Can the specters of the past help them catch a killer before they wind up dead? *Of Breath and Blood*, which starts an exciting new story arc for our detectives, follows. Their investigation into a cult leader who attracts followers with supernatural gifts risks Daniels' sanity and Remalla's life and they'll have to rely on each other to survive. *Of Body and Bone, Of Mind and Madness, Of Power and Pain* and *Of Love and Loss* continue the storyline.

And last, but certainly not least, get ready for a crossover series with the Daniels and Remalla books, featuring a character introduced in *Of Breath and Blood*. *The Redstone Chronicles* includes *Lost Souls, Lost Dreams, Lost Chances* and *Lost Hope* and features the exploits of gifted, but troubled, paranormal P.I. and former Texas Ranger Mason Redstone and his sister Mikey. They'll take the cases others won't and risk their lives in the process.

A NOTE FROM J.T.

....

I hope you enjoyed *Red-Line: Mirrors*. Of the three books in the trilogy, this one is its emotional heart. I loved the development of Ramsey and Sarah's love story and depicting what they're willing to sacrifice for each other. It was also fun to put Ramsey through a bit of trauma. He is always the tough guy and protecting others, but now he had to be the one to accept the help and endure his weaknesses. It was a nice element to add to his character, and it provided his and Sarah's relationship more depth. I know some readers prefer the action and fast-paced thrills, but I love the lighter and more delicate moments in this book. It makes my heart happy. Don't worry, though, the action and thrills pick up again in *Trust Destiny*. Y will show how far he's willing to go to get what he wants and there will be a lot of ups and downs for our characters, so get ready.

Reviews are a huge plus and big help for an author, as well as potential readers. I would love it if you could please take a couple of minutes to leave a review for *Red-Line: Mirrors*. Add if you'd like, please leave a few comments, too.

As always, thank you for your time and readership. It is deeply valued and appreciated.

Now, on to the next book!

ACKNOWLEDGEMENTS

....

Again, this book would not exist without the support of my family and friends.

Thank you to Mom, Dad, Cathy and Nick for all your love and support. I am grateful every day for each of you. I could never have done this without you.

To my amazing friends – Crissy, Gwen, Fay, and May. You continue to hang in there with me through this journey and your belief in me keeps me going. Thank you so much for your continued love and support.

To my extended family and friends – Jessica, Alex, Suzzie, Jack, Anne, Artur and the staff at Aboca's Italian Grill (if you're ever in Richardson, TX, you should eat there), the awesome GNO ladies, the amazing book group women and my cohorts at Emler. All of you played a part in this and I thank you for continuing to encourage me.

To Mayza Clark at Mayza Clark Photography for making me look good with a great author photo.

And of course, to my nephews and nieces – Taylor, Alex, Sydney, Colson and Leighton. I'm so glad I get to share this with you. I can't wait to see what dreams you will follow, whatever they may be. And Colson, I know you want a book with pictures. Well, I'm working on it.

ABOUT THE AUTHOR

Born and raised in Dallas, TX, J. T. Bishop began writing in 2012. Two years later, the Red-Line trilogy was complete. She's not done though. J. T. continues to create new characters and story lines to entertain her fans.

J. T. loves books that explore characters' unique abilities and origins. A touch of the supernatural with a side of the paranormal is a theme she finds intriguing and provides a wealth of inspiration for her books. But an absorbing murder mystery, suspense story interwoven with powerful charismatic characters provides the drama, angst, passion, and humor she craves. A little romance doesn't hurt either.

J. T. loves hanging out with family and friends, traveling when she can, and spending time in nature (despite the heat in Texas). Getting up in the morning with a cup of coffee, ready to write, is the start of a perfect day.

BOOKS IN CHRONOLOGICAL ORDER

....

Although recommended but not required, in case you like to read in order...

Red-Line: Prelude to the Shift, a short story (free at jtbishopauthor.com)
Red-Line: The Shift
Red-Line: Mirrors
Red-Line: Trust Destiny
Curse Breaker
High Child
Spark
Forged Lines
**
The Girl and the Gunshot, a Daniels and Remalla novella (free at jtbishopauthor.com)
First Cut
Second Slice
Third Blow
Fourth Strike
Haunted River
Of Breath and Blood
Lost Souls
Of Body and Bone
Lost Dreams
Of Mind and Madness
Lost Chances
Of Power and Pain
Lost Hope
Of Love and Loss

....

TRUST DESTINY

Ramsey emerged from the office, looking worn and tired, as if his sleep had only added to the weight on his shoulders. Speaking on the phone, Hannah looked up. She'd been helping Declan follow up with those out on the street searching for Sarah. As people called in, she noted their progress and then sent them to wherever Declan indicated next. Declan and Leroy sat in the kitchen, looking over maps of potential new areas to look.

Hannah hung up the phone as Ramsey walked toward the table where she sat.

"Any news?" he asked. His sunken, unshaven cheeks and puffy eyes portrayed his weariness and worry.

"Nothing new," she said, and watched him deflate. "When's the last time you ate a solid meal?"

"I'm not hungry." He stood by the couch. "What can I do?"

She told him what he didn't want to hear. "You can go take a shower and get something to eat."

"I can shower and eat later. Where's the next search area?" He searched for his keys, preparing to leave the moment Hannah answered him.

"We've got plenty of people looking Ramsey. You need to rest."

Ramsey's fragile nerves stretched thin. "Dammit, Hannah. I don't need to rest. I've rested enough. I can't just sit here. I have to go out and look for her."

"You're not going to do her any good if you collapse while you look. You have to keep up your strength."

He continued to look for his keys. "Forget it. I'll head out my own."

Leroy and Declan came out of the kitchen at the sound of Ramsey's voice. "Sherlock?" asked Leroy.

"What, Leroy?"

"You need to take it easy. You're pushing yourself too hard."

Ramsey's last reserves snapped. "Will you all stop telling me what to do? While I'm here resting, Sarah's out there dealing with who the hell knows what. I'll rest when she's back here safe." He searched the room without success. "Where the hell are my keys?"

"John," said Declan, feeling his brother's frustration.

"What, Declan?" Ramsey retorted as he swiped at some papers.

Watching his brother dig through a pile of discarded maps, Declan stilled himself and tried to project some measure of calm toward Ramsey.

"Stop doing that," said Ramsey, feeling the wave of energy hit him. "I don't want or need your interference."

Declan remained passive. "John," he said. "She's going to be okay."

Ramsey's head whipped back at him. "How the hell do you know that? You don't know where she is or what she's going through. God knows what he's doing to her."

Declan didn't let Ramsey's outburst stop him. "She's going to be okay."

Ramsey stopped for a second, but his manic energy wouldn't still. "You can't be sure of that. If she fights him or refuses to comply, he could hurt her."

Declan kept up his affirmation, knowing that Ramsey needed to believe in something. "She's going to be okay."

Finally, Declan's words seemed to pierce through the wall of fear that Ramsey had erected. He stopped and stood, as if he carried a hundred pounds of weight around his neck. His frantic, searching gaze managed to stop long enough to find and hold Declan's.

"You don't know that," he said.

Declan didn't hesitate. "Yes. Yes, I do. I feel it in my bones."

Ramsey studied him, feeling for any indication that Declan might be lying. Feeling some small amount of weight shift, but not disappear, he felt his fatigue hit him and with quivering legs, he found the armrest and lowered himself down onto the couch. Releasing a deep breath, he found himself shaking and he clasped his hands together to keep them still.

"Sherlock," asked Leroy, "You okay?" Both he and Declan moved into the room.

Ramsey didn't answer. He took in lungfuls of air as his body continued to quake and his vision spun. He leaned forward and closed his eyes against the dizziness.

Hannah was up and kneeling next to him. "Hey, what's wrong?" she asked. Reaching for his arm, she felt his cold and clammy skin.

"I don't know," he answered. "I can't seem to get enough oxygen." His breathing picked up and he turned pale. Another wave of dizziness hit him and he closed his eyes.

Declan and Leroy kneeled next to him. "Take it easy," said Declan.

"I think you're having an anxiety attack," said Hannah. She looked at Leroy. "Leroy, do you have a paper bag?"

Leroy headed into the kitchen and returned with a brown paper lunch bag. He handed it to Hannah. She took and opened it.

"Breathe into this," she told Ramsey. He did as she asked, breathing shallowly at first, but then deeper, and his breathing began to slow.

"Feeling better?" asked Hannah.

Ramsey managed to open his eyes and saw three concerned faces looking at him. "A little," he said into the bag.

"Take your time. Are you dizzy?" she asked.

"Yes."

"It should pass in a minute or two. Just keep breathing."

She kept watch and even though his breathing returned to normal, he was still pale and despite his cool skin, beads of sweat popped out on his forehead.

"I know you're not hungry, but something in your stomach would help. You need fluids, too."

He took the bag away from his face. "I'm fine."

"You look terrible," said Leroy, studying Ramsey's haggard face. "If Sarah walked in here right now, she'd give you an earful for not taking better care of yourself."

Ramsey stared over at his friend. "God, I wish she would." He dropped his head and looked down. His vision slowly began to clear and he blinked his eyes. "I don't know what I'm going to do if…" He took a deep breath.

"Stop thinking like that," said Declan. "I know it's easy to think the worst and your imagination is running wild, but you have to remember something. He's not going to hurt her. He wants you to suffer, but not her. Even if she refuses to do what he wants, he won't harm her. But what he will do is hold her until he drives you stark raving mad, which I suspect is a big part of his plan."

"Well," said Ramsey, finally feeling his dizziness lift. "His plan is working."

"So, don't give him the satisfaction of falling apart," said Declan. "You do what you need to do to find her, but you have to take care of yourself in the process. You keep going like this and you won't last long enough to enjoy it when we bring her back."

"And I don't want her yelling at me for not taking care of you while she was gone," said Leroy.

"I've seen her temper," said Declan. "Nobody wants her angry."

Ramsey allowed himself a brief smile. "No," he said. "Nobody wants that."

"Olivia made some soup," said Leroy. "Think you could handle some?"

Ramsey sighed and sat back on the couch. He knew they were right. No matter how much he wanted to spend all his waking moments searching for

Sarah, he couldn't neglect his body for too long without consequences. "Okay," he finally gave in, "I'll try some soup."

"Good," said Leroy, heading into the kitchen. "I'll bring you some water, too."

Hannah kept an eye on Ramsey and would have preferred a little more color in his face, but overall, he appeared to be doing better. The phone rang and she rose to answer it. "You stay where you are," she told Ramsey. She picked up the phone and followed up with another searcher calling in to report his progress.

Declan continued to monitor Ramsey and when his earlier frantic energy did not return, he sensed that Ramsey had achieved some measure of acceptance and hoped that meant his brother would be a little easier to handle. He rose to stand when he heard Ramsey speak.

"Declan?"

Declan stopped. "What?"

"You meant it, didn't you?"

Declan sank back down and put a hand on Ramsey's shoulder. "Yes, I did. She'll be okay. I wouldn't lie to you. "

Ramsey said nothing, but Declan watched his lost look return. "Hey," he said and Ramsey looked back. "You eat all your soup and take a shower, I'll give you my piece of Olivia's chocolate cake.

Ramsey's lost look faded. "You don't eat chocolate cake."

"I know, but Leroy does."

"You're taking your life into your hands."

"I'm willing to do it, if it will help you feel better."

"That must be one hell of a piece of cake."

Leroy walked into the room, holding a bowl of soup and carrying a tray table. "Anybody touches that last piece of cake, they'll pull back a stump."

Declan chuckled and Ramsey couldn't help but allow himself a short-lived smile.

Made in the USA
Las Vegas, NV
29 November 2022

60674584R00185